For my Mom and Dad ,and all their love and support.

In memory of Ray Harryhausen.

Forgemaster

Edited by: Aaron and James Dalzell

ISBN: 978-0615821436

Forgemaster

by
Aaron Dalzell

"…sit quietly stranger, and listen,

for the tale I tell…is a story for the ages."

The stranger listens in earnest, as the old man tells his tale…

Prologue:

Agonan's Pail

'Cooling of the tongs...is not the end of forging!' A gigantic, burly, overweight Gormon yells; he's sitting at an old rickety table within Agonan's Pail, a piece of furniture that is accustomed to the sheer, massive size of the Gormons, much larger than the normal scale and size of the Civilians, who sit at the regular tables. Across from him, he yells at a Gormon woman, stocky and shapely she is, just as tall and just as brawn and manly looking as the Gormon. Her blonde hair is braided down her back with metal wire tassels. She frowns broadly from plump cheek to plump cheek back at the wooly fellow.

'AH! You stupid arse, you don't know what yer talking about! You cool the tongs once finished with yer piece, and place 'em within yer rugged apron! Thus marks yer finished, once you have cleaned up! Because all is done, what else is there to do, eh? I ask you. So please tell me, Mr. Smithy! When do you consider yer werk to be done, eh?! We're all listening!'

And Mr. Smithy, the burly Gormon, is about to tell the woman just what he thinks. He squints his eyes, and grits his teeth. Looking about, he notices they both have caught the attention of the other patrons who have minded their own business about them, until the business of the two Gormons have interrupted them, so now the patrons can't help but listen to this argument between the two bickering Gormon. Even the Gormon, who stands watch behind the counter, turns his attention away from his customers and eavesdrops on the discussion.

'I'll tell you exactly when the forging ends yah broad. Get the metals and alloys out of yer ears and shake the anvils from yer skull, and listen carefully to what I'm about to tell ya! Are you listening?!'

She simply glares in response to the fool's question, thinking of all the curses in her head she's going to tell him once he's finished speaking.

'Good! So listen up, and I think the rest of ya will agree with me on this, at least those of yah who have half a brain and mind about yourselves.' He stands up from the table, knocking his chair back and to the ground. 'The craft of forging is never done, never finished! From the time when you put on yer apron and dawn those gauntlets of thick and proud leather, to when ya prime the bellows with yer boot. The coals heat and the irons boil, into a lovely golden liquid, almost looking good enough to drink!' From the back of the Pail, behind the oak counter, an old woman's voice caws out like an elderly crow.

'Not half as good as my drink I'll wager!' The rest of the company laughs, and the Gormon's cheeks blush, embarrassed.

'Not at all Madam of the Pail, not any drink could possibly be as frothy, warm, and quench the throat of a thirsty Gormon such as yours!' He replies in sweet kindness and apology.

'Alright you glut! Go on with what you were sayin!' Skip all the theatrics and get to yer point, my drink is getting cold.' The brawny, blonde Gormon woman irks him on to finish his argument. He rubs his beard and shakes his fist at her. 'Half a moment you, I was just about to continue! You have as much patience as the blinking of the eye.' He takes a deep breath, huffs and gurgles a bit, then continues.

'My point woman, is that forging is a craft of a life time's work! Your first sword and your last will never look the same, but as we go on, we become more proficient in our craft. Once you hold up that finished armor or weapon above one's eyes, for all the stars and the moon to gaze upon in awe, for the sun to glisten her light upon the shiny steel, and that warm ray of light in the early morning is reflected down upon the steel face like a heavenly glow, casting neither wear, nor showing any signs of blemish and scratch, and all your hard work throughout the night has been polished and glistens proudly... ah, that is when you know that your masterpiece...is complete.'

He looks off into a trance, imaging such an image, him standing upon the highest of mountains, and the morning rays at his back, calling upon the weapon in his hands, for each of them to join in song and celebration. The burly Gormon takes to his heels, for he is very nimble for a pudgy Gormon man. He begins to sing, in his husky, musical voice, in his ancient native tongue, the proud song of the Gormons, the lyrics that have been passed down from ages and eons, since the ancient times of Fausengard and all their people. In translation to the common language of the Civilians, this is how the song goes:

"The bellows thunder, and the furnace roars!

When hammer clashes upon anvil, and fiery sparks soar!

The Forgemaster Melds,

The Forgemaster Bends,

Turning iron and steel, into the mightiest weapons,

In all the land!"

All at once, for a time, the other patrons join in with the chorus, singing away to the words and chants, enthralled by the majestic beauty and staunch powerful words that are held within Gormon poetry. But then, like all good times, they must come to an end, and the Gormon lands his eyes upon the fowl looking and bored Gormon woman of his, sitting in her seat, refusing to join in with the song, pouting and frowning, and those brown eyes of hers glaring up at him in disgust.

'You can butter these people up all you want with yer songs and wurds! I for one will not be whittled and fooled by that false charm of yers! It may have worked on me as a young lass, but not anymore, now that I have become awake to notice it! I see right through you, you glut!'

The burly Gormon growls at her, pulling at his beard in rage. He stomps his feet about and dances around, a different sort of dance, not one of any celebration, but far from it. This is a Gormon who can't keep his feet when angered, so he'll dance around until he thinks up just the words he can use, once the angry fog has rolled away out of his thick, furry head. This is not new to the other patrons hanging about, watching with fanciful joy and entertainment, for this is just a usual night for these two, and the others know what will happen next.

'Damndable Woman! You make me so! Argh!' He stomps about and stomps about, pulling at the beard, biting his lips, throwing and waving his hands about in a goofy charade, the others laughing and looking on, waiting for it, just waiting for the show to start.

'I make you what! Go on and say it! Stop yer stammerin' and give me yer best shot, you big ole Arse!' And the burly Gormon jumps over the table and tackles the Gormon woman with a massive elbow, and tosses her with a shrug and suplex. She goes careening into the table. The Gormon reaches down to grab her, but then she latches onto the beard. 'Ha, my turn ta pull yer ugly mug!' She gives him a straight shot to the family crest, and he falls over in a whimper. 'Now what do ya think of that, you glut?!' She spits on him and walks by, her powerful arms swinging to and fro. The Gormon gets to his feet and charges from behind, wraps his arms around her waist and they both go flying through the door, knocking over those who were either about to leave, or the unsuspecting ones who were on their way in.

The crowds chase them outside to see these two giants wrestle in the streets, wanting to see who would have the upper hand this time around. Many were taking bets on the victor.

'My gold is on Grawn, I think he has a shot this time.' While the other man next to him says in reply. 'Not a chance, look at Eulesa's arms, their much bigger than his. Besides, she has a better winning streak.' Grawn and Eulesa, those are the names of the bickering pair. The two Gormons toss about, and roll across the ground, not much of a fight, but more of a comical wrestling match. 'How long have they been doing this?' One of the onlookers asks. 'They've been doing it as long as they've lived here, as far as I can remember.' Says one of the elder folk. He continues, 'They hate each other's guts, but they both share a passion for the forging of metals and contraptions, so passionate, as you can see, they get and this leads them to disagreements between one another. That's their forge beyond yonder!' He points over across town, high upon a tall and mighty green and rocky hill, where a strong foundation of stone and brick carries upon it, the walls of Y`hul's forge, a tower ruin from days of old. For neither ivy, nor fungi can been seen upon its cracks and mortar, nor about the yard kept behind an old fence of iron, for the up keep Grawn and Eulesa perform daily, is a passion almost as strong as their passion for forging. *"The Sunder and the Thunder"*, is what Grawn and Eulesa call their jewel of a home.

'You can say what you want about Grawn in front of Eulesa, and speak your mind about Eulesa within ear shot of Grawn, but never talk about *The Sunder and the Thunder*, unless it's good news.' The older man adds. The other man cracks a smile at the name and chuckles to himself. 'Sunder is right. Look at them go!'

Their brawl continues all the way down the cobbled road, and across the paved streets. They reach an embankment upon the hill west of town, pass the local housing and many shops held out upon the streets. More and more they pass, and the larger the spectatorship becomes. Cheers and hollers cry out, and the curses roll off of Grawn and Eulesa's lips and tongues at one another. Eulesa strikes to the ribs, and Grawn head-butts, she bites with her less-than-shiny, yellowed teeth, and he holds her into a right smelly armpit hold. They grapple and hold, roll and tumble, until they go just a little too far, and off they go, down into the spring beneath the hill. The cold, dewy water seems to snap them out of their frenzy, and they let go of one another. They take in full, heavy breaths, soaking and dripping wet.

They get to their feet, and climb out of the river. As they pass, they pay no attention to those who gape upon them with wide jaws and funny eyes. Their boots clop and squash from the waters as they stomp by. They turn to one another, each eyeing the other up shamefully, and then face away into opposite directions. 'Consider this a draw?' Grawn asks in a hustled, gruff voice. She coughs and hacks, her throat still choking on a mouthful of water. She spits up a long strand of grass from the stream. 'Admit your wrong!' She roars in a low whisper only he can hear. He clenches his fists, almost about to repeat his silly dance of frustration. 'Alright, alright, fine! You've won, there, are yah happy?!'

She scoffs with laughter. 'I wuld of been happier, if you wuld have drown in that water back there!' She retorts. 'I'd have stuck yer head down to the fishes first! I bet yed say I wus right then, wuldn't yah!' Grawn lashes back, and then Eulesa slugs him across the mouth. 'Ah, shut yer face, glut!' And they walk away, off towards their hill.

The inhabitants and townsfolk of Y`hul, watch as they continue down the road, and up the path and hill, hitting and yelling still at one another, until they finally close the door of *The Sunder and the Thunder*, behind them. 'So, who won?' The two betting Civilians asked each other.

Aside from the quarrels and the constant bickering of those two, most utterly charming of Gormon, life was peaceful, and all was tranquil about the land. Y`hul was built some time ago, nestled several leagues south of Fausengard and the lands of the Gormon. Even though the village is mainly made up mostly of Civilians, the two Gormons Grawn and Eulesa run a steady, and well organized trade in rare metals and armors, swords, axes, as well as other weapons too. Also, there is Ragnar, the Gormon who runs Agonan's Pail. Many travelers who pass these parts, those who bring tales of legends, stories, and even news from distant lands, no matter what their business, nor wherever their paths may lay ahead of them, they always pay a visit to Y`hul, to view Grawn and Eulesa's wares, and to trade in gold and ancient stories. They also come to pass their time in Agonan's Pail, one of the finest establishments in drink and food throughout the land of Aura, and where the best tales and most valuable information can be heard, some if the coin is right to the one who bears these stories and rumors to be told, not simply given away.

One may wonder how and why this establishment received its name, for that is a most interesting story in its own right, but I will try to keep my words short, or I may have to charge. But anyway, it goes something like this: "The Pail, as those who frequently spend their days within its broad wood and stone walls call it, plays an important role in Gormon culture. Thousands of years ago, during the second eon of Aura, the great battle between the Gormons and the Rauks raged on in the far northern lands of Fausengard, back when the two great lands Aura and Raukmar were one.

During the battle, the Gormons were stranded in forgotten valleys and deep, dank caves within fissures and mountains, with no food, nor water. The Rauks hurled rocks and boulders at the peaks and summits, causing avalanches and rock slides, preventing the Gormon armies from escaping, and day after day, thousands of Gormons were dying from starvation. The Rauks are made of nothing more than titanic clumps of stone and granite, they need neither nourishment, nor rest, and can keep fighting on and on for as long as time allows them. One Rauk, however, felt pity for the weary Gormon, and helped them from being completely eradicated, providing for them whatever he could: food, water, but this was still not nearly enough to permit the entire Gormon armies to fight on and survive.

Just as all hope seemed lost, and the Gormons all but scattered and beaten, the Aurora, Agonan, intervened. He came to them in their valleys and caves, their prisons of death and to those who were fading away, their sarcophagus. He came bearing a large pail, crafted out of massive planks of solid wood, and riveted together by two hardened plates of steel banded all the way around the circumference of the base and head of the pail. Built by the Aurora Gonun, the pail was filled to the brim with refreshments and exotic platters of food and game, hunted by Agonan's mighty sword and bow. The pail would never go empty, and lasted the Gormons through to the final days of the war, and to victory, just as the mighty hammer, Maulur, wielded by Gonun himself, struck down into the ground, and a vast and engulfing crack, separated the two realms on either side of the Great Divide."

It was this great battle, that Ragnar the Gormon, named his tavern after, for he, like many Gormon, are descendants of those ancient soldiers of Fausengard.

The floors beneath the patron's feet, are tan marble stone, the counter is made of sturdy lumber, with a nickel-plate riveted and welded across the top, and engravings written in ancient Fausengard, are etched among the edges in script of a more archaic dialect from that time long ago. Ragnar, a large burley fellow, with a belly beneath his animal-skin vest that jiggles with every laugh from one of the patron's jokes or anecdotes. He bears mighty sideburns upon his humble cheeks, and a curled waxed mustache across his upper lip, and a mane of black hair, and large grey boots at the foot of his bulky structure. He knows all too well the quarrels between Grawn and Eulesa, for he is usually the one who will have to break them up, if they cause to much damage to his business, or interfere with the safety of his guests.

Some question if the Pail truly exists, and if the rumors of him keeping it at the back of the tavern are true, but time and time again, he assures all, that it does not. But he could be lying to the patrons, and the rest of us as well.

Later on that night, as midnight came upon the land, and the Pail sat quiet and only a small handful of guests were left seated at their tables, Ragnar decides to walk outside for a sniff of fresh breeze. Off straight ahead of him, he can see the moon over the eastern mountains, the gray tips, become darkened and silhouetted in front of the pale, icy glow. Turning to the other end of the streets, he can see the smoke rising up from *The Sunder and the Thunder*, for those two kin of his will be hard at work throughout the rest of the night.

"Cooling the tongs, is not the end of forging..." He repeats to himself, laughing, thinking about the quarrel those two engaged in, over such little things as a comment, disputes, or disagreements with one another, how silly and futile those two have become, as their days ramble on as much as they do.

The rays of fading moonlight dampens slightly, a silhouette upon the ruins of their forge, what was once the watch tower of Mal Sudor, which was used by the Asyndians to help keep watch over the lands in strategically mapped places across Aura. Over the years, Mal Sudor fell into disrepair, crumbled and broken mortar and bricks were scattered across the rocky hill it sat upon. The ashen brick had crumbled to only a quarter of the size it once was, but ever since Ragnar sold the property to Grawn and Eulesa, they have, over the years, worked wonders upon the ruins, creating a forge for crafting weapons worthy for many travelers to come and pay visit, for their fame has spread throughout both Othetica and Fausengard, and the rest of Aura. They have also brought a little green to the hill, planting trees and grass about the landscape, and bushes around the fence and about the posts.

Within, the furnace of tarnished iron roars, and the flames churn to power the sparks and flames. At the heart of the forge, are two accomplished blacksmiths, who from dusk, until dawn, hammer away at steel and iron, creating some of the finest armor and weapons around, the likes of which can only be found within *The Sunder and the Thunder*.

Ragnar drifts off into a fine day-dream, laying his head back upon his arms, and crosses his leg over the other, and gazes out upon the green pastures off to the north, the mountain peaks reach high and mighty along the far edge of the forest, and somewhere beyond the borders, the oceans mirror the majesty of the dome and high rim of Tundrok's sky. The stars shine out brightly, and Pry's moon shimmers and glistens with the night, in all its majestic glow and sparkle, and once another quiet night has passed beyond the far reaches of the horizons of Aura, the morning sun, the eye of Lota, will rise again, across the calm and misty grass of the dewy sweet morning, the kind of morning all the inhabitants of Y`hul can taste upon their lips and tongues. In the afternoons, a brisk rain will shower the array of colorful flowers and other types of lush flora, and will sprinkle the trees with a light drizzle. The evening wind will run her long icy fingers across the ground, and at the setting of the sun, the air will turn warm and inviting, like a pleasant fire upon the skin, and a ghostly fog will dance and sway, like a supernatural fire rises from a spark of dry brush and bramble of brittle autumn leaves.

These thoughts remind Ragnar of a poem he once heard some time ago from one of his patrons, he never remember the young woman's name, but he remembers her voice, as beautiful, as it was chilling, though filled with sorrow, the way she sang those words, it filled him with a warm feeling inside, almost as though death was not the sickle-wielding intruder he has always been made out to be, but should be viewed as a distant friend who you have not seen in ages, and has walked for miles and miles across distance and time, to pay visit, and to go off on a long walk together, one you will never return from:

The seasons will come, and the seasons will go,

The leaves will fall, and the grass shall grow.

A light will shine upon Aura's birth,

As the forests grow to burn the stone hearth.

For when Winter comes with chilling, cold nights,

The sun will shine with the warmth of Summer's lights.

And burn the glaciers into the open sky,

How sudden, the seasons keep passing by.

The ages move forever on,

Another leaf falls, another day gone.

In the dawn of spring, the blossoms shall bloom,

At the dusk of Fall, they crumble, and fade to their doom.

The seasons move forever on.

When night wanes, the sun will again rise,

Another day comes, another day dies.

Whenever Ragnar thinks about the poem, or hears the pretty voice of that woman, a tear falls from his sad eyes, for it reminds him of time, and how fast time moves, for one in tune with nature can tell just how far the days have come by the fall of a leaf, or the warm air that turns to cold winds, and one can tell the age of a man just by the creases and wrinkles upon his cheeks, and the shadows cast under his eyes.

While engrossed within these questions, deep inside the vaults of his mind, a flicker of a red flame dances upon his eyes, a flame that stretches out from the north. Fires arise and sweep across the land, burning trees and charring the roots of the mountains and ancient structures that lay between Y`hul and the northern horizon. 'Fires that burn', He whispers to himself. 'Fires...fire...fire!' Ragnar leaps to his feet and hurries through the streets, warning all of the oncoming inferno. 'Fire, a fire comes from the north!' Not just flame invades the quiet town, but looming overhead, high into the sky, engulfing the clouds and clean air, is a storm of ash and soot that speeds quickly towards them. All leave their homes, and scramble about in mad panic, gathering what provisions and belongings they can carry.

Grawn and Eulesa hear the commotion carrying on outside, among the tangs and clonks from their hammers hitting the anvil. 'What's going on bout, out there! Are those rabble still goin' on bout us!' Grawn peers out the shutter of the window. 'What yah see, glut?!' Eulesa asks in the middle of her hammering. 'Can't quite tell frum all the smoke...and will yah quit that hammerin', I can't hear!' He retorts. Eulesa stops her hammering, and again asks Grawn what's going on outside, what all the commotion is. 'Maybe you oughta turn that blasted smoke down a bit, we're probably sufficatin' em down there!'

He slams the shutter close, and eyes Eulesa up with a dirty glare. 'Yur the one who's been wantin' the heat turned up! You turn it down!' She holds up the hammer and waves it at him in a threatening motion as though she were going to bash his skull in. 'Don't you go startin' with me now! You wantin' ta be O fur Two taday?!'

He picks up an axe from the holder in the corner and grips it tightly in his grasp, ready to use it at any moment, if only she drives him further over the edge. 'I'll cleave yah in two, if yah...!' Before he can finish his sentence, a sound startles their bones cold, and makes their hair stand on end. 'By Gonun, what was that?!' Grawn yells, startled by the blood-curdling roar. They rush out of the forge, and stand upon the hill, witnessing the entire town of Y`hul being burned all around them by some unseen foe who hides within the thick clouds of smoke. Eulesa cries out, 'Look, down there!'

Grawn looks and he sees Ragnar crawling along the road, injured and bloody, his leg appears to be broken and part of his face burned away. Then, from out of the smoke, something snatches him away, and they hear his screams as something tears him apart.

The same fate can be said for the others, the Civilians run through the streets, panic stricken and disorganized, the smoke flows over, and something hunts them in the shadows, taking them into the thick of the smoke, just as Ragnar. Eulesa grabs Grawn upon the shoulder from behind. 'Get yer armor glut! We're goin' in!'

Grawn and Eulesa bind their calves with iron, band their chest with steel and plate-mail, wear their helmets, Grawn's helmet bears two stag antlers of many points, and Eulesa's has a thick braid of hoft hair flowing down the back, and several crests of wondrous jewels. Their boots iron, and gauntlets of durable copper, the ends of each piece coated with animal furs and underneath they wear a layer of chain-mail. Grawn arms himself with his mighty Wall Shield, and Eulesa, a spear some fifteen feet in length, with a three foot long spike of stainless steel at the tip, The Skewer, she calls it. Often enough, she threatens Grawn with it.

They pound their heads together for good luck, bash metal knuckles together, then trudge down the rocky slope of their hill, and head straight on into the smoke and ash that now covers Y`hul completely. Even to their stout, Gormon hearts, whose bravery isn't easily shaken away or wavered by fear of anything, but even the gruesome sight of the pieces of bodies and entrails of the Civilians, who have been torn away, burned to a crisp, partially devoured, and skewed high upon the rods crowning the roof tops and down upon the fences closer to the streets, ripped out through the windows of their homes, and tossed against the solid, brick walls and cobbled streets, even stepped on and trampled.

"What sort of monstrosity could have done this?" They each thought to themselves. Neither said a word, only a slight gasp and disgust at what they were witnessing.

Then, after walking for a time, the charred remains of Agonan's Pail stood in front of them, and Ragnar was nowhere to be found. 'I can't believe that thing burned the Pail...it's gone! Our friends and fellow Y`hulin's are all dead! Eulesa?!'

This was one of the most sympathetic words Grawn every used towards his Eulesa, for she too, was devastated that all had been destroyed and decimated. 'I too, can feel it Grawn, it wears me down to where I can't feel anything, or maybe I just don't know what to say, or how to feel in such a situation, for sadness, shock, stunned, appalled... these words cannot describe the feelings I have!' This two, was the first time she has called Grawn by his name in a long age.

Grawn reaches for her hand, 'I...I am so surry.' He says, as a tear leaks down his cheek. 'I too, Grawn.' And they give each other a hug of forgiveness, an act of kindness each has not had, again, for some time, not ever since they first met.

Through the smoke up ahead, they hear the snuffle of a long snout, as something shuffles about the stone street, something with clawed feet, for the jagged nails scrape and scratch across the stone. They look into each other's eyes and nod to one another, ready to face this abomination head on.

Grawn and Eulesa go into fighting stance, and enter into where the smoke is thickest, and the gurgles and cries of the beast are fiercest. But, it seems odd to them, maybe it's just false hearing, but they swear there is the echo of a man's footsteps, walking towards them, along the cobbled streets, somewhere, just off in the distance. They call into the dark, but there is no answer, only the growl of the beast.

PART I:

Terror of the Drog

Down a long, barren road, surrounded by twisted trees and dark woods, walks a lone, sullen man. He wears a crude, dented suit of plate-steel armor, and in his right hand, carries a blade encrusted with dry blood and thick strands of decayed silk from a massive web. Within the leather belt across his waist, is his smith's hammer Niron, and thrown over his left shoulder, is a burlap sack full of an assortment of metals, pieces of armor, and unfinished weapons. His name is Hernan, Civilian of Aura, the Forgemaster of Othetica, in the distant land where the Aurora Othetian rules, in the lands where the mighty empire of the Civilians stands.

Just over the trees, about a few miles due north over the hills, he sees smoke rising up into a thick black cloud which looms above. He quickens his pace, steering away from the path a little, and taking cross country off in the direction of the smoke. Rushing past thickets and long grass lands, up over a tall, clover-abundant hill, and down again, into the woods, Hernan notices the trees become more and more whittled away and the trunks burned and black, and he kicks up thick pockets of ash from trees that have been burned down. After a while, he comes to the edge of the charred wood, which opens back up to the road where it has turned north on his original trek. The dirt road and landscape around seems to have been met by the cruel brutality of an unyielding inferno.

Hernan continues once again on the northern part of the road, and after a mile long sprint, up ahead, at the end of the road, upon a low-lying acropolis of burned grass, smoke rises up from what appears to be an abandoned village.

The remains of the sign post read: *"Y`hul, one-half mile ahead."* He has been to Y`hul before, but it has been some time, for he used to come to the Pail with his master Kerrun. Now, he barely even recognizes a pebble of what is left of the town.

As he walks through the streets, the marble stones beneath his feet are charred, the homes have been burned asunder, down to piles of ashes. The corpses of the inhabitants have been thrown about like rag dolls, the smell of charred flesh is still fresh in the air, their twisted limbs and faces of pain hang from steeples and windows, some have been partially devoured and others torn away until nothing but a skeleton remains, with the bones scattered about. In the distance, he hears the faint sound of someone's voice call out, but it seems far off. *"Could someone have survived such an attack"*, he wonders to himself.

The smoke ahead of him is still fairly thick, and blinds whatever lies in front of him, but just up ahead, he hears the cries getting closer towards him, and he breaks into a run. Then, his hopes are dashed away, for through the fog of ashes, Hernan sees a fiery light attack, and the cries for help turn to screams of pain, he hesitates for a moment, then quickens his pace towards the fire. All he can hear now is the clanging of his armor and footsteps. He stops and kneels to the ground, listening for any more voices or sounds.

The winds begin to pick up, and the smoke swirls round him like cyclones, forcing the cancerous winds down his throat, choking him, making the air hard to breathe. The flutter and swooshing of large wings echoes in the night, a roar shatters the silent air that looms over Y`hul. Hernan recognizes the cry of the beast all too well, and the dark shape takes to the sky and flies away, up towards the black clouds, and off away to the mountains that border the northern lands. Upon the crest of the mountains, a tall black peek juts outwards, looming down upon the village with an opaque shadow of doom. This peek is where the tower of Ausgard stands upon a fortress of black obsidian, the sister tower of Mal Sudor; Ausgard guards the north, while Mal Sudor watches the south.

The winds of the beast has cleared away some of the smoke, and the town becomes more visible. Hernan walks about the ruins, examining the destroyed homes. He comes to the ruins of Agonan's Pail. He remembers going into this place, the array of colorful characters, the hearty owner, a Gormon the same as his master Kerrun, and the eccentric Gormon man and woman, who ran the forge of Y`hul, always fighting, always hitting each other, but between the two of them, could make a hell of a weapon or a piece of armor. He thinks hard, to try and remember their names, *"Ah, Grawn and... Eulesa, I believe was the woman's name, a feisty lady she was."* The memories of going into their forge begin to enter his mind. *"I wonder if the forge still stands."*

Marching up the road, on the other side of the smoke screen, there it stands in front of him, out upon the hill this tower has stood upon for all these years, there *The Sunder and the Thunder* still is, though it looks as though to have been touched by the flames of the beast as all the other buildings, but has fared better luck, for it still stands, and its foundation still looks strong and sturdy as he remembers the forge to be when walking through the doors with Kerrun all those years ago, when he was but a young lad.

Within, everything still seems to be pretty much the same as he remembers. The racks off to the left still bear, in order, the axes, then the spears, then swords, and at the base of the spiral stairs, are the shields, broad and wide, small and buckler size. Upon the other wall are the suits of armor, from boot to helmet, and all the other pieces: pauldrons, greaves, cuirass, and gauntlets in between.

Each set is varied and crafted specifically for certain wearers; for one size did not fit all, each suit has its own specific function and style. Above the armor suits, hanging on iron holders nailed into the paneled interior walls, were the war hammers, battle hammers, maces, and morning stars, and flails. At the far end of the tower, on the other side of the wall, behind the counter, through a tall and broad doorway, was the forge, where Grawn and Eulesa crafted these magnificent pieces of weaponry and defense. Inside, there is the large tarnished furnace, the coals have become exhausted, the anvil sits blackened by soot, and a massive grind stone stands in the corner, upon a mechanism that utilizes a foot pedal, which powers the wheel. The ceiling has caved in, and debris is scattered about the floor, along with shards of splintered wood, and crumbled stone from the walls.

The hours pass deeper into the night, and the sun has long set into the northern mountains. Using what trees he could salvage from the charred remains of the forest, dragging the massive logs to the forge, using his mighty strength, and trimming them with an ax so he could fit them through the back door. With a spark of two pieces of granite, fire has once again been brought to *The Sunder and the Thunder*. Using oils he finds in some old bottles upon the shelves, he polishes the anvil to its former luster, and primes the grindstone for sharpening, for he has much forging to do before heading into the shadow of the mountain, where the winged beast had flown. Hernan guesses that this creature has made its lair within the walls of Ausgard, for he has followed this creature now for three days eastward and has finally found where it dwells. The creature is an ancient beast of the old world, the days when Aura and Raukmar were joined. The beast he chases for, is a Drog, and he will not stop until it is slain. *"But why would a drog fly three days away from its lair?"* Hernan asks himself.

Hernan works into the night, blasting raw steel, clenching glowing iron with tongs, and hammering his own weapons and armor into repair, with a few signature adjustments, all created with his own hammer, Niron, given to him by Kerrun. Sweat flows down his brow, drips onto the hot iron, and singes into vapor. With one final slam upon the steel, he quenches the molten axe blade into a trough full of ice water. He raises the blade up into the flicker of the torch light, examining the surface for any blemishes and cracks, or any brittle spots. Inch by inch, moving the blade along the grind wheel, and pumping the stone with the peddle, he smoothes away any of the blemishes he examined for earlier. With a slash and jab, a whirl and spin, then cutting into an old log of wood, the axe is balanced and straight.

He hammers and wails heavily upon his armor and shield to test their durability, so to protect his skin and muscle, flesh and bone from harm. Making sure all his gear is in working, functioning condition, and everything fits tightly upon their appropriate areas, he lays down the hammer upon the anvil, and his work is complete. Hernan crashes down upon one of the beds in the room upstairs, exhausted, for he has not had any decent sleep in days.

Dawn creeps over the misty hills and jagged mountain peaks. The orange rays of the sun, the aurora of Lota shines over the southern lands, but cannot pierce the thick, volcanic clouds that cover Y`hul and the northern lands, as though some ominous force is protecting the drog within its lair. The fiery light streams through from the east, flooding in through a beam in the ceiling and shines upon Hernan's eye, awakening him from his slumber. He grabs a nearby bow and a quiver of arrows from the stand, and marches out into the woods, with nothing on but a pair of slacks and leather boots found in a chest upstairs. He wonders out into the eastern woods, where green still existed. He has been tracking his game now for about a half hour, when he comes to a tall cliff, overlooking a cluster of forest below.

The smell of oak and pine blows upward from the valley. He takes a deep breath, and immerses himself in the scent and fresh air while he could, through his nostrils and into his chest, as though it would be the last, for tomorrow, this part of the forest, may look like the northern forests. How ironic, that the Ash trees, have literally turned to ashes. This is a lush green and fertile hill, a place the spring and summer lights would never miss, even the early fall, when the last of the sun shine is out and about, streaming forth from behind the gray clouds, would smile upon this area, for flowers flourish here, reaching down into a meadow. Through this meadow, is a lake that runs under the trees, here the beams of light stream through the leaves and reflect a golden sparkle off of the surface of the lake.

"Take a good look at them now, the flowers, the emerald caps of the trees, for soon, they may no longer be here, for tomorrow to see." Hernan says to himself. He climbs down a natural stair, carved into the side of the cliff, and follows the woods off towards where he saw the stream from the top of the cliff above. Crossing over the terrain, leaping over thorn bushes, brushing passed rock formations, and ducking under low-lying tree branches, after about a half a mile, he comes to the wide lake. He kneels down, sets the arrows next to him, and dips his hands into the water like a cup, and retrieves handfuls of water to quench his thirst. Then, in the reflection of the lake ahead of him, he sees, standing off upon the far edge, the animal he has been tracking. He looks up and a golden fawn, with curved horns and a golden fleece that shines by the day light, stands mighty and proud upon the far ridge. Its chest puffed with white fur, the neck arched up, and head held high with pride. The fawn dips its mouth down, and laps at the cool water.

Hernan clutches the long bow in his hand, removes one of the arrows from the quiver, places it upon the resting point, positions the thick string into the notch, guides the arrow, and draws back as far as he can, aims...yet before he could fire, the fawn seemed to look directly into his eyes, with its dark brown eyes, as though it spoke to him. He lowers the bow down; he could not bring himself to shoot the fawn. He tosses the bow to the side, gathers some large fruit native to the area, and some berries from the nearby bushes, and makes his way back to Y`hul. For the remaining hours of the day is spent roaming the remains of the town and keeping watch for any shadows and beasts that would attack him unsuspectingly, until the time comes for him to move out, for the true hunt is about to begin.

He waits for nightfall, dawns his armor and hoists his shield over his shoulder, places his axe in a holster upon his belt, gathers his hammer Niron, some torches and other provisions, and sets off for the Ausgard fortress. He storms as fast as his legs can take him, bursting through the burned trees that crumble before him as he tears through the ruins of the northern forests. Then, after miles of running, he comes to a high cliff overlooking a deep fissure below, where a dank and muddy stream runs at the very bottom. Out over the far side of the fissure, is a long and barren wasteland, where steam and poisonous gas gushes up from geysers and volcanic craters, and out to the north, are the peaks of the mountain, and the fortress of Ausgard which stares down upon Hernan, like a deathly idol worshipped by the black shadows that lurk and slither far below. At the peaks, above Ausgard are the clouds of volcanic ash that blankets this part of the land in darkness.

Pass the fissures, and across the barren, poisonous lands of noxious gas, he travels through a remote valley of charred debris and a strong, pungent smell of sulfuric gas. The landscape is dotted with ancient ruins and crumbled towers bearing insignias dating back to the ancient Fausengard culture. He crosses a wide bridge made of polished jet obsidian, inscribed with ancient writings and hieroglyphics. At the far end of the ridge, there is an entrance to a cave that leads into the base of the mountain. Hernan stands in front of the cave and gazes within the darkness, listening...and then a stark roar echoes outward from deep within. Hernan lights one of the torches he carries in the burlap sack, and ventures forth into the caverns.

The ribs of the mountain run deep. Upon entering, the torch light dances upon the stone bowels and innards of the mountain's domain where the drog dwells, the beast he has been tracking now for days. At the far end of the tunnel, there is a stairway carved out of rock that extends upwards, further into the mountain. At the top of the stairs, is a barren area of crumbled ruins, that stand upon either side of a long obsidian walkway. The caverns stalactites and stalagmites grow opposite of each other, like vast rows of razor sharp teeth, an open jaw prepared to engulf its nourishment being lured in. Littered about the ruins are decayed bones and skeletons, mig webs are strewn about in thick clumps and networks, along with old remains of torches long extinguished from the civilization that once used them as a means to light these dark tunnels.

There is another stair, and from above, he can feel wind upon his face. He climbs the steps, jumping over the middle, which had crumbled some ages ago. He muscles his way up a steep wall onto another platform, and then from here, to reach the next landing, he removes a long coil of rope from the sack, ties a loop, and with a strong swing of his arm, tosses the loop above and manages to hook the rope upon a sturdy cliff face.

Pulling himself up for a stretch at a time, he can see light getting closer and the breeze getting stronger. He can feel the burn in the muscles and tendons of his arms and legs, reaching out with his right arm, he clutches a firm grasp upon the ledge and pulls himself up onto the platform.

From here he can look out through a large crack in the mountain wall, and he sees far below, miles in fact, to the distant lands, and the forest that lay far away, back towards the east, and the town of Y`hul now looks like nothing more than a speck of dust, swallowed on all sides by the charred forests, covered by the shade of the black clouds which emit forth from this mountain. He turns and sees a red glow streaming down a long tunnel. He follows the corridor till he comes to a dwelling with a high rocky ceiling and charred granite walls and shaded, marble floors. A roar trembles the walls, the beast is near. Within this room, stands a passageway, some thirty feet or so high, with a gate blocking the way.

This is the entrance to Ausgard, the black fortress perched upon the mountain like a bat embracing the sunless recesses of a cave. Upon each side of the gate, stand two statues, depictions of Fausengard warriors about as high as the gate. They stand in a battle position, as though they were alive, guarding whatever is in the room beyond.

On the right side of the gate, is a large mechanism, a turning lever, with a thick bronze chain to hoist up the gating. Hernan slowly, with powerful shoves and turns, putting all his strength into the rusted contraption, forces the lever to turn. One crank after the next, link by link, the chain rattles upwards, and the gate screeches open, as though letting loose a thousand wailing demons from their covens. Smoke and steam pours forth from the dismal room beyond, covering the floor with a thick blanket of fog. The heat makes the armor hot to wear, and swelters beneath the metal, piercing his very flesh, making his surroundings unbearable to dwell in for too long. He heaves a large boulder under the lever to keep the gate from closing. With the grating mechanism held open, he picks up his torch and delves on, into the lair of the beast.

Hernan follows a marble hallway, decayed by time and blackened by flame. The sulfuric smell of the mountain turns to a poisonous fume that corrodes Hernan's lungs with each inhale. Up ahead, a red glow beams through.

Within the inner chamber, stands mounds of crags and rocks. The walls of Ausgard have been built into the mountain to fortify its resistance to any attacks. Scattered about the ruins, are fallen structures of a once mighty fortress of war, now but a figment of what it once stood for. Huge monolithic pillars reach high up to the ceiling, holding the watch tower with its strong arms, while other pieces and broken pillars lay scattered about and around the obsidian tiled floor. The rooms and guard quarters lay behind locked doors, and resides at the base of the fortress and high up on cliffs. A treasury sits at the center, with its secret and forgotten treasures, gold and jewels, and other artifacts as well, laying deep within under mighty locks of titanium, and the keys either no longer exist, or are lost on some ancient Gormon corpse, somewhere in these vaults.

Weapons and skeletons lay scattered about, armor racks overturned, crumbled buildings and caved-in walls lay on top of forgotten secrets only the ancients once knew the answers to, written texts and scrolls that are inaccessible to any visitors, or intruders alike. Hernan cries out 'Captain Cezius...!' But there is no reply. He calls out again, and still only silence, except for the echo of his voice, spreads throughout the hollow cavern. And then a low grumble, and a slobbering roar echoes back. The sound of teeth clenching together with a stinging, poisonous hiss fills the molten air with dread. Hernan looks above, and high upon the far palisade wall, stirs two sets of yellow eyes, burning with fervor. Hernan draws his axe, raises his shield, and prepares himself for attack.

The creature sleeks back into the shadows and disappears. Hernan stares intently, but cannot find where this fiend could be, he could be hiding anywhere. He can only hear the scraping and crawling of the drog's talons upon the rocks, as though a thousand blades where being sharpened in intervals. It's gurgling surrounds him in a perimeter, the beast eyeing up its prey, those glowing yellow eyes watch every movement Hernan makes, each step, every lift of his axe, and swaying of the shield, everything is being monitored by the drog.

Hernan stops, and waits intently, shield held at eye-level, prepared for anything. Then, at that moment, all movement on both sides stops. Hernan could no longer hear the drog, nor could he tell what direction the beast would be attacking from. The only sound, is that of the molten activity taking place in the chambers far below, where rivers of magma run through the veins of the mountain.

Hernan scans the area, whips around to check his back, then again from the front. Nothing stirs in the dark. He looks up to the crater in the ceiling, where the mountain opens to the outside, the Ausgard tower stretches high up to the peaks of the mountains, from where he stands Hernan cannot see the top of the tower. A faint blue glow from Pry's moon highlights the tower from the east. Hernan, however, has starred for far too long, and has not been paying attention to his surroundings.

The roar of the beast echoes forth, with a sudden shift, Hernan turns to his left, as a huge reptilian drog lunges from the darkness and attacks with claws pointed forward like ten drawn swords, aimed at Hernan's throat. He raises his shield and deflects the incoming claw swipe, but falls upon his back, his axe sailing across the floor. The drog slices again and again, with a relentless flurry of strikes, but can barely scratch Hernan's mighty shield. With all his force, Hernan lands a mighty jab with his fist across the drog's poisonous jaw.

The beast recoils and flies to a higher platform of rock. Hernan can clearly see that this is the beast that decimated the village of Y`hul and killed the villages entire company of Civilians and Gormons, this is the same beast that carried away

Captain Cezius Cabriel, a brave and mighty soldier that once served Aurora Othetian, the beast carried him away to its lair, this mountain, this fortress of darkness.

Hernan and the drog stare, locked eye to eye. The beast flies in and lands, breathing its wreathing flames and fiery bellows upon Hernan, who deflects the blast with his shield. The drog knocks over the columns and pillars upon Hernan, trying to trap the warrior so he can devour him, yet Hernan dodges and evades the incoming monoliths.

The battle rages on, the drog claws, Hernan retrieves his axe and slashes back with mighty blows, having trouble landing a solid hit to pierce the thick scales upon the beasts flesh. But then, the drog raises upon its hind legs, and Hernan answers by removing a long knife from behind his shield, and with a charge and all his might, rams the point through the scales, and plunges the weapon deep into the fell, beating heart. With a last cry of agony, and a wail of defeat, the beast contorts and falls dead.

The dark clouds that have loomed above part ways, and Hernan can now clearly see the starry sky and Pry's moon now just above the mountain, and the tower a silhouette bathing in its light. Hernan has studied the properties of drog scales, and knows they can make a powerful, and nearly impenetrable suit of armor. He removes the knife from the drog's corpse, and one by one, plucks away the scales, placing them into the large burlap sack. After he removes the final scale, only a naked and lifeless drog corpse remains, slowly to be eaten away by the acrid and corrosive gasses and fluids of the mountain, and whatever other creatures will crawl out of their dwellings and holes now that the beast that has terrorized them is dead.

Hernan rummages about the area, but cannot find a trace of Cezius anywhere, no body, no blood, no armor, nothing. He even climbs to the Ausgard tower and explores about its ruins and forgotten halls and hidden corridors, and as in the fortress, there was no sign of Cezius Cabriel anywhere. He places the bag of Drog scales over his shoulder, and heads back down the way he came, to the entrance of the cave, for the exertion of the heat upon his flesh, and the sulfuric burn of the gas upon his throat was becoming too difficult, for even someone with his strength, couldn't possibly handle much more.

Once outside, Hernan feels the relieving touch of the cool winds of the night air. As for Cezius, Hernan does not know what fate has befallen him. He only hopes that Cezius was able to escape the drog and is still alive somewhere. Whether he would see him again, he was not sure. Hernan must continue north to Stonehaven, home of his old master Kerrun, and Kerrun's son Roaur, who is a mighty Gormon warrior and an old friend of Hernan's.

If Hernan follows his current course, and travels by the constellation of the stars, he should reach Stonehaven within a week. Kerrun is old and wise, and knows much about the rich and deep history of Aura, and would be able to answer the questions Hernan seeks, for the secrets back within the tombs of Vos`ul in Fausengard has left him with many more riddles and a vast puzzle with many pieces that needs put together. The situation at hand has made things far too risky to return to Othetica for a time, especially alone. He needs Kerrun and Roaur's help to proceed further. The clock and the hands of time, shall turn back some, and more shall be told of Cezius and his soldiers of misfortune.

And so Hernan travels on and on, to the north, and to the home where the Gormons of Fausengard dwell, through valleys by day and night, the horizon of his destination will soon be in sight...

PART II:

Chalice of Cidom

The sun slowly dims upon the final days of the season. The cold chill of Escalion, the winter, the season of the bitter moon, bites the winds with ferocity. The final light of Somerion, the summer, fades behind the western mountains in a fiery dirge. The last rights of warmth have been done away with.

The blood of the light exposes the snowy peaks and rocky summits, of the limitless pinnacles that seem as though they stretch ethereally into the misty clouds above them. The charred flames reflect upon Hernan's searching eyes, blank and emotionless to their surroundings, but deep in thought and searching of the mind and body for an answer, to be able to grab hold of something, a memory, a feeling, but unsure of what or why. He builds the flames higher with some old foliage and sticks. He gazes pass the flames, and looks westwards to the trees below him, and to the horizon beyond, and recounts and ponders the last few weeks. Thinking about those he traveled with, how he had to lead them away from their protective walls of Novilon, and across a landscape he knew all too well to be perilous to those who weren't ready for its savagery and risks, and to a place with a past so sinister, that it made even the bravest of warriors cringe at its name.

He should have never taken them, he should have refused, he warned them, but they did not listen. If he did not take them, they would have died anyway, in the wilderness of starvation, after roasting the hofts they would have brought with them, then they would have ate one another. But that would have been a merciful death compared to the fate they suffered. Kandarius should never have sent them, but what were his real motives behind the expedition? What role did Kandarius play in this higher purpose that Isifier spoke of, and if Kandarius is involved with Isifier's plans...?

***

Within the long golden throne room of the palace, the walls of fine and polished marble surround from all sides. Tall and mighty pillars reach upwards to long and deep cut arches and grooves, inscribed with the scriptures and images of ancient times, fierce battles, brave warriors and heroines who have lived in days long past. Strange sensations and mist flowed in and out of the open balcony doorway, a triangular window with a rounded top at the point, and silver handles that pulled the doors open and close. A sacred spell is being held over the brows of every guard and servant to the Aurora Othetian, who sits upon a throne of gold with silver trimmings and decor, and sacred minerals native to Aura, mined from the chasms and dirt on the outskirts of the vast city. Along the arm rests and the monolith of stone where Othetian leans his back, are encrusted with jewels of varying colors as bright and vibrant as a rainbow. Below his feet, about the throne's base, runs a small stream clear as a polished crystal or opal of ocean blue, and within this stream swims fish and other life sacred to water and Othetian.

Othetian would usually spends his days walking among the flora of his many gardens of high trees, rich soil, a dazzling array of flowers, yellow and violet, red, blue, cyan, and colors most of which have never been seen or discovered by Civilians. With a wave of his hands, the spring and summer breezes would sift and rustle through the ivy and bushes of jade and emerald leaves and shrubs. Now he spends his days locked away, his mind clouded, for dark have been his dreams of late, the hours that rest upon his shoulders, crumble away with the time that flows from his closed eyes, he has become ill and begotten with the ugly spawn of dystopia upon his eternal mind.

The great and elder being is overseen by his adviser Kandarius Lockmore, a tall and lithe man, dressed in aristocratic robes of maroon and purple, bearing a necklace with an insignia hanging from it, a man who whispers little secrets into his master's ear.

Far across the polished floor, on the other side of the throne room, the mighty golden double-doors open, and a staunch warrior clad in the silver ceremonial armor of Othetica, bearing mighty wings upon the helm, and the Othetian Crest upon the breast-plate of the armor, and at the shoulders, upon the pauldrons, two more decorative wings are placed. By his side is a round silver shield encrusted with a pattern of knobs and rivets, and a singular blue opal at the center. The armor glistens from the sunlight streaming in from the vast windows, and as he passes across the light from the balcony, he is enveloped with a shine that sparkles like the body of a mighty Aurora. The man stands in the presence of Othetian, and kneels to his honor and fealty.

'My Aurora, guardian of all Othetica, the land which has earned your name in honor of your many deeds, I have come at your orders.' His bowed head looks up upon the distant and unaware Othetian. His name is Cezius Cabriel, captain of the Othetica armies under the Grand General, and protector of Novilon, the capital city.

'My Aurora, I have returned as quickly as I could, and when I was able to. We have driven back a majority of the Mirym savages, but many smaller bands still insist on making petty and futile skirmishes against us. They amass raids on caravans, burning our smaller remote forts, but all should be under control soon enough, for this is nothing that we can't handle. It appears as though there has been some sort of civil dispute amongst the clans and we seem to be caught in the middle. Ironically however...our presence seems to have banded many together against us, and now their war is on our doorstep.' Cezius explains.

Othetian is slumped over the hand that braces his gaunt cheek, with a conscious that is unaware of any words, or any other outlying activity around him. He only stares back at Cezius, with neither response, nor reply. Kandarius steps forward to speak. The advisor sends a chill down Cezius's spine. The man's voice, on the other hand, describes a completely different being, for his tone is deep and powerful, almost hypnotizing, using his sentences like a snake, and alluding to the listener like a spider that sings a sweet song to the unwary fly, inviting him into the web. 'The Mirym are savages and a threat to our civilization's outlying towns, the provinces of Cysiiros near Greenhaven in particular. Not to mention our Civilians!'

'I do not question the wisest of Aura, but we only escalate what was not our business to begin with. I have lost many good soldiers for a cause that is not ours. The Mirym are back behind the borders for the most part, if we station a watch, build some defenses, then if we secede from the Northern Provinces, we can end this needless bloodshed! Let those savages solve their own disputes!' Cezius replies.

Kandarius's tone grows questionable. 'I thought you told me, here in the presence of the Aurora, just a moment ago, that you would be able to handle yourself, and yet now you talk of retreat?! To leave our lands and people behind, vulnerable to attack?' Cezius interrupts, 'I just told you we will station a small battalion of guards, and build up a defense, a stronghold, to keep the remainder back behind their borders...!'

Kandarius raises his hand to silence him. 'Forts and strongholds take time to build. How many soldiers and builders will be overrun, killed, slain in the night by the hordes of Mirym, while we focus on building useless structures?! Ah, it does not matter, the Aurora has already decreed that your presence is no longer necessary.' This is shocking news to his ears, Cezius can feel the serpents tail rattling, and the scales tightening. 'What are you saying?' He exclaims.

'I'm saying your command is going to one of your fellow officers, for I have another assignment for you, and our mighty Aurora Othetian has given me the permission to assign you for this duty.' Kandarius explains to the angered captain.

'You just can't take me away from my duties! We are on the brink of an impending war with the Mirym, and you want me to run some errand for you?! Surely you jest?' Cezius retorts.

'That's enough captain! The officer I have assigned is on his way to your post as we speak to take command. I will make sure, the situation GETS under control.' Kandarius looks wide eyed upon Cezius.

'But I can't...' Cezius stammers in refusal, but Kandarius interrupts him.

'Now, if you will follow me, I will brief you on what needs to be done. Do not get to upset captain, this quest is of the highest importance, and I need someone I can...trust to handle it.' Kandarius motions for Cezius to follow him. They go behind the throne room, through a decorative, sturdy wooden door that leads into a living area with a window overlooking the entire city of Novilon and all its limits, as the buildings and tall structures and towers reach out towards the horizons in all the cardinal directions, and the system of streets below, looks like nothing more than a grid with tiny Civilians that go about their business for the day. Kandarius gazes out with his bright eyes, staring down below like a hawk perched upon the cliff's edge, his hands together, and long fingers interlocked with each other. His back turned away from Cezius.

'Alright Kandarius, what are you playing at?!' Cezius asks in a stern tone. 'If you and Othetian deem my skills at war to be so insufficient, then why do you ask me to do something, you claim, to be even more important for you?'

'I do not play games, nor do I joke Captain Cabriel. You see, that was war, this is a bit different. I...as well as Othetian, feel you have become war-weary, and this assignment will give you a change of pace.'

Cezius replies with anger. 'War Weary! Humph...I don't need a break, there is never a break from battle! I need to be with my soldiers, as they need me!' Kandarius turns a deaf ear, as though to ignore Cezius's last few words. 'The matter I speak of, will save Aurora Othetian, and our entire civilization...if you care to quit being so defiant and listen to what I have to say, I will inform you what that matter is.'

Cezius gives Kandarius a scorn look. 'Very well...what do I need to do?' A grim smile forms upon Kandarius's face. 'Good, we have very little time, so listen carefully.' Kandarius turns to face Cezius, and walks over towards him with a brisk stride, as though he were floating. 'I've recently become aware of an artifact, a priceless treasure that has been lost for centuries, that artifact, is called the Chalice of Cidom.' Cezius gives him a confused look. 'The Chalice of Cidom? I've never heard of such a thing.' He replies.

Kandarius continues to explain. 'It's a sacred item of legend, a mighty goblet said to hold the essence of healing.' That same familiar look of disgust engulfs the Cezius's face.

'This is your grand scheme?! You want me to chase after some legend, an object that may not even exist! Some symbol straight out of a children's tale!'

‘The chalice exists, I have studied the ancient scriptures and have charted a map of its location.' Kandarius hands a rolled up piece of paper to Cezius which contains the hand-drawn map of the entire northern lands that border onto Fausengard. Cezius looks over the map. 'Some time ago, I have sent my advisor, Isifier, and a large group of excavators to Vos`ul to dig for the chalice, but I haven't heard from them in about a month, so I need you to go and find out what happened to them and bring me back any news of the chalice.'

'What do you suppose could have happened?' Cezius asks.

'I haven't the faintest idea, but if they have found something...that is why I need you to take your best soldiers and go to Vos`ul. Take the map and find your way.'

Cezius flashes a cold glare. 'My best soldiers are in the cold northwest...dying to protect this land.' Kandarius makes no effort to reply to Cezius, but ignores his words as though nothing was spoken. 'Do this captain, and I will personally see to it that you are made Grand General of all of Othetica's armies, and that you return to your soldiers, and your name will become legendary among Civilian stories and tales. What say you?'

Almost falling into the pool of Kandarius words, Cezius brings his head above water. 'There is nothing you can say that I believe, but if this chalice does exist, and if it will save the Aurora, then I'll do what I can to locate it, and to bring it, and out people, back *(If they yet live...)*!'

Kandarius grins and nods. 'If I may suggest, the terrain of Fausengard can be quite unforgiving, and hard to navigate through its maze of rock patterns and twisting mountain paths. There is however, one I know of who would be able to help you, one who, as I understand, knows his way about Fausengard...'

Smoke rises from the forge, and the heat of the furnace blisters the air, as Hernan creates his latest weapon, a steel gauntlet with three blades of jagged iron riveted above the fingers, upon the knuckles. Hernan wipes the sweat from his brow. The bell rings to the door in his shop, a visitor has come. Hernan lays down his hammer upon a wooden table and walks out to greet them. He finds Cezius, the captain of the Novilon guard and northern armies standing in the lobby surrounded by many soldiers clad head to toe in armor, armor that he forged for them.

'Ah, Captain Cezius, I see my armor has served you and your troops well?'

Cezius does not respond, but only walks in and seats himself at a corner table. Hernan sits upon the counter of his shop, while the soldiers slowly fill in the vast space of the room. 'Yes it has saved mine, and many other lives.' He looks about the shop and gazes upon the finely crafted creations of the Forgemaster, trained under the craftsman Kerrun. Strong, durable, hand crafted swords, axes, spears, half-plate mail, full-plate, chain-mail, any kind of armor or weapon that can be imagined, the Forgemaster has created it and has it displayed within his shop. Upon the far western wall, full suits of the soldier and guard armor are displayed with the appropriate weapons of their ranks on the stands, even a few foreign designs that the people of Othetica have never seen.

'What piece is that?' An eager soldier asks, pointing to a very exotic piece on the far right of the displays.

'That is a rare design I learned from the Baldushan people of the Isa Desert. I traveled there years ago with my master Kerrun, a Gormon of Fausengard. He wanted to broaden my mind on the subtle variations and intricacies on the many ways protection of the skin, the preservation of life, can be made. You see captain, when you call, what I create as armor, it's an art form, it's a craft. But when you dress up men and women to go to war, you are no longer creating art, you are making a life preserver.'

'It's not just a good piece of armor that saves lives, Forgemaster...it also takes great leadership, and brave men and women who are willing to give their lives for those who cannot protect themselves.' Cezius replies.

Hernan nods in agreement. 'You are absolutely correct Captain Cezius, there are many factors in life and death that intertwine with one another, for the outcome...of what may. I have my skills...and you have yours. Now, what do you want from me? A new sword...or maybe that rust spot on your left pauldron needs a good shine? For surely you and a host of soldiers didn't come here to just look at my wares, or is this a show and tell?'

Cezius shrugs off the sarcastic remark made by Hernan. 'I find your acetone sense of humor the least amusing. I am here on a mission from Kandarius Lockmore, Adviser to Aurora Othetian...'

Hernan interrupts, 'A slimy man such as him deserves no spoken title...'

'I hate it just as much, but I am here because the Aurora is ill, and my soldiers, and myself are leading a search to find the Chalice of Cidom...'

Hernan's ears seem to lift up and his eyes open at the words he hears. 'The Chalice...I have heard of it, but only in legends of old.'

'An expedition was sent some months ago and none have been heard from. We have a map here that will lead to the location. They may have found something, so we are going there to get the chalice and find out what happened to our people.'

'Why have you come to me? I want no part in the affairs of the Aurora and his lackey! If its weapons and armor you need, that I can help you with, but anything else is...' Cezius cuts him off. 'You have a knowledge of strange and exotic places outside of Othetica. I know you've spent several years in Fausengard, and that is where we need to go, and you know the land up north and its people better than any other Civilian in Novilon.'

'Where exactly is this location?' Hernan asks. Cezius hands him the map, Hernan unrolls it and looks over the scrawled landscape with wide and intent eyes. He thinks upon the circled area, he lowers his brow, and turns his attention to Cezius. The captain can feel the dread that fills Hernan's stern eyes. 'Captain...do you have any idea where you're going?'

'A place called Vos`ul, do you know where it is?' Cezius asks, hoping the Forgemaster would be able to lead them there.

'I do...but...'

'But what? Can you take us there or not? We are running out of time!' Cezius grows impatient with Hernan's hesitation.

'I can...but I'll ask you again, do you know where you're going?' Hernan repeats his question.

'No...I don't know where this place is.' Cezius looks about him, the courage in the eyes of his soldiers begins to wane. 'What is this supposed to be, a test of some kind?' Anger fills his voice.

'It's not a question of where, but what Vos`ul is. Vos`ul is an ancient burial catacomb of the warlike lords of Fausengard. Sadistic and malicious in their ways, they were. There exists things in those halls and tunnels that have no words to describe them, for those who have breached Vos`ul's secrets, never tell their tale...except for one! One, who just moments before his last breath, told a bone-chilling tale that no ears should ever hear...fifteen years ago, a Gormon mining troupe was sent to excavate the vital minerals that were said to have been within Vos`ul...'

When Hernan finished telling the last words of the Gormon, the color in every Civilian faded from their flesh, all except for Cezius.

'I'm not believing this! You speak of fairy tales, whilst you tell one yourself.' He stomps over to Hernan and rips the map from his grip, rolls it up and grips it tightly in his hand. 'Fall into your ranks, we are leaving!' The soldiers shake away their fear, because they are more fearful of their captain when he is angry, and they clumsily file into their ranks and wait for Cezius to give them their orders to march out the door. Before Cezius can call out, Hernan speaks. 'Are you that eager to get you and your men killed?'

Cezius doesn't turn, but sternly replies, 'We leave tomorrow morning at Lota's first light, with or without you.'

'Very well then, we leave at first light, but before you go, you and your soldiers might want to leave their helmets with me.' Hernan replies.

Cezius turns with a confused look. 'If I may ask...what do you want with our helmets?'

'Because if we are going to Vos`ul, and if we go into those catacombs...you need something to light your way.'

'We have torches.' Cezius replies.

Hernan laughs at Cezius. 'You'll never pierce that darkness with torches...you need real light to see in Vos`ul!'

'I suppose you have what we need?' Cezius asks.

'Leave your helmets with me, and you'll find out tomorrow.' Hernan replies with a smile.

'What's your cost, Forgemaster?' The tone in Cezius's voice is wearied and tired of Hernan's mockery.

'Ha, if we walk out of those tunnels alive, you won't be able to afford it!'

Cezius motions for his soldiers to drop their helmets on the floor in front of Hernan. By the time they are finished, there are dozens of helmets in front of Hernan's feet. Cezius gives the word, and the soldiers of Othetica, followed by Captain Cezius, march out of the forge in a line, and head up the vast circuits of streets back to Othetian's palace.

Hernan works late into the night, casting fittings for the dozens of helmets in his possession. He opens a specially, tightly locked door, and rummages through some sturdy chests, that are also locked up. One of the chests emits a bright light and streams throughout the room of the forge with a blinding fluorescent glow when Hernan opens it. There sits the secret light to break the darkness of Vos`ul. Even more powerful than the orange dawn that will rise and emit forth from the mountains in the east.

At first light, Cezius and his soldiers ride up the marble streets on their armor-clad hofts, heading for the forge. Just ahead, standing below the mighty stack of the chimney, Cezius sees Hernan awaiting them, clad with a steel breastplate over a brown cloth tunic and hooded cape, steel boots, leggings, and thick leather gloves. He leans against the cool, gray brick of his forge. Cezius can see next to him, laid out upon mighty racks of metal, are all the soldiers helmets, including his own, which is designated by the symbol of an Othetica captain. He notices there has been a strange notch added to the top of the helmets, about where the forehead is. They ride up alongside him.

'You're late, first light was about an hour ago.' Hernan says.

'I take it you are ready then?' Cezius replies.

'I like to be prepared.' Hernan says.

Cezius steps off his horse and walks over to Hernan. Hernan looks him up and down, then looks over his shoulder at the tall, white hoft he dismounted.

'Where are you going with that thing?' Hernan says motioning to the hoft.

'It's a long journey, so we are taking our hofts along...do you not have one?' Cezius asks inquisitively.

'No, I'm scared of them...you won't make it far with that

thing. The northern lands are treacherous, rocky, full of valleys and craters, you'll never make it passed the border on the back of one of those. You and your men will have to walk along with me.'

'Now look here...I give the commands to my men, not you, and no one but Aurora Othetian may give me commands!' Cezius retorts.

'And the Aurora's lackeys...' Hernan laughs, but Cezius ignores the comment, only giving him a smug look of anger.

'I know those lands like the back of my hand, you don't...if I say leave the beasts...leave them.' Hernan says curtly.

Cezius motions for his troops to dismount their hofts. 'Very well, if you say so...we walk.' Cezius turns and looks at the helmets upon the metal racks, he finds his own and picks it up looking directly into the notch. He fumbles about with it, and notices a little slider on the side of the notch. He goes to slide it, but Hernan stops him.

'I wouldn't do that...at least not while looking directly into it.'

'What will happen?' No sooner does Cezius ask his question, does he get his answer, for one of his soldiers fails to listen, grabs their helmet, and slides back the notch, and with a bright flash, the soldier falls to the ground covering his eyes, screaming out in pain.

'What has happened to him?!' Cezius asks in earnest.

'He's going to be blind for at least a month, maybe only a few weeks depending on how good a blast he took. There's nothing that can be done except get him to a bed, and let him sleep until it wears off.' Hernan replies to the immediate question.

'Get him back to the palace', Cezius motions for two soldiers to carry the man away, 'And send back someone to get the hofts.' (To Hernan) What is that contraption you placed on our helmets, it just blinded one of my troops?!' Cezius demanded an answer.

'That little gem on your helmet is going to help what little chance you have in Vos`ul, I would give you a demonstration, but I think your boy there already did just that, in fact, it just saved his life. He may be blind for a while, but at least he'll soon see another day. Now, are we ready?' Hernan asks.

'We march!' Cezius calls out, and their quest for the northern lands of Fausengard and the Chalice of Cidom begins.

For days and nights, they trudge along the smooth roads of Othetica and the remaining lands of the Civilians, for within the next few days, the roads begin to grow heavy with debris and rocky, gravelly, dirt. The thick, lush green of the tree tops and grass turns to granite crags and boulders, with dead yellowed grass growing here and there in patches across barren plains and tundra. The climate changes into a clammy, bitter cold, with daunting gray skies looming above that let in very little light or warmth, or protection from the bite of the wind.

They reach the top of a high and mighty acropolis that looks out upon a vast area of Fausengard, which lays out in front of them, stale, lifeless, nothing to see for miles and miles but cold plains.

'Once we climb down this plateau, we'll be in the lands of the Gormon.' Hernan points outwards off in a particular direction. 'If we head further westward beyond those hills, we should arrive at Vos`ul within a few days, but the winds are against us.' He can see the miserable looks upon the soldiers and Cezius. 'It only gets worse from here on.'

They mustered their wits and made their way down the steep acropolis, passing into Fausengard, crossing the long stretch of plains, and once they reached their goal beyond the hills, Hernan could not have been more correct, for the terrain would never have supported their steeds, for every step, every drop, led down into vast craters of spikes and teeth of granite and stone. For the trek, they pay close attention to every step they take, for one misstep and they would fall. When at rest, they looked about their surroundings, gazing upon the impressive mighty citadels of the ancient Gormons that once inhabited this part of Fausengard millenniums ago. One of the soldiers asked Hernan many questions about this strange race of people, for he has never seen a Gormon.

'Forgemaster, sir. I noticed the doorways and openings upon these structures are immense! The Gormons must have been about ten, fifteen feet in height.' The soldier asks.

'They are a mighty race, ranging from seven, to maybe even ten feet or more in height. That is why their structures are much larger, and spacious than a Civilians. After living for so long in Fausengard, I grew so accustomed to their lifestyle, that when I returned home, our own lodgings seemed so cramped, if you could believe that.' Hernan gave a laugh.

'Do any still exist?' The soldier asks with great fascination.

'They do, but they are very secluded further on north of here. It is very rare for anyone living outside of Fausengard to have ever seen a Gormon, it's rare to even be able to lay eyes on their architecture. Consider it a privilege to see such marvels standing before you this close.'

'I think it's absolutely amazing what they've accomplished... Forgemaster, sir? If I may ask, if...if we do make it back home, could you teach me more about these Gormons, I'd like to know all you could tell me.' The soldier asks shyly.

'Young man, consider it something to look forward to, for anything that can give you hope in these grim situations and conditions, always helps.' Hernan replies giving him a pat on the shoulder.

Cezius intervenes. 'Of course were going to make it back. We're getting the chalice, were getting our people, and were getting back to Othetica. Go ready yourself, as for the rest of you, make ready we move out.' He gives Hernan a look of disapproval. Hernan glares back.

The following morning, while traveling along an emptied ravine bed, one of the soldiers scouting ahead finds something laying obtrusively on the bottom of the shallow stream where some water still resides in shallow pools. The scout takes a closer look and is aghast that the shape is of a dead figure, he rolls them over to see the face of a Civilian, drained and old-looking, his skin gaunt and pallid white, his limbs feeble and insipid. Cezius, Hernan, and the rest of the soldiers huddle around to examine the corpse.

'He must have suffered severely, look at how twisted the face is. I wonder what happened to him?' Cezius asks to himself, but out loud.

'Is he one of the ones who went with the expedition?' Hernan asks.

'Has to be, there's no one else he could be. He must have strayed from the convoy and got lost. It looks as though he's been laying out here for some time, he must have starved to death...' Cezius says.

Hernan gets closer and touches the flesh. 'The flesh is dried out, but this is not the progress of decay, nor did he starve to death.' Hernan replies.

'What are you saying, he had to of, there's no other explanation.' Cezius retorts sternly. 'Do you know what happened to him Forgemaster?' Asks one of the soldiers.

'No, but I wish I did. This is odd. I've seen many strange things in my travels, but this is new to me. However, I have one idea, unless you don't believe in fairy tales and ancient legends.'

The scout calls Cezius's attention to him. 'Captain, what's this?' The scout draws their attention to a sticky film covering part of the arm. 'It seems even the migs have found a home in this barren waste. Amazing how such tiny creatures could survive, where a race of giants could not.' Says one of the guards in a joking manner. But there was something about that silky strand that made the flesh on Hernan's arm crawl.

'Is the Forgemaster afraid of a little mig?' Cezius snorted.

'It's not the little ones I'm afraid of...' Hernan whispered to himself as his eyes dart from left to right and he looks all around and behind them.

Beyond a stretch of cliffs and some rocky pitfalls, Cezius and his band rounded the corner into a low lying valley, which seemed to be eaten away with corrosion and an unusually hot breeze. 'Where is that hot wind coming from?' Asked one of the soldiers.

'There is volcanic activity nearby. The Gormons used the natural power of Aura to fuel their great and mighty underground machines. Many have long been in disrepair, but some actually still run after all these years.' Hernan answers the soldiers question.

Up ahead, on the far ridge of the high path, the scout yells and waves his hands wildly. 'Over the hill! I see the encampment!'

They head to the top of the ridge, and sure enough, on the other side, is what remains of the Civilian mining camp. They head down for a closer look, but what they find, or what they don't find, startles them, for the camp is abandoned. It seems as though a struggle had taken place, there is blood, armor, shattered weapons, broken shields, tattered clothing, tents that were either emptied or overturned, pickaxes and equipment lays scattered about, but not one body is to be found.

Cezius picks up a bloody helmet. 'What happened here?'

One of the soldiers walks over to Cezius holding a weapon bearing the substance that was found on the Civilian's body in the ravine. 'Sir, you'd better have a look at this.' He hands the sword to Cezius, who examines it with a worried look upon his face.

Hernan, who is also looking at the blade says, 'Not

afraid of a little mig are you?'

Cezius ignores the comment, but simply replies in a cold tone, 'It's...it's the same as on the man's body.' He turns to Hernan.

'Is there something we should know about these mountains and hills, Forgemaster?'

'Like I said, not unless you want to hear more fables and legends, but be aware of the foul shadows that lurk in the deep, dark recesses of the mountains.' Hernan replies.

They go about searching the camp, Hernan goes to examine the large cavity in the rock where the Civilians were digging, which appears to uncover a large entryway.

'Captain, over here.' Hernan calls out.

Cezius stands in front of the cavern entrance and grips his mouth and nose tightly, blocking from a foul stench that emits from the darkness. 'They must have found something. It smells like something foul has been living here for a while.' Hernan comments.

'There's only one way to find out...' Cezius exclaims. (To soldiers) Everyone, we rest here for a while, then we'll make ready to head into Vos`ul.'

The soldiers took a tent accordingly, most sharing one, some staying outside, Cezius stays in the largest tent, while Hernan stays in one that's in the far corner of the ridge. He lays his equipment down and lays back upon the sleeping roll. Out of the corner of his eye, he sees a strange book laying on the ground next to him with the pages open, face down, as though someone was reading it, and then left in a hurry. He flipped the book around, and noticed by the scribble, that it was someone's journal. He skims through and reads some of the more interesting logs that were recorded.

Journal:

Day 5,

After days and days of travel behind us, we've finally reached the site of where the chalice is supposed to be hidden.

I wonder what this chalice is that everyone is whispering about? Isifier tells me that us scrappers aren't supposed to talk about it. Why...I wonder?

Day 16,

Misery...! How miserable could a person become?! Weeks have gone by and this rock could not possibly clear any more slowly, we have already lost two of our party from strain and exhaustion! Isifier drives us till our bodies refuse to budge any further.

Day 27,

We've finally made it! The rock is clear, but many more have died in the process. Isifier has been silent...the only person he has spoken to, is a messenger to send back to Kandarius, to give him an update, and to tell him the work is almost complete...The only thing left to do, is to explore these caves.

Day 28,

Some of us scrappers have finished clearing away the rest of the dust and debris. Down in the depths of the shadows beneath the mountain, stands an ancient door of crude metal, with inoperative gears and levers that were once used to open and close it. The sight of its carvings and monstrous faces turns my blood cold. I don't want to go any closer. Some of our strongest men hook chains to the mighty latches and pull...a shrieking sound of metal breaks the silence and could be heard for miles. The door is opening...

Day 32,

It's been four days since anyone has seen Isifier. He, and a group of soldiers went into the tunnels behind the door, and none have come back. I hope they don't! Those bastards have punished us enough! I say we should just leave, but everyone is afraid, I can't blame them, because I am too. The shadow of the iron doors upon our faces dampens everyone's spirits. How much longer will it be...?

Day 33,

I have been hearing strange sounds at night, scuffling sounds upon the dirt, shifting and moving rocks. Could just be some small mountain creatures, maybe a loon? But loons howl...

Day 34,

I see them...I don't know what, but I see shadows shifting at night, moving about. I see the ground moving, as though it were opening and closing...Am I going insane?

Day 37,

One of the soldiers have returned, I don't know what happened to her, but she is bloody and her armor is torn apart with deep bloody slashes covering her flesh. One of the healers removed the armor, which seemed to almost be fused to her waist. While removing it, she screamed and writhed with pain and agony. What happened to this poor woman I wonder? The only sign, is a massive bruise completely surrounding her waist, as though something had a hold of her and did not want to let go. Her words were incoherent, but she claimed they found it, they found the chalice! I thought we would be leaving, but as darkness closed around her, she said...Isifier had drank from the cup...the source of the altar! What followed chilled me to the bone, I know not the words to describe what she spoke of... Before she could finish, she was dead. Some of us took her to the spot over on the other side of the ridge were we buried the rest of the dead.

Day 38,

I awaken to something strange. Judging by the cool dampness of the air, and the faint smell of the early wind...it should be morning, but the lights are out. No sun shines, Lota does not watch us. There's something sticky? Am I sticking to the ---------------

The journal ends.

Hernan closes the journal. The revelation is astonishing, the chalice does exist. All the legends and tales he heard years ago were all true. But if someone has already drank from the chalice, would it still be of any worth to them, has their quest been in vain? Hernan takes the journal to Cezius's tent, he must report what he has just read. He bursts through the tent to find Cezius sitting at a small table near candlelight, looking over the map Kandarius gave to him. Cezius jumps, startled by Hernan's abrupt entry.

'What is it Forgemaster?' Cezius asks.

'They've found it! They've found the chalice!' Hernan replies with excitement.

Cezius gives Hernan a puzzled look.

'I have a journal of one of the scrappers, he documents the entire expedition here! Read it and you'll see!' He tosses the journal upon Cezius's table.

Cezius flips through the journal and reads it. He closes it and his eyes open wide. 'Then it was a success...it's here, but Isifier? The dog! Why would he be so foolish as to drink from the chalice?!' Cezius rubs his beard in thought, then slams his fist into the table. 'That bastard, he may have jeopardized everything!'

'Who is this Isifier?' Hernan asks.

'As you would phrase the word Forgemaster, he is a lackcy to Kandarius. He must have sent Isifier in his place so he could remain at the palace.' Cezius speaks in a whisper, then he looks at Hernan with a worried stare. 'I have a bad feeling about this entire mission.'

'I had a bad feeling as soon as I found out we were trying to get to one of the most dangerous places in Fausengard. If this Isifier has drank from the chalice...judging by what happened to him, things did not turn out to well...What now?! What do we do captain?' Hernan asks.

'We delve into the catacombs of Vos`ul, find the chalice, find our people, and if he still lives, we make Isifier talk!' Cezius replies. Cezius looks upon Hernan's face, which has grown very placid and confused. 'What's wrong?' Cezius asks.

Hernan looks about the tent and his surroundings with a nervous stare. 'What time would you say we reached this camp...about late noon?'

'Yes, why?' Cezius tries to figure out what Hernan was getting so worried about.

'If it's late afternoon, then where did the light go?'

Cezius notices this startling revelation as well. The light should be shining, but there was nothing. Fausengard is cloudy, but to have no light at all around the afternoon, did not sit well with the two of them. At that moment, one of the guard's cries from outside the tent.

'THE SUN FADES...THE SUN FADES BEHIND DARK CLOUDS!'

Cezius and Hernan rush from the tent to find that the sun has been engulfed in darkness above, and the valley has grown black as night. The soldiers run about in mad panic. Cezius and Hernan can see the horror upon their faces.

'What sorcery can control the natural elements of Aura?' Hernan asks with confused dread in his voice. Cezius only gave him a look, but said nothing. However, deep in thought, Cezius had some idea of what was going on.

'It's just like in the journal! I have a feeling we're going to have some company.' Hernan says.

In a thunderous, commanding voice, Cezius cries out to

his soldiers. 'Prepare yourselves for battle! Prepare yourself Forgemaster...I have a feeling we've walked into a trap!'

The soldiers form together in scattered groups, watching each other's backs. Cezius heads to the foot of the ridge, while Hernan heads towards the entrance to the caves. They stand in the dead silence of the dark colossus of the mountain, waiting for something to happen, waiting with all their inner instincts of primordial fear eating away at them, all except for Hernan and Cezius, two warriors who were ready to face any foe, not matter how big or veracious they may be, but this eclipse of darkness would loom as a shadow to them the rest of their days, for the horrors they were about to face this evening, terrors they would behold, would not be so easily forgotten.

'WEB!' A soldier cries out. Below their feet a sticky web begins to form about the ground. The ground shifts, and a cry of death rings out. One of the soldiers has disappeared.

'Captain, what's happening?!' Another soldier cries.

'We were set up!' Cezius replies back in rage.

Another scream, and a soldier disappears from beneath their feet, as though the ground had swallowed him up. Then another scream, and another. A trap door camouflaged by dirt and rock opens up, and a giant tunnel mig erupts forth, snatching a soldier, and pulls him in. One of the beasts leaps forth from its tunnel and lands upon Hernan. With a mighty blow, Hernan slashes the mig in two, spilling its greenish guts all over top of him. One leaps for Cezius, but he pierces the creatures eye, and slices off one of its large crab-like pincers before driving the death blow into its face.

'Captain Cezius...watch out!' Hernan calls out, but Cezius doesn't notice the trap door opening to his right side. The creature springs up and grabs Cezius by the leg and tosses him against a large rock, knocking him unconscious on impact. Two migs close in to tear him to pieces and feast on his flesh. Hernan leaps in between the migs and Cezius, with a mighty kick, he sends one of the migs spinning onto its back, and the other one he slices the head clean off, sending it flying over the edge of the cliff. The migs surround them. Hernan rushes to his tent and grabs his helmet. Using the slider upon it, he slides back to reveal the jewel and blinds some of the migs that try to attack, they begin to scatter and head back to their tunnels. Above his head, the light breaks through the darkness, and blisters the nocturnal eyes of the migs. They recoil and retreat to their dens.

Blinded, Hernan covers his eyes and looks above to see Lota shining brightly upon the mountain. He surveys the battlements, and sadly, he is the only one who stands. All have been killed by the tunnel migs, or taken away to their den, all except for himself and the barely conscious captain. He lifts the captain by the shoulders and drags him over to his tent and lays him upon the cot inside. Before leaving the tent, Cezius speaks.

'Forgemaster...I know we have not become the best of allies in this endeavor, but I must ask a favor of you if I may?'

Hernan fixed his attention on the captain and listened to what he was about to ask him.

'If Isifier has found the chalice and has taken its power, then he must be stopped! He must not be allowed to spread whatever terrible atrocities he has planned for Othetica. I've watched you take down those beasts out there with bare fists and some of the finest weapons skills I have ever seen in a Civilian, that's why I am asking, no...pleading, go into Vos`ul and kill Isifier! You're the only one who has the skill to do so, my leg is shattered and my ribs are broken, I cannot go with you. I know you will succeed.'

Hernan nods in agreement. 'I must ask you one question captain, you said we were set up...set up by who, does Kandarius have something to do with this?'

Cezius tries his best to stay conscious, but feels the pain overcoming him. 'I wish I could tell you everything Forgemaster, but there is very little time. I've had my suspicions for some time, but today confirms what I have longed feared. There are events transpiring before us that we have no control over, a long forgotten war between good and evil has once again awakened, a fear that should have been left forgotten has once again become relevant. And those who would see this fear come to be, have shown their faces. I feel the chalice has a small part to play in things to come. We were not meant to return from this farce. However, if worse comes to worse for me, I...you must make sure that nothing happens to Aurora Othetian, for he and the other Auroras keep us safe from the darkness outside...' Cezius is overwhelmed with pain and goes unconscious.

Hernan leaves the tent, readies his armor, sheaths his blade, and carries a large battle axe in his hands. With veins pumping fight, and eyes burning with concentration, Hernan descends into the darkness of Vos`ul.

The caves were black as night. The distance Hernan traveled had only been a few yards before all the light of the outside faded behind him, and the cool breeze was gone. Hernan slid back the cover upon his helmet and the light crystal vanquished the darkness around him, surrounding him in an ethereal field of light. further into the bowels of the cave, he enters into a vast cavern, with a sliver of sunshine from outside emitting from the ceiling high upon the furthest side of the cavern. Within the darkness upon his right hand side, he can hear the familiar creaking, scratching, and crunching of the tunnel migs. He shines his light and can see the foul mass of web that spans the entire width of the cavern, and below is an empty pit of opaque darkness.

The migs crawl upon their thick wires of web, feasting upon the flesh and blood of their prey, the fallen comrades from his party, once mighty soldiers of Othetica, now wrapped cocoons to be eaten by fell creatures. The remains of skulls and pieces of bones are strewn about with the desiccated corpses. The creatures sense Hernan's presence and crawl to attack him. He shines the light crystal upon them and they scatter away into their catacombs within the mountain walls. Up ahead, at the edge of the cavern, there is an entrance that leads into the inner chambers.

The inner sanctum of Vos`ul has marble floors, cracked and eaten away by acrid liquid that drips from the ceilings, coffins line the lower walls with urns and treasures, offerings to the ancient Gormon warlords they belonged to. Upon the high acropolis cliffs sit ancient mausoleums which belong to the more aristocratic and higher up warlords. The air is thick and heavy, Hernan has a difficult time breathing, for the air has a putrid, rotting odor that looms like death and the decay of millenniums. Against the northern wall, there sits a mighty stone altar with a basin of liquid, which seems to emit an odd glow of light and a strange, sweet smell. Hernan walks over to take a closer look. He readies his battle axe to prepare for anything, for the room seems too quiet.

While trekking across the decayed marble, he kicks something upon the ground, sending it rolling across the floor. By the sound, the object is something metallic. He shines his light to the floor and sees a twisted metal object of faded bronze and crushed remains of rare jewels that Hernan has never seen before. He picks up the object, and looks at it closely, and thus realizes, he is holding the Chalice of Cidom, or at least what remains of it. The cup seems to have been crushed by something with a strong and mighty grip, for the metal was thicker than any Hernan had ever seen or worked with at his forge, and was stunned by its durability, but began to worry about who or what crushed such a mighty goblet.

Something moves, but not just in front of him, or behind, but all around him, many shapes seem to surround him. Hernan is prepared, on edge he waits for the thing to strike out at him from any corner, at any moment. He swore the sound was coming closer from behind, and turns to find nothing there. Then, he hears a splash come from the altar. He whips around and sees the glowing liquid dripping from the altar.

Approaching with caution, he sees something stirring, a

bulbous, writhing shape constricts around the altar, and with a grotesque, sick, scaly greenish hand, the thing laps up the water with huge handfuls. Closer to the altar, Hernan could see the thing seemed to be surrounded by many tentacles with long, slimy articulate fingers on the ends. The foul creature lapped the liquid, Hernan could hear it gurgle and belch, as it swallowed and gnawed its jaws together.

Hernan takes a few steps closer, ready to strike the beast while it drank, but he could feel something tighten around his waist and he is lifted into the air by one of the tentacles. The creature stopped drinking, and looks up at Hernan. Hernan could see the beady eyes of a man, upon a face that has been twisted and distorted, cursed by the liquid of the basin, and his head swollen to gigantic size more than triple the circumference of a normal Civilians' head. The hair was thinned and decayed, and hung in long strands, the body was morphed and disfigured, and there were hundreds of tentacles where legs should be. This was the cursed form of Isifier that the unknown Civilian wrote about in his journal.

'WHO ARE YOU?!' Isifier speaks in a gurgled, wretched voice that echoes throughout the cavern, his two yellow eyes glaring at Hernan.

Hernan writhes with pain as Isifier crushes the answer out of him. 'I am Hernan, Forgemaster of Othetica, and the one who will destroy you!'

'Don't be so foolish, FORGEMASTER! I am above your feeble skill! But I am amazed you managed to get passed my creatures!'

'Your creatures?! Those things have dwelled in this place long before you ever came here.'

'Just a little gift from my masters beyond the realm of Aura!' Isifier tightens his grip. 'The chalice has given me the ability to touch their realm and gain some of their power! Thus allowing me to control those beasts like slaves by giving them the darkness they need to shelter themselves from Lota and Pry's harsh gaze, so they can feast as they please. For when I return to that feeble land of Othetica, I shall use all the creatures of night and terror to discard of the weak Civilians. I will take care of Kandarius and that pathetic Aurora, then I will claim my throne and all of Aura will cower before me! The Hexagus will once again walk the realm that is rightfully theirs! You hear me, I will release you my masters, may the Hexagus Realm take its threshold of supremacy once again! Down with the Auroras, HAIL MAZ DREGOR, HAIL THE HEXAGUS LORDS!'

With quick thinking, Hernan shines the light into Isifier's eyes, blinding him. He tosses Hernan across the inner sanctum, hurling him into the coffins and urns of the western wall, smashing the light crystal on impact.

'I will make you suffer for that, you vile thing!' Isifier roars.

Hernan tosses his helmet and struggles to get to his feet. 'At least I'm not as vile as you!'

Isifier strikes Hernan across the chest and face with a solid blow, sending Hernan into more coffins and scattering the treasures of the tomb, and kicking up dust that has laid dormant for thousands and thousands of years. While laying in a daze, Isifier lands blow upon blow down upon Hernan, then picks him up, and tosses his limp, broken, body across to the other side of the sanctum, then lifts him once again and hurtles him head-on into the marble altar, causing some of the water to fall upon Hernan. Some of the liquid drips upon Hernan, and he gets taste of it. Almost immediately, he feels something, something strange is taking place in his body, as though his shattered bones, scars, and bruises are healing themselves. He leaps to his feet with new rejuvenation.

'You cannot destroy me! The power of my Lords runs through me!' Isifier cries with sadistic laughter.

Wiping a trickle of blood from his lip, 'I've seen some strange and ugly things in my travels, but you have to be the strangest, and the ugliest!' Hernan retorts back at Isifier.

Isifier swings at Hernan, but Hernan leaps away with

great stride. He draws his sword, and prepares for the onslaught about to come.

'You're testing my patience thing! When I grab you, I'll eat you piece by piece, absorb your skill, and then we will no longer need the Forgemaster for our higher purposes, for I will bring Azalir into this world by my own hands! Feel honored Forgemaster, for your part in this story ends here, for it is I who will fulfill the ancient prophecies and tales of old! How amusing, for all these years...the Forgemaster was right under our noses, but we didn't even realize it! We could of had Azalir long ago, but we were too ignorant...so here you are now in my grasp! Not even Kandarius could find you, but I have! We expected to find one of the Gormons or Asyndians, never did we realize, the Forgemaster we were searching for...was a mere Civilian! (Sadistic Laugh) Ah, this is to perfect...It will only be a matter of time! Now try not to struggle or squirm , as you fulfill your true destiny, and become part of our divine order and serve your Hexagus Lords!' Isifier unleashes several of his tentacles at Hernan.

Hernan dodges each of the tentacle hands as they struggle to try and get a hold of him. A rage ignites in Hernan's eyes, a fiery anger and swelling hatred burns inside of his veins. 'I don't know where my fate lies, but I know one thing will come to pass, I will fulfill my promise to Captain Cezius Cabriel, leader of the armies of Othetica...I will destroy you!'

With the force of a Skahljhen Fire Tank, the rage of a Desert Prowl, the fearlessness of a Gormon soldier, and crying out the battle hymn of an Asyndian, Hernan rushes forth, head-on to attack Isifier, showing no mercy, and all focus. Hernan clutches a mass of tentacles and slices them to pieces. Chunk by bloody chunk, Isifier is left with nothing but bloody stumps instead of the long tendrils that were once a part of his body. Isifier's eyes turn to fear as the Forgemaster charges straight for him with blood lust in his eyes. Hernan tosses the sword to the marble floor and tackles Isifier to the floor, like a battering ram hitting the heavy doors of a palace. He clutches the bulbous, deformed head of Isifier with both hands and lifts the writhing face up, and then slams it to the ground, crushing the skull and mincing the brain into gelatinous waste. Hernan grabs the large earlobe and lands blow after blow upon Isifier's face with bloody, steel gauntlets. Hernan reaches in and tears one of Isifier's eyes from its socket. Isifier wails in pain, screaming to the black for his death. He grabs hold of the crumpled chalice and shoves it down Isifier's throat, causing him to convulse and choke. Slowly and painfully, Isifier's remaining eye rolls over white, and the deformed shape finally dies. Hernan gives him one last kick to the face and spits upon him in disgust.

'Where are your Hexagus Lords now?!' Hernan picks up his sword and heads for the entrance of the tomb.

At the foot of the exit, Hernan hears a screeching roar, and the heavy flutter of wings lifting off into the air. He rushes out, but is too late, the beast, a drog, fly's away with Cezius in his clutches, away to the west, over the valley and beyond the mountains. Hernan grabs the rest of his equipment from the tent, picks up a few leftover pieces of gear from the bodies, and chases after the drog...

***

And now Hernan sits upon the high cliffs of the mountains, looking out through the misty air at the tree tops below, his fire burning bright into the night. Far to the west he can see the mountains that divide the border between Mirym and Fausengard. It's the water that streams down from the icy summit that creates the lakes and rivers in the valley below that makes the forest so lush and green in such a barren part of Aura. Dotted across the vast landscape in key strategic places, are the ruins of the ancient Asyndian watch towers, and at the center of Aura, far to the south, just barely a sliver of a shape in Hernan's line of sight, is the ruins of Gammafir `ur kmme, the tallest and mightiest structure in all of Aura, built so long ago, that no written history of its creation exists, nor does anyone know for sure who built the structure. Many Aura theologians believe it was built by an ancient ancestor race of the Asyndians, as sentinel protectors for a mystic force that they protected and worshiped. There is an old saying Hernan once heard on his travels years ago:

And the tower leans, and the tower sways,
High above the clouds of Tundrok,
over leagues of vast and endless plains.

Gazing with eternal sight,
Gammafir `ur kmme, protector of
the Azalian light.

Hernan wondered if it had something to do with what Isifier mentioned about 'Azalir', and what did this have to do with him, what were these prophecies? With many questions on his mind, he heads north, to the tower of Stonehaven, home of Master Kerrun.

PART III:

Stonehaven

Before continuing on over the valley, Hernan stops and rests within a lone barren field of jagged rock walls within a crater-like area. The ruins of a lost Fausengard civilization surrounds him, and looming over upon the far eastern ridge, is the ancient tower of Bal Sador, once belonging to the Aurora Tundrok, who commands power over the storms and sky, but he has longed abandoned those ruins, but the shadow that reaches out upon the rocks gives him an odd feeling, as though something is watching him.

Black clouds hurdle over, a storm begins to brew, and the rain comes down. Hernan sits in silence, the only sound, is the sound of the rain dripping upon his armor, making a consistent tick, tick noise. He pulls his hood over, and waits patiently for the storm to pass so he can move on to Stonehaven, for the place lays just about half a day's march through this valley and over some rocky hills.

His ears pick up something, a sound, but he's not sure with the rain beating against the rocks, but he swears to himself that he hears something moving about the area, around him, maybe even more than one. He stares off to the mountains again, looking upon the ruins of the tower, but then he hears the noise again. This time he's sure of it, something is there, and its getting closer, it seems as though the sound is coming from behind him, then, at the foot of his back, the shuffling stops dead. His muscles tense, and the grip upon the hilt of his blade tightens. With his fastest reflexes, he turns, but is not fast enough; the shape of something malevolent erupts from the shadows and knocks him unconscious.

He awakens, feeling groggy and unbalanced as though

he was drugged or poisoned. Stripped of his armor and weapons, his hands bound by some unnatural silky thread, he looks about his surroundings, but everything is the wrong way, the floor is the ceiling and vice versa, until he realizes he is hanging upside down by his ankles, also bound by the silky substance. His head begins to clear, and the sight is all too familiar, he is caught within a mig web similar to the one at Vos`ul. He looks around, he recognizes he is within the walls of the tower. The vast web stretches across the tower floor and from wall to wall, all the way up to a gaping dark tunnel in the ceiling made of mounds and clumps of the web.

From the corners of his eyes, Hernan can see two black shapes, two migs are creeping across the web towards him, with salivating jaws and snapping pincers. It was the poison of the migs that made him so disoriented. A loud hiss echoes forth from the ceiling, and the migs stop dead in their tracks. He gazes up to the hole and sees shiny, scaly mig legs crawling outwards from the darkness, and attached to the legs is the body of a thin, pale woman with blood-red hair and burning red eyes. The people who once dwelled in these parts named her Miglas.

'Awaken...my prisoner... I invite you into my warm embrace.' Miglas speaks in a hollow, scratching voice of seduction. She lets out a high-pitched laugh that echoes throughout the ruins.

'Your smell reeks of my brood and their spilled blood! I've been tracking you since Vos`ul, and now I have you right where I want you! My sisters and I normally give our prey sweet dreams while we feast upon them, sparing them the pain, but you...oh yes, the warrior who survived and escaped Vos`ul, you will feel the puncture of my sisters as they chew away at your skin, and you will feel the excruciating pain as we suck your veins dry of your life's fluid! You will feel the itching and crawling of my young hatching inside of you, tearing away your insides, to be born into a world where they will be one with the shadows, and bask in the darkness to feast on those who dwell within the light, but are unlucky enough to walk into our webs when they are blinded by the night...'

She hisses, and the two migs close in as Miglas watches on with her fiery eyes of blood lust and wrath. As one of the migs begins to strike, with pincers dripping venomous juices foaming from the tips of the fangs, Hernan rears his head back, and when the mig is in range, he thrashes forward with all his force and drives his forehead into the skull of the mig, forcing it to lose hold of its webbing and falling to the marbled floors below, splattering on impact.

Miglas lets out a shrieking scream, and the other mig closes in to strike. The poison has now worn off, and Hernan rips his hands free from the web shackles, winds his arm up and lands a hard right hook across the face of the mig, shattering its eyes with an explosion of greenish goo, and then falls to the floor. Hernan breaks the strand of web holding his ankles, falls and catches onto a hanging strand of web, uses it as a rope and safely climbs down to the floor.

Miglas, with cat-like reflexes, lands upon the tower floor. She rears up to strike, her and Hernan lock eyes, but with a loud clasp of thunder, a great and mighty being appears from above, and crashes to the floor, smashing Miglas under his large steel boot.

'Miserable creatures!' The being roared. He lifts up his heel and scraps Miglas away using a gigantic dagger. He places the dagger back into his hilt and looks down upon Hernan. 'You seem to be able to handle yourself pretty well, my small friend.' He chuckled.

Hernan looks at him, and notices the Helm of Storms upon his head, and the Rings of Lighting and Thunder upon his fingers. Across his waist is the Belt of Rain. He is Tundrok, the Aurora of storms, and he has returned to his tower.

'You are Tundrok.' Hernan asks.

'Of the wind and storms, the thunder and the clouds is my realm. I've built these towers ages ago to keep my priorities in order, but events are changing, and many of my towers, now sit abandoned like this one, and despicable creatures such as these now inhabit them, so I'm doing some maintenance.' Tundrok looks inquisitively at Hernan. 'What brings a Civilian such as yourself all the way out to these remote parts?'

'My names Hernan, Forgemaster of Othetica. I came out here with a band of Civilian soldiers to Vos`ul. We were attacked by creatures such as these, and now I'm the only one who remains. I'm heading just over the hills to Stonehaven where my master Kerrun lives.' Hernan replies.

'Kerrun? He is the ancient hermit that lives east of here, I have noticed the tower on my many travels, and Forgemaster...? There was an old story told years ago about a Forgemaster, but I don't remember how it went...ah well. If I may say, if it's forging and weapons you do, you should head to the east a ways, then go north towards the Great Divide. My brother Gonun has his forge there, you've probably heard of him.' Tundrok reaches into a sack tied upon his belt, fumbles and reaches around, then removes a rolled up parchment of paper, which seems tiny in between his thumb and index finger, but is of normal size to Hernan. 'My brother keeps hidden away and likes to keep to himself, that is why his forge is often called the Lost Gonun Forge.'

'I've heard of the Lost Forge, no one has ever laid eyes upon it, so many consider it to not even exist. Kerrun told me about it in a story when I was younger.' Hernan says.

'That is what Gonun wants everyone to think, but the forge does exist. Only myself and Agonan, our youngest brother, know of its location.' He tosses the map down to Hernan. 'This map will show you it's location. Only the wisest of the Gormon people are able to decipher its symbols and directions, and from what you say about your master, he should be able to read it with no problem. Gonun may not be happy with me, and he may be bothered by you at first, but I think after a time, he'll take to a Forgemaster such as yourself.'

'I thank you mighty Tundrok, and I will take your word

to go visit Gonun.' Hernan replies.

'Your quite welcome Forgemaster. And now I bid you farewell, I must head back to Mirym, there has been some conflict, and I have to figure out what is going on. They've been raiding Civilian forts and invading Othetian's territory, which will not be tolerated if I can help it. The Auroras have maintained peace within Aura since the Aura War eons ago. If I may ask one more question before I go, how has the old Aurora been? What is Othetian doing about these attacks? Have you any news on this situation? It has been some years since the Auroras have had a gathering to discuss events, and it's usually Othetian who calls us to order, but there has not been any word from him or any of the other Auroras. I'm troubled by all of this.'

'The only thing I tell you, is that the day before we left Othetica, our captain, Cezius Cabriel, mentioned that Othetian has been clouded by some kind of darkness, and his adviser, Kandarius Lockmore has been in charge of things.'

Tundrok's voice shifted into a low roar. 'To take control over the authority of an Aurora...!' He didn't finish his sentence, but went into a silent stare, after a moment, he went on. 'There is something wrong....this makes no sense to me, except... if...if what I think is about to happen....!'

'What is going to happen?!' Hernan asks.

'I have to leave Forgemaster, I wish you well in your travels.'

'It has something to do with Maz Dregor and the Hexagus Lords doesn't it?!' Hernan shouts aloud.

Tundrok turns and gives Hernan a grim look of death, his broad face goes white and pale. 'Where did you hear that name?'

'Never mind how, I know it, but I don't know who or what he is or who these Hexagus Lords are.' Hernan replies.

Tundrok stomps closer to Hernan and kneels down closer to him. Feeling a little intimidated by the giant being, Hernan steps back. 'Listen carefully to me, if what I think will happen comes to be, it will be the end of all Auroras and Aura as we know it. The Auroras fear nothing, no beast nor being, except for one, a monstrous, undying entity born of Wom, everything that is black and dark within the realms of the Galakaos. His name is Maz Dregor, the Destroyer! He will bring about the end of Aura and all the realms of Galakaos would soon fall to his reign. I speak of a passing, a new age of tyranny, and a return to a world that was once engulfed by chaos and death, slaughter and torture, a time when the Hexagus once ruled, and will rule again. These events are the Grey Age. I cannot stress enough...we cannot let the Grey Age come to pass...the Hexagus Lords must not be allowed to return to Aura!'

'And what of Azalir?' Hernan asks.

'I'm not the right one to answer that question, ask Gonun, he can tell you everything about Azalir, that is... if he chooses to.' And with a clasp of lightning, as fast as he arrived, Tundrok was gone.

Hernan puts on his armor, and gathers his weapons. He leaves the tower and makes his way towards Stonehaven. After a few hours march, across the winding valley, and the barren tundra beyond the cliff faces, the haven was in view. Smoke arose from the chimney pipe at the very top of the tower, and gears moved the hands of the giant clock face, for Kerrun always had a fascination with time. Hernan grasped the map tightly in his hand and made his way down the hill, hoping the entire trek, that Kerrun would be able to decipher the ancient symbols.

Hernan walks to the ancient looking tower in the valley, a high marble structure built into the cliffs, armed with machinery and gears turning, creaking, and a massive forge built off to the side smoking and bellowing an elongated black cloud stretching upwards into the sky, the forge where Hernan first held a hammer, and pounded upon steel, and melted iron into the shape of a blade. The place where he built piece by piece, his first suit of armor.

Hernan stands beneath the massive, monolithic doors of solid metal. To the right of him is a large hanging rope, as he pulls the rope, a loud gong-sound rings out. A tall, well proportioned figure with a mighty beard down to his belt and a flowing mane of hair opens the doors, and reveals himself to be Roaur, Kerrun's son and one of Hernan's old friends. Roaur peers out, and opens the door with caution.

'Why...I can scarcely believe my eyes! Hernan, is that really you?!' Roaur asks, excited to see his old friend again.

'Hello Roaur, it's been some time. You were expecting someone else?' Hernan replies.

'You might say that, but, please, please come in, come in!' Roaur waves Hernan into Stonehaven, closing the mighty doors behind them.

Hernan looks about the tower, everything seemed to look the same, it's as though Stonehaven has been untouched by the finger of time, and the decay of age. The tower stretches upwards for miles, at the very top within the highest room is where Kerrun spent his days. Roaur leads Hernan across the stone floor and up the long and dizzying heights of the stairs. In the hallway at the very edge of the furthest wall, adjacent to a wide and gaping eye of a window, Hernan could see the flicker of light emitting from Kerrun's study. They stop at the foot of the door.

'How has your father been?' Hernan asks.

'I hate to be the one to tell you, but he hasn't been well. Within the past months, something has come over him, weakening him.' Roaur replies, giving Hernan an ill favored look.

'Is he ill?' Hernan asks in a concerned voice.

'I...I don't know how to explain it. He seems well enough, he spends his days shut away in his room, reading old tomes, gazing over old maps, but he has a hard time moving about, and his body seems to be wasting away, getting thin and pale. I don't know what this plague is that haunts him, but I can feel something as well, it's something that goes deeper into the roots of us all. I can smell it in the air, hear it whispering in the wind, I see it in the ever changing and shifting skies...'

'Has it anything to do with the Grey Age?' Hernan asks.

Roaur looks upon him with shocked and haunted eyes. 'Then you already know of what I speak?' Roaur replies, and Hernan nods in agreement.

Roaur leans closer to Hernan and his voice grows to a whisper. 'Three months ago, a strange man came to Fausengard...a man draped in a shadowy cloak. I didn't like the looks of him.'

'Who was this man?'

'Not sure, he just shows up here at our door, the same way you did. He demanded to see father, but I sent him away and warned him that if he ever came back I'd kill him!'

'It was around this time Kerrun had fallen ill?' Hernan asks.

'I know that man is responsible, curse him!'

Hernan thinks to himself for a moment. 'What did this man look like?'

'I'll never forget those eyes, those coal black eyes rolled over white. And his face sunken and pale, but the strangest thing about him, was that pendant upon his neck, some kind of symbol. Just by looking at it, I could tell it was something...something sinister. It blew an icy wind over his shoulder. Gave me chills, it did.'

A faint familiar voice speaks from the room. 'Roaur, who is there with you?'

'Be right there father.' Roaur calls back. 'Come, father will be glad to see you.' Roaur leads Hernan into the room where Kerrun waits.

Hernan and Roaur walk into Kerrun's room, and there he sits in a large chair, covered up in a large blanket and reading through a hefty-sized book. He turns around in his chair and is shocked and amazed at seeing his old pupil standing before him.

'Gonun's Anvil! I...Hernan! It's been ages my boy. How are you?' Kerrun asks with as much glee as his weak body can produce. Hernan stands next to Kerrun and shakes the Gormon's mighty hand. Kerrun's height sitting is the same as Hernan standing.

'I'm still hanging in there, how 'bout you, old fellow?' Hernan politely asks even though he already knows the answer.

'Oh, I'm having trouble getting out of this chair, my bones ache, my mind comes and goes, and I'm cold all the time, but not cold by the winds or the weather, just...an odd feeling of cold. I know this may sound crazy, but it feels like something is looming over me, like I have a pair of eyes watching, burning through me...' Kerrun goes silent, and returns to his book. Hernan and Roaur look at each other worried. Hernan places the map Tundrok gave to him on the table in front of Kerrun where the candle light shown.

'This was given to me, master Kerrun. It's a map, but I cannot read it...and I was wondering if you could?'

Kerrun sets his book down upon the table next to the parchment. He sits still for a moment, then reaches out with his feeble hand and picks up the map. He turns it, examines it closely, and holds it up to the light. 'Why, this is an odd piece of paper, it feels strange, I've never seen anything like it.' Kerrun removes the strand of tassel that binds the roll together, and opens the map. His eyes go wide and brighten. 'Hernan....where did you get this?!'

Hernan hesitated for a moment, then spoke. 'I received that map from Tundrok.'

Kerrun whispers to himself. 'The Aurora of weather and storm, the one who's territory is Mirym...Incredible!?'

'He said that only the wisest amongst the Gormons would be able to decipher the symbols and markings scrolled upon it.'

Kerrun reached for a looking glass with many levers, lenses, and contraptions upon it, the device ticked and spun, whirred and clicked together. He wrote and scribed onto another piece of parchment like a madman, only making minor comments and whispers out loud. 'Incredible...astonishing....I don't believe....,IT IS!' After a few more words and symbols, scribbles and murmurs, for the first time in months, he leaps from his chair in astonishing excitement. He jumped about the room as though he were a new man. 'It is, it is...after millenniums, all who have searched, all who have failed! At last, I have found it, I have found it, oh bless the Auroras! I have figured it out, it's here within my hand!'

Roaur could not speak, his eyes look on in complete shock, then Hernan speaks. 'You've found it, you've found the lost forge of Gonun?!'

'I have, I have! I knew it existed, I knew, I knew, I just knew it!' He laughed and bellowed until even the mighty structure of Stonehaven began to shake.

'Tundrok told me we should go to the forge, there is more there we can learn about what is going on.' Hernan said.

Kerrun's excitement grew to no bounds, and he bellowed aloud shaking the entire chamber. 'Then make yourselves ready, we'll take whatever supplies we can. Hernan, you've had yourself quite a long trip, relax for a while, and when you're ready, we'll make the final arrangements we need, and head northwest, to the Forge of Gonun! Oh, and Hernan my boy, take this.' Kerrun hands him a scroll with plans and diagrams to a suit of armor. 'Those are plans to forge Drogscale armor with golden chain-mail and heavy steel and silver rivets. It's taken me years to figure out the best formula and proper structure in which to shape, build, and bind the set together, and I've finally done it. I see from that satchel of scales you have there you haven't forgot what properties I've told you to watch for on your travels, and I have a feeling with the long journey were about to make, you'll need all the help you can get. Just like old times. When you two are ready, make use of the forge and help each other out. Make ready, for the road is long, and I feel time is short.'

'Father, do you think it's a good idea for you to go, do you feel you are well enough?' Roaur asks in concern.

'I have strength enough for this.' Kerrun replies.

"The Final Age...The Final Doom...The Final War...and The Last Hero."

Under hammer, the roaring pour of metal, and the power of muscle and sweat, Roaur grasped the steel with heavy tongs and Hernan hammered down, blow upon blow, shaping the metal and drog scale into a new, even more powerful and defensive armor according to Kerrun's schematics and diagrams. And so it was done, hung upon iron rods and hangers, is the Kerrun-Drog scale armor, forged by Roaur and Hernan the Forgemaster. It's spikes and horns were about a foot or two in length, with a ribbed, gold and bronze breast-plate, and a helm, pauldrons, leggings, and gauntlets made of the melded scale material.

PART IV:

Ruins of Otoni

Dawn breaks over the furthest mountain, and a sharp beam of sun clasps upon the windows of Stonehaven, and so it was north they went, to the furthest reaches of Fausengard, into uncharted realms that no Civilian or Gormon has ever been. They took caution of the road and all the dangers that lay in wait, yet there is excitement and adrenaline rushing within their blood. As they walked along Kerrun began to speak in ancient Gormon. Roaur understood a little, as did Hernan. The words translate to an old verse, speaking of Gonun and the lost forge.

In Civilian:

"O hurdle, O hurdle, come find the lost place,
where all has become lost and hidden away,
O wonder, O wonder, the far distant lands,
to search in vain for Gonun's sacred place.
O smoke, O thunder, O splendor and scourge,
O if only we could find, Gonun's lost forge...!"

In Ancient Fausengard:

Uoo rummel, Uoo rummel, doun dendo est ghotoshk
wer elun decou testgok Gonu yhelen dogto,

Uoo Vundr, Uoo Vundr, est furthr ghands,
tusk eresquo iasu Gonu erskdvr sckais.

Uoo koff, Uoo rvvrdr, u diaunder hin scrrge,
Uoo tys vrv elun Gonu Uuulos Fvrg...!

'It was a traveler's chant for the road. Long have those

Gormon of ancient Fausengard wanted to find that forge, hidden away, far beyond the rim of those mountains and plateaus way eastward, were all time and age is forgotten, where only mountains grow and snow falls eternally. Soon, we will lay eyes upon the hidden grotto, were the weapons of the Auroras were forged, the weapons that helped drive out the scourge of Hexagus and their Dregor minions!' Kerrun's voice grew louder with excitement; he could barely contain his joy.

'At least you're feeling better father.' Roaur said.

Kerrun takes a deep breath. 'Ah...I've never felt better in my life.' He unfolds the map to look at their progress. His face changed to alertness, which seemed to trouble Hernan and Roaur.

'We need to be on our toes, according to this map, there seems to be Trau`l territory over beyond that hill, but if we take this right at this rock here... and circle around, we could avoid them, but it would just make our route longer. There is an old ruined fortress this way called the Ruins of Otoni, we will take shelter there.' Kerrun says.

'What if there are worse things within those ruins than Trau`ls?' Roaur asks.

'What are you worried about Roaur, what's one of those Trau`ls going to do, poke you with a fork, ha!' Kerrun replies. He hits Roaur across the shoulder. 'What do you think Hernan?' Roaur asks.

'I say we take the risk, and then we'll deal with what comes.' Hernan replies.

After a mile stretch of abandoned, rough, and treacherous road, they come to the ancient ruins, out over a steep cliff-face, and down over treacherous hills, the vast ruins, that stretch out for miles, built upon layers of dirt and brick, laying down within fissures, and stationed above the far northern horizon, by the base of the mountains, were the Ruins of Otoni, once one of the greatest strongholds, and central power of Ancient Fausengard.

They follow, for about half a mile, a long and twisting stairway, crumbled and cracked, covered by erosion of wind and the ashes of all those who have died in war and battle. Across the battlements and fallen towers, charred brick, and destitute holes and quarters were the troops of Gormon were stationed, are the remains of bones and skulls, rustic armor and battered weapons of this war-torn nation.

'How long will this route take us?' Roaur asks.

Kerrun studies the map, and looks at the route closely. 'Well, I'd say about three days, maybe four, that's if we don't get lost. It appears we have to take that tunnel over there, and by dusk on the fourth day we'll end up on that ridge on the far side to the eastern part of the ruins. It's a shame our times is so short, I would love to take a moment and study these ancient scriptures and hieroglyphics, they could teach me, and reveal much information about our ancient heritage, maybe uncover some long lost secrets.'

'If we survive to see these coming days, and if these ruins still stand, we may be able to return and do just that.' Hernan says. They continue northward, and then turn towards the east, were they come to a ruined tower with a set of stairs, and upon that tower, built from an ancient shell of the beasts of the northern sea, is a looking glass, a way for the ancient war-lords to keep an eye over their empire, and for the guardians to watch for incoming invasions. Kerrun rushes up the stairs. 'Up here you two, take a look at this, an ancient telescope, a looking glass created by the Ancient Fausengard, a marvel of their time, no one had anything like it, except maybe the Asyndians, who had their wings and far-seeing eyes. But for us land beings, this was an advanced little gizmo to have. I tinkered with one of these once at Stonehaven...'

'The only thing father saw from it, was a bird picking a worm from the ground at the first drop of Spring rain from ten feet away…' Roaur mocked, and Hernan followed with a light hearted laugh.

'Well it worked, did it not?' Kerrun retorted, seeming a bit embarrassed. 'Here, Hernan, I want you to have a look, see for yourself.' He moves away, and allows Hernan to look through. 'You just use these levers to lower and raise it, here let me lower it down for you…there we are, and you just turn those knobs on the side there…yes that's it…now, you should be able to see all the ruins, at least passed a thousand yards or so…' Hernan gazes outwards through the powerful lens, and can see every detail of brick and ivy that wraps about, and the many stairs and ledges, corners and crevasses. He gazes up into the sky, the sun is bright, and the sky is clear, the air is crisp, and the wind blows with a steady calm. Hernan lowers the looking glass to one of the far darker corners due west, and for a moment, thought he saw something stirring, but when he looks back, it is gone. He removes himself from the eye piece.

'What is it Hernan, you look as though you saw something?' Kerrun asks.

'I'm not sure, off over there, I thought I saw something moving about.' He replies.

'Could have been anything, who knows what sorts of beasts dwell in this place now.' Kerrun says.

'Trau`ls, that's what!' Roaur adds. 'One on one, Trau`ls are no problem, but in groups, that's a more complicated situation, we need to keep on not just our toes, but both our feet.'

They march ahead for about twenty kilometers, and turn the winding corridors and forsaken halls and tombs of Otoni, until they stand in front of a gaping portal, like a giant, toothless mouth, whose throat leads downward further into the obscurity of these ruins, and to whatever awaits beneath them.

Hernan looks upon each of them, 'Are we ready to descend?' He unsheathes the mighty Drogscale Battleaxe; Roaur levels his hammer in front of his piercing eyes, ready to smash. He nods, and is ready. Kerrun shakes his head in agreement, his powerful mace at his side, beneath the heavy fur coat. They descend downward, into the forgotten vaults and many tunnels of old mines and creaking walkways and metal bridges.

As the darkness closes around them, Kerrun lights a few torches and gives one to Hernan and Roaur. The tunnels stretch high above for miles and miles to the surface, and upon each side of the narrow ledge, surrounded by a guiding rail, are vast chasms with overhanging chains and mining equipment where the ancient Gormons used to dig and excavate for their materials. Up ahead, they hear the creaking of an old machine once used to move along buckets of heavy iron and banded steel to dig heaps of dirt over and over in a consistent loop. They cross over the chasm onto sturdy ground, with glittering walls upon each side, instead of an endless fall. They find the machine that echoes in the deep, and the natural gas propulsion keeps the gears running, but the belt for the mechanism has long snapped, and the buckets no longer turn. Some are missing the bottoms, and all of them are corroded with dirt and soot.

Scattered across the grounds, are the sharp, jagged and sophisticated tools they used to drive the mighty roots of Adimantium metals and alloys from the walls; some in the form of picks and scrappers, others are chisels and mechanisms of grinding iron and pistons. 'This is Adimantium metal, this is what was used to craft the Aurora soldiers weapons, it's not as powerful as Aeridric, used for the Aurora weapons, but you could ask for no finer weapons, unless Gonun crafted them from Aeridric himself, but he had assistance, and the strong men and women assisted with these weapons and armor. Since the Gormon have long abandoned this place, there's no telling who or what may have claim to these priceless walls and vaults now.' Kerrun says.

'Abandoned…or driven out…' Roaur says in a whisper to himself.

Resting here and there, keeping shifts for watch, about three days go by and so far there path has been straight, and fairly smooth, no entanglements with any hostiles thus far.

'Okay, I'd say by my internal clock, that we are about due for our final rest here, in a few more hours we will head straight on just east here, through that tunnel down there, and reach the other side of that cliff face upon the far ridge of this chasm.' Kerrun kicks a rock down into the long, dark abyss below. 'Let's hope we at least don't roll over and fall down there, eh?' His laugh echoes through the tunnels and caves, waking a pack of bats and rodents that screech down the far end within the tunnel, and fly through the cracks of the caves, to the outside. 'Hernan, you keep first…' Up above their heads, they hear a loud rumble, and the caverns begin to shake. Debris and dust from the ceiling crumbles down upon their hair and shoulders, covering them in a light film of soot. They cover their eyes, as they look above, wondering what made that sound. Then, after a few minutes of silence, the sound booms again, this time even stronger. 'What's going on up there?' Roaur asks. 'It feels like these walls could come down any moment if this keeps up!' Hernan replies.

'No, these walls aren't going anywhere.' Kerrun ensures. 'But in any case, Hernan, you take the first watch, Roaur will relieve you in two hours, and then I will take the final watch. If this ceiling does go, and I know it won't, but just don't hesitate to let us know…there's a good lad.' And with that, Kerrun quickly falls into a deep sleep. 'Don't worry Hernan, I'll have one ear open…listening.' Roaur says. Soon he drifts to sleep.

Hernan wondered the corridors, not too far, always within sight of the other two, and within ears reach so he could hear any activity shuffling in the dark. Upon the far wall, Hernan slouches down with his back against the cold wall, his axe across his chest, tightly gripped in his hands. He cannot shake away the lure, the sleep, the soft voice of the dreams, and the call of the soft soothing singing of the Woman of the Night, who guides us hand in hand into an ethereal world of unexplained visions of our mind. But this was not a dream, nor is his sleep soothing and calm.

He ascends a mighty stair, and there is the mirror of thorns and spikes, the horns of a dark beast and a mouth of pure crystal, reflecting a broken and tattered man, bruised and bloody, his face looks so familiar, he's seen this man before. The light shifts, and the shadows play games and sinister tricks with his mind. He stands at the center of a great pit, and there before him, is a shining light, and before the light, a shadow stirs the dark silhouette of some being, he cannot see its face or body, just an eclipse, and an outline of bright light that engulfs it. The shadow moves forward, and quickens its speed, and breaks into a run. A hand lunges forward, not a hand, but a fierce claw grips his neck tightly, and he struggles, trying to pry the vice away...

Hernan wakes up, and finds he is hovering over the vast chasm below, and a hulking Trau`l has hold of his neck, ready to release him to his doom. Regrouping his composure, he grips the Trau`ls wrist and hand and wrenches the beasts carpal bones apart. The Trau`l lets out a painful cry, and lets Hernan go. He grabs onto the edge of the cliff, and hoists himself up upon the ledge. The Trau`l grabs hold of its arm tightly, cursing the Civilian. His fiery eyes look upon Hernan, the bones tied around its neck rattle from its heavy breathing, and he throws off his head dress of heavy leather and crudely sewn eyes and placed antlers, and tosses it to the rocks below. Its nose is pierced with a fierce jagged bone shoved straight through the cartilage, and several jagged bones were torn through the skin like pins, in some tribal design or meaning. The Trau`ls purple skin glows red with anger, it grabs for the bludgeoning cudgel upon its loincloth, hanging by a loose belt or rope created by dried intestines of some beast, raises the weapon, and charges at Hernan. The Trau`l towers over Hernan some ten feet, Hernan ducks away, and when the beast is right in front of the cliff, Hernan leaps forward with a mighty ramming head-butt, and the Trau`l is sent flying, but with Hernan's helmet lodged into the Trau`ls stomach. He can hear its bones and flesh shatter upon the jagged crags at the bottom.

Hernan quickly returns to Roaur and Kerrun, and finds their sleeping sacks empty. He calls to them, and hears a faint reply, a struggle down the left corner around and down a far tunnel. He rushes after them as fast as he can, cursing himself for falling asleep. He follows the tunnel, and turns inward, into a large room, which once held a throne of power, where a great Gormon War-Lord would have once been situated and would have ruled from these chambers, giving commands to his soldiers, keeping an eye on the miners and scrappers, and demanding his orders be followed through with, or else execution would be in order, and the Ancients of Fausengard would not shy away from their torture. Beyond that room is where the grunts and struggle is coming from, for inside the room is an old assembly line, where the molds would have been filled with molten Adimantium metal, into bricks to be placed within the treasury.

The Trau`ls have Kerrun and Roaur hanging upside down by their ankles, tied to massive hooks, their hands bound and mouth gagged by moldy bandages and torn material, and on the opposite end of the room, the Trau`ls pull them by a large grating chain, rusty and long since it has been oiled, to a burning blaze of an oven, used at one time to smelt the metal, but now is to be used to cook the Gormon, melt their armor, fry their beards, and blister their flesh to a rotisserie goodness for the Trau`ls to sink their teeth into.

Kerrun and Roaur look over and see Hernan, they mumble curses and tell him to hurry up the best he can. With only his fists, Hernan leaps upon the belt of the assembly line, and rushes under Roaur and Kerrun, towards the Trau`ls. Two of the beasts let go of the chain, and charge towards Hernan. He gives one a heavy kick, and sends the Trau`l down into the molten pool below, the other he leaps over, grabs the beast by the arm, and tosses the bulky monster into the oven to burn. The others let go of the chain, and the chain stops the mechanism. He sends another into the furnace screaming in agony, and the last he grabs the mace from its belt, and cracks the skull wide open with a mighty swing across its face, and it too, takes a dive into the burning liquid below, to bathe in the agonizing death of melted Adimantium metal.

Hernan releases his two companions from their binds, and pleads for them to forgive him, for he did not mean to fall asleep, it could not be helped. Kerrun approaches him with a smug look upon his face; he raises his hand above Hernan, and pounds him hard, knocking him unconscious and limp to the ground. Kerrun and Roaur gather their belongings that were taken by their captors. 'Roaur, pick him up and let's go!' Roaur hoists Hernan over his shoulder, and carries his hammer in the other, and trots closely behind Kerrun. They track back towards the throne room, and head out the far tunnel. Once through, they take the eastern tunnel as planned, and break into a run. Just up ahead, they see a faint light, followed by a long arched stair over another chasm. Hernan begins to stir. They stop for a moment, and Roaur sets him down.

Hernan rubs his soar head, and looks up at the two of them. 'What happened, I remember the Trau`ls and then all went black…ah, my head is throbbing.' Kerrun grabs Hernan by the arm and hoists him up. 'You clumsy oaf, you were fighting the Trau`ls and tripped over your own boot lacings! Bumped your head on a rock you did! Now hurry up and let's get out of here, there's the bridge up ahead, and over the bridge is the stair out of here. Now go, go…!' Hernan shakes himself off, and breaks for the bridge, Kerrun gives Roaur a wink, and the two follow after him. The Trau`ls are in pursuit.

Hernan, Kerrun, and Roaur cross the bridge, and begin to ascend the stairs. The sunlight pierces in brightly, and they can feel a bit of wind across their skin. Roaur stops and heads back down. 'Roaur, what are you doing, we don't have time for this!' Kerrun shouts. 'Half a moment, this will stop those bastards!' He stands at the tip of the bridge, and on the other side, legions of Trau`ls gather about. Then, above their heads, the boom and crash echoes even louder. Large chunks of ceiling falls. As the Trau`l mount their attack and begin to cross, Roaur raises his hammer high above his head, and then another large chunk of ceiling falls, crashing through the bridge, and sending the foul beasts into the abyss. Roaur turns to the others, 'So much for my plan!' Hernan and Kerrun wave him on to get moving. 'Roaur, stop fooling around and get a move on will you!' Kerrun yells, and the three exit the caves as most of the ceiling begins to collapse behind them, and closing in their exit just as they slip through.

Upon the surface, they stand among the familiar crumbled tower ruins and buildings in collapse. Upon the left side of the road ahead, is a large river that separates the two halves of the ruins. They hear a commotion up ahead, a dozen or more voices cry out to one another, an army, but not an army of Trau`ls. 'It sounds like there's some fighting going on…come on Hernan, let's hurry up and get in on this!' Roaur cries excited, and rushes off ahead of the other two. Hernan follows behind, and Kerrun curses Roaur's impatience. 'Blasted lug-head! I know he's a great warrior, but we have to stick together.' Kerrun trots along down the stone road, and catches up to the other two, watching a battle taking place.

Crouched behind huge rocks, rubble and abandoned towers are battalions of stationed Gormons, clad in heavy armor and battle ready. One of them upon the highest tower shouts orders to the soldiers below, some who launch chunks of debris with make-shift catapults at their targets beyond their perimeter. Hernan, Kerrun, and Roaur could see they were surrounded by legions of Trau`ls, who have taken over the entire other half of the city, which was divided by the murky river of water at the center, and were throwing large boulders and hurling trees at the Otoni fortress. The three rush in closer to take cover next to a group of Gormon.

'What has happened here?' Kerrun asked one of the troops. 'I thought these ruins were supposed to be abandoned!?'

The soldier turned, his blond beard was half burned by flames, and a deep red scar covered part of his face where he was burned. 'We received word from the Asyndians about the Mirym attacks upon Othetica, so we've come westward from Fauldsgrad to set up watch at the borders in case they decide to invade Fausengard, others have gone on ahead to join up with the forces gathering there. Our superiors thought the abandoned ruins of Otoni would be a good base of operations, but this place is over run by Trau`ls! If this keeps up, we'll all be dead before the Mirym reach here! They've done nothing but bombard us day and night with rocks and trees, but we've managed to collect some of their projectiles and use 'em to build these catapults, and give them back a taste of their own medicine!'

'You said forces are gathering, what forces?!' Hernan asks.

'Airical has called for troops, something about old alliances, that sort of thing. I don't know much about it. Seems like a big waste of time to me, the old alliances haven't existed for ages! Something big must be afoot.'

'Something is indeed.' Kerrun replies.

From the tower above, the leader of the Gormon soldiers yells charge, and the blond Gormon, along with the other troops, charge at full speed in the direction of the Trau`ls. Before they even knew what hit them, boulders and rocks fell from the skies, smashing and killing the Gormon on impact. The large, red-bearded Gormon leader jumps down from the tower and stomps toward Hernan. His name is Hideron, general of Fauldsgrad.

'You! What are you doing here? This is no place for Civilians! Can't you see we are at war with a legion of Trau`ls?!' He looks upon Roaur. 'You look like a strong and well built Gormon, get in there with the others and fight!' He then looks at Kerrun. 'And you, old man! This is no place for you either...!'

Roaur stands up to Hideron and they stare eye to eye. 'Watch what you say about my father!'

Hideron growls back. 'How dare you, just who do think you are!? I am your superior in command, and you dare speak back, after I have given you an order!'

'You don't give me any orders. I am Roaur, the greatest warrior Fausengard has ever seen. Your position means nothing to me, so you'd better step down, now!' Roaur replies back with double the intimidation.

'Some warrior you are, I've never heard your name before, now you'd better get in there or I'll...' Before Hideron could finish his sentence, there was a loud thunderous boom hitting the ground over by the bridge leading across to the other side of the ruined city. They all rush to the top of the fortress ruins to find out what was happening. In between the second wave of charging Gormons, a large being stands in front of them, and the opposing Trau`ls. He stands about twenty feet in height, wears tarnished bronze armor and an animal skin cloth across his waist, upon a thick chain across his chest is a horn, and he wields a sword that spans about fifty or so feet in length. He is beardless, and upon his blind left eye, was a deep scar that ran from his head to his cheek. He blows into the horn that thunders across the sky and shakes the entire city causing rubble to fall, he cries out a bloody roar, raises his sword high into the air, and leaps upon the Trau`ls before they knew what was happening. Hacking and slashing, the being whittled down to nothing but puddles of blood, goop, chunks of meat, and piles of splintered bone. The rest, who could get away, fled from the city limits, back to their burrows and caves on the other side of the hills. The being turns, tramples through the piles of guts and slime which now litters the ruined streets of Otoni, and walks towards Hernan and the others who stand upon the top of the palisade.

'Which of you is the Forgemaster?' He asks.

'I am the one you seek.' Hernan steps forward. Hideron rubs his head in confusion.

'I am Agonan, Tundrok has told me about your meeting, unlike him and his busy mind, I am aware of whom you are, and I have come to help you get to my brother's forge safely. That map will only lead you on the dangerous path. Us Auroras take it for granted, because we fear nothing. Even with a map, Gonun's forge was never meant to be found. If what Tundrok has been telling me, and the Grey Age comes, then it's imperative that I take you to Gonun immediately. We must be prepared for what is to come.' Agonan turns to Hideron. 'Your troops can safely occupy the ruins now; I don't think the Trau`ls will be back for a while.' Hideron bends on his knees, thanking the Aurora over and over, praising him for his intervention.

'If you are ready, we are off. Unfortunately, we must travel on foot, for if I take you the way I travel, well...you don't want to find out what would happen to your flesh.' He laughs.

'Unbelievable! I never would imagine I would one day travel side by side with an Aurora, let alone to the secret forge!' Kerrun says to himself.

PART V:

The Drog Riders

The wild winds blow fierce as ice, and as cold as the reptile's blood. The wings of the great beast carry the weakened and limp body of Cezius within the talons of its feet. Cezius feels a rush of pressure against his face, as though he were traveling a hundred miles every second, the atmosphere seems to take him up higher and higher, then with a sudden sweep, dives back down again, and the unscheduled patterns continued over the course of this odyssey he has been swept away on. The sharp motion, and the tearing pain within his back, begins to stir his long and darkened sleep.

His bright blue eyes open, his hair sweeping wildly in the winds, and that's when he looks below, far below, gazing out over mountains that appear as small as little dirt piles children create upon the floor of a muddy forest during the spring months. Vast lakes weave in and out of the green mounds and valleys like the veins upon the elderly that have sagged and become varicose with age. The clouds they soar through create screens of mists and water vapor which seem impossible to see through, or in which direction he was heading. He turns his neck up, and sees the dark green scales of the flying creature. It's long, double jointed legs hold him up, and inward close to its chest and abdomen area, it's long muscular arms are stretched outwards. But as terrified as Cezius felt being gripped by this beast, even he would admit that the mighty wing span of this creature was most impressive, for they must have measured some twenty to thirty feet in each direction. They forced pressure downwards, catching the strong updrafts, and keeping its large figure aloft in the air on a glide across the setting sky, and the red of the sun dazzled across the scales in a million sparks of gold and lightning clashing across the atmosphere.

The sights were overwhelming him, and he began to feel dizzy, and darkness was taking hold again, he could feel his eyes begin to close again. Before he faded, he could hear a voice, a woman's voice cry out against the muffle of the wind, 'Hang in there captain, we're going to land!' She began to speak to someone else, for it must be the beast she's speaking with. 'Their they are Fenzir; let's head down to those cliffs!' As for the young captain of Othetica, all goes black.

Down below, the creature circles about the area of heavy forests of golden wood, rivers that are needles in width, and a raging water fall on the cliff face, which supplies these rivers with their ample water distribution to the northern oceans that flow around Mirym, and just barely touch upon the Fausengard borders in the east. The creature lays the limp passenger upon a soft patch of weeds and grass, then lands just yards away. Cezius rustles about and twists and turns upon the grass, hearing many voices talk amongst each other, sounding muffled and out of focus. In the background of their discussions, is the crackling roar of a fire. He grips his sore arm, and cradles it within the palm of his hand, and gets up to his feet, limping, taking very slow and careful movements, for he still feels his head throbbing and his eyes turn the landscape about him.

He looks around at several faces looking upon him; they are blurred and unfamiliar to him. Before him, a tall and proportioned man stands, his armor brass, and his cape a golden yellow. He wears a helmet that bears the symbol of the Asyndians, the Athil carving above the brow etched into the polished brass. The others are dressed in their own specific armors, some dark silver, aged gold, copper, scale, and chainmail, and either wearing varied helmets of their own make, the other two rest their helmet, cradled under their arm. As Cezius's eyes clear up, he sees now there are five figures surrounding him, each wears a scarf around their neck. The four men wear red, green, brown, and white, but they are complex in their design, as is their armor, for this is how the Asyndians once made their wares, items, arms and armor, before their dark days came about. But off to the right, behind the rest, is one woman, a tiny thing in stature. Her hair is a long, light brown, cascading over a suit of green-scale armor, a skirt of gold scales is about her waist, and her scarf is as yellow as the rays of the sun. Her one ear, the one on the right is longer than the other, and the tip is pointed, and under the left eye, is either a scar or an odd tattoo, though looks purple in color. She, as well as the others, looks upon this injured Civilian she has brought from the east.

Cezius eyes them up, and thinks hard, searching for the words to speak, but could only come up with two of the most simple, and probably, for his situation, the best questions he could ask, 'Who are all of you?', and 'How did I get here?' The man in the brass armor speaks to him, a smile shines upon his face, which seems to be warm in its tone and grin, for he does not try to strike warning into Cezius's heart. 'Feeling any better, young captain?' He said with a joking tone and a chuckle that becomes a laugh amongst the group. 'Shoranna tells me you had a bit of a bumpy ride getting here, for you, like the rest of the Civilians and Gormons, and just about anyone within Aura as well, aren't accustomed to flying.' He walks over and helps Cezius trot his way over towards their fire, where six rocks have been placed in a circle, like six thrones of rock. The man seats Cezius upon one of them; the others sit down accordingly around him. ‘The powers of the drog have helped heal your body, but you’ll still be soar for a time.’ The man says to him.

Cezius just stares at them. 'Is he still able to speak, sir?' Asks the old man in the dark, silver armor. He scratches his long white beard, trying to figure Cezius out. The man in bronze armor replies. 'He's perfectly well, just give him half a moment to take everything in and let go of the shock of being so high up in the air.' He turns the conversation to Cezius. 'You weren't too lucky then, my friend, for the drog fly so fast, that many just go black at take-off, but the fact you were able to actually wake up in the middle of flight...? You must have some strength about you, Captain Cezius Cabriel.' And this is when Cezius broke through the course dryness of his sore throat, and spoke to them. 'You know who I am?' Cezius asks, where the man replies, 'Of course, how else would we have searched you out?'

'What about the other, there was another Civilian with me! He went into the crypts to find the chalice?' Cezius asks eager to hear if they had any news of Hernan. Shoranna replied in a grim tone. 'You were the only one there with any life when I found you. If your friend went into those crypts, then he probably died in there.'

Cezius retorts at the very thought. 'I don't believe that! I've seen that man fight, he was side by side with my troops and I, he battered down those giant mig's as though he were swatting flies!'

The man in brass armor intervenes with the conversation. 'You'll have to excuse Shoranna; she's…been through a rough time…we all have.' Shoranna heads away from the group to the edge of the woods. 'She doesn't know your friend, or who he is.'

'Hernan?' Cezius adds.

'Yes, Hernan, the Forgemaster. We can tell you, however, that he is alive and well, as of yesterday he passed north of Fausengard in the company of two Gormon. He must come by a different road, for he has another task set before him.' The news is glad to Cezius's ears, for he will be a valuable ally in the fight to come. Cezius looks around, for the beast that brought him here. 'A monster…something big brought me here, what was it? Where is it?'

The man motions for him to quiet down. 'Shhhh…they might hear you.' He looks about the skies above. 'The drog are our allies, but these in particular are very sensitive to being mistaken for other drogs of a less than savory nature, for not all are friendly.' Cezius looks in the sky, 'Where are they at, I can't see them?' He asks.

'They go where they please, and are summoned only when we call for them.' The man takes off his helmet, as do the other riders, and they reveal they each have a specific tattoo around their eye, and an ear that is longer than the other and pointed. 'We are the Drog Riders, a sacred group who patrol the skies, land, and seas. We are spies for the west, an extra pair of eyes for Asyndia, for we take our orders from Airical and the sacred lady, Y`nahlia.' The man says with great pride in his voice.

Cezius looks upon them and their strange markings. 'What do the tattoos mean, and the ear? And, if you're from Asyndia, why do you not look like the other Asyndians, you look as though you were any other Civilian, except for the mentioned tattoos and your ears.'

The man stands up. 'To answer your questions, I will give you a brief lesson in our history, but first I think our names are in order. My name is Durg` the Blessed, the old one with the beard is Augr` the Winded, the tall one over there, with the brown locks and beard is Hurg` the Legend, the bald one with the side burns is Arro` the Bold, and you already know Shoranna the Legacy.' Cezius nods to great each one as Durg` introduces them. 'The tattoo is a birth mark, when the drog fly at speeds beyond light and time, they permit us to see where we are going, and our ear, allows us to hear what the drogs say when they speak, for drogs are clever and can understand any language spoken to them, but only us select chosen can listen and understand them, for their speech is as old as Aura itself. They were taught to speak by the sacred lady, but over the course of eons almost all of them turned feral and forgot this sacred language, but during certain stages of Pry's moon, and Lota's sun, on a specific day during the seasons, a drog and a rider will be born at the same time, they are destined to be one, and will meet by fate, we hear their call, as they are drawn to the power of this mark, for it calls to them.' He says pointing to the tattoo upon his eye.

'You said you were part of a sacred order, where are the rest of you?' Cezius asks. Durg` and the other three bow their heads in sorrow, then Durg` speaks. 'We are all that is left of our kind, us five are the last of the Drog Riders, for many were slain during the Raukmar Wars, some died of old age, for when either the drog or the rider dies, the other will die as well. And many were persecuted, hunted down for trophies, our ears and birth signs would be sliced away, and our drog's butchered and segmented into a pile of wings, bones, scales, whatever the perpetrators could sell to those willing to pay the price, but we have suffered the highest price for our services to Aura, and now we are all but faded into a passing tale told by campfires and beside a child's bed.' Durg`'s words fade into the crackle of the fire, he looks up and sees that the stars now brightly glitter.

'I am sorry, if I may, I have a few other questions to ask.' Cezius says to Durg`, not wanting to intervene with his deep thoughts upon the past. 'Go on young captain of Othetica, for the night is still young, the hour not so late, and the past is only the past. So go on, ask what you will, for we'll be happy to answer.'

'How did you locate me, I mean…me and my troops were in one of the most remote and uninhabited parts of

Fausengard. What made you fly there?' Durg` and the others laugh. 'We are constantly everywhere, we can fly as fast as we choose and cover the entire realm of Aura with incredible time. Shoranna simply flew over your location, found you unconscious, and brought you here, it's a very simply matter for us to find someone.' Durg` replies.

'Why were you trying to find me?' The five stand up and at attention, facing Cezius proudly. 'We were waiting for when you would ask that question, for it is the most important one of all.' Durg` says. Augr` walks over closer to him and places a hand upon his shoulder. 'Because, when the Grey Age comes, you are the one, to lead the armies of the three, the armies that gather as we speak!' Augr` stands back at attention.

'Army of three, what army is this you speak of?'

'Yes, as Augr` has mentioned, the army of three. Long ago, a last union of Asyndians, Gormons, and Civilians joined together to face Reignkiing, the ancient foe, summoned to blanket Aura within the confines of the first Grey Age, but thanks to the efforts of all, this did not come to pass, only Asyndia was afflicted. Now, the darkness stirs, the enemy has revealed itself, a new Grey Age is upon us, for I believe you already know of what I speak of, for you have seen this first hand.' Cezius thinks for a moment. 'You mean…' Cezius shouts. 'Yes, Airical and Y`nahlia have begun to renew these old alliances and have made contact with those who have not abandoned the old ways, for west is where we are to take you, to lead the new alliances to war, the Runegard troops have been summoned and await the command of their grand general.'

Cezius takes a moment to absorb all this news, a bit of shock comes over him, then he begins to feel anew, a sense of pride about him, for when he was taken away from his duties to the north, he felt low and ashamed, thus these feelings begin to creep back into his conscious mind. 'I…I feel honored, for your sacred Auroras to have chose me as their general, for such a responsibility…but I was pulled away from my duties, torn from my troops, my brothers and sisters, demoted to a mere errand boy! For a war wages on our borders with the Mirym, and apparently, I was not worthy, and my leadership insufficient.'

Durg` gives him a glare. 'The Lady and Airical know of your skills and of your deeds and victories as a general! You are not insufficient, your departure was not your doing, for sorcery and trickery of a dark, and more sinister kind was at work!' He goes silent for a moment. 'As for your troops, your war with the Mirym, it is all over.'

This sudden news comes as a horrifying shock. 'What do you mean over?! Did we win, were my soldiers pulled out?! What happened?'

'Hurg`, Arro`, you want to tell him?' Durg` looks at the two riders who sit with their heads looking away in any direction but at Cezius. 'What!?' If something has happened to my troops, I will have you tell me!' Cezius demands them to speak, it takes them a moment to find the right words, but no words can subdue what they are about to say, so Arro` the Bold, stands and breaks the bad news to the captain. 'Two weeks ago, Hurg` and myself were spying out the land, when we intercepted them, legions of them…'

'Legions of what?!'

'Dregor,' Hurg` answers, 'Thousands of them, led by Athian Dor. They surrounded the Othetian troops from all sides. They could not be helped, there were too many! Then the Mirym finished up the rest…it was a blood-bath!'

Cezius's face begins to contort with anger. 'That was who replaced me! Once I was out of the way, he would send in the black armor of the Dregor Legions to wipe out my men?!

That scum, that bastard! He killed them all, all those good men and women…men and women I knew for most of my life, who followed under my command, who would die for me, and I for them!!!!!!!'

'Your soldiers fought bravely captain; they died fighting in your honor, and the honor of all Othetica! There death was a tragedy, but was not in vain. It has revealed to you what you must do, and you will have the vengeance you seek!' Durg` says. Cezius does not reply, but his thoughts read upon his face like an open book. He goes away off into the trees, and sits down upon a large, knobbed root, overlaying a vast steppe, and below an array of green shrubs and low laying branches.

'Leave him alone for awhile; he's been through enough for one day.' Durg` says to the others.

'What about Shoranna?' Arro` asks.

'We'll let them both be. Call the drogs and put the fire out, we will patrol the area tonight and return in the morning, they'll come back and we'll meet them here.' Durg` commands. The four remove a special instrument, a lute that echoes each note with the pluck of a string. After only a moment of waiting, they hear the rush of wind, and the flapping of wings. Their drogs appear just over the trees, and land upon the cliff where their camped. Durg` rides upon a large red drog, Arro` upon one of deep grey, Hurg``s is dark blue, with light cyan highlighting the scales and under the eyes, and Augr` rides upon an old brown one, slump and not as agile as the others. They kick off, and they roar out into the night sky as fast as they arrived. Shoranna watches them as they leave, and heads through the woods to find the captain.

For most of the night, Cezius sleeps by the tree, having nightmares under the pale stars in the sky, he can hear their voices, hears them calling out to him, calling his name as their butchered and hacked down to pieces. The shade of the pines and oaks clouds his thoughts and veils the already darkened night. He is stirred by a rustle in the bushes down the hill, in the green valley of shrubs and bushes.

Cezius descends down the steep hill to check what is about the area. At the bottom is a thick overhang of trees and brush with bushes and ivy strewn about and overhead like a tunnel. The captain follows the tunnel into a opening were the moon light trickles across the grass with a pale blue glow and upon a low hill is a lone tree, thick and hardy, it's trunk scraped and scratched, worn and torn from birds, bugs, burrowers, and time. A lonely, sullen old man in the moonlight.

He walks about the tree, running his fingers across the bark, remembering when just as a young lad, how he used to climb them, when time meant nothing and the days were less dark. He and his two older brothers were in the woods, tossing rocks at the lakes, warding off sea monsters, and poking trees with sticks like spears created in a child's mind, pretending they were the legs or necks of mighty beasts, and horrifying creatures. Off on adventures they would go, to other places, other realms.

Until one night, that's when everything came to pass, for that moment came rushing back to him, after all these years, how could he have forgotten? *But was this his memory, or someone else's he was remembering, for he doesn't remember his brothers leaving him*, they left him alone in the dark shadows of the monsters, beasts, and sea monsters that surrounded him. The sun was going down, and he heard a voice call to him. He called for his brothers, 'Piaus…Ezirius…!' But they did not answer his call. Were they calling to him, trying to find him, but it was not Piaus's voice, nor Ezirius's voice. He called back to them, no answer. The voice called again, calling his name, but he ignored the voice, but the more he tossed it from his mind, the stronger and louder it beckoned to him. Was it simply his imagination? *Were those his brother's names? He doesn't remember any of this.* Thus, he gave in, and followed swiftly, through the dry leaves, along the paths, the closer he came, the stronger the winds blew, but they were cold, not the autumn winds he was accustomed to, for the smell of the air was not right, it seemed stale and feverish.

'…over here…' Said the crackle of a strange voice. Cezius could not tell whether it was male or female, it was raspy and soft, very low in volume, as though it spoke without lips, but with thought and cunning. He did as the voice said, and turned, looking off to the south, beyond through the trees, encompassed by a black wind and pale light, a being stood, wrapped in darkness and shrouded in mystery, for who this figure was, Cezius could never figure it out, *for he does not remember this memory*. The face he could not see, only an incorporeal shell of something sinister watching him, speaking to him. He remembers the figure approaching, *or does he?* But was not walking, but floating, hovering above the wind. The figure began to reach out…

and the next thing he remembers, are his two brothers hovering over him, trying to wake him from the nightmare, yet the image seemed so real. *But why was he seeing these things, he never had two brothers, he had a sister that died young...who were these eyes...that he was seeing through...*

At that moment, out from the trees and ivy, leaps a monstrous beast, the drog that brought Cezius to this place. Cezius looks upon the creature, as the drog looks upon him. It's crouched upon its hands like a quadruped animal. Its wings are withheld, tucked in upon its back, next to its spine. The drog gurgles, smoke seems to puff from the two elongated nostrils at the tip of its nose with each breath. The drog stands upon its hind legs, the emerald scales sparkle majestically under the pale moonlight; the beast spreads its wings. Cezius readies for an attack, not knowing what the beast may do. Yet, in an odd turn of events, the drog takes a bow.

Cezius looks on, amused by what he is seeing. Then, a voice speaks from behind. ‘Go on, he’s waiting for you to bow in return.’ Shoranna says. Cezius looks at her confused, and then looks back at the drog, who is awaiting his reply.

‘You want me to bow back to this beast?’ The drog snorts and growls, for he understands every word Cezius is saying.

‘I wouldn’t call him that if I were you. Fenzir makes for a fierce ally, but an even deadlier enemy.’ She says. Cezius steps back a bit, afraid of Fenzir’s reaction to his comment. ‘Well, so Fenzir is your name?’

‘Unlike the more feral drog, Fenzir can bow, just a friendly greeting, a tradition amongst the ancient drogs, a way of courtesy, so go on, before he’s offended.’

Cezius steps forward, takes a deep breath, and returns the bow. Fenzir returns to his upright position, and then crouches back upon his hands and legs. Fenzir nods. ‘He accepts your courtesy…congratulations, captain, it is always wise to be in the good graces of a drog, especially one as smart and as cunning as Fenzir.’ Shoranna adds with cheer.

Fenzir makes a few grunting sounds and hand motions, using some form of sign language while speaking. ‘What is he saying?’ Cezius asks. Shoranna is silent for a moment, watching Fenzir’s hands and listens to what he is saying. ‘He says he is glad to meet you, Captain Cezius Cabriel, of the Othetica armies.’ Shoranna answers, after deciphering the complex language of the drog, which only the Drog Riders can understand.

Cezius's eyes go wide with surprise. 'He knows who I am, he knows my name?!'

'Your victories in war have spread to the ears of many beings and creatures within Aura.' She replies, then moves closer and continues to say something else, in a quieter, more subtle tone. 'And I want to apologize for being so despairing about your friend, and that I was relieved to hear he was still alive.'

'I was upset, as I understand now you were also.' Cezius replies. She remains silent, Fenzir grumbles. 'No Fenzir, it's alright…I…I knew someone who was close to me, she died in that battle. I knew her for a long time; she was like a sister to me. We grew up together; she was the only one who accepted my oddities, this ear, these tattoos, and this mark upon my face. I haven't seen or spoken to her since I left with the Drog Riders, and when Hurg` and Arro` told me of what happened, my heart fell, now she is dead.'

Cezius takes her hand. 'I am sorry…If I may, can I ask her name?'

Tears stream down Shoranna's face, as she remembers her friends face, her smile, the time when they were children, to when they were separated; everything came rushing back to her. She began to feel dizzy, and Cezius leans her against the tree. 'It's okay…just take a moment, you don't have to answer if you don't want to.' He says.

'No, no I'll be alright,' She stands to her feet, but her legs still feel buckled from the mental burden she carries. 'Mira, her name was Mira.'

Cezius shines a light hearted smile. 'She was a soldier of mine, and a brave one at that. Sadly, I was not close to her. I took the time to remember each and every one of my troops, and I remember her name, for I was the one who placed the

Golden Crest of Bravery around her neck, the highest reward for honor that any soldier of Othetica could achieve.'

Shoranna cleansed the tears, her nose snuffled, but from the rain and the storm, a rainbow in the form of a smile emerged from the frown upon her lips. 'That is comforting to know, but I only lost one…you lost all…I can't even imagine, or begin to fathom how you feel. When I heard she was killed, slaughtered by those beasts, I wanted to rush in and slay them all, I…'

Cezius interrupts her with a stern hush, 'Don't, you don't want to. You only bear the weight of one, don't carry the weight of an army. For I, more than anyone, wants to rush in and destroy every last one of those Dregor and Mirym! But I have to hold back, because a good general has to keep a clear head, and know when to attack. I know my soldiers didn't go down without a fight, and they died defending what they chose to protect, that which they held most personal to them, closest to their hearts.'

'So how do we know when to attack?! How do we keep our anger from blinding us, our hatred from getting ourselves killed?!'

Cezius thought for a moment, and an idea came to his mind. 'Let's ride out!'

'Ride out?' She was trying to figure out what he meant.

'Yes, take me north to the Dregor encampment, we'll spy out the land, scout the area, see what our options are, and plan a strategy. When the time is right, that's when we'll make our strike. What do you say?!' The familiar fire of a captain and a general was once again burning in his blood.

Shoranna nods, 'Yes, yes that sounds like a plan, a fine plan indeed!' She turns to Fenzir, who has been listening to the entire discussion, and he knows what is to come. 'Fenzir, we ride!' The drog sprints across the ground, and lifts Shoranna and Cezius upon his back, and glides into the air, heading north, high above hills and mountains, off towards the cold regions of where the Mirym tribes dwell. Cezius returns to the war he was pulled away from.

PART VI:

Thogmig

'Just over this ridge, that is where they fell…'

Shoranna pointed northward, just over the pinnacle of the furthest hill. Fenzir kept his speed under control, not flying to fast, so Cezius is able to maintain his composure. Cezius notices something unusual, as the sun begins to rise, and the rays glisten upon the leaves of an unusually large tree, its vast branches stretch upwards into the eastern skies like roots reaching for a calm pool of water. 'Does that tree seem unconventional or is it only me, for I don't remember seeing a tree that size while I was stationed here?'

'Every tree is like a child, and like every child to be born, there is a mother. Every forest has a mother tree; I would say that tree is it.' Cezius agrees, and they continue onward.

Just up ahead, hovering high above the hills, is a large cloud of smoke, and an atmosphere of soot and gases, and poisonous fumes. They land upon the high ridge and walk through the stretch of woods, or what was once a wood, now all the branches are dead, the ground burned, leaves disintegrated, and the grass eroded with swampy marsh water and charred dirt.

Established below are the dark tents stained with fresh blood, and heaving bodies of heartless, malicious legions of black armor and jagged weaponry. This is where the Dregor are camped, the armies of Kandarius, and their snorting, thrashing Slaths are chained to the trees. The Dregor fire is a burning red and the beastly figures surround the flames, snorting and drinking a foul liquid from cups made of bone.

Their thick shaven jowls would swallow the liquid and spew and spit, and regurgitate from blood-thirsty sadistic chants. Their voices speak the ancient tongue of Dregor and the Hexagus Lords.

"Burn their flesh, better than raw!

Rub their bones together to make our flame,

And eat the slain, as their homes burn and their cities crumble!

Blind their eyes, bind their hands,

For the sport and for their pain,

Hunt them all down, and watch them stumble,

Then gut the lame, and eat the slain, for our stomachs grumble!

Slay the children, slay the women, and slay the men,

For no Gormon, Asyndian, or Civilian,

Will ever see another dawn again!

Our dark lords have come, when the jaws of Daskar have opened..."

The Dregor finish their vile song, Shoranna and Cezius look at each other, wondering what the Jaws of Daskar meant. They move closer, and see the horrible revelation, as the Dregor are devouring the soldiers, roasting them over fires, taking the bodies from stacks and piles they keep nearby to their fowl-smelling tents. Shoranna can see the hatred and rage on Cezius's face. 'Those are my soldiers…my brothers and sisters…Their eating my soldiers!' Shoranna grabs his mouth to silence him. 'Shhhh, they'll discover us…I can't even begin to imagine how painful this is, but we had to see this, it is what you said, we have to be level-headed, we can't rush in!' She says to his ear in a whisper. He lays his head upon her shoulder, drowning in tears and sorrow, she wraps her arms around, and tries to comfort him, but after what he has seen, there is no comfort to be had. He tried to charge out, but she held him back. 'We need to get out of here, we stayed to long, we've seen too much.'

Before they leave, there is a sudden commotion from the legions, they all leap to their feet, and stand at attention. 'Cezius, something's happening!' He looks on, and the two crouch back down into the bushes. Standing high upon the ridge is a tall figure in heavily dented and cracked armor, held together by thick leather straps. A wide black cape flows in the cold winds behind him, casting a shadow across the Dregor's faces. Upon his face, is half a metal mask, bolted into his flesh over a placid white eye, and upon the thick iron is inscribed the many curses of the Hexagus linguistics. His thick black and slightly whitened hair rustles violently over his furrowed brows. And at his right and left side, are two black drogs, Abhor and Femog. Their necks sweep the area, and their red eyes glare across the many in the legions and ranks of Dregor and Mirym. He speaks out to them, in a low and gurgled voice, but brawn and projected outward in a roar. The Mirym, who share the base, circle around, their Civilian faces gaze up at the figure, and their wolverine-like features, their ears, their tails and claws are down.

'Today, we have achieved what has begun the downfall of this illusion called Aura! Built upon the false hopes and the lies of these Aurora's who have stolen…taken away from the true lords of the land, the Hexagus! Chief Glenheim, as a token of Kandarius's friendship and good will, he grants these lands be returned to you and your kind, in exchange for your continued service to his will.' The burly, husky Mirym chief steps forward, his eyes are fiery red, and his features are more bestial than the others. He shakes the hand of the figure.

‘I thank you, Athian Dor, and all the Dregor! Our people are liberated from these accursed Civilians, but we have one more obstacle in our mists, the Treefort, the main base within Greenhaven! Once we rid ourselves of this machination that has tried to drive us out permanently of our former lands, driven us to a cold and hellish life, wondering like nomads and scavengers under forsaken glaciers and frozen hills! My people die around me, and I watch them suffer; watch their life pass before me! Once Treefort has burned, then can we have our freedom, for freedom will be regained! Tomorrow, the Mirym tribes march on Treefort! Tomorrow, the gnarled roots of that foul place will be no more, all slain, and none will be taken alive! But there is one, one who will be taken, far to the north, in the most forsaken hole in the mountain; there we created miles into the ice, a prison, unbreakable, impenetrable. There, we will place the naked body of the captain, Cezius Cabriel, the one who has led this attack upon us!’

The blood boils in Cezius’s veins. He swears to himself he will have the chieftain’s head, and all the heads of those who have slaughtered all his men. But, he has learned a key piece of information, the Treefort is to be attacked tomorrow, and time is running out. ‘We have to leave and meet the others back at the pinnacle.’ Shoranna insists.

‘We should head to Treefort and warn them as soon as we can, they have to be warned!’ Cezius insists. ‘We need the others, with a force that large; the other Riders will be able to help hold them off.’ Shoranna replies.

‘Very well, but we have to be fast, time is short and we’ll need as much help as we can, that was no mere militia army, this is war, they slaughtered my Icerym forces, and now they’re going for Treefort. They're making their way into Othetica, next will be Cysiiros...and then Novilon, the capital...’

She hops upon Fenzir and holds out her hand to Cezius. 'Then we better move…' Cezius grabs on, and they ride off back south to the pinnacle to meet the others, but the Drog Riders have rode off, so they will have to find some way to get their attention and contact them to return, so that they may decide what to do next.

They glide upon the winds, and Fenzir begins to pick up speed. Cezius begins to feel the darkness close around him. 'Don't worry about me; just go as fast as you can…' And Cezius collapses. But just as Fenzir began to pick up more speed and gust of the wind, everything came to a stop. Shoranna was tossed away, and something catches her in mid air, as is the same for Cezius, his body is thrown clear of Fenzir's back, and catches onto something sticky. Fenzir tries to cut himself free, and struggles but his wings are held down.

His struggling wakes Shoranna from her momentary black out, and she looks down at the vast forest and valley below. Off above towards the sky, hanging near a titanic long branch is Cezius, who is still passed out. And over to her right, Fenzir still struggles to break free of this wiry trap they are in. Shoranna looks about, and tilts her head as far back as it can bend, and she sees the massive tree trunk, the mother tree. *"It can't be possible"*, she tries to tell herself, but it seems the tree has moved, it moved to intercept their path, whether by its own accord, or by the forces of something else, she wasn't sure. And the sticky threads could only mean one thing. When she was little, she once heard tales that a mig, the queen of them all, cast her webs across the dome of the sky, and that none could escape her grasp. She is the terror of the skies, the one pest Tundrok could never fully exterminate. She is Thogmig, and this is her web. And from a large hole in the tree, the queen of the webs, the widow of the mother tree, with many legs and thousands of eyes, reveals herself, sensing the struggle taking place within her web, the little flies trying to get away.

As Thogmig drew closer, Fenzir sends forth an atomic fire beam, and scorches the web away. Cezius still hangs unconscious above, and Fenzir and Shoranna are sent hurdling towards the trunk of the tree. They collide, Fenzir flies up and grabs Shoranna, her web tears and she falls, but is caught just in time. He sets her down at the crown of the tree. Shoranna rubs her head, soar from the impact. They each look about the area; Thogmig is nowhere to be found. But then, they look above and see the vile God-Monster crawling across the limb of the tree, heading for the unconscious body of Cezius.

'Come on Fenzir!' She leaps upon Fenzir's back, and they take off towards the high branch. Fenzir scorches Thogmig, a duel high above towards the clouds. He cannot burn through Thogmig's thick exoskeleton, but ruptures dozens of eggs she carries upon her abdomen and horns, that explode with green, red, and bloody globs of puss and vile fluids. She screams in pain and anger for the loss of her young. From her crusted throat, she sprays a thick web over Shoranna and Fenzir, and they fall back into the web below. Cezius begins to stir, and as he awakens, he sees the horrible, twitching, creaking legs, and many eyes in front of him, crawling closer. He scrambles, trying to pry himself away, but he cannot, and he is trapped within her webbed prison.

Thogmig sizes up her mark, and creeps in to swallow Cezius whole, her mouth open, and fangs spread wide. He can smell her foul, ancient breath as she begins her attack. Her throat smells as though a billion rotting carcasses are screaming forth from their digestive pain of the rancid, putrid stomach. She rears up, her mandibles twitch and crunching; the incisors pump their decomposing juices around him. But something draws her attention away, and she backs up into a defensive crouch, ready to strike at something.

A large red streak flies in and knocks her bulbous shape back. Then another strike, and a flash of burning embers scour across her face. A final blow from two more streaks of force and energy, and she is knocked off of the branch, belly up onto her web below. The objects whirl around as fast as they came forth out of the sky, and they fly in and begin to burn the web away, a final flash of a blade, and the sizzle from a powerful force of energy, and Thogmig, the God-Monster, falls from the Mother Tree, to the vast forest of Greenhaven below.

Upon the branches above, by the crown at the top of the tree, lands the four Drog Riders, who have returned from their scouting of the western and southern lands. They glare down upon Shoranna as she and Fenzir free themselves, and climb their way up to a nearby branch.

'What were you thinking…coming this way?! We've been looking for you for hours now. You get yourself caught in Thogmig's web, and you place yourself, and the Grand General's life in danger! What were you thinking?' Durg` scolded.

Before she can explain herself, Cezius interrupts and answers the questions, after being freed from the web by Arro`. 'I told her to bring me here, this was my idea. Not to be caught by the mig, but to spy out the lands, and the Dregor camp, gain information of what will be their next move.'

'Dangerous and foolish a move, but never the less, did your plan work, have you found out anything?' Durg` asks.

'We have found out a crucial move of the enemy, Athian Dor and the remaining Dregor and Mirym, plan to attack the main fortress of Treefort!' Cezius replies.

'That means we must make for Runegard immediately, and alert Airical, to prepare for an early strike upon us!' Durg` suggests.

'No, as I have told Shoranna, we must reach Treefort as soon as we can. I know her battlements well; the soldiers there are among the bravest ever conceived within Othetica's boundaries, and one of my best men is stationed at Treefort, he will be able to assist us further. We can use the environment there to our advantage, and besides, we only have twenty four hours to make a plan, for they will be moving out soon, they will be at Treefort by tomorrow!'

'Then let's go and drive back those Dregor, once and for all!' Cries Augr`.

The riders cut away the remaining webs and strands that blanket Shoranna and Fenzir. They mount their drogs, Cezius rides with Shoranna, and they head east to Treefort.

PART VII:

Lost Forge of Gonun

After what seemed like an eternity of travel, taking hidden paths, dirt roads, sacred crossings were they would walk on water, ethereal passages through the solid rock walls of mountain summits, and hidden stairs that lead up into the sky and clouds, and then down through deep low laying valleys, and underground canyons. They trudge the last mile or so of steps up from the underground passage, which places them at the center of a thick, surrounding of forest as far as the eye can see. Agonan leads them through a vast maze of trees, and specific paths amongst the thickets and walls of frost-bitten ivy. The ground begins to head upwards and they find themselves in a vast clearing through the trees, walking across a barren tundra, and far off to the left they can see the eye of Lota, suspended in the air above the rocky cliffs and pinnacles, not setting, nor any rotation or motion at all. It's as Kerrun said, this is a place where time is meaningless, and never passes, were everything stands still. After traveling miles across the tundra, they enter the other side of the forest.

'If this is the easy path, I'd hate to see the hard path.' Roaur says, huffing from being out of breath.

'I don't think we would have even made it that far.' Kerrun replies.

'Agonan, how much further is it to the forge?' Hernan asks.

Agonan turns and looks upon them, laughing at their weariness. 'I see you fellows are worn out already. What you are standing in front of, is the Forest of Ages.'

'Why is it called that?' Hernan asks.

'Because if I was not here to show you the way, it

would take you ages to find your way through. With that map, maybe a hundred years or so, but without a map, or me to help, a millennia, thousands of years if you were lucky.' He laughs again.

'But we'd never make it, we'd be dead way before that!' Roaur exclaims.

'That's why the forge is lost.' Agonan replies. He leads them onward, through the twisting trees, and fallen logs, deep, dark moats of water, and pitfalls hidden behind hills. Until, finally at last, above the next hill, and far over the rim, there they see, the cloud of thick smoke rising up from Gonun's forge, high above the trees into the sky. The closer they get, the thicker the snow falls around them. They pass the final tree into a clearing, with a cold, icy lake off to the left, and at the foot of the lake, a mighty wheel spins, pumping the bellows of the forge, which sits upon a stone platform for a base, and upon it sits a massive furnace, as well as an anvil the size of a small house, and leaning upon the anvil is the largest hammer Hernan, Kerrun, or Roaur have ever seen in their lives. The hammer is of a strange shape, at the front of the hammer, is the carving of a face, with a curved tip in the shape of a wing, the shaft is wrapped with thick leather, and at the base of the shaft, is a multi-colored opal stone, in which the colors seem to move and rotate with an ominous glowing light shimmering forth.

'They have nothing like this back in the forges of Fausengard!' Roaur says.

'Be very careful, Gonun is very impatient with strangers, I think Tundrok already warned you Hernan. As long as your with me you should be fine, it's been many, many eons since Gonun has seen your kind, I don't know how he'll react, not well I imagine. Just speak only when he speaks to you, make eye contact and be powerful with your words, and I cannot overstress enough, under any circumstances, do not... do not touch his hammer! The three of you wait here behind these bushes, and don't move until I get back.' Before they could ask him where he was going, Agonan disappeared into the trees.

From where they stand, they could feel the powerful heat blasting forth from the furnace, and hear the roar of its fire. The heat melts all the snow around the base of the forge, no snow or frost can gather nor fall nearby. Kerrun is mystified by what he is seeing, he could not help himself, for he had to get closer, he has to see the forge. He rushes out from behind the bushes and runs to the forge. Hernan and Roaur rush after him.

'Father, it's too dangerous...!' Roaur calls out.

'I have to see it...I have to see...!' Before Kerrun could get to the stairs, a huge, hulking beast leaps out in front of Kerrun, tripping him up, and he falls to the ground. The creature is a quadruped, with scaly legs and tail, and the body covered with stubbled fur, a long jaw and snout, and a gaping wide mouth snarls and snaps at them with razor sharp teeth biting and grinding. Around the creatures neck is some form of collar, with a massive chain attached; as the beast moves, it drags the chain across the ground. The creature crouches, and in the blink of an eye it pounces. Roaur and Hernan jump in front of Kerrun to protect him, but the chain catches, and knocks the beast down, gagging it.

Hernan and Roaur help Kerrun to his feet, and he dusts himself off. The beast snarls and barks with rage, slobbering all over as it moves it's jowls open and close with ferocious, snapping, force. From behind the trees, they hear the monstrous footsteps of something colossal approaching.

'Is it Agonan?' Roaur asks.

'I don't think so...' Hernan replies.

'Back behind the bushes!' Kerrun yells, and the three rush back to their hiding place. The limbs shake, and the snow falls from the branches revealing the green of the tree leaves. Stomping forth from the shadows of the forest, is a being twice the size of Agonan, carrying a mighty dozen or so trees upon his left shoulder, and a large double-bladed axe in his right hand. His beard braided into several sections, under his ears are mighty side-burns, and his head is bald. He wears a thick metal breast plate and his arms are bare, chain leggings, and thick, hardened leather boots. He stops and his deep, dark eyes scan the area, he walks over to the forge and places the trees upon the ground near a large pile of cut logs. He pets the beast upon the head, and walks up the steps to his forge, where he sits at the grindstone to sharpen the axe, his back turned away from them.

Without hesitation, Hernan marches forth towards the forge, followed by Kerrun, then Roaur.

'Aurora Gonun! My name is Hernan, Forgemaster of Othetica. It is imperative that I speak with you.' Hernan calls out.

Slowly, Gonun turns, the rage and agitation burns within his eyes. He grabs the hammer and stands up from the grindstone. Hernan, Kerrun, and Roaur stop dead in their tracks. Gonun towers high above Hernan, looking down at him, surprised by the Civilian's courage.

In a roaring voice that shakes the forests all around, Gonun speaks. 'What did you say you are?!'

'I am...' Gonun interrupts Hernan.

'I did not ask who! I asked you...what did you say you claim to be!' Gonun replies.

Hernan takes a deep breath and stares directly into the enraged, glowing eyes of the Aurora. 'I am a Forgemaster of Othetica...'

Gonun squints intently and looks him over. He holds the massive hammer in front of him, hovering over Hernan, then releases the weapon. Hernan stands without flinching, Kerrun and Roaur brace themselves for the impact, but when they open their eyes, the hammer has shrunk down to their size, about the length of a large, two-handed war hammer. Hernan stares into the sullen, blank eyes of the hammer's face, almost as though he were in a trance. Kerrun and Roaur wonders what is happening, then Gonun speaks.

'Pick up the hammer, and prove who you say you are!'

Hernan, with a mighty grip and a shrug, without second thought or hesitation, lifts the hammer up above his head and holds it high for all of Aura to gaze in wonder. Roaur and Kerrun's eyes go wide and they gasp at the sight.

'He did it...!' Kerrun says.

'What does this mean father?' Roaur asks.

'It means son, that we just might have a chance...we just might...' Kerrun replies.

Gonun is astonished by what he is seeing, for this Civilian, has proven himself to be the true Forgemaster.

'I expected a Gormon, or an Asyndian, but it seems I was wrong. So...at long last, the Forgemaster of legend has truly shown himself here today, and he appears in the form of a Civilian. I'll be honest with you, I never thought very highly of the Civilians and their ways, but I sense something different in you, you have an air of self-dignity about you, a sureness of your strengths. Most of the denizens rely upon us Auroras to save them from everything and all at every bend in the road of life, but you keep to your own...selfish, but I respect that you are not relying upon others, where you can simply help yourself. By lifting that hammer, you have shown me who you truly are, for only a true Forgemaster can lift it.'

Agonan has returned from the forest. 'Brother, I told them to wait for me...!'

'It's fine Agonan...this Civilian, and these two Gormons are my welcomed guests. They speak strong, and keep stout hearts.'

Agonan is a bit surprised by his brothers words and behavior.

'...for the Forgemaster is in our mists, and I will help him, and his friends in any way that I can.'

'Of course.' Agonan replies.

'Come my friends, I will prepare a place for you to sit. When I came to this grotto, I never thought anyone would ever find this place, which is why I settled here, seclusion and absolute, complete isolation. Only Agonan and Tundrok come here. However, when I came here I brought some things with me, let's see what I have.' Gonun walks over to the forge, with Hernan, Kerrun, and Roaur following behind. Agonan heads over and gives them a lift up to the higher platform, since the steps were much larger than the three of them. 'Warm yourselves by the furnace while I try to find you something...I know I put them in here somewhere...' Gonun begins to talk to himself while he digs through an old beast-skin sack filled with what looks like old carvings and sculptures, small to Gonun, but the same size as Hernan, Kerrun, and Roaur. 'Ah, here we are, you can sit upon these, I sculpted them some years ago.' He removes some wood carvings of chairs and a table. The three sit upon them, relieved to be sitting upon something that's not the ground after months of travel.

'We will talk for a time, and don't worry about my pet, he is harmless. He has never seen anyone other than myself and my brothers, so he's just a little anxious and curious.' Gonun lets the beast off the chain, which then runs up to the forge and sniffs the three of them. He is particularly fond of Hernan, he lays next to him and Hernan scratches his ear.

The hours pass, Kerrun and Gonun do most of the talking, for Kerrun has many questions, and Gonun answers many of them. They discuss Fausengard and Aura lore, the time when the Auroras crossed the mighty bridges of the Galakaos from their former worlds, to come to Aura. They discussed the Aura War, when the Hexagus Lords were diminished from Aura to the outer reaches of Galakaos. Hernan speaks about his ordeals, about Vos`ul and how he came to be part of this story, though he had questions of his own about what part he had in the event of the Grey Age, though he had his own ideas, he wanted to hear them from a being who has seen more time, and ages than himself.

'What is my part in the Grey Age, all I know is that it has to do with Azalir, but who or what is Azalir? Tundrok said you would be the one to tell me.'

Gonun takes a deep gulp of a mug full of hot liquid

distilled from the sap of the trees. 'Why of course I know, I was the one who forged Azalir.' Gonun answers, wiping his mouth and beard.

'Then, Azalir is a weapon.' Hernan says to himself.

'A blade, once the most powerful weapon in all of Aura. There was once a powerful warrior, stronger than any being alive. He was born of Justice and Light, Honor and True Heart. He was the chosen of the Auroras to lead our armies against the Dregor. Upon the peak of the highest summit of Aura, this warrior used Azalir to strike down Maz Dregor. The blow was so powerful, that the blade shattered, and only part of it remains. That blade is the key to opening Wom, and unleashing the Hexagus once again upon this realm.'

'What was this warrior's name?' Hernan asks.

'It has been ages since I last heard it, for I do not remember. Agonan, do you?' Gonun replies.

'I'm not sure, but in legends, he is referred to as the Hero of Ages.'

'An incredible tale, no scribe or tome, nor record I have ever read before can compare to hearing the words from the point of view of the Auroras themselves.' Kerrun exclaimed.

'...and so no Dregor or their worshipers could get hold of Azalir, the ancient Asyndians constructed Gammafir `ur kmme, the tallest structure in all of Aura, which can be seen from anywhere in the realm. The Asyndians placed Azalir at the very top of the tower so no one, only an Asyndian could reach it.'

"...and the tower crumbles, and the tower falls,
from sky, and from grace upon Aura below,
By the destruction of Dregor, the flags of our foes!
There is no more hope, there is no more light,
Azalian has been taken, Gammafir has lost all sight!"

'The minions of Dregor, the hands of the Hexagus could

not reach the blade, so they destroyed the tower and stole it by force, removing Azalir from its sacred place, and now it is gone. It's been missing for a millennia, and if the enemy still has it, which seems likely, then they will try to reforge it, and only a Forgemaster can do so...'

'Then, the Dregor will be searching for me. That is what Isifier was speaking of...' Hernan says.

'You must be extremely careful, the Dregor worshipers are a crafty bunch, infiltration is their most dangerous weapon, sneakiness is their sword, and lies are their shield. Two outcomes can occur, either the blade is forged, and the Dregor use it to revive their Hexagus Lords, or...we use the blade to fight back! To destroy and wipe out the Dregor indefinitely!'

'Can we not destroy what remains of the blade?!' Roaur asks.

'It's not so simple, the blade is essentially immortal, even though the blade can be broken, the essence is eternal, so we must locate and reclaim the essence, though I don't know where you should look. Hernan, from what you tell me about Othetian, I would suggest you head back to Othetica and start there. It seems there's something deeper at work than just an Aurora having nightmares.'

'But how would I be able to reforge the blade, how can I recreate the power of the essence it once had?!'

'Ah...you are a Forgemaster, the one thing you posses is craftiness and the ability to take scraps and create a one of a kind piece of work.' Gonun gets up and adds some wood to the furnace. 'For your final lesson, I'm going to bring out your full potential of this skill, for it's not just a matter of creating simple weapons and armor, but these skills go deeper. I will teach you things no other living Aurora, Civilian, Gormon, Asyndian, or any other denizen of Aura knows or has ever witnessed. Your time is short in your world, but here time is eternal, and what I teach you will remain eternal, for when you leave this grotto, we will never meet again.'

Hernan nods in understanding. Kerrun and Roaur agree

as well.

The season is long and rigorous. Gonun grants upon them vast and limitless knowledge of his skills that no other being has ever known. They dissect the components of armor and weapons down to intricate and the tiniest of minuscule parts and create master works compared to anything that has come before. Thus, the season, based on Gonun's comprehension, comes to an end.

'Well, I think the three of you are ready, and you know what you must do. Hernan, that hammer is yours, for I used it to forge Azalir. You now posses my skills and knowledge, for I pass my legacy onto you. The three of you will keep the equipment you made, for all of your hard work, you do me proud.'

Before they part ways, Hernan and Roaur ready their gear, but Kerrun does not.

'Father, are you ready to leave?' Roaur asks.

'I'm not leaving son, if it's alright with Gonun, I will stay here. You go with Hernan and help him.' Kerrun turns to Gonun, who nods in agreement with Kerrun's decision. 'I choose to stay. You and Hernan must go on, I think there is more to learn about this place, for while my mind goes ever on, my body does not. I'm too old for adventuring, I will be much better off here.'

'I understand, you know what is best, and my heart shall miss you.' Roaur replies.

'As will I.' He places his hand on Roaur's shoulder. 'You take care. Watch out for Hernan...and yourself.'

After saying their final farewells and taking one last look upon Gonun's Lost Forge and the grotto, Agonan leads them out of the sacred land, to the outlying borders of Othetica.

'This is where I leave you, farewell.' Agonan parts ways with them, and heads back towards Fausengard.

'Come Roaur, let's get back to my forge. There we can figure out what the next step will be.'

They travel across the hills and up over the horizon, the

towering gates and structures of Othetica's architecture comes within sight, they notice encompassing the city from above, the clouds getting darker and growing thicker, as though a storm were approaching from the south.

PART VIII:

Curse of the Grey Age

At the entrance to Othetica, Hernan and Roaur notice the gates are wide open, without guards or sentries on the watch.

'Is this common for Civilian's to leave their cities unguarded?' Roaur asks.

Hernan stares puzzled. They hear crowds of people within yelling and roaring.

'Must be a riot, let's hurry and see what's going on.' Hernan replies.

They rush through the gates, when they are stopped by a passing group of soldiers. Littering the streets ahead, are large mobs and crowds of people yelling and throwing, bearing weapons, and hurling epithets and threats through the air.

'Forgemaster sir, you have returned! Where is the captain, where are all the others?'

'I am the only survivor, we were ambushed in the mountains...' Hernan replies in regret.

'Ambushed, by what? A group of these Gormons?!' The soldier snorts in disrespect towards Roaur.

Roaur steps forward gripping his hammer in agitation, but Hernan holds him back.

'He is a friend.'

'This is just what we need! First the Aurora, then the captain and our people, and now were siding with Gormon! Could things get any worse?'

'What's happened to the Aurora?' Hernan asks.

'Not long ago, the clouds above Othetica grew dark as night, and a violent storm screamed lightning and roared thunder, tore through the city. Strange occurrences began to take place, there was something, an odd sound like someone's voice, a chant of some sort. I don't know what was being said, it was a strange language unlike any I ever heard before, sent a chill through me! The voice echoed throughout the streets and alleys, then the shriek rang out into the air, the cry of a woman's blood-curdling scream. It came from the Aurora's palace. We hurried as fast as we could run, and when we got there, I...I cannot believe what I saw.'

'What did you see?' Hernan asks.

The soldier looks silently off in the direction of the palace and points. 'Up there, upon the highest balcony.'

Hernan and Roaur gaze upward, and there, as the soldier had said, on the balcony is Aurora Othetian, frozen in stone. The two of them were speechless.

'And just this morning,' The soldier continues, 'these Asyndians show up, preaching about the Grey Age and the end of Aura. The people are restless and civil unrest infects every street of Othetica, us soldiers can barely maintain control, and Kandarius hasn't shown himself for days. The Asyndians have everyone in an uproar. I don't know what's going to happen, so some of us are leaving, and if you're wise, you'll do the same.'

The soldiers walk pass them and leave the city without looking back. As they pass, behind their shoulders, and further on down the street, gathered in front of the palace and an adjacent building, are huge masses of Civilians, crowds and crowds as far as the eye can see, and surrounding them and barricading against them, pushing and shoving, are what is left of the Othetian guards. Hernan and Roaur pass empty shops and homes, looking as though they had been ransacked and destroyed by the mobs. Hernan's forge is on the outskirts of the city so he hopes it is still in one piece as he left it.

Hernan and Roaur push their way through the screaming, roaring crowds, closer to where the three Asyndian's are perched, high upon the roof of the building adjacent to the palace. Roaur looks up at the palace and marvels at its wondrous architecture. The Asyndian's are an aviary, bird-like race from Asyndia, now called the Greywaste. Two male guardians stand by, while a female Asyndian with an ornamental head dress speaks.

'You ungrateful Civilian's show all signs that you deserve what is coming, but the Grey Age will affect us all! Our people have suffered already once, and we are here to help you! Your Aurora is frozen, your people die around you, and you dare to bite the hands that reach out to help?!'

The crowds throw debris and objects, booing and cursing the Asyndians.

'And where is your leader, where is Kandarius! If he would be so bold as to show his slimy face, we could get to the bottom of this! Come out of that sarcophagus Kandarius, meet us in words!' The Asyndian screams.

The Civilians continue their onslaught.

'You are not Civilians, I spit at you! You are more barbaric than the Mirym! Your heads are filled with more rocks than the Gormon!' She traverses across the roof closer towards the palace. 'Come out Kandarius, let the people truly know what is going on! They want help, they want leadership, than come out and force feed it to them, like a school of bratty denizens, greedily, callously grabbing with their filthy paws! Taking and not even bothering to say thank you! Though I wish they would take what is good for them, for you did this to them, spoiled them, fattened them up for the kill! Oh, if they only knew...!'

'You know nothing of Civilian matters!' A Civilian screams. 'Just leave, go back to your waste land!' Another Civilian cries.

'You Dogs! I should let the Grey Age take you, crumble your buildings, wash your history away, drag you down to your tombs...!'

Then, the people fall silent, and all look up, including the Asyndians. Atop the balcony of the palace, stands the thin, pale figure of Kandarius. His eyes stare with scorn down upon the Asyndians. He turns to his people, who look up at him, his scorn turns to a relieving smile. He waves his hands for the Civilians to calm down.

'Why, my proud Civilians, Aurora Othetian would be proud of those he has led.' He turns to the Asyndians. 'It seems that those we have thought to have been our closest allies, would dare come to speak ill of myself and the Civilian people? Why, this is an insult to the Aurora himself, you dare speak this treason in such a public way? Can you not fly yourselves up here and we can talk in a civilized way?'

'Look around you Kandarius, there is no civility to be had when the Grey Age comes!'

'Grey Age, you speak such nonsense. You bring this uproar and distress, if you would just leave us now, then all could go back to the way it was.'

'I stand here now, before Othetian and his people, to bring you out of the shadows. No more can you hide, Airical knows who, or should I say...what you are!' The Asyndian cries out. 'I plead to you, Civilians, we are here to stop what has happened to us a millennia ago, from happening to you and the rest of Aura. No one is safe from Him and what he is capable of...!' She points to Kandarius.

Kandarius is silent, then lets out a laugh that all within the city can hear. 'It seems to me that your race and your Aurora are jealous...jealous of what Othetian has accomplished with the Civilians, living in peace and harmony, unlike your kind, living for eons in war and squallier, constantly running and begging, hiding, fighting. You Asyndians always thought you were better than all, until you became greedy, tampered with the essence of the Auroras, and unleashed to your people eternal darkness across your lands. Dead ashes now cover what was once green. Blue skies now run red with Asyndian blood! You come here daring to preach about help, when all you cause is chaos, you are the ones who will start the Civilians on the path to another Grey Age...' Before Kandarius can finish, the

Asyndian leaps into the air, spreads her wings, and lashes out at Kandarius in a blood-crazed frenzy. But before she can land a blow upon him, from a dark shadow of the city, an arrow shoots forth and pierces her chest, sending the Asyndian spiraling to the ground. The other two Asyndians fly to the streets to retrieve the body, but are surrounded by the angry crowds.

Hernan sees something move out of the corner of his eye and turns to see a shadowy figure retreating through an old alley. Hernan and Roaur follow him in pursuit. At the end of the block they duck down behind some old crates and see the figure talking to a tiny man, who cowers in fear of the cloaked figure. The figure threatens him, points in their direction, then back at the tiny man, who then shoves him over and disappears down the corridor. They wait for a moment as the tiny man walks in the opposite direction. Hernan and Roaur follow him to where he is unlocking a door to his home. They corner behind him. The man turns and is terrified by their armor and weapons, and of their vast size compared to his.

'Who was that man you were just talking to?!' Hernan asks.

The man whimpers and begins to cry, begging and pleading for his life. 'Please...please don't hurt me! Take what you want, just leave me alone!'

'All we want is information, we're not going to harm you.' Hernan replies, trying in vain to calm the man down.

'What....what do you want to know?'

'That man...who is he, were is he going?' Hernan asks.

'I can't....he'll kill them if I tell! He killed my brother, then he'll kill my wife, my daughter, he'll kill all that I have left that is precious to me! He's taken everything from me, forcing me to keep him in the darkness...I...I can't bear him anymore!' The man yells hysterically.

'What is your name?' Asks Hernan in a soft, less threatening voice.

'Barrel...the Civilians call me Barrel. I'm not from here,

I'm from the north, near the borders of Fausengard, I own the tavern and housing for the poor of this area, though I used to. I moved here with my family, we were traveling merchants before we decided to settle down in Othetica. I owned the business with my brother Oar...then, then that monster came, took everything I owned for himself, forced us into the slums. My brother tried to stand up to him, and...that bastard took my brother's head, cut it clean off in front of me! He said my wife and daughter would be next if...' He breaks down into tears.

'Barrel...we promise to you, if tell us were that man went, we'll make sure he never bothers you or your family again, and you can have your belongings returned to you. What say you?'

'But...he is cunning and dangerous! How do I know he won't kill you then come back and finish the rest of my family and myself?!' Barrel replies.

'Believe me, me and my friend Roaur here have seen and faced worse than a cunning assassin. I've fought drogs with my bare hands, drank mig acid, spit in the face of a Trau`l, and ripped the limbs from a Dregor beast!' Hernan replies.

Barrel's eyes widen. 'You've...you've done all that?!'

'Want me to prove it to you?' Hernan replies crossing his arms.

'No, you look more than capable! Okay, but not here, come inside and I'll tell you what you want.' Barrel opens the door and they walk in.

'My wife and daughter are not here now...thankfully. I don't know how they would react to this, or the angry mobs and revolts in the palace square. What are these times coming to...?' He pours himself, Hernan, and Roaur a mug of hot liquid, a sweet drink made of a special recipe prepared by his wife, then sits down exhausted into a chair, takes a deep breath, and swigs the drink. Hernan and Roaur sit opposite of him. Hernan sits in a chair, while Roaur sits on the floor, since the room is so small for his size.

'I'm sorry my quarters don't quite accommodate you

master Gormon, nor do I have a mug of your size, but I very, very rarely see your kind around Othetica.' Barrel apologizes.

'It's quite alright. Your wife's drink is delicious by the way!' Roaur replies.

Hernan sips the liquid, then sets it upon the table. 'You said you would tell us about that man.' Hernan says.

Barrel takes another deep swig. 'I don't know too much about him, he never told me his name, he said "*it was none of my business, and to stay out of his*"... The only thing I know is that he comes from the deserts in the south...'

'Isa?' Hernan interrupts.

'Yes, he is here on someone's behalf, I don't know who hired him or why, but this person, whoever he or she is, gave him my name, and that's when he found me out, took everything for his own, threatened my life to keep me quiet.'

'Were is he hiding out?' Roaur asks.

'He roams freely from place to place. This area used to be crowded with people, but he's slaughtered anyone who comes sneaking around, now no one comes down here. Though, there is an abandoned warehouse just down the street from here, I've seen him go in their more than anywhere. I've actually tried to follow him there once, to see what he was up to...but he caught me and told me that if I went in, his pets would feast on my flesh. I don't know what horrible types of things he spoke of, but I never went back. The building isn't locked, I guess whatever is in there, keeps the intruders silent, that a lock isn't necessary...' Barrel finishes telling his tale of the stranger, only to see the faces of Hernan and Roaur to be unflinching. 'The two of you seem to be unafraid.'

'Let's go Roaur, we know what we have to do.' Hernan says.

'Right with you Hernan.' Roaur replies.

'That is good, more courage is needed for our people, to help us through these dark times.' Barrel says to them.

'I thank you for your time Barrel, I doubt our path will

lead back this way, but I hope all gets better, and your profits flourish once again.' Hernan says to reassure Barrel.

'Thank you, I wish there were more Civilians and Gormons like the two of you. May Othetian, wherever he may be, keep an eye on you two.'

Hernan and Roaur leave Barrel's home, and head in the direction of the abandoned warehouse. Off in the dark corners and sides of the streets, they see the piles of bones and corpse that Barrel had to push aside and hide away, to cover for the Skahljhen assassin. Not far, up ahead of them, in the blackest corner of the alley, stands the rickety structure were the assassin hides away. Without wasting anytime, they charge forth, and burst through the door, to only enter a pitch black room. From what they can see, there are a few barrels, crates of supplies, beams holding the structure in place, piles of old webs, but the odd thing is, the temperature of the building is scorching hot.

'Something in here is making it feel like the desert.' Roaur comments.

Then the door slams behind them. 'Hernan, did you close the door?!' Roaur asks.

'I didn't touch it...' Hernan draws his weapon. 'Something's in here with us. Where are my mining helmets when we need them?'

Roaur draws his lumbering hammer. The two of them walk in fighting stance around in a circle perimeter.

'Roaur, your eyes are better in the dark than mine, can you see anything?'

'Do you want the bad news or the worse news?' Roaur asks.

'Bad news.' Hernan replies.

'Migs...several of them. They're all around us, descending from the ceiling as well.'

'Then what's the worse news?' Hernan asks.

'Their stingers. Sun Migs from Skahljah.' Roaur replies

with a gulping lump in his throat.

This means trouble for Hernan. There are different species of mig: The Tunnel Migs of Fausengard are armored with pincers, heavy and slow, the Water Migs of Sasparia are non-poisonous, but wicked fast, and have razor teeth and a painful bite, however; the deadliest migs of all, are the Sun Migs, their stingers have a poison that kills instantly. These migs do not spin webs, for once their prey dies upon injection of their poison, the group ravage and tear the limbs from the joint, rip the flesh to pieces, crunch the bones, slurp the blood, and leave behind nothing but a slight stain upon the ground. These creatures are among the deadliest beasts within Aura, and are feared by all, even Hernan and Roaur are cautious by what they face.

'It's no wonder why the Skahljhen didn't lock the door.' Hernan chuckles. 'You've got me covered, right?!'

'Just keep your head down, and let me do the swinging!' Roaur replies. With that, Hernan ducks his head, and Roaur with a violent thrust, wheels the hammer around in a circle, splattering the migs' blood and guts all across the wall and floor beams. 'Hernan, roll to your left!' Hernan rolls out of the way, and Roaur's hammer crashes through the floor, splattering one of the migs to a pulp, splashing the venom and legs over Hernan. 'Just don't get any in your mouth or eyes, and you'll be alright! Hernan, rush towards me, now strafe right!' The hammer goes down, and the last of the creatures is decimated.

'That's the last of them.' Roaur announces.

'Can you see any way out of this room?' Hernan feels around trying to find a door or a passage. Roaur looks about, and over in the corner, beneath some old supplies sees a trap door. He grabs Hernan by the shoulder and guides him. 'Over here, there's a trap door.' Roaur opens the door, and a strong light beams forth. Hernan goes down, and Roaur squeezes through, busting away some of the boards to fit better. Below, they enter a long stretch of tunnel, where the sound of a powerful furnace seems to roar.

'The heat is getting more and more unbearable, I think we're getting closer to something.' Further down the corridor, and rounding the corner, they enter a large prison room with cells and the faint flicker of torches lighting each corner. Rotten tapestries hang down from the ceiling, some lay dry rotted on the corroded brick floor. At the far end of the room is a large double-door with bolting mechanisms and bears the hollow face of some ancient creature upon it as some form of crest or guardian.

'Roaur, through here. Help me get these doors open...' They pull and thrust at the doors, but before they can get them open, a monstrous shape leaps down from the railings above. It's a gigantic, fire-spitting prowl, a cat-like beast with a serpents tail, also from the Isa desert. It spits flames upon Roaur, who just momentarily leaps out of the way, only having his beard get slightly singed by embers.

'Are you alright?! Hernan cries out.

'Sure!' Roaur replies, struggling to get up. The prowl leaps in front of Roaur, crouches, ready to pounce upon him, but then Hernan, with full force, tackles the prowl to the floor, the serpent tail strikes at his face, but Hernan grabs it, and lays a powerful back fist crossed its face, knocking out the teeth. He then uppercuts the serpent, and knocks it out cold. The tail lapses, and the prowl shakes off its concussion, and swipes Hernan away, leaving a wide and bleeding gash across his arm.

'Is that the way you want it, then let's finish this, your move.'

The prowl orients itself, notices its dead tail, turns to Hernan and hisses, it leaps high into the air and pounces upon Hernan, but a violent force swings through the air, and sends the beast crashing with bludgeoning force into the wall, smashing the structure to pieces. Hernan looks up to find the blow came from Roaur's hammer.

'I had things under control!' Hernan shouts.

'I just needed my revenge, he's all yours...' Roaur motions for Hernan to attack. Before Hernan realizes what hit him, the prowl strikes, Hernan is on his back, the prowl clawing at Hernan's armor, trying to pry it off, it's claws being ripped away and its toes bleeding profusely. Hernan grabs the beast tightly by the chin, and throws a powerful blow, leveling the prowl to the ground once again. Hernan takes out his blade, raises it high into the air, and sticks it tightly into the beast's skull with a crunch, killing it instantly.

The two continue to pull at the door, and force the rusty hinges open. The darkness leads through an obsidian tunnel that reeks with smoke fumes and a burning stench. There are a few torches lighting the way, and eventually leading to a spiraling stair that ascends endlessly upwards to their destination.

At the end of the tunnel, light shines through to the bottom of the spiral stair. Within the room, dotting across the walls of a mighty tower, are thousands of windows, small in diameter, and spaced close together. Hernan and Roaur look up through the dizzying heights, then begin to traverse upwards.

They trudge forth for hours and hours, stair after stair, which seems like a never ending march upwards. The roar of the crowds and mobs begins to die out the higher they go, until only the sound of the wind is all they hear. Through the windows, they could look out below and see all of Othetica and how it stretches outwards towards the horizon. While they gazed out and pondered the many thoughts within their minds, they did not know that something stirs in the darkness, something is watching them.

'Shall we sit here for a moment and rest?' Hernan asks out loud.

'I'm in agreement. Of all the beasts I've encountered, these stairs are more treacherous and dangerous than any foe.' Roaur remarks.

The two sit down upon the stairs, though their rest is cut short, for Roaur leaps up to his feet, and walks to the edge of the inner circle. 'What was that?!' He stares off to a far corner above them, surrounded by shadows.

'What did you see?' Hernan asks. 'Wait a moment, I hear something...'

There are tiny scratching noises moving about and around them.

'Whoever built this place, surely didn't want intruders skulking about.' Roaur says.

The faint hiss and a whistle sound, a gurgle and cackle pierces their ears. 'Now what?!' Hernan exclaims, wondering what terror they will have to face next. At that instant, three creatures leap forth from the shadows and attack with cunning and stealth. These beasts are lanky and smell of sludge and coagulated blood that stains their claws. Their faces are similar to Civilians, but more twisted and bestial. They wear tattered and shredded pants, torn from abnormal growth and deformation, and rigid claws have torn through the old dried out leather of their boots. They shrill a wicked laugh as Hernan and Roaur swat at them while the beasts hover in the air on massive wings twice their size in length.

Feeling that surge of anger rush through him, Hernan makes a running jump from the stair and catches one of the beast's by the wings. They land upon the opposite side of the stair, and tumble down a few flights to a small and narrow landing. He beats down the beast with steel and iron knuckles, and the creature tries in vain to fight back, but it's no use. Hernan wrangles the beast and snaps its neck with a rough twist, and the spine, bones, and nerves within shatter and splinter. The beast twitches and convulses; Hernan picks up the creature's body and tosses it down to the darkness of the bottom. 'Let the abyss take you!' He cries out.

Roaur smashes another against the wall with his hammer, and the splattered mess of the creature's oozes down the wall in a thick, gooey slop with veins, bone and crumpled flesh. The final monster grabs hold of Roaur from behind and slashes at his face, ripping his helmet from his head, and scraping a large gash across his thick eyelid. He grabs the creature in his one hand, and throws the beast to the ground, and using his large boot, stomps on and smashes the head to a bloody pulp, then kicks the body over the edge, he then reaches down and picks up his helmet and places it back over his scalp.

They reach the top of the stairway to a platform with large windows at hexagonal angels. Out beyond the horizon, the sun begins to set, and the sky gushes red as blood over the hills and mountain tops. The walls of the chamber are jet black and opaque with the shadows of bestial figures and faces protruding from their adimantium structure. There is a lone double door within a beasts mouth on the far side of the tower wall. As they near the doors, they can see the eyes of the beast glow red from the many ruby eyes studded throughout the head, and steam erupts from the nose with a hiss.

'I'll assume this is our path.' Hernan says. Roaur nods in agreement.

Within the inner chamber, the architecture is brooding and dark, they hear heavy footsteps marching behind them from down the corridor, and getting closer. Hernan and Roaur take cover behind a sculpture, twisted and suffering with anguish is cast upon its face. From around the corridor, two soldiers walk pass, though these soldiers are not of Othetica. Their armor is black and rustic, made of gears, sharp thorns and spikes, they each carry a shield bearing a strange insignia upon it, a twisted triangle which points up, and a horned triangle inverted within the other, to form the symbol of the Hexagus.

'Hernan...that symbol! The man I told you about...that's the symbol he bore upon his necklace!' They look about their surroundings. 'Where are we, what is this place!?'

Hernan's voice is quiet and sincere. 'I...I think were in Othetian's palace.'

'Why would an Aurora have such brooding architecture?' Roaur asks, confused by what he is witnessing.

'Let's follow them, they made lead us to the assassin.' Hernan suggests, and the two proceed.

They follow behind, not to close, nor to far, always keeping them just within sight. They head through a doorway turning to the right, going into a much larger, more eloquent room. The two soldiers march down a long carpeted throne room, the once throne room of Aurora Othetian, the room where Cezius Cabriel marched to speak with the Aurora and Kandarius at the beginning, before the tragedy at Vos`ul. The throne room once gold, is now black and corroded, above the obsidian throne of black diamond and crystal, hangs two large fire braziers and in the middle, the same symbol the two guardians bear, the symbol of Dregor, of the Hexagus Lords, the symbol which hung around the man's neck, the man who was shielded by a deep and brooding darkness, this symbol hangs upon a black tapestry over the throne, and the stream of crystal water and living fish, is now black with sludge and littered with bones that have been eaten away.

Whatever malevolent being that has taken over here, is absent. The soldiers stand in front of the throne, on opposite sides of the hall, facing one another. The sinking sun falls to the west, and casts the brooding shadow of Othetian's statue across the floor of the room.

The guardians stand motionless. Hernan walks out from the shadows, with Roaur close behind, their solid footsteps echo across the floor, and to the beams of the ceiling above.

How unusual, the guards don't move, they seem to not even notice them, and are unaware to their presence, as if they have been shut down. Hernan stands about eye to eye with them, Roaur circles them, looking down with hammer at the ready, in case the guardians were to awaken at any moment.

'What kinds of beasts or contraptions are these?' Roaur asks.

'Their armor is strange...unlike any craft I have ever seen. The pieces have been formed into the shapes of shifting gears and leavers, yet their flesh is cold and blue. Their emitting an unusual presence of heat. These fittings, and this here', Hernan points to specific key areas on the armor of the guards, 'It doesn't make any sense to me? No hammer or soldering, no melted metal, no melding, no riveting? No signs of hammer blows... This armor just isn't right...I don't understand its make, who made it, and how?'

'Look at those eyes, there white as death, pale as the sickest flesh.' Roaur says.

They go to the balcony outside. The terrace stretches outwards for miles it seems in all directions, and out upon the very edge, stands the towering statue of Aurora Othetian. They walk out to look closer and examine it. The statue towers above them, the face withered, the teeth grit in pain and agony, the right hand clenches at the heart, while the left is held high into the air, the crown and armor are frozen with him.

'How are we going to undo this Roaur?'

'It cannot be undone.' Says a slither of a voice behind them. They turn to see Kandarius standing behind them. Next to him, is the assassin whose name is Grenan, and two heavily armored beings, one may be Civilian, but the other, much larger one, is neither Civilian, or any other denizen, nor bestial, but a machination and mechanical being. These are the Persivators of Kandarius, his personal body guards. One is female in build and shape, with a broad metal helmet covering her face, with protruding horns, and a long pony tail pulled through the top of her helmet and down her back. Her eyes are soulless and covered by darkness, she carries a mace with thick, poisoned spikes at the tip. The other is twice as big, with golden armor, and a sword about ten feet in length attached to his hand. He walks in a slump, for one of his shoulders is heavily deformed, but covered with a full-plated pauldron which seems to cover almost a quarter of his body, and pulled over top is a raven-colored cape. Kandarius stands straight in posture with his hands crossed one over the other, and his eyes seem to glow with an ominous blue blaze. Hernan looks to Kandarius's feet, and notices a little creature crouched at his ankles. The beast is a little furry creature about two feet tall, and the face of a sadistic old man, with an evil little smile and pale white eyes.

'So, the Forgemaster finally returns to Othetica. A shame the captain was not as fortunate. I always knew he wasn't worth anything and couldn't handle himself.' He laughs. 'My little friend here has been following you, for I see what he sees. Your journey has been quite impressive so far I must say. But are you ready for your final chapter, your final destiny that awaits!?'

'What have you done Kandarius?! What is this sadistic scheme of yours all about!?'

'Scheme? Why, you've misinterpreted me. I only want to return this land to its former glory. There was once a time when power and rule truly meant something , when Aura ran red with the blood of legions, when command and conquer meant a stronger, more disciplined rule, and enslavement... meant a controlled society.'

'The Grey Age will only bring about the end of Aura and her cultures! You will have nothing to rule!'

Kandarius retorts with a wicked laugh. 'You cannot believe the lies of our history spilled by the worthless speeches of Gormons and Asyndians...for you truly don't know the meaning of the Grey Age. The Grey Age is rebirth, when our only true masters, the Hexagus Lords will be reborn from Wom, the mother. She will conceive the sons and daughters of a millennia who ruled with true power, the power of tyrants, not these feeble Auroras!' His roar echoed through the skies. 'For these denizens need true leadership, they need to be structured...enslaved!'

'And what will you do about the Auroras! They will not go down without another fight!' Hernan shouts.

'Look upon him, this is the power of your Auroras!' He points to Othetian. 'They are weak and feeble, they had their moment, their fun, but it's time for them to move aside, the realms belong to the Hexagus and the Dregor beings! Soon, all of these...inferiors, will be cleansed of.' Kandarius walks over to the statue. 'The once Aurora of life and hope, the face of the

Civilian people, now a symbol of decay, suppression, yet hope...for those who wish for change, and want true leadership and structure in their world.'

'Without the essence...without Azalir in your hands, you will not succeed!' Hernan says.

Kandarius laughs again. 'But I have Azalir, I intend to succeed. The blade is quite safe and out of reach, and when the time comes, I will be able to use it as I please.' Kandarius replies. He is tickled by the fear that grows upon Roaur and Hernan's face. '...and you are going to reforge the blade for me!'

Hernan refuses, but something comes over him. The pale blue light within Kandarius's eyes turns red as flame, and he can hear Kandarius's voice in his mind, he cannot resist the plea for help, the voice is that of a child.

'Please...help me! These Asyndians will use Azalir to turn Othetica, and all of Aura into the Greywaste, my home will be gone, and I will...we will have nowhere to go...I don't want to die! Please help, you're the only one who can...'

Roaur watches in terror as Hernan falls prey to the trance. He can see the necklace upon Kandarius's breast glowing red. With a roar, he leaps forward, hammer above his head prepared to attack, ready to strike, but the small female Persivator, Krel, steps in between, and with one powerful strike of her mace, sends Roaur flying back and shatters his helm into pieces. He lands upon the marble unconscious. The helm protected Roaur from the deadly poison, taking the full force of the blow.

Within Hernan's trance: *'Are you going to help? Please, reforge the blade...so we can cleanse Aura of this menace that blights us...'*

Hernan doesn't reply, his thoughts weaving in and out of consciousness, delving further into madness, agony, and torture. Then, with a sudden surge, his body is overcome with pain. The voice changes from a child, to a gurgling beast. This voice was different, could this be....could this be the voice of the Destroyer? The one whom the Auroras fear the most, the ancient being who once enslaved the entire Galakaos in a tyrant's grip? Is this the voice of Maz Dregor?!

'I will not kill you Forgemaster, but I will make you feel such pain, the likes of which you've never known or could possibly imagine! Your heart bursts forth with lesions, your skin itches with plague and pox, your blood runs sour with toxins and venom, your head swells, your bones shatter, your mind breaks down, all your memories dissipate!'

Hernan screams and writhes with gushing pain, he cannot bear what is happening to his body. *'Your paralyzed, you cannot walk, you cannot move, you are blind, all your vision is of night, and the black abyss! No stars guide your path, no sun shines upon you Forgemaster! You will forge the blade, you will bring forth Azalir reborn! We will walk within our realm once more, and for eternity!'*

The onslaught of Hernan's body continues. A shout echoes like thunder through the sky like the cry of a hawk, a burst of lightning strikes from above. When the smoke clears, an Asyndian stands upon the balcony, and the assassin Grenan lays dead, charred, turned to smoking ashes and bone, and protruding from his chest, is the arrow he fired at Y'nahlia, the female Asyndian. The Asyndian holds an exotic weapon of two golden cudgels with blades, attached in the middle by a silver chain, the weapon gives off sparks of lightning. He stands ready for battle, he is one of the Asyndians who guarded the Sacred Lady, Y'nahlia, the female Asyndian with the head dress.

The interruption of the Asyndian breaks Kandarius's hold over Hernan, who after some minutes, regains his original state and composer, rubbing his renewed eyes and gripping his throbbing head. Hernan looks over at the Asyndian, amazed by his appearance.

'Are you alright Forgemaster?' The Asyndian asks.

'I'm fine now....I think.' Hernan replies as he looks

down at his flesh which seems to smoke as though it were burning.

'It will take some time for the touch of a Dregor to wear off.' The Asyndian informs him.

Hernan looks over to Roaur, who mumbles and turns about, slowly regaining composer.

'Roaur?'

'Oh...my head.' He feels around for his hammer, grips it, then uses the shaft as a crutch to get to his feet.

Kandarius's eyes burn with rage, and his teeth grow sharp and blood-thirsty. 'You dare interfere Asyndian!' He screams.

'Your assassin killed our sacred lady, our mystic, our queen, the wife of Airical! Y`nahlia! If I would not have retrieved her body from those denizens, I would have caught that assassin much sooner, for I caught glimpse of his movements in the shadows as he ran off. Your Civilians stabbed my brethren to death and burned him! I will make sure they are avenged! The darkness and fear you hold over these Civilians is powerful indeed.' He turns to Hernan. 'You are lucky Forgemaster, no one returns from a Dregor chant the same person, most do not return at all.'

'He is the one who will not be so lucky!' Hernan cries out.

'Keep your distance Forgemaster, you've only felt a taste of what this man can do! Do not risk it!' The Asyndian warns him.

'I want you two to kill the Asyndian and the Gormon, but beat the Forgemaster down till he can barely stand.' Kandarius orders the two Persivators. And with the speed of light, they leap forth and attack. Krel attacks Roaur, while the golden machine, Othyus, attacks the Asyndian.

The battle grows intense between them. Still feeling a bit weak, Hernan and Kandarius stare each other down.

'Please Forgemaster...do strike at me, strike with what

feeble power you have left, for it will do you no good. Soon you will have no choice but to do as I say!' Kandarius laughs.

'Hernan! Your hammer, use it on the statue!' The Asyndian cries out.

'WHAT!!!' Kandarius cries out.

'The statue Hernan! Use the hammer on the statue!' The Asyndian pleads.

Kandarius smiles. 'Yes...do it Forgemaster! Strike the statue, I dare you to!'

Hernan draws the hammer upon his back, and with a mighty sprint, he leaps into the air, and strikes the stone. He strikes again, the rock begins to crack, again, and another crack splits the stone, and once more...the rock begins to crumble. Kandarius waves his hand. 'Now your dark spirit will awaken, you obey me now...my Aurora! HA HA HA!'

The debris scatter, then behind Hernan's shoulders, a strong current of wind blows from the east and encircles them upon the vast balcony, the stone circles into the wind in a cyclone. Hernan, Roaur, and the Asyndian look on in horror. The Persivators retreat behind Kandarius, who holds his hands to the sky and his fingers move about like the legs of a mig, manipulating and conjuring the daemonic form, of the fallen Aurora Othetian.

Othetian's face begins to take shape, his carcass, arms, and legs form together and fuse into the winds, two wings spread outward some twenty feet. The form is not solid, but an ethereal shadow of what Othetian once was. He is under the control of Kandarius's power. Othetian holds his arm up, and the black clouds that hurdle over swirl downwards into his palm, burning with a black flame, forming a weapon of the most deviant and malicious power. His once immortal gold titan's armor now corroded and drips black sludge and bile fluids from the broken carcass. The pain he feels is severe and tormenting, his screams damage the ears of all across Othetica and the lands beyond, even those of Fausengard, The Greywaste, and the Sasparians to the south, beneath the ocean depths they can hear his cries of torture. Othetian's red eyes glare down upon the three of them. Hernan, Roaur, and the Asyndian ready their weapons and prepare for the most difficult battle they have ever fought, against their most deadliest foe.

'What is this?! What has happened to the Aurora?!' Roaur cries out.

'He is controlling the essence that was imprisoned within the statue, he is controlling the essence of an Aurora!' The Asyndian replies.

Othetian strikes down, sending them flying in opposite directions; Hernan to the right, Roaur to the left, and the Asyndian into the sky. Kandarius looks above, and uses a powerful blast of energy to cripple the Asyndian and send him spiraling to the ground. The Asyndian hits the ground with a thud and cannot move.

'Now, strike him down!' Kandarius commands Othetian.

Othetian raises the blade, and with a powerful blow, strikes, but his swing is momentarily brought to a halt. Hernan, using the hammer, blocks the strike. Othetian recoils and bellows a blood-curdling roar. Othetian strikes again, and Hernan fights back, a duel between the titanic Aurora and the Forgemaster ensues. The clouds thunder, and lightning clashes through the sky, the magnitude of the battle sparks the very fabric of the land, and the stability of the land basks in the uncertainty of collapse, the end broods over the heads of every Civilian who watches and awaits for what is to come, but many take to their heels and run for their lives as the debris crumbles around them.

'You cannot win Forgemaster, it is useless to fight back!' Kandarius threatens, placing more energy into the control of Othetian.

'I'll die here in battle before allowing you to free the Hexagus!' Hernan, without warning, with the fastest reflexes and all the speed he can muster, whips around, and hurls the

Hammer of Gonun at Kandarius, who is to surprised to react, and the hammer lands its blow with deadly precision, sending Kandarius back through the doors into the throne room.

This however, causes a two sided effect, for Othetian has become unstable, he begins to self-destruct, his eyes melt away, the stone blisters, his limbs and body swell, and with a last scream of agony, he explodes into pieces, the ashes catching the wind and showering all of Othetica in a downpour of his remains. The blast cracks the structure of the balcony, and it breaks away, sending Hernan and Roaur to the ground in an avalanche of debris, dust, and stone. Hernan falls, and all goes black.

A while later, Hernan hears a voice calling to him. 'Forgemaster...awaken Forgemaster, we are safe now...Forgemaster?' Hernan's eyes open slowly, only to see the stars in the sky and Pry's moon gazing down upon him. Another voice speaks to him. 'Hernan, are you okay?' It's the voice of Roaur. He sees the two silhouettes move in closer and stand above him. 'He seems to be coming around.' Says the Asyndian.

Hernan sits up to a campfire ahead of him in a small hollow with hills around them, and on the far ridge are some trees and the mountains stretch far beyond.

'I'll help you up.' Roaur picks up Hernan with one hand and sets him upon his feet. Hernan rubs his head in confusion. 'Where are we?'

'As far away from Othetica as I could carry the both of you. Come over to the fire, and we will talk more.' Roaur and Hernan follow the Asyndian over to their camp, where Hernan sits upon a fallen tree stump, over grown with moss and fungus at the base. Roaur sits to the left of him, and the Asyndian sits upon the ground with his legs crossed, in a meditative style of sitting. His wings are folded back and his feathers are settled.

'Now, I see you carry the Hammer of Gonun. You truly are the Forgemaster, I sensed it as soon as I discovered your presence in Othetica.' The Asyndian says.

'The hammer...I threw it, what happened to it?!'

The Asyndian points to the hammer. 'It's over there, where you laid unconscious. It appeared next to you about an hour ago. The hammer follows you, and only you can retrieve it. I saw it disappear before Kandarius could lay his hands upon it.'

Hernan walks over, picks up the hammer, and returns to the fire.

'What were those two fiends that protect Kandarius?' Roaur asks. 'The one looked so tiny, but gave me a blow that would have knocked me into next week if not for my helmet.'

'Those two are extremely dangerous, you are truly a great warrior to stand in a fight against them. They are the Persivators. Othyus, the large golden one, and the smaller is called Krel, a fierce female spirit, corrupted and seduced by Kandarius's dark power, Othyus is her brother, and together they protect Kandarius.'

'They were once warriors of ancient Runegard, and loyal guards to Edrin, the ruler of Runegard before its downfall. Kandarius placed into their will corruption, and poisoned their minds with severe pain and torture, until they became the monsters they are now, lifeless, machines that only exist to serve their master's will.' The Asyndian mentions.

'Kandarius was able to summon a dead Aurora, how is that possible?' Hernan asks.

'The Asyndians have vast knowledge, and we know many things, but this is something I did not expect. My people have dealt with Dregor worship before, but we have never come across someone with power such as his...at least not for millenniums, not since...' The Asyndian's voice lowered to a whisper.

'Is that why you and your people came to Othetica?' Hernan asks.

'Before I go on, I will first introduce myself, my name is Falkon L`or, you do not have to tell me your names, for I know both of you already. My brother and I are, or were, guardians to the mystic lady, Y`nahlia. Our Aurora, Airical, sensed a presence here in Othetica, he could see into the mind of Othetian and knew something was wrong. He feared a resurgence of Dregor, for we could all smell it blowing on the wind. He knew the time had come, The Grey Age was upon us, for us Asyndians, this was all too familiar a feeling, only this time, more is at stake than before...circumstances seem to be much more dangerous than all those millenniums ago.'

'My father taught me about the Grey Age, how it turned all of Asyndia, the most precious land in all of Aura, into a barren wasteland, where only the Asyndians can inhabit the mountain tops and cities in the sky, places where only they can reach.' Roaur says.

'It destroyed most of the ancient races, some escaped. The Gormon to the north, the Civilians to the east, and the Sasparians to the southern oceans...It is as Kandarius spoke, many of our own, those who are fallen and twisted, live day by day, fighting, begging...we delved to deep into our studies, and we paid the price...we have some allies left, but most have never forgiven us for what we have done.'

'What caused the Grey Age to happen? What caused the Greywaste?' Hernan asks.

'It was many millenniums ago, when our ancient ancestors inhabited the glorious west, a jewel, fresh water, crisp sky, sturdy forest, peace as the Auroras gave to us, free of the Hexagus. But there were some who were too greedy, those who wanted to know the true nature of the Dregor and their Hexagus Lords, those who should have left events and history be. There was at one time two ancient and extremely powerful beings, an Asyndian by the name of Naumokron, and a Civilian named Malkahz. They were the practitioners who studied the essence of the Auroras and the Hexagus, understood it's properties and what made them, what they were and are, and how they came to be.'

'According to history, it was a brooding, storming night, and Naumokron discovered a rip, a way to use the essence to break through into other dimensions, travel to other realms, though the power to open one of these portals would have to be great, greater than any force within Aura. Malkahz knew Naumokron was going too far, and told him to cease his work, but Naumokron killed Malkahz, stole his heirloom necklace and created a transmitter, a beacon to tap into one of these dimensions. Through this necklace, he could communicate with the Hexagus Lords. He fell deeper and deeper into madness and under the control of Maz Dregor. It was he, who told Naumokron, that with the essence of Azalir, only then could they walk Aura once again, for that which makes, can unmake, as is the reverse, that which aborts, is used to reborn.'

'They twisted Naumokron, feeding him power that surpassed anything upon Aura. He would stop at nothing to get Azalir, but he knew the blade was kept high above, within Gammafir `ur kmme, guarded by enchantments devised by the Auroras themselves. One thousand years before the Grey Age, Naumokron went to the ocean that bordered Asyndia to the south, he flew to the highest mountain top he could find, and there he disappeared from sight, hid away from all, and there within that cave, for one thousand years, he summoned forth a blast of energy from the realms beyond, and cast the energy, the smallest essence of Hexagus power was all he could summon, cast the energy into the watery depths. That is how powerful, and how difficult it is to use the essence of the Hexagus, for the weakest of spells take a thousand years or more to charge. The blast created a summoning portal, and from this portal, arose something colossal, something monstrous, something no being in Aura can comprehend or describe unless you were there to see it! Naumokron, had summoned forth, an ancient foe… Reignkiing had awakened from its slumber, the dreaded foe, the swallower of oceans, Foameater, Ragulkaugkahn, whatever language his name was translated into, all would be interpreted as death! For it was this unstoppable force which decimated all of Asyndia and created the Greywaste.'

'Reignkiing was a crustacean, as big as a continent, as powerful as the Auroras, he was an ancient creature, created by the Hexagus, in a process so painful, so dreadful and horrible, no pain in the world could compare. He dwelled under the molten oceans, a guardian who only came when awakened by his masters, when his essence would be pulled from the depths of the Hexagus realm.'

Molten tidal waves ripped through Asyndia, flooding and destroying everything. A last defense of Asyndians, Gormons, and Civilians took to the mountain tops and the highest towers, while the Sasparians took to the seas, who, unfortunately, were burned away by the heat of the water, but their efforts were useless, nothing could stop Reignkiing, not even the Auroras could pierce his impenetrable shell, then Airical came up with a battle plan, a new strategy, that maybe a small force could infiltrate from within, so Airical summoned to his call, twelve of the most powerful, mightiest Asyndians. They were the guardians of the Twelve Altars of Y`nahlia. They were the Sentinels.'

'As the Asyndians passed overhead, the soldiers of Aura cheered them on, chanting the sacred words, the ancient song, The Praise for the Sentinels:

" The twelve warriors spread their wings,
Gliding over land and mighty tidal waves,

Guardians of the twelve bells that ring,
For your victory and our freedom we sing!"

Reignkiing grumbled and shook all of Aura, shattering mountains, boiling the seas, which in turn nearly wiped out and destroyed the entire Sasparian race, and the mountains collapsed under the Civilians and the Gormons. The Auroras, Agonan, Tundrok, Gonun, Pry, Lota, Sasparia, and Airical attacked full-force from all sides to cause a diversion on Reignkiing, while the Sentinels hovered about in attack formation, waiting for their opportunity, and when his gaping maw opened, they flew in with lightning speed.'

'They made their way through the mouth, the throat, and towards the lungs, then the heart. That is where the final battle took place, inside the belly of the beast, for at the center of the vast chasm of Reignkiing's entrails was the rotten, beating heart, pumping the thick black sludge of Dregor essence and malice. Organisms were alive, fighting off the Sentinels with rage. The organisms killed a few of the Sentinels, some were killed by the poisonous breath of Reignkiing. All but one was destroyed, one who brought down the final blow, an Asyndian crafted arrow that tore straight through the beast's heart.'

'Who was this Asyndian?' Hernan asks, momentarily interrupting the story.

'Myself, for I flew into those bowls and chasms with twelve of my closest allies and friends, and I was the only one to come out alive...'

Hernan and Roaur look upon the Asyndian in amazement, for his age and strength is greater and more powerful than either of them could fathom, and he carries the wisdom of ages and millenniums within his mind, has seen time come and go, many who were born, and many who have died. He falls silent for a moment, remembering his fallen comrades, then continues the tale.

'Reignkiing fell, causing tidal waves and storms, chaos echoed and spread throughout Aura, the God-Monster's death was felt by all. With the centuries and eons to follow, migration took place, the Asyndians that were left, built their cities further up into the sky, eventually the waters subsided and Reignkiing's remains were washed out to sea, where they can still be seen, which now look like an island that has been burned, charred, and decayed by the sickle of time.'

'The land of Asyndia would never be the same, a barren

wasteland, lifeless and bleak, the waters around Reignkiing, have become poisoned by his blood. No vegetation, nor flora and fauna would ever grow or evolve again. My home, is a barren land of ash and death. For that is why we came, this is what we must stop from happening to the rest of Aura. If the Hexagus return, the situation will be ten-fold compared to what Reignkiing had caused to Asyndia.'

L`or has finished his explanation. Hernan thought to himself and pondered their situation.

'If Kandarius has Azalir hidden, where would he be keeping it locked away, in the palace?' Roaur asks.

'No, that's too obvious, he would not keep it somewhere so simple to find, it would be somewhere impenetrable, and deadly to even look upon with a chance of getting killed, somewhere that crossing is implausible, somewhere inhospitable.' L`or replies.

'Skahljah, across the sands of the Isa Desert!' Hernan exclaims.

'Yes, it would be perfect, and I think I know just the place. There is a Dregor fortress there, located at the center of the desert, upon a high rocky plateau upon a black pit of sludge that surrounds its base. The gates and towers are guarded by sentries and traps, legions of Skahljah, and the sand creatures that reside throughout the desert, sun migs that hunt at night, and the desert prowl that skulk about during the day and at the brink of dusk, not to mention the many hundreds of deadly beasts and foes that also skulk about the sands.' L`or replies.

'We'll start tomorrow then, at the first ray of Lota's sunrise.' Hernan says.

'You and Roaur will go, I must return to the west, to let Airical know what has happened and to tell him of the situation at hand, for our ladies death will be mourned for a thousand years and more. I do not know how I will break the news to Airical or what is going to happen. Asyndians know much, but we unfortunately do not have the knowledge of all things, including when our long life will no longer exist. We can live on for years, centuries, millenniums...but we could die tomorrow without any knowledge of our passing.' L`or says.

'I understand, and I am sorry for your loss.' Hernan replies.

‘Then I take my leave...and I wish your travels across the dunes and dry seas well.’ L`or flies into the air, gliding on the western winds, heading back to his land of desolation, to deliver dark news and the lady Y`nahlia's body, which he has kept hidden away in a safe place. Just as they planned, at dawns first light, Hernan and Roaur take the road south, to the Isa Desert, and the land of the warring Baldushan and Skahljah.

PART IX:

Y`nahlia's Song

Far above the charred foreign land, basking in the light of the shadowy Greywaste, within mighty clouds and golden skies, where only the Asyndian flies, is built the majestic city, the empire a crowning jewel of its former glory, Athilnovia, the new Asyndia, where the Aurora Airical resides upon his marble perch, overlooking the entire land of Aura through the mighty windows, without glass or frame, from the mighty towers for which only the most royal of Asyndians can fly to, far above the deadlands, where many criminal Asyndians struggle to survive, the fallen, the down trodden, those that have once served their master of the black arts, Naumokron, the Dregor worshipper, the bringer of Reignkiing.

For L`or, Athilnovia is his home, where he has presided over his Mystic Lady and Aurora as their protector, the Last Sentinel, the last great warrior, of a once great history of aviary creatures, whose land had been sold and desecrated, destroyed by the powers of Naumokron, and the desolation of Reignkiing. He now serves as a messenger within the golden city and towers that float within their magical essence created and maintained by Airical's vast powers, flying back and forth throughout the skies and across the vast realm of Aura, yet his main duty still, as it has always been, as he has always done, is to serve as protector for his Mystic Lady and his Aurora.

He now returns with the corpse of his Lady, Y`nahlia's body wrapped in a sacred white sheet, and her golden essence, now faded dust, scatters across the shimmering ivory towers that glow within the sun's rays as he flies her across Athilnovia, to bring Airical's beloved, her cold, dead soul, back to his arms. But, Airical knows, for his moons and stars have grown bleak and slowly dwindle, flaring out of power and exhaust their light.

In the distance ahead of L`or, the candles flicker, and a mass, a vigil gathers around the twelve statues of the Auroras, The Temple, the Twelve Altars of Y`nahlia, the vast halls of this mausoleum, this sacred place where Y`nahlia presided over, maintaining and protecting these most precious of Asyndian artifacts and culture, these shrines that give comfort and protection, powers to those who use and take advantage of their blessings. Now they will serve to guide the Sacred Lady to the halls of an alternate future, a future place and time created, imagined by the Asyndians, an alternate plane of existence where the wings of the sacred guardians go to, and now the queen will watch over her subjects, and serve as a guiding hand to those who become lost, and wish to seek these very halls and domes of clear blue skies, a sight even more beautiful, more majestic than that of Athilnovia.

Surrounding the embankment of the temple are trees of bronze tipped with a lush bushel of yellow leaves, the branches are strewn across and wrap around like golden hands and lithe bronze arms, embracing the warm structure, the roots grow down into the mists and dissipate. Upon the rails of silver, a mesh of vines with sacred fruits and olives grow, that were used as offerings for the Aurora shrines, picked by Y`nahlia herself.

Groups of hundreds of Asyndians, of all different colored feathers and wings, like a pastoral rainbow in the morning sun that glisten the falling drops of dew from the bronze trees and the golden leaves, gather around in congregation and camaraderie, in the presence and prestige of the twelve statues of perfect marbles, of perfect shape, carved from the sacred materials of stone that were mined from the tops of the ancient mountains that protrude through the clouds near Athilnovia.

Now I have gone into detail already, and have talked at great length about what some of the Aurora's throughout this tale, who they are and what they look like in description. But the shrines have been carved differently by the ancient Asyndians who built them, and dedicated them to their Lady. Against the temple walls of gold, under a colossal overhang, a canopy of solid spectral marble that reflects the sun's bright rays, stand the Twelve Altars of Y`nahlia, as follows:

Airical, is depicted as he is, a being of sacred glow, with wide spread ivory feathers and sacred robes of smooth marble and jewels adorned upon his carved diadem, The Sacred One, his name translates to in common Civilian Language. Gonun is depicted as machinery, gears and leavers, his body an assembly line, and powerful steam engines crank and turn his beating, metal heart. Upon his eye, is a looking monocle of very fine magnification to preserve the detail of every one of his pieces and creations, to be of the finest quality, without flaw, without blemish, the finest craftsmanship, and gigantic pipes which release thick clouds of steam. Agonan, the Soldier, is clad from head to foot in scaled armor, for his face is covered in bronze and copper scales with broad polished, jet black wings at his back, his armored body is ironbound, and his sculpted sword and shield are riveted to his arms by sacred nails and liquid nickel. His pose is that of a relaxed, frozen state of saunter.

Tundrok, the force of nature, and the realm of the skies, commander of lighting and lord of the thunder, has been cast in cold nickel with his Crown of Storms imbued with gleaming sapphires and the crown itself made of twisted coral set to the nickel plate, he is seated upon a stand with arms and legs crossed in a seated pose. Sasparia, the keeper of the seas and sands of Sasparian islands, the domineering queen of the

Sasparians far in the southern seas, is posed upon her stand of sea rock, smooth opals, hand placed one by one to simulate scales of her fish-like body, are held together by an impenetrable caulking made with a secret Asyndian technique that has died with the ancient ones who made these sculptures. She has a long, curled and cascading fin upon the bottom half of her body, from the waist down, and a scepter of water elements with a carved serpent's head and decorated marine life adorning the shaft, while the serpent's eyes are two pearls. Shemoga, of the Baldushan people, and the keeper of the mystic eclipse, and the slain sister of Sasparia, her shrine, or what was once left of its structure, has long crumbled down into rubble and scattered jewels, now nothing more than a faded gray pile of rocks and stone.

The shrines of Lota and Pry bear their corresponding ambiance surrounding their altars. Lota stands rising in the eye of the dawn's breeching sun, with a single open eyelid pouring light upon her statue, and her wings spread to soar into the skies to the sprinkle of stars across the night air and fill the coming morning with her gaze over the brink of the mountains. Pry is crouched upon a solar moon, and a shade of night entices and surrounds his silhouette in shadows and mystery, as he coils himself within his coal black wings and hides his ethereal, hooded form. Lota bears a painted tattoo upon her eastern eye when open, and Pry has the same tattoo upon the western eye when closed, to symbolize the rising and setting of the sun, and the materialization of the pale eye of the moon, a whispering orb of the night, like a willow the wisp.

Closer to the middle, are the two larger sculptures, the shrines of Kathaxes and Asyndiis, the Father of the Voids, and the Mother of Aura from whence the Auroras and the Hexagus have came forth into the realms across the Galakaos. Kathaxes's many hands reach forth from a gaping black form of a dark abyss, and Asyndiis is draped with the ivory pigment of her robes and the painted clay sky above her head rains the elixir of life, the fluids to suckle and grow all flora, all fauna, and all beings alike and different. Her cat-green eyes, and several layers of wings, draw the white birds of peace to her warmth and protection, as they nestle and huddle under her solid structure.

On the far end of the other Auroras, is the mysterious and secluded Aurora of the mountains and dirt, soil and the growth of trees, is Niffrok, the forgotten one, the one who hides from the day and the night, from the elements of rain, snow, thunder and lightning as it strikes and crashes upon Niffrok's surface and burns his trees and engulfs the forests and grasslands. His only friends, are his trees and pet mountains, the few that speak to him and tell him secrets of the realm, for the mountains are the eldest beings, even older than the trees, for if we could hear the mountains and listen to them, they would tell us a story or two. Niffrok's shrine is nothing more than a large lump of clay in the shape of the Aurora, though his features are clouded by mists and a bit distorted because very few, even the other Aurora's rarely see him, and most of them have forgotten, hence the name Forgotten One. But his distinctive feature, is the lone tree which juts from the back of his shoulder, the first tree he ever created and planted, the first tree he fed rain, and grew into a full, living, white oak some hundreds of feet tall and fifty or so feet in width, a tree that could drink and sop up an entire ocean, along with several rivers, streams, and lakes.

At the center of all the shrines, is the altar where Y`nahlia, the Mystic Lady, sat upon a throne of jade and diamonds, with golden trim. Many exotic birds and plants surrounded her throne, vines would hug the legs and armrests, while peacocks and Rain Divers, small blue birds which swoop and fly through the sky and drink the rain drops, would rest by her head and upon her shoulder. Quails and Red Fires nestled by her talons, next to birch tree seedlings, that were warmed by the decorative, low-hanging lamps with clear wax candles burning a magical glow within each of them, usually there are six lanterns or so hanging upon six hooks welded into and arch and molded together by the poles, and this decoration would be placed into the floor at the back of her throne. Now her pets have fled away to other resting grounds, other homes, or have died and will pass on into the realms in which Y`nahlia will soon travel.

L`or eases his landing upon the balcony of the temple. He walks over to Airical, where he holds the body in front of the Aurora, and for all the others to see. Airical approaches L`or and places his hand upon his shoulder. No words are spoken between the two, L`or simply places Y`nahlia within Airical's arms, and walks away to the front of the crowds where the hundreds of Asyndians stand, their heads tilted down in sorrow and weep for the loss of their Sacred Lady, the Jade Throne has faded.

Airical is shattered by the loss of his loved one, though he does not show his emotions, he keeps his weeping hidden under the shadows of the cool willows that engulf his mind and thoughts. The rain falls from dark clouds and blankets his cheer, and dampens his spirits.

Her body is prepared and decorated with adorning jewelry and a sacred dress of fine silks and spun lace and heavenly threads and beads. Her limbs are wrapped in sacred gauze, and a head dress of cascading feathers and a tiara of the purest diamond and opals, is placed upon her head. The arms of Y`nahlia's corpse are crossed in an X pattern, with each hand holding a key in its death grip. One key is for the Doors of Time, and the other for the Doors of Eternity as she passes into the realms of the dead. Airical gives her the last rights, the Asyndians kneel on both knees with hands across their chest. They whisper sacred words, as Airical chants the final words, the song of Y`nahlia, will ease the spirit on her journey forward and far beyond.

Bells, horns, and drums begin to play, and flutes whistle. A low, ominous voice of tenors and bravados begin to murmur and chant, followed by the higher octaves of the divas and their arpeggios. Airical's voice is heard at a volume above all others. In the Ancient words of the Asyndians, within the clouds far above the Greywaste, over mountains and into deep waters of the oceans, his voice, his song would be heard by all. Within the heart of every Asyndian, the song of Y`nahlia echoes:

"Golden rivers, feathers on the tide,

The colors of her eyes expire, as she's laid down,

For her body and time has subsided.

Autumn leaves turn to snow,

Feathers burn to ash,

Those ashes blow in the fires of summer,

Her wings spread and the winds carry her,

Into the afterlife, for happiness ever after.

***

Gazing through her eyes she'll find,

There's a place beyond space and time,

Where the Asyndians and majestic beasts fly.

Let her ashes soar.

***

Her wings glide towards the ivory towers,

Which touch the sky,

To sit upon the thrones among the guardians,

Of the divinity and embrace the return to serenity.

Outward plains of green grass, clouds,

And hills roll on, forever moving by,

Let Y`nahlia's ashes flow with the river's tide,

As her body and essence becomes one with Aura's eye.

***

Gazing through her eyes she'll find,

There's a place beyond space and time,

Where the Asyndians and majestic beasts fly.

Let her ashes soar.

***

From a world that's soon out of time,

Y`nahlia, I release your soul and mind,

And I know your way you will find.

And let her ashes soar.

Soar out to infinity, let her ashes soar."

As the song comes to an end, Y`nahlia's body is placed within an altar; she is submerged into clear water that settles within. The Asyndians surround the altar of clear, pure water that ripples with the cool breeze. The waters lead from the altar, into a stream that will carry her ashes across the waters, under a waterfall, and then into the tomb beyond where the Twelve Altars reside. The fires around the altar are lit, and after a period of time and a long vigil by Airical, L`or, and the many Asyndians, her ashes break down and spread throughout the waters, turning the pure water cloudy and gray like the foreboding clouds that gather around them. The stream carries the ashes through the waters and flows down into the canals, passed the water falls that cover the doors to the tomb, and the portal into the next realm.

After the Asyndians gave their final goodbyes and respects, they flew back to their towers and perches high above and around Athilnovia. L`or and Airical stay behind, for they have events to discuss.

'I'm sorry my Aurora, your loss is felt by us all. I miss the Lady already. The shrines and temples will go dark, and the Altars will decay, for they have already begun their decomposition into the black voids and darkness, fading with the setting sun, fading with our Sacred Lady.'

'I miss her L`or, she was the light of all light, and not afraid of any foe or coming darkness. She died trying to save others and ourselves from a second darkness. Kandarius will pay for his atrocities, he has to! But his darkness and tangled thoughts clouds my own foresight and judgment. He grows more powerful with each passing day.' Airical explains.

He continues. 'You are the greatest amongst my soldiers and generals, and of all the Asyndians, Falkon L`or, you've defeated Reignkiing, delivered the body of my beloved safely back here for proper burial, and you've had an important role in keeping Athilnovia golden and bright, but I fear our strength wanes, the source of our lasting life is failing, and unless Kandarius and these omens are stopped, then the Hexagus will reign again.'

'You will take part in his downfall. L`or, you must return to the Forgemaster, for I have important information he must know, information only Gonun has told me, but has long forgotten. I fear he did not tell the Forgemaster.'

'What information shall I carry on to the ears of the Forgemaster?' L`or asks.

'Tell the Forgemaster, that he must head for the Southern Isles, from once the Civilians came on ships and tide, and waves of blood and war. The Forgemaster must know there is a sacred relic hidden on those islands, an anvil. With the Hammer of Gonun, the Forgemaster will be able to reforge the blade. Unfortunately, Gonun never shared the secret of where to find the ancient mineral to reforge Azalir, but I feel he will find the answers there, at the anvil, that he seeks.'

'And…I feel something is about to happen that has not happen since the days of darkness, when light banned shadow…the sacred warrior, the one…The Hero of Ages is close, for he has returned, I can feel his presence is near, he is close…he is on his way, and will soon reveal himself to us. But as to his identity, that...will only be revealed in time.'

PART X:

Possessor

Far to the southwest, at the very edge of the Greywaste, near the remains of Reignkiing, standing upon the highest black peak, carved out of eons and decay that has formed the black spires of the Castle of Solument, deep into the rock face is the fortress and within the lifeless eyes of the windows, tattered curtains stained with blood, ripple with the wind that howls through the withered halls and rings the chimes upon the steeples, the chimes that cry out like the sound of whining animals in pain. The dead walls surround, protect, and hide the inner sanctum of Naumokron.

Long has he been forgotten, long has he sat upon his dark perch, long has he watched from the empty windows the rising of the tide of the sea, and from the sphere of opal upon the center pedestal far beneath his perch, the tide of war and the blood of lifetimes.

Far below, under the shadow of the colossus, stands the tall, pale shape of Kandarius, his robes of blood-red twist and writhe in the cold wind, which blows across the wastes. The ashes of the old lands barrel across in dunes and dust storms. Off to the west, moving northeast along the spine at the center, where many remains lay of skeletons, and the ribs and necks of large beasts that once bore the burden of the ancient Civilians, Gormons, and Asyndians, he could see the urchin creatures move and stalk about. Long has the ashes eroded over the deaths of millions. Kandarius gazes out over the vast stretch of land; a sinister smile curls over his blood-red lips. The gray skies above blot out the sun, for no light has shined upon the Greywaste in millenniums. He turns his gaze up to the black spires where the old Asyndian of darkness dwells, his old master.

Up above upon the thorns and ledges, featherless, pale-eyed Asyndians, twisted and fallen, flock about and gaze down upon the visitor to their master's fortress. The vulture-like Asyndians gather about and eye up Kandarius, examining his intentions and smelling the air about him. Far below at the base of the mountain fortress, there is no door, for Asyndians have only their windows and perches they fly up to far above, miles and miles a ways up to where only they may reach. The mangled Asyndians pack together tightly around the spires in flocks and unbelieving to their eyes, the stranger vanishes before them.

They scatter about the area, searching for him. Their milky white eyes search and hunt, flying all about the mountain from base to pinnacle. At the top of the palisade, there is one gate, a large iron bound heathen of a mechanism, pulled by two fallen Asyndians who may never rest, for attached to their faces, are large casts of metal formed to the shape of their lower beak and mandible area, and upon their upper beak, curving over and pointing towards their heart, hangs a huge metal spike, and if these twisted, wingless Asyndians ever failed in their duties, and grew weary, letting their heads fall, the spike would drive through their chests, causing a slow, painful, and agonizing death. These fallen ones look upon the strange being, and they cower before his presence.

'You will open these doors, for I demand to see Naumokron. An old friend comes to pay him a visit.' The fallen ones stretch out their wide arms, the shackles upon their wrists pull the chains of the door, and with a shuffle, and one leg after the other, they pull the mechanism and the doors begin to open. The doors to the long, dank, and moldy entrance hall open with the screams of creaking and squalling as if a thousand animals where being slaughtered and innocent people were being tortured.

Kandarius is approached by a hunched over, wingless servant of Naumokron's, the gangly creature looks upon Kandarius with its one pale blue eye and a cracked beak, and speaks in a crackling voice. 'You must be that tall fellow the master has been expecting, this way, just down the stairs here and through the doors at the end of the hall. The creature leads him down the stairs, through the dank and rustic castle of torture, pass the bodies and skeletons that hang from the ceiling, old prey swooped upon and caught by Naumokron's servants and brought back to be feasted upon, and coagulated in the crevasses of the stairwells, is piles of soot and fungus shavings leading down onto the rotten, and filthy floor.

The creature opens the charred iron doors, leading into the vast hall. The stalagmites erupt from the floor, stalactites break through the ceiling, pieces of rubble falls to the floor. The damp smell of blood is thick in the air, and the taste of iron is damp upon the tongue with every breath. The corrosive sludge is caked upon the obsidian floor in massive clumps. No torches burn, no braziers are lit. The only sound is the howl and shriek of the wind outside the obsidian walls and the insistent dripping of fluid, could be water, or maybe blood. Naumokron was nowhere to be found. Kandarius looks upon this twisted creature, this servant of Naumokron's with a sinister glare.

'Where is he, I thought you said he was through these doors.' Kandarius grabs the thing by the neck. 'Where?!' The creature struggles to get loose, but Kandarius's grasp is to tight, the beast simply points up. Kandarius tosses the pathetic creature aside. Up above, is a massive tower that stretches upwards, high above the peaks of the mountain. Perched high above, with thick black talons, a decayed black robe, and jet black feathers curled back, and glaring down with red eyes glowing in the twilight of the dark clouds above, is the vile wretchedness of the Ancient one, Naumokron. He leaps off, and soars downwards, with black wings stretched out turning dust into storms, winds into razor blades, and light into the blackest of shadow. He raises his twisted clawed hand, signaling for the servant to leave them.

Naumokron lowers his claw. 'The pieces are moving into place, the darkness is hurdling over, and soon they will fade to their doom… It has been a long time Kandarius; I trust all is going as expected?'

'It is only a matter of time, soon the Hexagus will be free, and all will be as it once was.' Kandarius replies.

'Excellent, you have done well Kandarius; I knew when I first found you, that you were the one meant to take on this task. Just a young lad you were, lost upon a long and dark road. You were lost, your family abandoned you, you had no friends, could trust no one...except for yourself. The amulet was drawn to you, it chose you, and so I took you as my apprentice, taught you what I know, for summoning Reignkiing took much out of me; I knew I was going to need someone to carry on the work of the Master, and you have. What else do I have left to do, but to see this through, to see the day when our kind will rule this realm once more?'

And then, time seems to freeze at that very moment.

Kandarius does think back, to when he was abandoned, his family, his friends, a beautiful lass whom he loved, a girl his age, that would smile and give deep meaningful stares and innocent looks into his heart, and his eyes would look to hers, as they would walk across fields and through trees without a care for time or age, they were each so young, so full of life. But then, he does not remember much, a cloud came over his mind, a shadow, and then...her blood was upon his hands, and how it got there, he did not know, he could not remember what happened that day, all those years ago. He left her, left her to the animals and the wild, in a place where no one would know, no one would ever see, where no one would remember, except for him, for he would never forget.

Then, he and two of his brothers Piaus and Ezirius, were out playing by the old farms, and the dead cornfields, fall was upon Aura, and the air was turning brisk and cold. The three of them were out in the darkest part of the woods, and they could feel a cool rain begin to fall, and they took shelter under a large tree, and at the base of the trunk, was a hide-away, a small cave deep in the ground that was abandoned by its previous inhabitant for some time. While his two brothers were in the cave starting a fire, Kandarius looked out from the entrance, at the old trees around them, and to the branches above his head of the old tree. The wind picked up and twisted and swayed the branches back and forth, left to right and all about. The many hands and long fingers waved with the icy winds, and creaked and rattled as if whispering some frightening secret that only the forest and the trees know. Then, that's when he heard it again, that voice, a deep raspy voice, not threatening, but comforting and soothing to hear, yet it gave Kandarius a creeping chill down his spine, there was something about the voice that made him feel afraid. It spoke louder and louder, as though it were in the distance, just over the hills, and was crawling its way through bushes and scratching tree trunks with long, sharp nails, working its way to Kandarius, and he would be confronted by some loathsome shape. Then, with the clasp of lightning, it startled him back into his own thoughts, and he could hear his older brother's voice telling him to come in, before he gets struck, for the storm was getting worse, and they would have to spend the evening within this dank hole.

That night, his mind swirled with nightmares and dark thoughts, he could see twisted faces taunting him, evil beasts biting and clawing, the people of Aura dying in genocide, a dark shadow engulfed the world, and the Galakaos, and buried all into the grave, bodies upon bodies piled high through city streets, without limbs or heads, some chewed and masticated, giant daemonic figures scoop up piles and dump them into their gaping maws, and swallow the flesh and bones, drink the blood, and wash away all of the Civilians and denizens upon Aura, all life ceases, all time dies, and the black shadows soar across the sky, and eclipse the red sun and obliterated the cracked moon, and there...one boy stands at the mists and terror of it all, upon the hills and dunes of flesh and skin that rot and stiffen with the decay of not time, but the dark influence that engulfs all.

He carries his sword, and a shield of courage upon his scrawny arm, the helmet upon his head barely fits, and obscures his vision. A black shape rises above all others, and stares down upon the boy with the new sun, the new star, and the moon of coagulation and dripping vile fluid into the sky, for the eyes Kandarius cannot look upon, for they are to vile, to horrible a sight to behold. He closes his eyes, and with all the might of his sword hand, charges at the shape of darkness, and slashes wildly, splattering blood, splattering pain, as the screams and smell of death are thick in the air...and that's when the young boy's eyes are open, he can truly see, he can feel the warm blood on his knuckles, as it drips down his fingers and to the cave floor, and clutched within his two fists, a dagger that is drenched with the lives of two he has loved, and the corpses of his brothers are chopped to pieces and butchered, their limbs scattered across the floor, a massacre, a terror of unparalleled proportions and a sight more horrifying than the black shape he had fought within his nightmares, he blinks...and wipes his face, and their blood stains across his cheek, and when a tear mixes with blood, all is done, and sadness and sorrow, regret and self-rage cannot be undone, the moment cannot be reversed, for the blood was already on

Kandarius's hands, but now the victims were more, and the psyche spirals more and more into insanity and chaos.

'I did it once, I did not want to do it again...I felt sorrow, I felt a sickness to my stomach that I never felt before...I did it twice, three times...I...my brothers, my own flesh and blood, were dead...I killed them! But there was this voice inside, a voice telling me that it was okay, it had be done! But why, I did not understand. My love, my one true love, I slayed her, but that too...was okay?!'

Kandarius roamed the forests for days and nights, not thinking, but lost in that dark part of his mind, a place the sun would never pierce through, never reclaim that sunshine of a young boy's mind, for the voids of chaos within his heart would only pulsate and become stronger, the puss would spew forth from the wound, and no one would be there to cure the infection, stop the deeper scar that was being formed.

'And that's when you came, the black shadow loomed over head like a rain cloud, and swooped down with silence and scorn in his eyes, and the predator showed his face to me...a winged beast, a man in the shadows, but the silhouette of a bird, and the one the Asyndians cursed, the begotten Naumokron stood before me...you took my hand, and within it, placed this amulet, and said that I was the chosen one, the fate of Aura was in my hands, the balance of tyranny and power was my destiny, for the blood was already upon my hands...all that was left, was to control it, and bend the blood and lives of all to my will...'

He just remembers that black voice, and then, the Asyndian appeared before him, introducing himself as Naumokron, the one who would guide the chosen to his true destiny.

Naumokron handed to Kandarius, his birth right, the symbol of Hexagus, the beacon, a connection to Aura and Maz Dregor.

Naumokron had vanished, the storm clouds dissipated, and the moon was full, casting a soft blue light across the bank of the river, and the waterfall that fell into the pool at the bottom of the cliff where Kandarius sat and looked at the necklace, not just looked at it, but studied it, wondered about it, for he took it without question, without the true reason or answers he searched for. Why did it come to him, why was he chosen for such a dark purpose?

He tossed the symbol and gold chain to the ground. 'I do not want this, my life is done, and my name will be spoiled by the tongues of all who will speak of it! I hate this thing, I will not accept this fate, for I throw my power away.' The necklace clangs as he tosses it over the cliff, and down into the waters below where the waterfalls empty into. He turns to leave the grotto, stomping through the dead leaves, wondering what will he do now? Where does his loyalty reside now, for his life has been stained and tainted, then, that voice once more, comes to him, speaks. This time it's closer, almost as though its right behind him. He turns, and there's no one there. Above him, he looks up, nothing. At his feet, no...not there. Then where? He wondered to himself.

'Do you throw this power away so rashly?' The voice says.

'Who said that? Who's there...show yourself!'

'Why...I did.' The voice replies.

'Who did, I see no one!' Kandarius says, paranoia begins to worsen.

'Me, down here...look below you, to the pool where all water falls into, I am here before you.'

Kandarius slowly makes his way towards the edge of the cliff, the water falls rapidly downwards into the pool of what was once foam upon water. Now, there is a warp, a deep pool of sorts, but not made of water, swirling inwards like a cloud of smoke, colored in dark hues. At the end of the warp, within a long tunnel which stretches back into the distance, and standing at the distant horizon, there is a shape, of someone dark and shrouded in mystery, a dark outline of a man, maybe someone or something else that looms in a sickness and greenish glow. His face is blank, and cannot be seen, just his movements when he speaks to Kandarius.

Kandarius kneels forward and looks closer at the swirling pool, the realm into another world, another place and time, where ages and eons mean nothing.

'Who are you?' Kandarius asks.

'Why, a friend, perhaps maybe the only friend you have, the only ally in this matter.' The Voice answers with a light hearted laugh, amused by the boys purity and innocence.

'Then answer me, friend...are you really there, or do I talk to my reflection upon a foaming lake, for I have wondered this forest and these hills for hours and hours without food or water?' Kandarius asks.

The voice laughs. 'Oh...I assure you I am quite real, I am in front of your eyes, and not a figment of your mind's imagination or your stomach's thirst and starvation.'

'Then...where are you? How is it I am seeing you, speaking to you?'

'Because, you have a power! A curse... some would call it, an omen, but to one such as me and you, it is a gift!' The voice explains to the boy, who appears deep in despair to the shadow, for the being senses he is still mourning over the death and brutal murder of his brothers and his love. 'Ah, mourn not for the weak that have perished, we all must evolve into a higher existence, and the weak simply hold us back!'

'Is this the gift you speak of?! A gift does not murder and kill, a gift helps to make things better for one's self as well as others, allowing them to flourish for years and years eternal...'

Kandarius is interrupted abruptly. 'You see, I once felt the same as you. I felt I was cursed and that I was destroying lives around me, those whom I loved, but once I enlightened myself, and saw the larger scheme at work, and grew to understand what it was I could do, once I knew what kind of power I had within myself, I no longer needed those around me!'

'You...you eliminated them, all your family, friends, all your people...everyone?' Kandarius pauses, and is aghast at the words the shadowy figure says to him.

The figure gave a brooding laugh. 'You see, my young friend, it's our choices and our own interests that make us stronger, and bring out the true power within ourselves as individuals. In order for us to become more powerful, you have to eliminate the weak around you, those who would seek to get in your way! Punish you for something beautiful they don't understand!'

Kandarius begins to grow fearful in the presences of this shadow; his words are haunting and terrifying to the young boy. This thing claims to be friends, but who is he really? 'I will ask you again, who or what are you?!'

'Please young Kandarius, I already told you, and I guess I shall have to say so again, I am a friend.' The voice replies.

'How...how do you know my name!?'

There is a long pause between them, as Kandarius hears the swirling, unnatural winds within the realms that exist within the pool, an unnatural holler and gust blows across black rocks and towering spires beyond his horizons.

'I've been monitoring you for a long time, your power radiates like a beacon, a strong, bright light in a field of darkness and weakness, oversaturated by weeds that need to be pulled and destroyed! Suffocated from the roots they breathe upon, and circulate their blood!'

'Monitoring? How?' Kandarius asks.

'There are many ways. This amulet binds a connection to this world, the power within, allows me to see into this world, to communicate through my many subsidiaries. Naumokron has been the bearer for eons, searching, waiting for the one...you to come, my chosen one!'

'What is my purpose?'

'You are the one who will bring order and rule once again, to a land that does not have it! They preach of peace and unity, but they do not have it, they are disbanded, against one another, a civilization in an uproar, which will soon collapse! And when it does, you will be the catalyst, the great emancipator who will rise up, and order will return...!'

Kandarius looks into the eyes of the Asyndian. 'And that was my honor that was given, bestowed unto me by the almighty one, the Destroyer of the weak and downtrodden, those who would be left in the dust of the Greywaste, to forever decay and decompose with the ash, and upon those ruins, a new civilization would be born, a higher order would ascend to the higher echelon, and as Maz Dregor said to me on that night, more than a lifetime ago:

"We will once more have order,

Through war we will conquer, through death we will cleanse,

By tyranny we will reign, and when the blood has drained,

At the dawn of a new age, the Hexagus will reclaim their lands,

And the entire universe will be clenched in a grip of fear,

As the fingers wrap around, in a blood-soaked hand,

No one will resist, there will be no last stand!

We will once more have order,

When my throne has been reclaimed, for I am Maz Dregor

My lands will be pure, for I am the Destroyer!"

'And that we will do Kandarius…and that we will do…' Naumokron replies.

Kandarius walks closer, and places his hand upon Naumokron's shoulder. 'All these long years of staying hidden away and cooped up in these towers has taken much out of you. When was the last time you tasted the air outside, and spread your feathers across the skies? I have learned much from you, but I am still but one.'

Naumokron turns. 'What is your plan Kandarius?'

That familiar smile scours across his lips and his brows slant, the dark eyes turn pale blue and begin to shimmer. Naumokron becomes paralyzed and is unable to move.

Kandarius grabs him by the throat and begins to drain his power away, 'Kandarius…! What is the meaning of…this!' The door to the room bursts open and his twisted guards fly in. Kandarius raises his hand and without effort, engulfs them all in a ball of flame, and the ashes of the bodies snow lightly upon the floor.

'Your purpose serves me now, my Master! For I have need of you yet…' The necklace around Kandarius's neck glows red and casts fiery shadows across the floor. Once all is done, the limp and lifeless body of Naumokron falls upon cold stone among the ashes of his servants as his essence courses through Kandarius's body with a flicker of lightning.

'So close now, oh so close we are! Just need to bring the final pieces together, and then all that is scattered will be whole; all will be one, under the rule of only one! It is only a matter of time, and patience…as my time grows longer, all others rush and will miss a step, miss a piece, HAHAHA!!!!'

The winds pick up, the warm air collides with the cool breeze that blows from the east, the dark clouds hurdle over the mountain, and a funnel begins to appear and take violent shape, the black twister rips into the mountain and tears and crumbles the rocks and boulders, driving the mountain down to nothing more than a pile of dirt, and the black walls and towers of Naumokron's fortress crumbles away, and exists no more.

Upon the far ridge, the robes of a tall, lithe, pale figure blows in the winds, Kandarius watches on, as his power is only just sipped and tasted by a realm whose very existence has just been questioned.

He looks to his feet, and Aumon grasps his leg. 'Aumon, I need you to go to the Isa Desert, and to Kaskopos, and keep an eye on our friend there. I don't want anything to go wrong, all is falling perfectly into place, and I feel Ja`kal has one more task, before he has lost his usefulness to me! Inform him why you come, but make something up...be creative!' He winks at Aumon.

The wicked little creature smiles, and gives a sinister, tiny laugh, as he wisps away into a black mist, and vanishes from the Greywaste. Kandarius looks on, as the final smoke from the rubble clears, and all is left into ruin, the fallen Asyndians, at his command and his whim, gather to him and bow before his will, for they are his now, they obey only one, the one true lord of the Dregor, Kandarius, their master, their meaning for existence, until he crushes them in his grasp, relieving them of their usefulness, or his enemies kill them, for they will, and must, die for Kandarius, they will die for the benefit and sacrifice of Hexagus and the rise of tyranny once more.

Yet, in the back of his mind, Kandarius thinks of the last words Naumokron said to him, for he did not understand what the Asyndian was squawking about.

"Beware Kandarius...when his time has come Kandarius...he will be hunting you down, searching for the blood...that you take from me....!"

Was he referring to Maz Dregor? Or were these the empty threats of a dying old Asyndian.

PART XI:

The Shaded Woods

The harsh winds of dry soil and dead flesh scatter across the plains of oblivion and barren waste, Isa Desert, where the Skahljah dwell, the destroyers of life, the warlords of death and destruction reside within palisades of smoke and ash covered brick, built upon the foundations of human bones, mountains of life they have torn away with blades and hatchets, scimitars and dai-katanas. The spires rise high into the night and thick polluted skies and ethereal darkness, poisoned by production and machine-run fortresses.

At the center of the desert, at the core of Skahljah's black conscious, built upon the bones of Shemoga, the once Aurora of Isa, once an empress and queen among the Baldushan people, upon her bones is erected Kaskopos, as heartless as a sadist, as malice as cold, bloody steel after a murder with no feeling of regret, glowing red with anger and engulfed in doom, an eternal gloom spreads through its halls in comparison to a disease, an ever-growing shadow creeps and spreads its bat-like wings, eclipsing the shifting sands, giving the terrors and monstrosities of this land the shadows they so crave.

Many centuries, long ago, the Skahljah overthrew the Baldushan dynasty, torturing and enslaving them, holding public executions by placing the Baldushan within Skahljhen coliseums where they would be ripped apart by the migs and prowls, but no fate was worse, than to die at the hands of the Skahljhen champion, Ja`kal, who has never been defeated in combat by any beast or being, for it was Ja`kal who slayed Shemoga by slicing her throat while she bathed in a sacred pool, The Spring of Crying Ashes. Her blood filled the waters, and turned them black and murky, now a boiling tar pit that surrounds the base of where Kaskopos has been built, for his name echoes far across the desert, upon each infected, crusty lip of every Skahljah warlord and being. His chant is empty, hollow, and emotionless, except for the emotion of fear and terror, as black as his conscious:

"Ja`kal, Ja`kal"
The blood of Aura stains your blade...
"Ja`kal, Ja`kal"
Your flesh is hardened by the pain you create...
"Ja`kal, Ja`kal"
Your right hand genocide, your left hand extermination...
"Ja`kal, Ja`kal"
Your voice a blood-thirsty roar, all cower before your annihilation!

To destroy Shemoga, Kandarius granted to him, The Bride of Dregor, a living, breathing sword that absorbs the flesh and blood of all it strikes. The weapon is impenetrable and can never be destroyed by any force, for the weapon is the daughter of one of the Hexagus Lords. Before the strike commences, The Bride speaks an ancient curse in the tongue of Dregor, the black plague linguistics of her father.

Beneath the bun of his hair, Ja`kal keeps hidden a dagger with poison that seeps from the oils in his hair follicles. When the legions ride out, they ride from behind him, galloping on their steeds, the fire-breathing prowls, and when the roars and the drums are heard from a distance, no one is safe, no man, woman, or child will survive their war path. *"ALL WILL DIE AND PERISH IN THEIR OWN BLOOD!"* As is the code of Ja`kal, as is the way of the Skahljah.

Just on the other side of the drowning oasis, a pool of deadly black poison, that feeds the cold, black roots of The

Shade, a forest that has existed long before the Auroras, riddled with secrets and a dark past that possesses the brutal murders, goring, and butchering of millions and millions of creatures and inhabitants of Aura, since the reign and tyranny of the Hexagus.

Hernan and Roaur stand face to face with opaque trunks of twisted and gnarled tree roots, carved with the deep gashes and claw marks of creatures that lips dare not speak of, but to scream from their very sight, bestial shapes we dare not witness and gaze upon, but to run for our lives, for their very existence is threatened by what haunts and dwells within these trees, or would the correct term be trunks of twisted flesh that rises up from the blackness of Aura's prehistoric crust. Hernan and Roaur have overcome many obstacles and faced many beasts and villains to reach this point, faced atrocities that others would surely die just watching.

'Roaur, which direction did we take, I don't remember this forest being here.'

Roaur, just as confused as Hernan, replies in a grim tone. 'I swore by the direction of the winds, and the smell of the air, that we were heading due southeast. I'm not sure what this place is, but it seems like these trees, or whatever you call them, looks as though they've been here for some time. The air...it's stale and sour. I don't like this, I don't like this at all.'

'Neither do I. Can you see anything? I don't even see any light piercing the trees, only a hollow night within.' Hernan says.

'There's...I don't know how to describe it. There's weird things moving, but I don't know what, or how to explain what I see.' Roaur replies.

Through the trees, the screams and cries of those trapped within rang out, not just of men and women, but of beasts and other creatures, screams of agonizing pain, and agony for these trees torture, bringing out of us our most dreadful and deepest inner fears and nightmares.

'No matter what's in there, we will enter and we will

face it head on!' Hernan begins to shout at the top of his voice at the forest. 'Do you hear me, we will pass and you accursed beings of these woods will not stop us!'

There was only the faint moan and creaking of the trees rustling in the slicing winds that blew an icy wind from the northwest, then, after a moment, a voice shrieks forth, turning their blood cold. *"HE WILL!"*

'I for one will not be afraid of this menace!' And with a sudden burst forth of energy, Hernan tramples through the jagged brush and twigs, and enters the shadows of the trees. Roaur follows after him, each of them using their weapons to clear their path.

From the ground emits a glowing, pungent smelling green steam, upon each side of the trees, heavy thick vines are tied tightly around the trunks, heavy weeds covered with thorns and poison stingers, and beneath the tendrils and steam, is a thick, crunching sounding soil, not the sound of rock or dirt, but the sound of crunching bone upon their steel boots, for the skulls and bones of the ancient dead, millions from countless ages of the forests existence is littered beneath their feet. As their eyes begin to adjust to the darkness and the green glow, they can see that the tendrils and vines wrapped around the trees, hold the carcasses of those who have died in recent months, for they moan and scream in pain, begging for their passers to kill them, to put them out of their misery. Hernan walks through a heavily thorn-laden bush to get a closer look at one of them, an old-looking woman; the life seems to have been sucked away from her, her face is pale-white with the green glow of the light highlighting her sunken cheeks and forehead. She screams at his approach.

'No...please stay away! I know you creatures...you can't fool me anymore, for I have been suffering here for ten years, for ten years you've poisoned me, kept me alive just enough to torture me, come to visit me in your Baldushan forms, in hopes of a rescue, but no one leaves this place, never...I never will, I wish my death would come, why can you not just kill me! I want to die!' The woman became more and more hysterical the closer he moved towards her.

'How terrible, they kept her here for ten years! Those Skahljah know no mercy, no bounds to how far they will torture!' Roaur growled.

'What creatures do you speak of?' Hernan asked the woman in the kindest voice he could, hoping to solve what has been terrorizing these people.

Slimy vomit spews from her mouth that she chokes up from her throat. Her eyes shift up at her curious on-looker. Hernan looks at them, they were pallid with cataracts, for the first time in her miserable ten years, she began to feel strange and a smile came over her. 'Then...you are not one of those things, for you look different, not the usual disguise they take on?'

'No, my name is Hernan, I am a Civilian, and this is Roaur, a Gormon from Fausengard. Who are you?' Hernan asks calmly.

'I...I don't really remember, for I have hung upon this tree for the last ten years, these jagged roots feed me poison and keep me alive, to suffer...I once, I remember...I came from the desert, I was with a caravan of my people. We were heading to Othetica, I was going to trade goods with the Civilians there for my husband's wares, for he is, or was a merchant for the rebellion outposts. We we're captured by a Skahljah raiding party and the beast-man, the biggest and most ferocious among them, threw us into these woods, I'll never forget the eyes of that man, red as a burning fire, built like a monster, armored head to foot like their tanks they have...!' Her head fell forward in a slump, Hernan climbed the vicious roots that trembled beneath his feet, imposing that they did not like him climbing on top of them. He held her head up in his broad hands.

'This forest, what is it, do you know?'

Her face becomes terrorized by his question. 'After only a few hours, we became separated, the vines shifted around, and the trees moved about like the pieces of a chess game, and we were the pawns, the first move, the ones who were getting jumped! These beasts seemed as though they camouflaged themselves into the woods, their skin was like the bark of this tree, they were smaller than us, quick and agile, they move about the trees like insects. They take the shape of whatever they want, whoever they want!'

'That is what haunts this wood?'

'These trees have a will, but they don't have a will of their own, something controls them, a power more terrifying than these beasts, more deadly than the warlords of the desert...his eyes are always watching, he sees and hears all!'

'Who, who controls these woods?!' Hernan asks in desperation.

She looks passed Hernan and Roaur's shoulders, and speaks in a whisper. 'He's standing right behind you...' The vine closes about her waist and crushes her to death, the blood flowing over the scales of the vines. Fearing what the woman had said, they whirl around, weapons drawn and in battle stance, only to find nothing, for only trees and darkness stood in front of them.

'Where is he Hernan, I don't see anything!' Roaur says.

'I don't know, but let's keep our eyes open.' Hernan replies.

They trudge along, getting caught up in traps made by the thorns and brush, then slicing them away with their weapons. Along the way were the wrapped up bodies and carcasses of dead creatures littered about the ground with vines wrapped around them, some even still alive and squirming to try and escape.

'It unsettles me, that every time I step on a twig, or cut a root, I hear something screaming!' Roaur says with a shudder.

'It's as the woman said, this place is breathing and something is here, we have to find out what this thing is and destroy it if we are getting out of here alive, before it tries to destroy us.' Hernan replies.

They are trapped wondering, for days it seems, slaying man-eating flora, escaping from poisonous serpents and slaying the blood-thirsty fish creatures that keep upon the murky waters to drag them under, as they traverse vast lakes with an ancient raft fastened from the decayed wood. At the opposite end of the far lake, as they fight off one of the monstrous fish, its gills and pins squirting poison, and its fangs shooting acid that hisses as it burns through their raft, its jaws sink deeper and deeper into the rotting wood. They leap away just as the beast pulls it down, but when they hit the shore, a gigantic, even more threatening loch serpent, with hundreds of heads and a massive finned tail in the shape of a large unbridled fan with spikes, engulfs the fish and their raft with one gulp, then submerges down into the dark depths.

On the other side of this lake, the woods stretch further onward, till they come to an area where the trees over head grow even thicker, a night with no stars and no moon, and the green steam rises higher, until the smoky walls of this jade mist covers everything, and a barricade of vines surrounds them from the right and left. Further on, they approach a twisted face upon a corroded stone rock. From the mouth drips a thick sludge, and upon closer look, runs the blood of someone or something, a voice screeches out from the mouth and the blood gurgles and spits upon them, a strangled, high pitched roar cries out piercing the roots and cracking rocks and shatters stone.

'Beware, for you enter this realm, this realm... for my realm, you will never leave, never see the sun again!'

The ground beneath their feet begins to writhe and move, red eyes look out through the darkness, around them twisted shapes begin to creep forth from their shadows, and then the hordes attack, they are surrounded by the creatures of the woods, legions and legions of Maneks, the shape-shifters, the deceivers.

'Get them...my fiends, my destroyers...tear them limb from limb! Feast on their flesh, gnaw at their bones! Leave

nothing left!'

Hacking and slashing, bodies piles upon bodies, corpse upon corpse, green and black blood covers their armor as they drive back the hordes of creatures that seek to bleed them of their hearts and eyes. The Maneks claw, hack, and slash at their armor, scraping but not hindering.

'I don't know how much longer we can survive this onslaught!' Roaur cries out, holding back the seemingly endless hordes.

One of the creatures leaps down from above and knocks Hernan to the ground, but Hernan kicks it away and smashes the head with a hard kick to the skull.

'That thing forgot to tell his fiends, that their not breaking this armor!' Hernan fights with even more force than he has ever done before. The slop of their blood runs down his face, Roaur begins to stomp upon the creatures, but they climb all over him like a statue.

'I can't keep them off me! What will get rid of them!' Roaur yells.

All of a sudden they stop their attack, and the voice calls to them once more. *'Show them, show them your trick that I have taught you...SHOW THEM, KILL THEM, show them why you are the deceivers!'*

Hernan and Roaur could not believe their eyes, for the beasts before them, began to change, morph, shift into...Civilians, Gormon, Baldushan, warriors of their past slayings, were taking form through their own wooden flesh, which was now the skin of Hernan and Roaur's fellow kin, these beings were ancient, their armor and weapons were of a style and make that had not existed for hundreds of years, centuries, even millenniums. It seems as though Hernan and Roaur were surrounded by the dead, ghosts of the past come back to haunt them.

'Just perfect, an army of now armed, and heavily protected warriors against two! How are we going to get through this?!' Roaur says.

'I wouldn't worry about a thing.' Hernan replies.

'What do you mean?' Roaur asks.

One of the creatures lunges for an attack, and Hernan cuts straight through the metal as though it weren't even there.

'You see, their armor is only an illusion, they can take the shape, but they cannot copy the properties and materials, so just do as you've been doing...smash these bastards with that hammer!' Hernan replies, and the fight goes on. Roaur lashes out and the pulp of the Maneks grows up to their knees, crushed and bludgeoned by the hammer of Roaur.

'Come and kiss the pretty hammer you filthy beasts! AH!'

The ground begins to crack, and breaks beneath them into a dank and deep chasm. Hernan and Roaur try to hang on to the roots of the trees, but the roots shake the two off, and they fall below, the Maneks fall with them, squashing upon impact of the rocky bottom. Hernan hits a soft patch of the piled bodies and roles to the bottom, while Roaur painfully bounces from the dirt walls, rolls from a thick root, and hits the ground harder. The two of them gripe and curse, getting to their feet with pain in their sides, backs, arms, all over their body. They survey their area.

'Well, at least these things are dead.' Roaur says.

'I wouldn't say all of them...'

Roaur turns to see Hernan gazing up, and Roaur can see at the top of the cliffs, the remainder of the Maneks, now returned to their bestial form, surround and watch, standing still not making an advance to attack.

'I wonder what their waiting for?' Hernan whispers.

'Come down and fight! What are you waiting for!' Roaur yells up at them.

'You will not leave here alive, for it is forbidden, it is my way, my will, the will of Lypriis bids you stay, bask in the poison and nausea of eternal torture and pain! Flee the shining sun, the eye of Lota, and bask in my Shade!'

At that moment, a spot of wall shifts ahead of them, and

the wall begins to crumble, leaving only a large hole. Something within twists its way through, screaming, hollering, the madness within its cry rings out through the trees. Thick claws or fingers grip at the tunnel, dragging itself along to the opened hole. It's massive arms reach out and it pulls itself out, the Lypriis is nearing, it's almost here.

'I...AM...HERE...AHHHHHHHH!'

The moment the thing crawls out, its dark green body, shaped like a root attached to a green man begins to bloat, and the flora-looking maw upon its head begins to grow outwards, and the teeth erupt with acids and juices melting away its floral look, and changing into a ravaged monstrous shape. Several limbs, including arms with poisonous hairs and claws, and long nailed feet, stretch out and stand upon the ground of the pit. The long, massive tendrils covered in ivy erupt from the ground, and grip several of the Maneks from above, and it proceeds to devour them, gaining energy and power from their masticated juices. From the things back, two massive hands with three fingers upon each, and clawed, erupt forth and slam to the ground.

'Hey Roaur, how do you kill a weed?'

'By tearing out the root, HA!'

They charge forward, avoiding the massive hands that attempt to smash and pound them. They cut and decapitate the many roots and tentacles that lash out at them, for Hernan has much experience with handling an obstacle, such as tentacles. The teeth of the creature snaps and snarls, following their every move, wrapping them into its grasp and tossing them about, but they get back up, and charge again.

'Roaur, try to distract it, I'll go behind and try to cut that root.'

'Over here, you ugly spawn of a Dregor!' The creature roars and hisses, chasing after Roaur who hammers away at the tentacles, but he does not see the hand looming silently behind him. Roaur feels the tight grasp and struggles to break free. The hand hoists him into the air and slowly drags him towards the widened mouth, salivating and the teeth within the throat shift about, making ready to devour the massive Gormon.

Hernan hears Roaur's cries for help, so he dashes away from his target and heads for the Lypriis's back, he grips the hulking spines and hairs and climbs towards the top of the mouth, he swings the blade left to right, blinding the many eyes of the creature. The bulbous, bloated eyeballs erupt with green toxins and the Lypriis screams in agony, its body writhes and shakes the entire chasm. Roaur is tossed to the ground unconscious, buried in the slime of the Maneks.

Hernan wastes no more time, he rushes down the creatures back, but, not being careful, he is stabbed by one of the spiny barbs upon the Lypriis. He pulls the spine out, and continues down the back, until he reaches the main root, where the Lypriis is attached, and with a mighty stroke of the blade, he slices through, but only goes half-way. He raises his blade, and strikes again, and again, and hacks and hacks until, the separation is complete. The creature crawls about upon the ground, writhing and turning about, like a fish dying for air.

A dripping puss spews from Hernan's arm. He tries to close his hand around it, but the liquid is hot to touch, and burns the skin around the wound. He can feel the toxin coursing through his veins, and begins to feel dizzy. He notices Roaur is still unconscious. His blood begins to boil and raise his temperature, his flesh fevers and sweats, as though the poison is burning through his entire body. Something falls upon his shoulder, it is a strange piece of something, something from the trees. The forest and the Maneks begin to crumble around him, decaying into ashes and blowing away in the winds. Hernan looks around him, the forest, the twisted trees, gone, and all he can see is the Isa Desert as far as the eye can see, and off to the left a ways away, is the dark oasis that once fed the black roots, now a clear pool. Only he and Roaur remain as proof of what just happened.

Nightmares fill Hernan's mind, and all goes black, but

he does not see the silhouettes of those who have discovered him, standing in the sun that now shines upon this part of the desert, for Lota's realm can now see the sands once again.

Within Hernan's nightmare:

'A voice beckons me, I...I must obey...No! I will not! There is a mirror, a mirror at the top a twisted stair, wreathed in fire and thorns, carved from black obsidian, a mirror surrounded in shadow and darkness, but the mirror itself shines as the ocean upon the sunset. There is a figure, a figure within clouds of smoke and swirling colored gases that surrounds him...his hands reach out...!'

PART XII:

The Council of Isa

Hernan awakens in a cold sweat that pours from his body, his armor has been removed, leaving him only a pair of slacks. He is in a small room, with walls made of sandstone and clay, the windows are primitive, carved from the stone it was built from. To his right, sitting next to his bed, is a lovely woman, her skin tanned from the sun, her hair is black with bleached highlights and is braided in an odd fashion, not like the women of Othetica, nor the warrior women of Fausengard, but the braid is raised up in the back, and hangs off to the side over her shoulder. She wears a gown the color of the sands and dark leggings. She wears large emeralds upon the lobes of her ears and an emerald ring upon her right hand, but it was her eyes that enticed Hernan, staring brightly upon him like two blue stars. She spoke in a soft voice.

'You see bad visions, for your sleep has been restless. But don't worry, the poison has been cleansed from your body.'

Hernan looks upon the woman, for she is of the Baldushan, those who once ruled over Isa. He is startled at first by her presence, but soon he cannot help but feel flattered by the sight of her, for he has not been in the presence of a woman who beheld such beauty to him.

'Where is this place, what has happened?' He mumbles.

'Safe, is where you are, as to what happened, well I'm not sure what happened to you, but we've found you and your companion. He was unconscious, and you were suffering from one of the deadliest poisons I have ever seen. You screamed for days, speaking in your sleep.'

'Those trees...the forest...' His words are slurred from weariness.

'I don't know what happened, the forest had vanished from our sight, and there we found you and your large friend laying in the sands half buried, so we placed you upon our Djohmbo and brought you here.'

Hernan begins to cough severely.

'Take this remedy, it will help soothe your ailing and recover your strength, for you must have the strongest will I have ever seen...you should be dead.' She hands Hernan a clay goblet filled with a sweet smelling liquid, the aroma fills the room. He sips it slowly, for it is hot upon his dry lips.

'Your skin has been burned from the sun, I will fix you a poultice that will treat the scarring and soothe the burn and redness, but for now, lay back down and rest.'

'I, I have so many more questions, I don't know where to start.' He replies.

'Your questions will soon be answered as best they can, but not now. Lay back and relax, I will return to check on you.' Says the woman, then she leaves the room.

But Hernan could not rest, nor sleep anymore, he had to force himself to move, to leave his bed and walk. His legs tremble as he scuffs across the floor, he finds the sleeveless top that goes with the slacks and places it over his body, but is a bit tight upon his muscular figure. He rubs his heavily stubbled face, within a few weeks, a heavy beard will be upon him. Upon the far side of the wall, he walks passed a mirror. It has been some time since he has seen his reflection. He gazes into the eyes of a man, an old and worn man, not decrepit, nor aged, just tired. Someone who has seen many winters go by. The dark circles under his eyes are tired from this quest, worn down by the cruelty of fate, and the touch of time, a poison more deadly than that which had flowed within his blood, but this poison cannot be cured, a disease that gets worse with age and only quickens its pace. His dirty blond hair shows spots of gray growing in, and the skin seems less taught around his face and limbs, muscular yes, but not a young man's strength, only an experienced fellow who has been chiseled by the hammer and the anvil, strength granted to him by the steel that guards his body, and reflects from too many battles to count...with foes who should have killed him, yet he has prevailed.

Young men gain knowledge and wisdom, strength, valor and honor from adventure, fame for their deeds, their name becomes legend, and their memory, eternal. But for Hernan...what does this tired man nearing the twilight of his life have to leave behind, but a few weapons and pieces of iron? This quest wears upon him, drives him closer and closer to his end it seems. Again he feels as though time is winding him downward, into a spiral like a twister, driving him deeper and deeper. Then, he hears a voice within himself, something speaks to him...his voice, his conscious, the true reasoning of all living things. He listens, to what the voice has to say.

'You cannot give up now. You ask yourself what you have to leave behind, but you already know that, you already know the answer...you have the thousands of men and women you've protected with your armor, and allowed them to strike back with your weapons. You've brought home loved ones to their families, who would have never seen them again. Your craft saved them. Not all survive war and battle, for that is their choice to make, but you give them a chance, protected their skin from complete annihilation, for you allow them to fight another day, giving them that chance to breath once more, you are doing your part, the rest is their own.'

'But now, you have a greater responsibility at hand, for nothing ever stays the same. Sometimes fate must intervene to take us down another road, sometimes a road we don't want to go down, we want to find a way back, find a shortcut, find an escape, but there never is one, so...it's up to you, to persevere, and face the journey you never meant to take. Besides, why are you looking at what's behind, stick to the task ahead of you, for look how far you've come, how much stronger, braver, more determined you are to face danger and challenge head on! No matter if they are a brash, young lad, or an old fellow like yourself, life is a special journey for us all, and we never know

what will come our way, and we never can tell what waits for us at the end of that road...'

Hernan can feel the hot desert wind coming into his room from the far door, crafted in similar fashion to the windows, open and without a door. He can hear a discussion taking place on the outside, for the night is clear, and the stars shine brightly in the midnight sky, a perfect scenario for fire and discussion. Hernan walks out holding his arm in the spot where he pulled the spine away, it was bandaged by the Baldushan woman, and by rubbing it, feels the thread that was sewn into his flesh to seal the gaping hole which bled profusely.

Sitting around a large fire at the middle of a fair-sized encampment, is the woman, and there is Roaur, whose head was bandaged and eye covered by a thick patch, and a strange looking gray man with dark skin, a pale turban with a decorative point at the top, and robe which seemed twice the size of his small and fragile frame. His face is wrinkled up like a rung out cloth, his bottom lip rolled out with a few piercings, and golden chains that hung down around his neck, and the piercings were also upon his ears in a few different places, and the cartilage in the middle of his nose had a golden loop, his beard was combed down and wrapped around his waist, even longer than Roaur's. The old man's eyes were a pale blue like the woman, so they must be related.

The woman and Roaur turn and look at Hernan in awe, though the woman scowls at him and how he should have remained in bed as she told him to, but he refuses. Roaur leaps up and gives him a mighty Gormon hug, lifting him into the air. 'I'm so glad to see your alive my friend! If you didn't make it, then I didn't know what I would do, but your alive and I'm happy, there may yet be some hope after all this! I knew we didn't come this far just to have something like this stop us! HA HA! Tough for a Civilian, I'll give you that!'

Hernan, though happy to see his friend, winces in pain

by the burns upon his skin.

'Indeed he is not like the usual, aristocratic individuals that used to come this way. I knew there was something different about you when we found you laying out there in the middle of this desert.' The old man said, his voice raspy with age and dust.

'As my daughter Asla may have already told you, no one should have survived what happened to you, but you did, and your recovery has been incredibly fast, but my daughter is an amazing healer like her mother was. It was her knowledge of medicines and herbs that has helped in a big way. Meanwhile, your Gormon friend here has told me quite a tale while you were unconscious, and I must say I am amazed to see that both of you are standing in front of me.' The old man stands up, leaning upon his walking cane, and stands gazing upon Hernan.

'So, I stand in the presence of the Forgemaster himself! For I have read the scriptures, and have studied the signs, and once I found out who you are, and solved your puzzle, you standing before me, does not surprise me in the least, for you were meant to come this way, you were meant to cross this colossus of Isa. I feel that we were destined to meet, by chance or by fate, by luck or coincidence, call it what you will...but I know what is upon us, I know what you seek, and if I can help you, I will, for you do not fight this battle alone, you have allies in even the most unlikely places, and we are here to serve you.'

And with these words, from out of the shadows of the surrounding buildings, armies of Baldushan warriors step forth, stand at attention in ranks, and salute the Forgemaster. One of them steps forward, introducing himself as the captain of the soldiers. 'Our numbers are few,' He unsheathes his blade, 'but we are brave and proud, and are willing to fight to our last, if only to see Aura free again from this insidious enemy we face.'

He holds the sword up high, and his warriors join him.

'If only to see our people, and all the races of this good land free again, free from the fear that *"Forever Night"* brings, and we may once again claim our realm! These foul Skahljah were only the beginning, but it shall be the end, their end.' (Forever Night is the Baldushan words for Grey Age).

That very night, council is taken in one of the larger buildings were the old man and his daughter stay. While the necessary accommodations are being made, Hernan gets ready in his room, putting on his armor. While he straps one of the pauldrons to his shoulder, he hears footsteps across the floor. Her turns to see Asla standing there, looking at him curiously.

'I'm sorry, I didn't mean to startle you. I only wanted to check on you, take a look at your wound and see how you were feeling.'

Hernan flexes his arm up and down and smiles. 'It's feeling much better, still a little bruised, but I'll live.'

She sits down next to him and runs her fingers around the wound, taking off the bandage and examining it. 'It's coming along, as you said, you'll live.' She tosses the bandage away. 'I don't think you'll need to wear this anymore.'

'You are skilled at medicine, where did you learn your craft? Your father said that your mother was a skilled healer as well.' Hernan asks.

Her face goes from a smile to a slight frown, but she is grateful to hear the question and the interest he takes in what she does. 'My mother showed me, she was a healer for our people during these years being exiled away, constantly hunted down and killed by Ja`kal. She mended them and saved many lives. She saw that I had the talent for herbs and medicines, so she taught me what she knew, and I have been forever grateful for it, because it is all I have left of her.'

'What happened to her?' Hernan asks.

'She and some others were going to cross the borders into Othetica, to sale some of my father's wares, for he is a collector of rare and precious items, the only things we have left of our old culture, but our supplies were running thin, so we were going to use some of these items, to gain profit and supplies to feed our people. It's been ten years since I last saw my mother, I was still but a youth when she left. She went as a healer in case if anything happened along the way, and for morale support, but none ever returned. Our men were sent out to search, but no one could be found, nor was there any trace of their caravan.'

Immediately the connection was made in Hernan's mind, the woman in the forest, the one he spoke to, the one who, in all her torture, who smiled in his presence, that woman who died such a painful death, was Asla's mother, she had to be. Though he feels that she deserves to know what happened to her, he did not have the heart to tell of her mother's final moments, for it would shatter her. Asla was trying to read the look upon Hernan's face, trying to read his mind.

'It's alright; you don't have to say anything. I know she's dead; you don't have to try and make me feel better. I've moved on, though I loved her, and I will never stop missing her. I still have my memories and I still see her face. My father says I looked so much like her.'

'If only I did have the words to say, but I'm afraid I don't.' Hernan replies. 'For I've seen so much horror, some days, it just feels like, there isn't any more words to say.'

She smiles at him and holds his hand. 'I understand, you have your own plights to deal with, you don't need to bear my sorrows as well.' She says to him.

'Whether I like it or not, I feel I already bear not only the world, but the fates, the lives, and the destiny's of everyone. All eyes are on me now.'

'Like my father said, you're not in this alone. He is here, our people are here, your Gormon friend stands with you, and...I am here to, if you need anything.'

She caresses his face with her soft hands, and they share a kiss together. Her lips are like silk and the air about her is sweet to smell, and her emotions sincere.

'At least there is one who can make a difference on our

side.' She stands up and gazes upon him with pride. 'I will see you later, for I assume my father will be expecting you shortly.'

'You will not be at the council?' Hernan asks, buckling the last strap.

'I'm going to bed early, for I feel sleep is almost upon me.'

'Then I wish you a good night then.'

She turns to walk away, but looks back once more. 'I hope your dreams turn out better tonight, than the ones you've been having.' And with that, she leaves the room.

Hernan places the shield around his back, sheaths his blade, but wonders where his hammer has gone off to. He heads for the old man's council to decide what will be the next phase of action. Outside, Roaur meets up with him. 'I see someone's been getting a little friendly.' Roaur teases.

'Knock it off Roaur, let's just get to the meeting.' He looks again at his eye patch. 'What happened to your eye anyway?'

'The blow that damn plant gave me, knocked my eye clear out! Now I'm half blind and have to wear this thing on me!' Roaur replies with a mad rage, clenching his knuckles till the color in them runs white.

'How are you going to fight?' Hernan asks with concern.

'One eye isn't going to stop me! I still have my other eye, and four of my senses to use! I can smell them a mile away, I can hear them creeping up from behind, I can taste their foul air, and I can clench my hammer and pound till no skull or face remains, so there's nothing to worry about!' Roaur cried out, with great pride of himself. 'It takes more than eyes to be a great warrior.'

'Indeed it does, and I wouldn't want any other by my side, even if they had a hundred eyes and could see backwards.' He pats Roaur on the arm and they head over to the council.

'I'll tell you the worst part about it Hernan.'

'What's that?'

He scratches at his eye. 'It itches!'

They walk across the way, and down the dirt road for a stretch till they come to a large stone-layered building, much like the ancient ziggurats of the old Baldushan dynasty, which very few still stand after the Skahljah invaded these lands centuries ago. At the base of the structure are several guards at their posts bearing spears and light copper armor worn by the desert warriors and their faces draped in the ceremonial desert garb, each bearing a jewel at the crest. They bow to the Civilian and the Gormon as they walk passed. Hernan and Roaur climb the steps of sand stone, which there seem to be about a hundred or so drawn out before them. At the pinnacle they look out at the area around them. The deserts run all the way south to the mountain borders of the sea, all the way west, just touching the base of Gammafir, and north to the southern tip of Othetica. Off further south, a dust storm brews and kicks about wildly. 'That storm will be here in about an hour or so.' Roaur says.

'I wish this was the only storm we had to worry about.' Hernan replies.

One of the officers rounds the corner where they stand. 'They are just about ready to start, we're just waiting for the representatives from the Azari to arrive.' Hernan and Roaur look at one another confused. 'Who are the Azari?' Hernan asks. 'I've learned of just about every race, every creature that has walked Aura for the last thousands of years, but I have never heard of the Azari, are they a group or band of Baldushan, another tribe?' Roaur asks. The officer looks off beyond his shoulders and points, 'Here they are now.'

Hernan and Roaur turn, and there, off to the south, and closing in fast, were a small flock of Azari, Azimoth who dwell hidden away far to the south in the mountains, beyond the sight of any other beings in Aura, which is why little to none have ever heard or seen an Azimoth before. They hover above the structure in a circular pattern, Hernan and Roaur look at them closely, for they seem to be very similar to the insect in which they are named for, their eyes are large and bulbous, and their faces furry and upon their brow stand two large antennas, except for the one at the lead, he misses the second one, cut away by some foe. Their bodies are built like a Civilian's, clad in loose attire of lavish robes and loose fitted slacks, some wear blue boots, some brown, others a deep tangerine color. They have multiple arms and clawed hands, each with a weapon upon their sash-style belts, weapons similar in craft to the Baldushan. The leader wields a massive staff, tipped with a smooth, curved spear head, which seems to almost give off sparks of thunder and lightning. He holds up the spear, and they proceed to land amongst the others that watch on from below. The bearer of the spear walks forward and greets them, his language is an unusual clicking sound, but within his mind, Hernan can understand the words perfectly clear, as can Roaur.

'Greetings, I hope we are not late for the council, and we are honored to be called from our lands to assist you in these trying times, for we have much to share.' The Azimoth says.

'Come with me, the council waits.' The captain shows them into the grand hall where the others are seated at a vast, round table. The old man and several of the other Baldushan stand up to honor their presence. The old man sits off to the right of Hernan, and Roaur next to him, on the other side is a Baldushan councilman and at the head of the table is a kingly looking Baldushan draped in ornamental robes and piercings, with tattoos across his arms and hands, and large golden earrings hanging from his lobes. He remains standing as the others seat themselves.

'I am glad that many have showed, and I would like to welcome special guests in our presence. From the south, our allies and friends, the Azari.' They bow their heads and thank his introduction. 'From the far northern lands, representing the Gormon of Aura, from Fausengard, I greet you Roaur of Stonehaven.' Roaur stands and takes a bow, then sits down. Then he turns to Hernan.

'And from Othetica, a Civilian who I feel needs no introduction, for we are in the presence of the Forgemaster. I, am called the Desert Seer, I guide this band of Baldushan that remain, for we are few and scattered. Ja`kal has hunted down most of us, but we have been fortunate thus far, and it seems fate has turned in our favor, for your presence gives us hope for the coming days.'

Whispers spread around the table, speaking of Hernan and the legacy of the Forgemaster they have only read of in the ancient texts. But now here he sits before their eyes. However one councilman stands up from the far table, 'How do we know he really is the fabled Forgemaster that we all speak of?'

Roaur stands. 'I have traveled with this man for months now; we have faced many challenges, many foes, obstacles, death that should have claimed us! If my words do not impress or convince you, then Hernan, show him your hammer!'

Hernan stands in front of the councilman and raises the Hammer of Gonun for all of them to see. They gasp, and the council man sits back down. 'It cannot be! That…that's Gonun's Hammer, only a true…' Roaur cuts in and finishes his sentence. 'Only a true Forgemaster may wield it! So, do anymore doubts pry your mouth open or unleash your tongue?!' The councilman lowers his eyes. 'No…none. I will say no more.'

The Desert Seer holds up his arms. 'We brought this council together to do something of this coming darkness, not fight amongst ourselves…now, I have the gift of truth and foresight, I have already sensed the Forgemaster's presence when he was brought here. There is no doubting needed. He is the Forgemaster; now, I know why you are here, why you have come, for what you seek is not far…'

'An Asyndian, Falkon L`or, said that the blade would be found in Kaskopos. How far is it from here?' Hernan asks.

The Seer speaks. 'Kaskopos, the Shadowed Colossus, the black spires of the desert, is on the other side of the rim, passed the spikes and mounds, over fiery sands and inferno winds. The dunes hide those that would eat our very flesh, not with our entire armies could we cross the desert, and no army has ever breached the black walls.'

'There has to be some way, I must get the blade…'

The Azimoth leader stands to speak. *'By the might of Moth`og, we could fly a small force from above by silence, and infiltrate from one of the towers.'*

'The trickery of the lying hoft, as it is called, it just might work, my Seer!' Says the captain of the soldiers. The Seer is quiet for a moment, and then speaks. 'My visions are clouded, and grant me no opinions of success,' He grasps his head for a moment and closes his eyes, then after a short minute, he opens them again, 'but if the rest of the council agrees, we will put the plan into motion.' He says. The Azimoth leader speaks again. *'We must create a signal, when the Forgemaster is within, he must let us know when we can strike!'*

'I don't know what can be done, but I will find a way, Roaur and I will find a way across the desert, and breech the walls of Kaskopos... when inside, I will find the blade, and send off some sort of flame, smoke... you'll know.'

‘Do you know where to look for the blade, for Kandarius is clever, and will not have it sitting out on a night stand.’ The Seer looks curiously at Hernan’s thoughts. ‘I know what it is you see at night, you see the mirror, don’t you?’ The Seer asks.

‘There is a mirror, a dark mirror, surrounded by two flames upon either side, and wreathed in thorns and spikes…’

‘The Mirror of Dregor…’ The Seer whispers to himself, as he grips his head once more. ‘That concludes this council.' He grasps his head again, this time, more severely and winces at the pain, he feels something coming over him... 'I want to thank those who have come. We will begin tomorrow, to the Azimoth, my subjects will see to it you receive proper quarters, as to all the rest, I bid you a goodnight, and may the desert winds keep out of our dreams.’

'Thank you Seer of the desert, but we will head back to our lands and prepare, then we will base ourselves were none may see us attack from.' He turns to Hernan. *'We will await your signal Forgemaster, and we will be ready for battle!'* And the Azimoth bow, and bid them farewell, were they head outside to travel back south.

One of his subjects turns to him, 'Seer, are you alright? Is something the matter?'

'I'll be alright...I just have a headache, something...I feel something, I don't know how to explain it, but it's almost like something...someone is watching us.'

'Is there anything I can get you?' The subject asks.

'No...nothing...'

The Seer turns to Hernan. 'I wish to speak with the Forgemaster in private council, there is a matter for which only he may hear.'

The others leave the room, and only the Seer and Hernan remain. 'Hernan, you have been touched by the Dregor; they are able to read your thoughts, as you are able to read theirs. Eyes are always on you…' The Seer speaks as though he is rushing, out of breath, trying to get as much information out as he can, before...he feels as though something is about to happen.

'What does that mean, Kandarius spied on our entire council?!' Hernan asks.

'He...he can see into my...my thoughts, I feel him forcing his way...into... my head...' The Seer grips his cranium and begins to squeeze, he stands to his feet.

The Seer begins to convulse and his eyes go blind. 'He's here! He's here with us now! AHHH!'

The ground shakes, and the structure pulsates. Hernan can feel shaking at his feet. Something seems to be approaching, something big and feels like many. He gazes in shock as the Seer rises up, and a red light flares. For a brief moment, Hernan sees the malevolent form of Kandarius, with those glowing eyes looking down upon him. A rush of razor cold wind begins to swirl and whip about the vast room. Hernan rushes outside where Roaur is, the dust storm is upon them.

'Hernan?!' Roaur cries aloud.

'I feel it Roaur, something's coming this way...!'

PART XIII:

Arena of Kaskopos

And everyone else feels the quake as well, for the refugees of the Baldushan, the soldiers, and the old man and Asla all come from their homes and shacks to see what is going on. In the distance, Roaur can see the sands shifting, charging towards them with swift speed and fury, a tremor approaches.

'Hernan, something big approaches...and that's not all, there's something else, a large army following close behind!' Roaur cries, seeing with his mighty eye.

Hernan turns to the old man. 'You need to get everyone away from here!'

A sentry yells from a tower above. 'Too late, there already here!'

The burrowing stops, and erupting from the sand is a gigantic, towering worm, with many coal black eyes and spines upon its side. Within its circular jaws it holds a large mass of Baldushan, and swallows them in a single gulp. The Baldushan soldiers rally together and throw spears and shoot arrows at the beast, but before they realize what hits them, the army Roaur spotted, comes barreling through them, slashing and hacking, their fire prowls ripping apart soldiers and every last one of the Djohmbos. Hernan and Roaur go into their fighting stance and do away with a few of the Skahljah warriors and their vicious beasts, Hernan decapitates one with his shield, and Roaur takes out two prowls with one swipe of his hammer. But the armies of the Skahljah and the hulking sand worm overcome and surround them, even taking the old man and Asla prisoner, holding daggers to their necks. The sand beast snatches up a few more unsuspecting victims and all settles down for the moment.

Hernan and Roaur are ordered to drop their weapons, for they will not risk the lives of anymore Baldushan, and they comply with the threat.

From out of the darkness, a larger, more deadly looking prowl walks forth, the hair is fire red and spikes curl back behind the things long ears, and upon this beast, Hernan gazes upon the terror of Ja`kal, the Annihilator, the hand of Genocide, basking in everyone's fear of him. His beast stops only a few feet in front of Hernan and Roaur and the warlord looks down upon them and laughs to himself.

'Most are wise to bow in my presence, for I demand a little courtesy and respect before I deal out pain and death!'

'We will not bow to a monster like you!' Roaur growls.

Ja`kal snickers and leaps from the prowl he rides, walks over to Roaur, who stands eye to eye with the gigantic Gormon. Ja`kal holds up his shaggy, clawed hand in front of Roaur and clenches a fist.

'I said bow, Gormon!' And with a hard swing, crushes Roaur's stomach into a pulp and the Gormon goes down to his knees with a long moan. 'That's better.' Ja`kal laughs. He walks over to Hernan and looks upon the Forgemaster.

'Ah, so you must be the Forgemaster that pissed off Kandarius. That was not a wise thing to do, not wise at all.'

'Ha! So your another lackey of Kandarius are you, I've already disposed of one of you. I know your reputation, you can torture me all you want, if Kandarius and his dark masters can't make me reforge Azalir, what could you possibly do?' Hernan says with a grin, then acknowledges Roaur, not looking away from Ja`kal. 'How are you Roaur?'

'Coughing up a little blood, but I'll be fine.'

Ja`kal laughs. 'Oh, now I hoped you would ask me that, because Kandarius doesn't need you anymore, so I get to do with you as I please!'

'He...he what?!'

'Just as I said, through his usual devious means, he's found something else to occupy his mind, another scheme of his! So when he sent word that you'd be heading this way, I was overjoyed, because now we have a celebrity to star in the coliseum of Kaskopos! Oh, don't worry, you will be dealt with, but I have to entertain the people and myself!' His laugh is like a razor that cuts the wind.

'How would Kandarius know where to find me? First by the Seer, and now you?!' Hernan inquires.

'He has eyes everywhere, you can't escape the shadow of his gaze!' Ja`kal replies.

Looking over Ja`kal's shoulder, he sees the same little beast, Aumon standing upon the prowl, smiling sinisterly at them, for this little beast had followed them after their escape from Othetica.

'So, I see Kandarius lent you his pet!'

'An ugly little thing, but extremely useful, I see why Kandarius keeps him around. Now, if you'll shut up, I have some new pets of my own that we've just caught for the arena, and I want to let them play!' He shouts to the rest of his Skahljhen troops. 'Round everyone up and chain them! We're going to have quite a show tonight!' Out of the corner of his ear, he hears Asla struggling to get free, for her father was beginning to fall over to the ground.

'Please, let me be with him, let me go! I need to be with my father!' She cries out.

With his sinister grin across his face, he marches over to see what the commotion was. He gazes upon the beauty of the woman and thinks she'll make a fine addition to his torture room, and will look even more stunning locked in shackles within his dungeon. 'You, woman! What are you cackling about?!' He looks at the old man, 'What? this old fool?!'

'You stay away! I only want to help my father, he's sick, can't you see?!'

Ja`kal looks down on the pitiful old man who barely grips his cane, and kneels upon one knee. 'What, not feeling well is he! I'll put him out of his misery!'

'NO!' She cries out, but it is too late.

Ja`kal is handed a large spiked club with a riveted iron handle, the spikes are stained with blood and rotten clumps of hair from previous use. With one downward lunge, he bashes the hold man's skull clean in two.

'YOU BASTARD, YOU MONSTER, YOU BEAST!!!' She tries to lunge at him, but Ja`kal knocks her backwards with a hard backhand. Hernan rushes over, but several Skahljah jump him, and wrestle him to the ground, binding his arms and legs.

'I don't know what you're so upset about, he's out of his misery, isn't he?! HA HA HA!' The bloody laugh of Ja`kal roars through the desert and the fear upon the eyes of every Baldushan grows thick like a black cloud, for there is no telling what fate this monster has in store for them, except for the nightmarish rumors that are carried upon the harsh desert winds, and spoken from dried-lip, water-parched denizens that suffer under his reign.

'Chain that woman in the dungeons, I will deal with her later! What are you standing around for, let's move these scum bags out, move, move!' Ja`kal orders, and several Skahljah lash whips upon their prisoners backs as they push and shove the Baldushan through the harsh desert sands.

Ja`kal looks upon the sand worm. 'The worm looks hungry, give him some meat, but not too many, save some for the arena!' And two of the Baldushan are fed to the worm, who slurps them down its gaping throat.

After three miserable days marching through the desert, the sands go rough upon their feet, as the sands turn to rough soil. The black spires of the Kaskopos fortress comes into view. Its high walls hang a shadow over them, dampening all hope of ever seeing Lota's sun again, for the clouds are dark for miles around. Upon the dirt to their left and right, dotting out across the land are the remains of beasts and beings, tossed away by the predators that have hunted them. One brave, but foolish, man bolts away from the march out into the furthest sands, but the Baldushan look on in horror as he is grabbed from below by a sun mig that strikes with its stinger and drags the limp, but still living carcass of the man down into its foul lair.

'Anyone else want to go their own way!' Ja`kal roars with a sadistic smile, and they continue onward.

They finally come to the front gate of Kaskopos, which has a corroded, rusted bridge of black iron stretching half a mile across the boiling pits of black sludge. The smell is unbearable for any of them to handle. The front gate rises about fifty feet in height, constructed of the same rotten and decayed metal as the bridge, with massive protruding spikes sticking outwards, in case if anyone is foolish enough to charge the gate, though no one was, for no one would attempt to contend against Ja`kal and his armies. They looked over the bridge into the pit, and could see some of the massive bones upon the surface, the bones of Shemoga could still be seen, which horrified them. Ja`kal called back to one of his troops.

'Throw a couple of them in, I want to watch them squirm, heh heh!' And obeying Ja`kal's orders, two Baldushan were pushed from the bridge into the boiling pit where they screamed in agony as they sank beneath the sludge, and boil in the Aurora's blood. Many Baldushan moved away from the edges and huddled together and cried for all their fallen friends and loved ones. But Ja`kal still kept that smile of deviance and hatred for life upon his cracked and scabbed lips, snaring his sharp teeth.

With a howling creak of grinding metal and twisting chains, the gates open into a realm of terrors beyond their imagination. There is no society, for a social structure does not exist here, only violence and maiming, violation and destruction. Plague and sickness runs through the streets and roads covered with carcasses and bloated cadavers, the smell even worse than the sludge pits. There are no merchants, there is no economy, only survival of the most primitive sort. Buildings are constructed from jagged metal and broken bones torn from freshly murdered bodies. The Skahljah who fight and stab one another, stop in the presence of Ja`kal as the army marches by dragging their prisoners. The Skahljah savages taunt and grab at the new prey the soldiers drag through the streets. They chant Ja`kal's name and gurgle his song, the noise they make terrifies the Baldushan as they pass.

Their march seems eternal, but they come to a halt in front of the massive black walls of the arena at the black heart of Kaskopos, and they are dragged by their chains down into the vaults of the coliseum. They are packed away into tiny, cramped cells where claustrophobia will soon drive them mad, they realize they will not live long enough to see or feel madness.

Echoing down the long corridors of the dark tunnels, they can hear the wails and roars, and the cries of whatever terrors that await them. Up above they can hear the screaming, cheering, chanting, and stomping of the crowds that fill the arena, eager to watch every last one of them get slaughtered.

For the first time in days, since they were dragged away as prisoners from the Baldushan camps, to this cell, Hernan and Roaur spoke of their situation.

'Well, is this really it? Is this how we're to die, as sheep being led to the slaughter.' Roaur says in a depressed whisper.

'I don't know, I don't know what to do. I'm supposed to be hope for these people, but I can do nothing. What can a solitary man, chained and bound, about to be led to his death in front of thousands wanting to see his blood be spilled do?! What can I do Roaur?'

For the rest of the time, he sat in silence and in thought, and that silence would haunt him for the rest of his days, that silence would be filled with the dying screams of every last one of his comrades, for one by one, or in groups, they were lead up to the arena. He could hear their screams, hear their blood splatter over the walls, he could hear the beasts and warriors rip them and slice them to shreds, and hear the chants and applause of the barbaric fiends. None ever came back, the cells began to empty faster and faster like an assembly line, until only Hernan and Roaur remained. Two Skahljah opened the latch to their cell, and they were escorted to the battlements.

To the center they are led. The arena stretched miles around, the sea of crowds and stands rose high up upon all sides around them, stretching hundreds of feet up, the arena is trashed with old ruins, splintered metal and armor, the ground stained burgundy of dry blood, but the sickest sight of all, is the pile of bodies left behind, for the dead Baldushan were not removed, but left were they met their horrible end, some stabbed, some in pieces, some you would never recognize, they were so brutally maimed. Hernan could not believe it, of all the horrors he's witnessed, this sight could not be comprehended, could not be stomached. He looked around the stands, searching for Ja`kal, as was Roaur, trying to spot the tyrant, wanting to call him out, challenge and do to him, the pain he has caused to so many. The crowds taunted and mocked them, throwing deadly objects upon them, until Hernan stepped forward and screamed so all of Aura could hear him.

'JA`KAL! Come down here, for I challenge you!!!!!!!'

Through the chatter and the taunts he could hear the laugh of one come through, it was coming from behind. They turned to see Ja`kal standing behind them, accompanied by two Skahljah, dragging the limp body of Asla. They toss her to Hernan's feet.

'She refused to scream as I wanted her to, whipping, branding, slicing, I even had my wretches kick her around and ruff her up a bit, well...' He laughs, 'A lot actually, to the point you see her now. No teeth, bloody gums, massive hemorrhage, broken bones, splattered brains, and bled veins, she's a tough one indeed, but I am bored, I want to see some more blood being spilled, her blood is not enough to satisfy my hunger!'

Hernan rushes over to where she lays unconscious. Scratches and bruises cover her broken body, her clothes have been torn and her body bruised severely. And her face, her beautiful face...! Hernan gazes with bloody fury into Ja`kal's lifeless eyes, eyes that laugh with the fire. Words cannot describe the fury and rage that burns within Hernan.

'Now, you must be patient Forgemaster, for if you want your vengeance as so many always do, you'll have to earn it like everyone else, by facing my twelve challenges, for I promised my denizens a show they would never forget, and a show I will give them!' He walks to the center of the arena. 'Now, what say you?!'

'I don't give a damn about your shows, your aborted brood, or this foul mass extermination you dare to call a game! I will fight you right now with my bare fists! But if you insist on this foolish delay to my beating you to death, then give me your twelve best, your deadliest, do your worst, I'll destroy them all, and when I toss twelve dead enemies aside, I'll be coming straight for you!' Hernan's tone seemed to resonate something within Ja`kal, which even terrified Roaur.

'Are you sure about this?' Roaur trembled.

'Stay back Roaur. I know you've stood by my side this far, but there is going to be a blood bath here, and I want you to stay away!' Not breaking his stare upon Ja`kal, as he speaks to him. 'Take the Gormon away, I will do this alone!'

Ja`kal laughs. 'As you wish!' He motions for the guards to take Roaur away, and they take him to the far side of the arena, but Roaur first stops and picks up Asla's body and carries her away also, they sit against the wall, were he holds vigil over her.

In his booming voice, Ja`kal speaks out to the Skahljah crowds. 'Wenches and scum, I promised you a show, and a show you will have! I present to you, from Othetica, the Civilian, Forgemaster!' The crowds boo him and throw more litter. 'Without his armor and weapons, the Forgemaster has decided to face the Twelve Challenges, twelve of the deadliest fiends and horrors that only the darkest corners of Aura can hold! Are you ready to watch him get torn to shreds?!' The crowds cheer. 'Then, it has begun! Bring out the first challenge!' Ja`kal leaps into the stands and sits back and watches in eager wait for the Forgemaster to die. A few guards come out and unchain Hernan from his bounds. Hernan stands his ground as the far gates open, to unleash what terror awaits within.

The gates open, and the sound of thunder echoes forth, heavy footsteps like the sound of an avalanche cracks the dirt, thus walks out, stomping up from the fathoms of the blood works, a titanic monstrosity that towers above Hernan. It's face is swollen and the neck bloated with layers of fat and pus. The arms and legs built like stocky tree trunks, and solid as iron. The cranium of his head is covered with thorns in the pattern of a diadem and a thick mane of shaggy hair. The teeth are worn down, and a good many are missing and broken from chewing and gnawing on the bones of his foes that he has slain. His armor is thick with boots of hardened leather, and fists battered and scarred, the size of large boulders. Within the bloated and battered hands, he drags behind him, a massive ball and chain of titanium, corroded and rusted, thick with spikes and jagged objects that have been welded on and dipped into pools of death, forged in the darkest corners of the furthest mountains and caves were molten lava runs with the blood of the Dregor, Auzh`komog, the Bone Decimator, is this weapons name!

The monstrosity bred in shadow, suckled on decimation and rage, clad in immortality and undying hatred, destroyer of love and happiness, laughter and the singing of nature, stares down on Hernan, eyes him up, and bellows the call of war, ready to tear asunder this pathetic creature who stands before him.

'What's this thing in front of me?! I came because Ja`kal promised me a challenge, for I have cleansed my lands of every last living thing, beast and being! Tore apart towns, ate warriors and their families, I became bored! And what do I get, a half naked Civilian without weapon or armor! I've faced foes far more armored than you, chewed on caged prisoners with more meat on their bones than this scrawny, pathetic excuse of a being! If your that eager to die, I'll pull your limbs apart piece by piece! For you dare face O`gog, the Dregor Juggernaut!'

Hernan chuckles and a sly grin rips crossed his lips. 'And the juggernaut shall fall!' He exclaims.

With a mighty roar at Hernan's insult, and the whirling sound of a hurricane, O`gog swings the ball and chain round his head, and with a violent toss, heaves Auzh`komog, tearing through the air, Hernan leaps away, and with an crashing explosion, the Decimator creates a large crater in the ground. Hernan, with the balance and agility of the prowl, which was unlike any opponent O`gog has ever faced, rushes with light feet upon the thick links of the chain, soars into the air, and with a single mighty blow of his fist, sends the Juggernaut teetering backwards.

O`gog staggers for a moment, dropping the chain, and to the amazement of the crowds, the Juggernaut falls back with a loud slam upon the arena floor. Teeth and blood splatters through the air, and scatters across the dirt. Using all his strength and a savagely bruised right hand, Hernan clutches the chain, pulls it away from O`gog's limp body, and steps back some yards. O`gog stirs and begins to get up. Hernan once, twice, spins the massive ball around several times. A dazed O`gog holds his head, reeling from the pain and cursing Hernan. He glares at Hernan, only to see his own spiked ball heading right for his face at full speed, he cannot duck, and the spikes rip through his face, shatters his skull, and splatters his brains to a pulp. Soon the twitching ceases, and O`gog, the destroyer of his lands, the Dregor Juggernaut, has been slain.

All is silent, as the winds scream through what seems like a lifeless stadium, then an uproar ensues, as the Skahljah cry out for Hernan's death. Ja`kal, simply snickers at the outcome, then rises from his place in the crowds. He raises his hand for silence. 'Assassins! Kill him!'

An arrow soars through the air, and strikes the ground just a few inches from Hernan's feet. The second challenge has begun. He rushes behind an old ruin and ducks out of sight until he figures out what to do. He looks up , and just ahead, in the crowds is a shadowy cloaked figure pointing a black arrow straight for his heart. He moves away, just as the arrow pierces the thick stone above his shoulder. The assassin leaps down and pursues after Hernan. On the opposite end of the wall, another assassin joins in the pursuit. To his right and at his left is an arrow ready to strike him dead, but as they each fire simultaneously, Hernan jumps away, and in a twist of fate, the arrows strike the opposite assassin. They have killed each other.

'WHAT!' Ja`kal shouts allowed, and the crowds' fury inflames even more that this foe from Othetica is still alive.

'Bring up the prowl!' Ja`kal calls out with ferocity.

The gates open, and a fire-breathing prowl, covered with armor and a rider upon it's back, rides out to attack Hernan head on, the prowl spewing deadly flames and poisonous gas, the Skahljhen warrior slashes his battle blade through the air, ready to cut down Hernan if the prowl doesn't get to him first.

Snorting fire, breathing acid and poison, the prowl leaps forward to strike, Hernan ducks away just a split second early. He rushes over and grabs one of the dead assassin's bows and rips the arrow from the carcass, he pulls the drawstring back, and crouches, ready to release the arrow. The Forgemaster is not only an accomplished crafter of armor and weapon smith, but is also has prowess with a bow and or crossbow as well.

The prowl and rider circles around for a second attack. Hernan releases the shaft, and with a howling scream, tearing through the still and dusty air, with deadly precision, the bolt strikes, gouging the Skahljhen's eye, ripping through the brain tissue. The rider flies off his mount and the blade is tossed away from his hands with a violent throw, and the bones and his spine crack and splinter as the carcass roles across the dirt. The prowl stops and begins to tear away at the Skahljhen's flesh.

Hernan yanks the arrow out of the other assassin's body, draws back, then fires into the thigh of the beast. Angered, the prowl charges shooting flame, blazing the ground, and charring the ruins abound. Hernan throws away the bow, and rushes for the Skahljhen's blade, parry's away to the left, then leaps onto the back of the beast, just escaping a whirl of fire blown in his direction.

The beast bucks back, trying to get this pest, this intruder off his back, but to no avail. Hernan grips tightly to the fiery mane of the beast's hair and sharp spines that jut from the beasts spine down its back. Hernan raises the blade over his head, while clutching to stay upon the mount, but retracts the attack, for he is almost tossed away. He rips a piece of the armor off of the beasts neck, tearing it away like a tin can, he proceeds to raise the blade one more time, he raises it high above him, and with a downward thrust, a cleave, and then another cleave, and then another, the spewing liquid burns away the epidermis part of Hernan's flesh, leaving a permanent scar upon his arm and chest. The beast's head is lopped away with the rough cuts through the bone and muscle, and a gurgling cry of pain. The body falls, tossing Hernan into a roll. The head tumbles across the ground, and the flammable glands within the beast's decapitated throat, engulfs in flames, then explodes!

Hernan turns upon Ja`kal, who's eyes seem to glow with fervor and malice. Soon, a large cart rolls into the arena, bearing a dozen or more large cages, and within those cages are starved, frenzied sun migs. Standing upon the very top of the cages, a Skahljhen minion, along with dozens more, armed with knives and daggers, cuts away a large rope, the cages are thrown away, toppling the rest of the Skahljah to the ground, the migs swarm and tear them to pieces, slurping the blood, masticating every last juice and piece of meat that was laden upon the skeletons from head to toe. Unsatisfied, and craving more blood, they crawl after Hernan, stingers secreting their venom, ready to strike, chattering mandibles ready to bite, and claws snapping, ready for attack.

The legion surrounds Hernan in a circle and close in, tightening Hernan's battle ground, so he is unable to maneuver. A stinger lashes out, Hernan grabs the tail and runs it through another mig attempting to attack from behind, killing the mig instantly. Using his arm strength, he rips off the tail and tosses it away, then drives his foot through the exoskeleton, splattering the head into goo. Three more of the creatures strike, Hernan leaps from the barrage. He pulls away a spear from a nearby body, and thrusts it into the mig, lifts it up, the legs and claws scramble, trying to break away from the grasp of the weapon, but the creature is tossed aside with the spear against some stone ruins. Another is splattered against the wall with a mighty toss, and the third is lifted above Hernan's head, and he drives down the mig into a back breaker, shattering it to pieces.

The rest Hernan either crushes with his foot, smashes with his fists and deadly punches and jabs, rips apart their limbs, or heaves them away to their doom. And with the death of the last mig, the fourth challenge has passed, and the fifth about to reveal itself. Ja`kal is curious to see just how far he can push the Forgemaster before he finally breaks. Hernan looks over to Roaur, who places the body of Asla upon the ground, bowing his eyes down, he looks upon Hernan and shakes his head no, in condolence. Hernan rushes over, Asla no longer breaths.

'I'm so sorry Hernan.' Roaur says weeping. 'She must have passed sometime during the last fight.

Hernan gives Ja`kal a look of death, and Ja`kal simply smiles.

'Is this all you can throw at me! Come on now, bring on the next fight!' Hernan yells, choked by his tears.

'Guard her body Roaur, once we get out of here, we'll

have a proper burial for her and her people, but vengeance must come first!'

Out to the stadium rolls another cart, this time carrying a massive wooden tank filled with dark and murky, frozen water. The crowd tries to look in, but they see only the black depths, however, Roaur knows all too well what lurks within.

'A Friemisk from the waters north of Fausengard. Be careful Hernan, these beasts bind you with their tendrils which freeze to ice, and never let go until you are fully devoured!'

Hernan walks closer to the tank and stands in front, waiting for something to happen. He prepares to climb and jump in, but there is a loud splash, then another, and several tentacles lash out from the water, grabbing Hernan and several Skahljah from the crowd, pulling them in.

All is quiet, aside from the occasionally splash, and several sets of bones being spat out covered with blood and the foul water. A loud squeal of something titanic screams beyond the boundaries of the water, Hernan leaps onto the side of the tank, he reaches down in and pulls up one of the massive tentacles, and the massive body of the Friemisk attached to it. Hernan holds the titanic beast high above his head, then tosses the scaly squid beast to the arena below, it's shell that protects its body cracks open spilling the insides out into a massive puddle of slime. It's flesh quickly dries away into dust from the hot sun.

Ja`kal stands up and points off towards the western part of the arena, high above the stands. 'There, face your next foes!'

Upon a balcony, two fire-breathing drogs tear apart a number of Skahljah carcasses and toss the bones into a pile behind them. The drogs hear Ja`kal's call, turn, and eye up Hernan. They spread their wings, and glide down below, swiftly past Hernan on both sides, knocking him to his feet. He gets back up, and snarls at the beasts.

'So, I get to fight these monstrosities again!'

They come around for another pass, and Hernan leaps upon the one to his right. Using the horns he steers the beast towards the other, they glide high into the air, far above the stadium and out of the crowds line of sight. The one drog, casts a breath of fire, trying to burn Hernan asunder, but engulfs its kin instead. Hernan lets go of the drog, and both fall towards the ground below, spiraling out of control. The audience can see a large ball of fire heading towards them and scatter, but the drog carcass, and Hernan land head on into the large tank of water. The water sizzles away with steam upon the drog's impact. All is quiet for the moment, then Hernan once again rises up from the water. The other drog spirals down towards him, rage alight in its eyes as it gains momentum, casting blazing smoke and flame at everything in sight. As the beast is right upon him, Hernan leaps into the air, passed the throat, straight into the drog's stomach.

The drog lands upon the ground with a thud, and all at once, the crowds of Skahljah cheer, but their celebration is short-lived, for the beast begins to convulse and writhe with pain, tossing and turning about the ground. Then, the rib cage cracks, and a hand bursts forth from the chest, and within the hand, is grasped a large heart attached to some of the arteries and veins, still attached on the inside. The drog falls dead, and erupting out of the stomach, is the rest of Hernan, covered in bile and foul-smelling fluids and liquids. He takes a large bite out of the heart, spits it away, and tosses the heart behind his shoulder. The Skahljah are rampant with hate, some try to leave their seats and attack, they hate Hernan, they curse the Forgemaster's name and his very existence. Ja`kal eases them, and simply tells the guards, 'Next!!'

Out comes a walking monstrosity, more ugly, and more terrifying than any of the others, a freak of nature. A two headed man-like beast, some twenty to thirty feet in height, pulled along by chains and several Skahljah soldiers tugging upon the other end of the chains. Upon the muscular body and broad shoulders sits two heads that spit acid, a vile vomit from its stomach, and pumped through the back of its heads by large tubes, surrounded by thousands of hair-like spines to keep those away that would attempt to rip the tubes out. Within its four, chiseled arms, it carries a different weapon to blister any foe into a bloody pulp. It carries a massive spiked club, an over-sized mace, a double-bladed battle axe covered with a thick layer of coagulated blood, and last, a sword, with a serrated, saw-like blade. Not to mention, upon it's back is welded and riveted a massive titanium shield, unable to be pierced by normal weapons. At that moment, Roaur calls to Hernan from behind.

'Hernan, over there! To your right!'

Leaning against the ruins, is the Hammer of Gonun, it has found its bearer at last. Hernan grips the shaft firmly with both hands, holds the hammer in front of him, pointing the face towards the creature. The eyes glow with a mystical, yellow light. Hernan is ready for battle.

Hernan has a hard time getting in close to strike, or find a suitable vantage point to survey his enemy's movements to find a weak spot, for this giant spits and vomits the acid across the arena, melting everything it touches, bodies, carcasses, the ruins, even some who are sitting in the front of the crowds. In a strange twist of fate, the hammer senses this, as though it were reading the very thoughts and feelings of its bearer. The hammer soars into the air, hovers for a moment, then begins to grow at a frightening rate of size and speed. The hammer, once again, is the size as when the Aurora Gonun held it over his head at the forge all those months ago. The crowds, and even Ja`kal himself, seem terrified by this turn of events. The hammer winds back, spins violently like a cyclone, and casting its mighty shadow over this fearsome beast, then, with a blow that could be felt some hundreds of thousands of miles away, the hammer strikes down, smashing the beast asunder, splattering its brains, guts, innards, everything was now nothing more than a pile of slop and acidic juices.

The crowds were thrown about and scattered, hiding behind their seats and others, as well as in the hallways and holes lined throughout the stadium. The remaining ruins have crumbled to dust, and a large crater was left within the stadium some yards in circumference. The audience, after their shock, looks up and sees this once mighty hammer, the largest weapon they have ever seen in their miserable existence, has now transformed back to its much smaller size. The hammer lays next to the bloody pile of the creatures remains. Hernan holds out his hand, and the hammer sensing him, returns to his hands.

Ja`kal stands above the crowds of cowered and fallen Skahljah and speaks. 'I must say, I am impressed Forgemaster. You have quite a few tricks up your sleeve, though I must say I do admire the determination you show much more, but you have not won, you still have five challenges ahead of you. I thought you would be hindered, paralyzed, killed, destroyed, mortally wounded, I never would have thought any who have stepped into my arena would ever make it this far, there is something else about you, your blood is different from any other Civilian. Congratulate yourself Forgemaster, for you grow closer and closer to your doom, I think these next few matches will prove to be quite entertaining, and even test your metal to its extreme!'

'Take stock and count your nine lives you slithering monstrosity, for its your doom that will light the days to come, break the darkness of this desolation. These walls will crumble around you, and I will make sure you never leave, even if I reside within the rubble of these ruins as well, clutching the sword that has been run through your chest and gouges your heart!' Hernan calls back, his voice shakes the darkened, smog-filled skies.

Ja`kal laughs with the utmost delight at the Forgemaster's threats that seem so empty and futile to his ears.

'Oh, some may say my life be wicked and miserable, but it's the simple joy of bringing misery and pain to others that gives me bliss! To watch as others cower and fall before my grace and being, to spread panic and terror, and others look on you as a monster, and envy me of my great and terrible power! Oh, I say I have all the more reason to keep on living, for so many before you have stood in front of me, kneeled and whimpering in their rage, cursing my name, speaking of me like a poison, an epidemic! So many who said they would bring about my demise...but really, Forgemaster? What would this land be without me to hold it in my black hand, my vice and grip, my tyranny that gives these crusty beings hope and salvation?! HAHAHA!!!!!'

Ja`kal points to the gate. 'Now, on with the festivities I say!' And the next challenge, the eighth challenge begins.

From the wide maw of the arena gate, where the opponents of Hernan have stepped forth, and all who have been defeated, a line of about twenty or so Skahljah walk onto the arena battlefield. These Skahljah are different, they are dressed in more lavish ceremonial looking robes, with helmets molded into the shapes and faces of celestial creatures and daemonic beings. Each carries a large, thick, pole the size of a tree trunk, about fifteen feet or so in height and with two handles, one upon each side, where they can carry the mighty pole. They walk with straight posture, and in a simultaneous march, in step with one another, they separate into two groups, and form a concentric circle around the arena, larger than the crater made by the hammer. The Skahljah stand at attention for a moment, the poles held out in front of them, blank eyes in trance and concentration. One of the Skahljah calls out a chant, a language so foreign and barbaric to both Roaur and Hernan, for this was the language of the Skahljah, in translation, it was a simple, powerful, two words:

" Commence Summoning!"

Then, in a specific sequence of pounds and drums upon the charred dirt, a sort of song, a song of doom and danger rang out through the hallowed halls, throughout the stadium. The crowds wild and wail to the beat, crying out in the chant along with the booms and pounds:

" Come, the lord of the sands, the swallower of bone!
Rise, above dirt, dust, and mortal decay, devour all creatures, chew on Aura's stones!
We bury the bodies, you swallow them whole, eater of life and death, burrower, digger within the world!
Arise...Arise...Arise!"

The sands begin to part, and the dunes twist and turn, the drums and pounds halt, and then... it arose, the serpent of the sands, the chewer of stone and bone, with thousands of rows of razor spinning teeth and a wide tube body that stretches in the air for miles above the arena, and the crowds chant and cheer, gazing up at the immortal creature of the sands, Bapheme, the creature from where all sand worms were born and descended from.

Throughout the far corners and the lands of Aura, there exists a specific race of creatures, which have existed, hidden away from all eyes, for they only dwell within their realms, their environments, surrounded by only their brood and servants. These are the God-Monsters, beasts beyond the size and age of any other creature or being, existing the same length of time as the distant realms, the Auroras, and the dark ages. The rise of Reignkiing was the first appearance of a God-monster, for he was the largest and deadliest, but the others for the most part remained unaccounted for. Reignkiing was born of the Hexagus, but the other God-Monsters came to exist and dwell within Aura, from the outside realms, across the vast and mighty bridges of Galakaos.

Now, the God-Monster of the sands has been summoned by means unnatural, Bapheme stretches its maw, and hundreds of sand worms lash out and writhe about. The creatures long, massive body bends downwards and its thousands of tiny pearl eyes looks upon Hernan. Upon its sides, millions of tiny tendrils twist and writhe about. The beast, with the gust of winds from its breath, sniffs and senses something about Hernan, something about his air, for even these ancient beasts knows who the Forgemaster is, and what he is to do. Hernan could hear a voice, a mental voice, a strange omniscient presence seemed to engulf within him, the powerful essence of the God-Monster.

'Greetings Forgemaster, your presence is known to most of our kind.' Bapheme spoke in a low rumble within Hernan's mind.

'What are you, how do you know me, how do you speak to me?'

'I am an ancient being, from the far reaches of another realm, as are the others. I came here from this horrible call, this horrible chant rang through me, I could hear something in it Forgemaster, not these simple words of these creatures that surround us, waiting for us to kill one another, not the words of this chant, but there is a spell in the air attached to the words. You know of what I speak, for I see you have felt it as well.'

Hernan nods.

'Your task has taken a burden upon you, not just a burden, but pain and loss of those you care about, those around you that you want to protect and defend. You know what is coming, and I can tell you know, we among the ancient creatures feel it too, as powerful as the Auroras feel it...if your challenge be success, this fight is not over, if you find the blade, the war is not done, for supremacy will not stop, until Aura and all the realms succumb.'

'I understand. I do admit I was hesitant to help Captain Cezius, to understand what I had to do, even though the curiosity was there, there was a thought in the back of my mind that I didn't believe, or how could I be this responsible force in the events of Aura, doubting my own reflection of a man who should have not seen another day.'

'There are many, may they be greater or lesser in our eyes, but in our own way, we all stay on the level with one another, and feel these same feelings and doubts in our own way, in our minds. Events happen, and if they cross our path,

we can run, but this makes us weak, but if we face these troubles head on, we become stronger. Think of where you've been, and look at all you have done...'

Hernan nods.

'I will leave you now Forgemaster. Never let change and despair take you, for it will destroy you in worse ways than these dark times and dreaded spells could ever do.'

Before Bapheme crawled back into the ground, he drew in closer to Hernan.

'Before I go, I want you to strike me with your sword.' Bapheme says.

'Strike you?'

'Don't worry, that old blade cannot hurt me! You want to win your challenges, don't you? You want to slay that bestial figure who eyes us both? Then let's give these monsters a show, eh?'

Hernan tosses the sword into the air with an elaborate throw, and couldn't help but grin. He catches the weapon, gives a fancy turn, and slashes with style, striking Bapheme across his massive face. Bapheme gives a dramatic groan and roar, throws his head back and falls back into his long tunnel.

Crowds roar with outrage. Hernan turns towards Roaur and nods with a smile, then proceeds back to the center of the arena, taking in the same familiar taunts and ridicule. Ja`kal, in all his rage and desperation he keeps held in, raises his hand and silences the crowds, while the next task is at hand. The doors open, and Ja`kal announces the next challenge.

'Hidden away, far beneath the tombs and caverns of Vos`ul, a being that was once feared by all Gormon, Asyndian, and Civilian alike, I present to you, a being who has not walked within the realm of Aura for eons, since the days of his ancient Fausengard denizens. Tul Ra`, Gormon Warlord, terror among the living, evil beyond the realms of the dead, now caught between both worlds, and not having a very good day I must say, HAHAHA!'

Out from the depths of the blood works, once residing

within his coffin, Tul Ra` charges out fully armed, covered from head to toe in a thick, decayed and ancient armor. His words and growls muffled and without understanding by Hernan or Roaur. The armor is covered in layers of spikes all about and around with jagged antler-like horns upon his helmet.

"Donusdo zrghrogd` dreskittu! Tuulbutk algodo yutt!" Growled the resurrected being.

'I can't make out the words Roaur, can you?!' Hernan asks.

'I can't, the dialect is so primitive and foreign to me. If this is the black arts of Kandarius, he truly has gone too far, for Tul Ra` many eons ago waged a campaign to cleanse the other races away from the ancient lands of Aura! I, I can't believe this. Be on your guard Hernan! Tul Ra has a bloody legacy among my people!' Roaur replies.

The translation into Civilian of what Tul Ra` speaks is this:

'Curse you of the Living! What sorcery disturbs my sleep and pains my waking existence?!'

The pale, yellowed and lifeless beams from his eyes glow, as he catches Hernan within his fiery gaze and charges with shield held in front of him, and like a battering ram, swats Hernan away like an insignificant bug. Hernan strikes back, but the blade hits the shield of Tul Ra` and shatters to pieces, shards of metal fly away, and he uses his massive boot, kicking Hernan in the ribs, slamming him back again to the ground. Hernan's chest collapses, feeling as though he were hit by Gonun's own hammer.

Yet once again, Hernan gets to his feet, grabs the mighty hammer, and charges back into the fight, this time able to strike forward and defend against the thick shield and it's heavy blows. Tul Ra` lashes out with his mighty mace, and lands a blow upon the hammer, which in turn, causes a powerful force to burst out, driving back the crowds with mighty winds and lightning. At this point, Hernan glimpses up to see the fiery skies and purple and smoky clouds turn to night, yet no stars can be seen through the thick atmosphere.

'I will enjoy tearing your flesh away and beating you to death with your spine and skull! I will shatter every bone within your rancid corpse you foul Civilian!' Tul Ra` roared in his native tongue.

Hernan wipes away the trickle of blood from his mouth, and smiles with busted lips, broken teeth, bruised cheeks, soar bones, and bloody gum's. 'I don't know what you just said, but I'll take that as a threat.'

Hernan and Tul Ra` raise their weapons and charge. Hernan ducks away from the slash of the mace, and hammers a throbbing blow down upon his foot, shattering the boot and the dead foot it encases. Tul Ra` drops his weapon and shield, crying out a long and wailing scream of pain. Hernan drives the hammer into his chest, splintering the cuirass, and bleeding the innards, and breaking the chest and ribs. Tul Ra` falls to the ground holding his body in pain.

'I have fallen to my foe, send me back to my sleep!' He says in a more sympathetic tone, and without second thought, Hernan drives the final blow of his hammer down upon Tul Ra`'s skull, smashing it like a tin can.

With a blinding flash and a swirling cloud of purple smoke, the body turns to ashes, and the armor seems to almost either crumble or burn away. The howling winds take the ashes upon their finger tips, scattering them about the arena, but Hernan swears he could have heard a stark scream in the distance at the death of Tul Ra`. Off away in the stands, Hernan begins to hear a single clapping of someone's hands, it is Ja`kal.

'I must admit Forgemaster, when I first laid eyes upon you, I did not think you would have much skill or this kind of power, but you truly have impressed me, you are almost worthy of challenging my greatness! But, you are almost there, you have made it to the home stretch, three more challenges to go, and I think you'll enjoy these last few. And I will say, don't disappoint me, because it has been a long time since I had a somewhat half-way decent challenge.'

This did not please Hernan in the least, for he could not wait to rip the heart from Ja`kal's chest, and the jests and taunts of his won't break his focus on the last three fights, the last three dangers he must face. His body is worn down, even though he has been resilient to these challenges and has survived way past any others who has been in his place, and if not for his determination and strength, he should be dead, but his Civilian bones can only take so much. Even one such as a Forgemaster, by hero standards, can take so much abuse on the body. Yet, in an odd sensation, the Hammer of Gonun seems to give him some power, but to think of all the challenges he has won without it, tells Hernan that the inner fight of one man and his own strengths can be a testament to show others that weapons don't always make a strong warrior, for without them, sometimes you have to use your wits and your bare hands, but a little help and assistance every once in awhile doesn't hurt either.

The sun has now set behind the arena walls and the far western mountains, though Hernan wonders when last he saw the sun, feel it he could, but he doesn't remember catching sight of Lota's mighty, burning orb which hovers over Tundrok's rim of the sky. Off to the far eastern rim, Hernan witnesses a strange glow of a burning eclipse, surrounded by an icy teal-bluish color and a burning black flame, the dark essence of Shemoga and her burning eye, the sister of Sasparia and the rhythm of the seas, blankets the skies in an uneasy darkness.

'Ah, my ladyship grins down upon us with her wicked glare! The Grey Age is coming...! But enough with world events, back to the festivities, "Release the Slath!"

Hernan hears no gate, neither the creaking of chains and levers he has grown accustomed to, now there is only the low growl and gurgle of something that blankets itself in the dark, shrouded by the night. Hernan cannot see outside of a few feet, only the dim light of torches from the stands and the glow of the eclipse. The crowds sit in silence, only chilling the air in a deathly whisper of silence. The gurgle and roars echo across the arena, as something encircles Hernan, something with pale eyes and a shadow body, paces about and stalks what is left of the ruins.

All of the sudden, Hernan can hear someone cry out, 'No, get away!' And there is a sudden sound of blows hitting something heavy and thick-skinned, then there is a snarl and a tearing noise like teeth biting at something. The voice is Roaur, he is hitting something, trying to drive something back. Hernan follows the sounds, and finds Roaur laying upon the ground, something has taken a large chunk out of his arm and he is bleeding heavily. Hernan tears a large piece of his slacks away and ties up Roaur's arm, trying to stop the bleeding.

'Are you going to be alright?!' Hernan asks.

'Boy, I think we're having a bad day, Hernan.' He laughs. 'I'll manage, but something took Asla's body, something just ripped her from my grasp, I couldn't see what it was, its fur was all black, but it's eyes are pale, glowing in the night like two dead moons. When I tried to stop it, it snapped at my arm. I'm sorry Hernan, I tried to protect her, but it dragged her off! I'm crippled by these damn shackles and chains upon my wrists!' Roaur lays back on the ground feeling faint from the bite.

Hernan leaves him and follows what looks like a trail, as though someone were dragged across the ground, and in the mists, are a set of large animal-like claw prints, something with four legs. But the unnerving clue, is all the blood being dragged as well. Hernan hears the ripping and tearing of jaws, and something chewing. He wanders around the corner of a ruin, and there, Hernan lays eyes upon the black beast that took Asla, a Slath of Dregor, a beast of the night, a monster from the past, summoned forth to terrorize and devour once again. The creature is similar in appearance to a large, skeletal black wolf, with short ears, and a long, thin snout, and pulled back, lithe face, with two dead eyes crusty around the lobes and sockets, and a stubby tail, as though something had torn it away or chewed it off. The creature gnaws upon Asla's body, tearing away her muscle, licking the bones clean.

'No...no...NO!!!!' Hernan yells and charges the beast.

The Slath turns and hisses violently at Hernan, growling with fervor. Hernan tackles the beast, the Slath yelping as Hernan tackles it to the ground, wrestling with it, the creature gains the upper hand and snaps at Hernan's face, its acrid slobber spills and drools over Hernan's face as its jaws aim in for the kill point upon the jugular. Hernan punches the beast away, and gives a right powerful kick upon its tough as steel bones. The beast gives a shutter and leaps away at a distance. The Slath lunges in, Hernan grabs the beast by the jaws as it tries to bite, he flips around, and drives the beast to the ground, holding it down from behind. The beast struggles to get free of Hernan's grip, but it cannot get free. Hernan rips away the mandible and upper jaw, breaking them apart with a loud crack, he twists and snaps the neck, killing the Slath instantly. He lifts the large beast above his head, and impales it upon a nearby jutting piece of splintered wood.

Hernan looks down upon Asla's mangled and chewed away corpse. Her blank stare gazes off, up into the night air. A million thoughts roll through Hernan's mind, and a million tears roll down his bitter face. Enraged and overcome with grief he marches over to Ja`kal, Roaur watches as he stomps by, he can see and feel the hatred resonating from his cold and icy glare.

'Let's go Ja`kal, call on your next dog! I can't wait until your guts are spilled, your head upon a spear, and your cold black, beating heart in the palm of my hand!'

'Still eager, that's good! At least my little pet got one last final meal before you killed it!' He grins savagely. Hernan only glares back for the time of the words is over.

'Only two more Forgemaster, you've really built

yourself up to something through all this death and gore! But I really think you'll enjoy this next fight, let's see if you can kill, what you can't see.'

This troubles Hernan. He crouches into his fighting stance and prepares himself for whatever monstrosity is about to show itself, or should I say, isn't going to reveal itself. Again, there is no gate, only the still whisper of the air, and the quiet murmurs among the crowds for they have been silent in the darkness now. Unknown to Hernan, but I feel he suspects, but these challenges, since the summoning of Bapheme, are the work of a darker power, that lays beyond the Galakaos, deep within the bowls of Wom and the Hexagus Realm, but Hernan, even though having his hands full battling monstrosities from across the realms, always kept in the back of his mind, what Kandarius has conjured with his powers that would allow the Hexagus to come forth, if Ja`kal had been ordered to deal with Hernan, for he begins to feel something else is going on, something deeper, than Ja`kal is leading on.

There is a scuffle behind Hernan, he turns and there is nothing. All the way on the opposite corner, he hears the sound again, then it rushes closer, as though it were right next to him, then it fades again. He grabs a nearby blade, and with hammer and sword in both hands, swings into the empty air. Then, he is lifted and tossed away to the opposite side of the arena, landing upon his arm and ribs, bruising them severely, and the hammer slips from his grasp. He holds his side in pain, clenching the sword in his right hand, his left arm hangs limp to his side. He gets up, and then, again from behind, something pushes him to the ground and begins to jab and kick upon him, causing his insides to burn, and once again, he is tossed about, though he is not sure, he feels there is more than one fiend running about. He thinks of what he can do, but is keeping mindful of the things that are lurking about, then off to the eastern side of the arena, one of the creatures is reflected from the light of a torch, he barely catches just a glimpse of what looked like the head, maybe an eye.

Then, off to the west, he can see a shadow reflecting, moving across the sands gaining closer ground, coming up upon his left. He stands still, and watches the shadow, and with a quick snap of his arm, lunges the blade into the things side, and it shatters the still air with a shrill scream of pain. The beast falls casting an imprint into the ground. The creature begins to rematerialize itself. It is a dreadful abomination, the likes of which Hernan cannot describe with simple words, only disgusting, long and twisted are the words he could use, gangling and bony, tortured beasts, fallen from whatever previous existence they once dwelled in.

Then another comes from behind and clobbers Hernan across the skull with what feels like a large blunt object. Hernan is dazed for a moment, for his hard head cannot easily be damaged, for his skull is as thick as the steel and iron helmets he creates. Whilst Hernan stumbles to his feet, he notices something odd about the crowds, even more strange and abnormal than before, for their eyes, their eyes simply stare on him, red as blood and glowing like thousands of flickering candles, only the orange flames are scarlet, and their silhouettes dark against the torches faint lights. It seems as though they were almost mutating, transforming, for the Skahljah race is difficult to describe, for their blood-thirsty history goes back to before when the Baldushan reigned throughout the desert, and these slinking, crawling, tortured tribes of the Isa Desert looked on, waiting for their time to strike. At the early dawn before their reign brought full force to Isa, it's not certain whether Kandarius had any part in their rise until later, when the death of Shemoga occurred, but by many early historians and the wisest of ancient Aura, it seems more than likely that his hands and will had something to do with these barbaric beasts conquering one of the mightiest dynasty's in Aura.

Then another blow strikes into Hernan's ribs, and then another, until he is once again beaten to the ground. He tries to reach out to grab the thing that was kicking upon him, but there is nothing there. Again, he gets to his feet, for no matter how many times you beat down a Forgemaster, he will always get back up. Hernan looks about his surroundings, and notices the fallen carcasses of his former opponents. He rushes over to the corpse of O`gog, hacks away at the arm until it is severed. The blood still flows.

He picks up the massive arm with both hands and waves it about, spraying a shower of blood, a thick and fowl smelling greenish plasma, all about the arena, and sure enough, the blood splatters all over the remaining two enemies. He can see parts of them, face, body, some of the arms and legs are revealed, as is their weapons, they carry massive hammers. Hernan tosses the arm aside, picks back up the sword in one hand and the Hammer of Gonun in the other, and charges after the beasts, who now cower away in fear now that they are visible. Hernan traps them within a corner; he cleaves one across the belt, and splatters the brains of the other asunder. He stands upon the ruins, holds both weapons up high above his head, and cries aloud, a scream, a bloody roar that thunders through the sky.

'Eleven dead, one more...to go! You have made it this far Forgemaster, but prepare yourself, for you have faced one, two, three foes at a time, you've faced colossal and insignificant, but now I present to you, an ancient inhabitant, who has dwelled within the spines and bowels, the dungeons and the deepest, darkest caverns of Isa, and all of Aura, a creature so powerful, so bent on destruction, it's hunger can never be satisfied! I hope you're ready, for you face a serpent of the rotten sands, where spices run bitter, and all that has grown, decayed! Twenty-five heads, six arms, and a Blind Keeper who is the only reason these crowds are not long dead, their bodies scorched, and all of Kaskopos isn't burned away. Come Forth! Oh master, keeper of the dark, bring your child forth! Bring amongst this audience and this Civilian, this "denizen", the son born from the wombs of shadow, torn out by the lifeless, skeletal hand of death, and the umbilical cord cut by time's sickle!'

Across the arena grounds walks a lame man, with a limp, and a hunched back. His eyes and face sunken in with age, some thousands of years old. His knotted hair and shaggy beard are a pale, faded red and he wears a tattered green robe, stitched together by ratty patches, and tied around his concave waste is a dusty old rope tied in a knot that has never been undone, for as long as the keeper has sat upon his throne of dark roots and gnarled trees deep beneath the crusts, at the core of Aura. The blind man turns, holds up his staff of twisted wood high above, chants the words of summoning, and from the depths beneath the arena, far beneath the blood works, the beast hears it's master's call, and it's coming, its broad, massive steps echo in through the catacombs and the jails. Hundreds of the Skahljah soldiers run out, and leap over the railings were the crowds' sit and leave the stadium. Ja`kal and the others stand and await its arrival.

Then, several sets of eyes appear, eyes of glowing reds, pale blues, noxious greens, glaring yellows, and disgusting flesh-like cataracts that catch the light of the flames. Some of the eyes have been fused over by scales and abominable birth defects, the beast exits and reveals its true horror, first just a few heads appear, then several more serpentine necks and heads, and one after the other, and group by group they stretch forth, and then the body upon a set of multiple legs, and six arms armored with gauntlets and broken chains. The twenty-five heads tower high above Hernan, and look down upon this insignificant being, and they give a low chuckle.

'Kill, my servant, my son, kill them in the name of your tortured mother, the bleeding darkness from once you were born! Take your revenge upon those that cast you away, down into the unforgiving madness of dementia and anger, the twisting mania of frustration and rage! KILL, KILL, KILL them all!'

And so the beast casts flame and fire, ice and snow,

lightning and thunder, the elements of death strike down upon the arena. The crowds run and flee as those around them burn and are cast down to piles of dust. All chaos ensues. The heads lash out, and snatch up dozens and dozens of the fleeing Skahljah, crunching their bones and swallowing them whole and guzzling the blood. The tails of the beast then lash out, and upon the tip of each tail, is a weapon of molten metal, branding and siring with each strike, melting the flesh away of any they touch. The stands burn and fire rises into the sky.

Bodies and debris fly and the turbulent winds tear and scream through the arena. Whirlwinds and twisters form on the outskirts and tear apart the surrounding areas and encampments. Ja`kal stands to his feet and cries a bloody roar, and in the distance, the signal is heard all around, and legions of Skahljah warriors enter in a rushing march through the arena. These soldiers are heavily armored and twice as deadly as the arena guard. They attack the beast from all angles. They jump down from above and hang upon its neck with hooks and chains, gouging their spears and blades into its many necks and throats. Through the wide open portcullis, the hulking fire-tanks of the Skahljah are pulled in by large creatures, bred to carry and tug at the massive iron machines. The bodies of the tank are built into the form of shells with spines that resemble sea beasts, the faces upon the front are of a prowl-like beast with ramming horns, and a long serpentine neck stretches from the prowl mouth, emits a serpent head carved from rusted iron. The tanks send out mighty blasts of cannon fire, bursting upon the chest of the twenty-five headed beast.

The keeper cries out. 'Fight all you want, use all the soldiers you can muster, you cannot hurt my son! He will kill all of you! You will all perish into a darkness worse than that in which my son was kept!'

Ja`kal's eyes glow red and he leaps down into the battlements. 'You...Damn...Fool! I'll teach you not to double-cross me!' With blinding speed, he charges forward and the Bride of Dregor is awaken from Ja`kal's sheath. The blade's suckers and thousands of mouths lap, their tongues ready to absorb their intake of blood. And with a slice, the keepers head spirals through the air, and lands rolling across the ground. The Bride of Dregor tastes the flesh of the keeper and absorb his essence and power. The monstrosity looks down upon his father's body and detached head being absorbed by the accursed sword, and cries out in sorrow. The middle head, the largest and most ferocious, snaps down at Ja`kal, to take revenge for his father's death. Ja`kal grabs the scaly lips of the beast, the teeth alone are larger than Ja`kal. He holds the top lip clenched in his fist, and with his other hand, he sends a deadly punch into the beasts face, severely weakening and causing it to go unconscious and limp. Ja`kal raises the Bride of Dregor.

'Hold this beast, I will deal with it!'

The Skahljah use their hooks to hold it's heads back with all the strength they can. Hernan watches on at what is about to happen. The Bride glows, and Ja`kal thrusts her into the beasts chest, straight into where the heart would be. The Bride devours away, taking the monsters last drop of blood and fluids. The organs shrivel and the veins and arteries collapse as does the lungs and the rest of the inner workings of this complex beast. The many eyes roll back into its many heads, the creature sways and with an devastating earthquake, falls to the ground. The Bride seems to tremble in Ja`kal's hand, wanting more, craving more life. Ja`kal feels more angry and agitated than ever. He looks above, and flying through the air, are the Azimoth, they have come just in time, seeing the disaster caused by the twenty-five headed serpent, thinking it were a signal from Hernan.

They glide down with spears in hand and attack the Skahljah soldiers. An all out war ensues, but the fight pushes back and forth as the Azari and the Skahljah decimate one another, and then the remaining Baldushan storm the gates, for the gates have been opened from the inside by one of the Azari, and fight their way passed the sentries and outer guard units.

Roaur uses his fists and his binds to clobber and break the necks of many of the enemy, and fights his way to Hernan, who cuts away the binds, and once again, they fight off the charging Skahljah legions side by side. After some hours, the battle comes to a standstill. Bodies of Skahljah, Azari, and Baldushan are littered about the area. Hernan and Ja`kal stand face to face, just within a few feet of one another.

Their breathing is heavy, but their strength and hatred is far from spent.

'I could kill you where you stand, but I want this to be a true warriors fight, no armies, no guards, just you and me! These challenges have concluded, Forgemaster! In one hour, meet me there, atop the highest spire, that is where we will meet, that is where your fate will be decided! Bring what you will, for I will be there and ready to kill! I will crush your bones, and She, my bride, will devour your being! In one hour!'

He rushes over the charred stands, and leaps away. He can be seen barely in the distance climbing up the tall, black tower that seems to reach up to the blackest of clouds.

'I go with you Hernan!' Roaur exclaims.

'No, once again, I must do this alone. Take Asla's body away from here, go with the rest of her people and the Azari, I will meet you later on, just outside the eastern fortress on the coast.'

'What will you do to prepare, for you fight on his turf?!' Roaur asks.

'On our way in here, I saw a forge beneath the Underworks of this arena. I am going to do what I do best, forge myself some gear, and I am going to go up to that tower, and do, again, what I also do best, I'm going to beat down that monster so severe, he'll crawl back into that dark void from once he came, though he'll have a hard time crawling when he's dead!' Hernan replies with a growl to his voice.

Roaur holds out his hand. 'I wish you well, and I expect to see you on the coast as we planned.'

Hernan shakes his hand with a powerful grasp. 'You

know it.'

The captains and generals and whoever else is alive after the attack, heads away from the arena, marching along together, holding their wounded, and carrying their dead and dying.

Roaur to, he takes off his cape, wraps Asla into his embrace, and carries her away as well. At one of the Baldushan outposts, the fires of the desert burn brightly tonight, as the vigil surrounds the many funeral pyres and burials. Many cry and many weep. Revenge is on everyone's mind, and they sing, sing in the name of Hernan, in the name of the Forgemaster, for his triumph over the savage brutality of Ja`kal.

"Hammer wielder, Sword Master, these words are for you!
You've seen horrors, and faced the nightmares of all time,
If there is anyone who can bring Ja`kal's reign down,
We know it will be you!
Armorer, Forgemaster, Defender of Aura and all her kind!
You have been granted the sacred hammer and the skill of Auroras,
If there ever was anyone who will release us from this tyranny,
Hernan, the Forgemaster, will bring us back to golden times!"

And the songs and the laments to the dead lasted into the night. Hernan, meanwhile makes his way down into the dark and dirty forges of Kaskopos, for one hour will come swiftly and he cannot afford to waste any more time.

PART XIV:

Defense of Treefort

As swift as the astral comet, leaving gusts of wind in their wake, scattered leaves and blades of grass that bow with the direction of the wind, the Drog Riders quicken their pace to reach Treefort. Off over the tops of the far rural country, hidden deep within the thick green forests, lies the pinnacle of Treefort, the tower that branches and curves in every direction. At the very top, a soldier on watch shivers with the cold wind that casts across his chest and limbs, not even noticing the passing Drog Riders, as they land under the trees, beneath his watchful eyes.

They land upon the forest floor within a clearing beneath the massive trunks, and ahead of them is the base of Treefort, its fortress blends within the trees in camouflage, a chameleon that lays in wait, waiting to strike from the shadows of the trees while Pry's moon is out, and Lota's gaze has fallen asleep.

The gate is surrounded by a ravine of clear water, and the sky above is completely covered by the tops of the woods that surround them. To the left and right towers, are built massive trebuchets and giant crossbow mechanisms to suppress siege armies before they can breach the gates, which are cast bronze over thick yew oak. A warning bell sounds out, summoning the battalions of soldiers to the front to see what the commotion is about. They look out and see the five drogs, and another man, a Civilian similar to themselves. A soldier to the far left flank cries out "Drog!" and to fire, but another voice orders for the marksmen to hold.

Down off to the sides of the fort, hiding behind masses of tangled roots and bushes, hundreds of archers and crossbowmen emerge from their hiding places. The captain of the fort, his name is Baeo, looks out at the visitors, then notices the sixth one that rides with them. 'You imbeciles, do you not know the Drog Riders when you see them! And a Civilian rides amongst them. Open the gates!' He calls to one of his guards. 'Kar, come with me, we will go out and meet them.'

The Baeo and Kar ride out on two brown hofts to welcome the Drog Riders. The six meet them in the middle between the forest and the fort. Captain Baeo smiles down at them from the saddle of the hoft. 'Well, I'll be...I don't believe my eyes! Captain Cezius Cabriel, am I ever glad to see you!' He dismounts the hoft and greets Cezius with a praise and a hug. He grips Cezius by the shoulders to make sure he is real and not imagining who he's seeing in front of his eyes. 'Once I heard you were pulled from the north, I thought we were done for. For a while we were, but we've managed to hang in here for a little longer at least.' He looks behind him at the Drog Riders. 'Once they got rid of you, did you decide to join the Drog Riders? I thought you had to be born as one of them?' He laughs, making fun of Cezius. 'So what brings you here, what has happened, tell me everything! What road has led you this way?!' He can see the grim expression upon Cezius face, and realizes something is wrong.

'We can't talk here. Let's go to your office, for I have much to tell, and less time to tell it in.' Cezius replies.

Baeo nods. Cezius and Durg` follow Captain Baeo to his office, while the others are led to their quarters to rest until a plan is made, and a small group of servants at the fortress are sent to take food and beverage to the drog that lay under the cool shade of the trees, their great, scaled bodies sprawled out over the mighty roots, basking in the moonlight.

'Incredible, I never did trust that man, but to think of all this destruction he is capable of...incredible! Our men to the north, all dead, slain by his followers and soldiers in black, and you tell me they are being led by Athian Dor? This is terrible news indeed.' Baeo replies as he listens to what Cezius has to tell him.

'It gets worse...Athian Dor and Glenheim plan to strike Treefort...they will be here by tomorrow night by dusk. We have to have a plan, strategize our troops, strengthen our defenses, make ready...and when they hit, they're going to hit hard, and we have to hit them back even harder!' Cezius says.

Baeo is silent for a moment, rubs his balding black hair, and then speaks. 'Then we have some work to do.'

They work late into the night, and by late morning, most of their defenses are readied. The troops are garrisoned into the trees above, and at the small alcoves within the bases of the massive trunks where small survival, one-manned forts are set up for each soldier to be stationed during a lengthy siege. The Drog Riders scout out the land from above, some fly back and forth in shifts to see how far away the armies are, and how many leagues it will be before they will arrive on the doorstep of Treefort. But they must be careful, because Athian Dor's two drogs, Abhor and Femog also patrol the skies over the marching Mirym armies that come from the west, going northwest, then south for a while, and then turning northeast again. According to the spying of Arro`, they will be at Treefort within two hours, and the sun begins to go down that evening. Augr` reports that the Dregor are unaccounted for, they cannot be found anywhere, for they do not travel with the Mirym. Hurg` cannot see anything south, and Shoranna finds nothing in the east. This unsettles Cezius, for he knows the Dregor will attack alongside with the Mirym, and that Kandarius will be involved somehow. He would send out scouts on foot, but he will not risk their safety, for the Dregor are crafty, and the scout, if he found the Dregor, would not live to make it back and warn them. The Drog Riders have the safest vantage point to scout the land. He begins to wonder if this is the trick they used to ambush and slaughter all of his men and women in the north.

The ballistae are loaded, the trebuchets armed, the soldiers are stationed in their designated positions. Swords sharpened, shields polished and held at the ready, pikes are set, axes and maces are ready to strike. The servants and others who are unable to fight are sent down into the cellars and tunnels to prepare for escape if anything should go wrong, or the battle goes ill.

Captain Baeo and Cezius look out over the vast clearing under the darkened trees, for throughout the fields, torches have been set to see any approaching Mirym or Dregor. At the far edge of the wood, a lantern flickers, a signal. The Mirym are approaching, they can hear their drums and chants in the distance, getting nearer and nearer to the battlements. They roar the battle hymn of the Mirym, passed down generation to generation by Glenheim's fathers, and their fathers before.

Gronkuld, our father of old,

Warrior, fighter, who said "a battle is a Mirym's gold!"

Our enemies die by our axe, and splinter their bones,

Cleave their skulls with ferocious blood-lust

and eat their beating hearts, roasted over hot coals!

When battle is over, war will never be done,

our freedom beckons to us,

Victory a sweet maiden,

that embraces us with her feral lust!

For our Mother Oukolda, we seek to favor you!

For Oukolda, our temptress we die for you!
We bring back honor to our mighty thanes and kings,

Oh Oukolda, grant us shield, while our weapons sing!

Through the trees, the feral wild denizens of the ice realm, rank after rank, line themselves upon the plain in front of the fort. The Mirym stand at attention, their grunting and heaving of their weapons echoes throughout the woods and trees. A low mist forms over the ground.

'What are they waiting for; they just stand there not attacking? What are they planning?' One of the soldiers says to the other who stands watch next to him. The Civilians form ranks closer, shields raised, and the marksmen have their bows drawn, ready to fire at the first motion of attack, for the air is thick with so much tension, that its weight bears down upon their shoulders, like too much water washed upon a dam or levy about to break and crumble, and that's when the death will rush in, the tides of war will break through.

The shadows begin to grow darker around the fortress. One of the scouts in the trees upon the high branch hears something stirring, something large, then there's movement off to the far left of the fortress, the scouts hear the breathing and shuffling of the large moving object or thing.

'You hear that?!' One of the soldiers stammers, he points to a wildly convulsing, shaking bush. 'Over there, in those shadows.' The two soldiers signal below, and some of the troops go to investigate, for they hear this activity as well. The troops huddle around with their spears and swords drawn, one of them pokes at the bush, and the movement stops momentarily, but then the large bush seems to grow higher in the dark, as a large black shape rises above them, and something with glaring eyes looks down upon them, and then it reveals its sharp, diamond–like teeth, rows of jagged swords upon opaque gums, within a yawning mouth that opens with a shrieking roar and cry that shatters the night.

The beastly shape lunges forward, and tears one of the soldiers to pieces, and devours the remains. Its black wings sprawl outwards by several feet in width, and it dashes at the others, trotting upon its clawed hands and talon-like feet. The claws are unsheathed like ten wicked swords, as waves of splattered blood scatters, and troops fall sick and dead from its diseased breath and ancient suffocating smell. The screams of the men and women are heard by the other armies, and then drowned in silence and gurgle as they are asphyxiated in their own blood and fluids from their mangled intestines. Femog strikes from the east. Shrieks and cries are heard, turning heads towards the west, as Abhor kills and slaughters their other flanks.

From the mists beyond the trees, the shadows of the Dregor army takes shape and reveal themselves to the night, as thousands of black armored soldiers surround the battlements of Treefort. At the center of the legions, is Athian Dor, he holds up his fist of cold hatred, and the troops of darkness storm the fortress, black mass upon black mass, like a cancer that spreads through the body, the dam has burst, and the murky waters begin to overflow. The Dregor are a symbol of the dirt that covers each and every grave that they will bury the Civilians in, dead or alive, a mass grave with dank smelling oil and red flames to burn them down, and keep a few hundred left over to chew upon the bones and meat.

The arrows fly forth and strike the Dregor at their hearts and necks. The Mirym and Glenheim charge forth in the wake of the Dregor. Ballistae's fire off flaming bolts that explode against the ground as the fire spreads and roars. Dregor crossbows send volleys at the high walls, and rustic spears are tossed, they arch in the sky, and turn downwards, striking Civilian ribs and chests, killing them instantly but painfully. The bolts strike, sending several hundred Civilians falling to their deaths, screaming as their bones are scattered across the dirt and their blood quenches the soil, and feeds the roots of the trees. Several large boulders are launched from the trebuchets and squash the Dregor and Mirym battalions to the left and right flanks, but it seems as though nothing can hold back, suppress, or slow down their assault. The Dregor and Mirym slash through the defenses surrounding the perimeter of the moat, and they reach the front gates, burning the bridge in their wake, igniting red flames and chanting the death of the Civilians.

The gates to Treefort open and the hoft soldiers ride out and storm to the front, crushing and stomping, and trampling the front lines of Dregor and Mirym, but they ride to deep into the enemies' territory and ranks, they trap themselves, as the Dregor and Mirym surround them, and encompass them within their shadowy death. The Civilians and their hofts fight bravely, down to the very last soldier, for the Dregor slaughter them all, the Mirym bash them to pieces, and their hofts; none are left to fight another day.

Following the hoft stampede, a troop of about three to four hundred foot soldiers rush out wielding shields like iron walls, dented from previous battles and carrying iron and steel weapons consisting of axes and hammers, heavy duty weaponry to put a pounding upon Dregor skulls and breaking down the feral Mirym lines and ranks. They traverse over the bodies of their fallen comrades, and break and blister through the ranks of Dregor and Mirym, the two sides hitting each other with the force of earthquakes and the winds of a thousand typhoons. They fight with no fear, no retreat in their hearts and thoughts. More troops join the crusade, led by Cezius Cabriel and the Baeo, Captain of Treefort, armed in their silver mail and plating, with their royal swords awarded to them for their bravery and leadership. Cezius wields his sword Wulfbane, a sacred blade that glows a faint blue light, given to him by the Aurora Othetian many years ago for his courage in battle. Cezius and Baeo attack and slay with fury and revenge. Cezius decapitates several Dregor and splinters their ribs, their cold burgundy blood splatters across the clean polished armor.

Cezius hears the swipe of a jagged blade and turns. Glenheim has cut down and splattered several troops to make his way towards Cezius, his true target in this war. Captain Baeo stands between them, and engages the Mirym chieftain in combat, but he stands no chance against the monstrous berserker of a being. Glenheim catches the blade in his armored hand as it is about to strike him, and crushes the steel. He shatters the Captain's knee-cap with his clawed feet, and drives him to his knees, where he kneels before the burly chieftain in agonizing pain. He grasps the top of the Baeo's skull, brings his sword back, and looks into Baeo's eyes with his emotionless stare of hatred. 'Die, Civilian scum!' And he cleaves Baeo's head clear off his shoulders. He holds the head up high for all to see, and his Mirym chant and holler in celebration of this blow against the Civilians and Treefort. He tosses the head away, as it soars through the air, showering troops in blood. The Mirym pass the head around and cover themselves in the blood, which gives them a bloodthirsty intensity and they seem to grow stronger and fiercer.

Cezius charges forward, and he and Glenheim are locked in brutal combat and fierce conflict. Glenheim's sword glows with an ominous grey smoke, and is icy cold. He strikes Cezius upon his arm, which eats through his silver armor, and leaves a frostbite mark upon his flesh. Glenheim's armor is made of a thick hide and fur, his helmet is rimmed with pieces of broken teeth from slain beasts, in the pattern of a sadistic crown, and a single stag antler, for the other has been broken away. His shield is a monstrous face of a bear, and he wears no boots, for his feet are covered in thick layers of fur, and his toes are jagged claws. His feral sideburns are tainted with gray streaks, and his incisors yellow with neglect.

Femog and Abhor soar into the thick of the battle, and slash away at the Civilian troops, but they are battered away by five blurring, dazzling colors, the Drog Riders swoop in and they clash in the skies above with the two black drogs. Their speed is so great, they only appear to be faint sparks of light, for they had to drive Abhor and Femog away from the other troops.

Below, Cezius and Glenheim strike at each other, their conflict rages on, as their troops die around them. Bodies pile higher and higher, and the death toll escalates, is this battle ever going to cease? The fates now reside with the two dueling leaders. The intentions of these two may tip the scale one way or the other. Each strike, each hit brings them closer and closer to the end, but to who's end, is yet to be decided. The battle above in the skies seems to have ended, and the two drogs have escaped. Athian Dor has vanished and is nowhere to be found. The Dregor forces, as silently as they appeared, are gone, disappeared, as are the bodies of their dead. Only the Mirym armies remain, and they are becoming over powered by the forces of the Civilians.

The Mirym become confused by these sudden events, and their defenses wane. Cezius finds a slip, a weakness in Glenheim's guard. He slashes Glenheim across the side, and drives the cold sword from his hands. He slams his fist across his face, and sends him to the ground. Cezius grabs Glenheim by his toothed necklace and unleashes a fury of blows upon the chieftain. The rest of the Treefort soldiers surround the Mirym. They lay down their spears and war drums, and hold their arms high above their heads. Glenheim submits, and accepts his defeat. Treefort still stands, the area of the forest has been charred, and the Civilians struggle to extinguish the flames. The Drog Riders use their mighty winds to assist in extinguishing the fire.

'Chain them up, and gather them over to the far side of the clearing.' Cezius commands. The Mirym are marched over, and gathered into a large group, their ankles and wrists are bound. Their weapons are collected into a large pile near where the bodies of the dead are gathered. Several of the stronger soldiers bind Glenheim and place him down into a large prison of thick steel bars.

Cezius stands upon the thick tree root above all the others, and raises the flag of Othetica high and it blows in the winds, and speaks in the booming voice of a general, tried and true. 'These lands remain in the hands of our Aurora, and remain a part of Othetica!' The Civilians of Treefort cheer his name, and he glares down upon the Mirym. 'You have been deceived! The deceit and lies of Kandarius has forced you against your own people and the Civilians of Othetica! We tried to hold peace for your lands, but Kandarius manipulated you with promises of retrieving land that he stole from you! It was all part of his scheme. As a member of the higher order of the Civilians and one who is close to Othetian, I will make sure what was once yours will be returned to you, but I have only one condition for all of you, will you march back to your lands bitter, and wanting revenge on us while you die in the cold wastes, or will you fight by my side, help the Civilians cut off the black hand of Kandarius that stretches from our empires and cities, then we can regain the order our realm once had many eons ago!' Slowly a few of the Mirym stand to their feet, one speaks; he is Brihem, the nephew of Glenheim.

'My name is Brihem, and if I may speak, my uncle has become ill over these past many moons, and his ill mind has been easily corrupted by darker powers above us all. I did not want this war to happen; I did not want to fight against your people, for I never trusted that sorcerer the moment I laid eyes upon him, when he came bearing promises of grandeur and power saying he would give us back our former glory, but I did not believe the cold chill that eroded from his voice! I know my uncle has committed many crimes, and if he must be punished, let him be so honorably as a true Mirym, for he is too far gone and will never join your cause. But if my people stand with me, I would be honored to right this wrong, for we have been defeated by a powerful enemy, but may a powerful enemy become a powerful ally this day.' He walks over and raises his chained hands in friendship. Cezius returns the gesture and they shake hands, and an alliance is formed.

'Brihem, for those who always thought your race were just barbarians of the cold wastes in the north, I say as witness to what I've heard, you do your culture proud, for you show honor where so many denied such behavior amongst the Mirym, mocking them, branding them with dishonor, but I don't think that is true, and I would be honored to have you fight at my side, and join the ranks of Gormon and Asyndian in the Runegard that forms in the west.'

'And what of my uncle, what will be his fate?' Brihem asks, showing no dishonor or discourse for what Cezius's decision may be.

Cezius bows his head in disappointment. 'I am sorry, but Glenheim has killed a Captain of Othetica, and a close friend of mine. By my anger, and the laws of our people, that bears the penalty of death, and at dawn he will be executed.'

Brihem nods. 'Then so it is, and let it be done. My uncle was a brave and mighty warrior; I hope his shame is not scorned in the eyes of our ancestors and our Fair Mother. But it is likely, he will be doomed, and I shall morn this night for him.' Cezius offers to let Brihem stay with Glenheim through the next few hours, but Brihem says it is dishonorable to show sorrow in front of one whose fate has come to be.

The mists begin to clear, and dawn's first ray of light breaks through the trees. A golden curtain, an array of streams of gold and white, flowers through Greenhaven like many suns and lamps. Glenheim's prison door creaks open in the morning silence, and he is lead back out to the fields where so many had been slain, many by his hands. Outwards at the center of the field was laid a stone slab of marble from the quarries nearby. The marble had a concaved piece removed from it where a head would be placed, and an executioner stands nearby in wait. Glenheim stands in front of the marble, staring off into the distance, waiting for his fate. Cezius stands by, and next to him is Brihem.

Without breaking his concentration, he speaks, not looking at either of them. 'Well, here I am Civilian, waiting for the thunder, waiting for Tundrok's rain your bringing…so put on your war paint... and kill me!' He sets his head upon the cool touch of the marble. The executioner steps forward with axe at the ready, but Brihem intervenes.

'No, the execution has to be done by you, General Cezius. You are the one who defeated him, and by our honor, you must deliver the sentence, you must be the hand of my uncle's fate!'

'Very well, in my heart my strike is for revenge, but for the sake of our realm, and the existence of us all, I seal your fate, for the honor of the Mirym!' Wulfbane is raised, and the tooth of the mighty wolf, the Hound of Othetica, bites Glenheim's head away from his spine, and rolls across the dirt. Only a faint silence and ominous whisper gather across the lips of the on looking soldiers and the horrified servants. That night under Pry's full moon, the Mirym create a large funeral pyre around Glenheim's body, and wear their sacred ceremonial head dresses and paint sacred symbols upon their faces. Brihem chants and the low rumble of drums beat.

"His ashes blow as Mirym's snow,

A warrior's pride spurned, a warrior's body burned.

May our Mother embrace him, may scorn release him,

For the road to the final Hall is now before him.

All dim, all pale…so take his winds from the pyre,

The war is over, and the lamps in his eyes, expire."

The fires burn into the night, and the next morning, Glenheim's ashes are placed into a sacred ceremonial urn, and a lone warrior of the tribe who was loyal to their chieftain, takes the ashes back to be kept sealed away in the frozen plateaus of the northern wastes.

Cezius gives his condolences to Brihem, and Brihem replies, 'The days of my uncle have come to an end, and I hope I can lead my people into a new existence, better than the one we have lived through these passed years.'

'Return to your people, and tell them this land is open to them. My men will be stationed here to keep things safe and in order, but our borders are open to you, and the Mirym may come as they please.' Cezius replies.

'I thank you general of the Civilians, and I hold my axe to you and your own. This will be tough for my people, to have to pack our homes, our belongings, and our lives and migrate once more, but they will be happier living among the clear air and soft grass under their feet. For many of the younger generations, don't even know what grass is.'

Cezius nods in understanding. 'I hope all goes well for them, and that they will be happy and thrive in Greenhaven, the Emerald of Othetica. And once you have everything settled, we will meet you in the west.'

'We will find you, and I thank you again, for giving my people, all Mirym, a chance.'

He watches as the Mirym gathers their gear and weapons, and Brihem leads them back to their frigid lands where there huts and tents, where their nomadic lifestyle lies. Cezius is approached by Shoranna, and the other Drog Riders are behind her. 'Well general, shall we set off for Runegard?' She asks. Cezius turns to his men. 'I want a troop of about one hundred to stay here and watch the fort, the rest will come with me. We head west.' He turns back to Shoranna. 'I will stay on the ground and travel by my soldiers; we will follow you while you fly above.' Shoranna can see that look of a general burning in his eyes, and she understands.

'Very well, we'll go slowly so you can see us.' And with those words, they prepare their drogs for flight, and the troops who are leaving with Cezius gather their belongings and their steeds, Cezius is given a mighty white hoft to carry him, which reminds him of his hoft he left back in Othetica all that time ago, when he and Hernan set off for Fausengard and the tombs of Vos`ul. Shoranna approaches him while he mounts the saddle of his hoft.

'Do you think the Forgemaster will find his way to Runegard, how will he know which way to go?' She asks.

Cezius smiles and gives a light-hearted laugh. 'I wouldn't worry about Hernan, there's more to that man than meets the eye. He may just seem like an ordinary Civilian, a regular weapon-smith, but he has a determination that makes him as immortal as the Auroras.

PART XV:

Mirror of Dregor

'A finely crafted weapon, is a true test of the metal, and a deadly blow to Ja`kal's heart will prove that death finds us all, and this foul being will fall!'

Hernan climbs a tall metal ladder into the rafters and pulls down a hanging chain, thick of iron, and deadly fast in its whip. Over in the blood-splattered corner, are some shards and leftovers of blades and crude weapons tossed away from those who have perished within the walls and gates of this arena. He blasts the furnace, heat and smoke fills the room, and whirls its way up through the empty halls, to the surface and the outer bounds of the coliseum.

Hernan hammers away upon the anvil and the molten iron and bronze, concocting his latest, and deadliest weapon to use against Ja`kal. He looks out above, through a small grating of rusted bars of a drain, and sees that the eclipse in the sky is almost full, and the hour is almost expired. He rivets, bends, melds, and bolts the spikes and nails into place.

He has also made some slight modifications to his armor; a spiked chest-plate is complete, glowing with a magical essence from Gonun's Hammer, as are the gauntlets, boots, and helmet. The mold of the new weapon is doused into water, steaming with a hiss, and Hernan takes a small hammer and chisel, and cracks the sandstone open. As he opens the mold, he pulls out the welded, heated blade. A little polish and it is ready for battle, a powerful throwing blade attached to the chain, a bright light and jagged thorns upon fan-like blades protruding forth out of the shadows, tearing through opaque skies with deadly winds. He calls it, Gleamdrill, burrower of a dark heart!

Hernan walks out onto the battlements and looks up to the black tower. Ja`kal, now clad in full heavy armor and helm of many spikes and thorns, beckons him, taunting him with a single glare of his red eyes, a blood-stained cape waves and streams upon his shoulders, up to the forbidden moons of Pry's eye, and whips through the malevolent winds. The eclipse of the largest moon blankets the sky, and a strange cloud makes way, and swallows the tower, shrouding it into a mysterious fog.

'The hour has come, and your death is nigh! Just up these black steps, to be ripped and torn asunder by my hands, and the Bride of Dregor shall feed upon Civilian flesh, the blistering sarcoma of the Forgemaster!'

Hernan marches along the edge of the arena, and through a large portal, down a stretch of tunnel, and up the black stairs of the highest tower. The spire stretches upwards into the low-laying supercell, the black cloud that has engulfed the tower in its gaping maw. Through the clouds, there is a reddish light, a storm of flickering red lanterns and flames burn. Hernan climbs higher, and enters the fury of the black mists and haze. The blood lights engulf him, and the smoke writhes and dances around him and about his body.

What he finds on the other side, is a world unlike any he has ever seen before, it's as though his nightmares and visions were coming to life, coming back for him, but this was no nightmare, he is awake. A few nights ago, he dreamed he saw the top of a jet black tower, engulfed into a storm of blood, and he walked up many stairs, within the spire…and through the clouds, the cosmos seem to open up, for around the spire exterior, laced throughout the sky, stretching back into a void of tunneling darkness back beyond the furthest rim, are billions and billions of blood-dripping candles, and upon the doorway of the spire, hang two lanterns of infestation and disease that swells into gas and fumes, curdles into the air, and the center is the lone, floating entry way to the spire's interior. The jagged crown upon the brim of windows, the many gloomy eyes, and the solid twisted face of the cold, metal wall, curves above and inwards like a malignant hand and nails stuffed with dirt and decay.

Within the walls of the spire, the space is vast, and larger than the outside suggests. Across the way, is a narrow bridge, shaped into a cross-like structure, and beneath is a gaping abyss filled with teeth and spikes, razors and flesh, blood and bone. Hernan balances himself upon the narrow walkway over the pit, and slowly makes his steps across. Upon the other side, sitting upon his throne surrounded by mounted heads and scattered body parts, and the flesh of many Baldushan warriors and slaves sewn together to drape over the throne, the monstrous being of Ja`kal in waiting, the Bride of Dregor floats in the air by his side. The sword pulsates and salivates, waiting to feast upon Civilian flesh.

However, Hernan looks past Ja`kal, and notices the far off stairway in the distance, and above the stairs, sits the Mirror, the mirror that has been haunting his dreams with the figure that torments him. Wreathed in fire, within an obsidian frame, covered with spikes, the still waters of the gigantic mirror, about ten feet in width and height, stares back at him blankly, which oddly, casts no reflection of the place, just an empty space of whatever ghastly realm which may reside within. The portal responsible for summoning some of the terrors into the arena.

'So what is it that has truly drawn the Forgemaster here? Is it revenge, obligation of hatred, to see my head smashed by that hammer, or is it your visions and nightmares, maybe it is fate and destiny…but I think there is something else that has lead you here, for Kandarius has foreseen your arrival. I care not for my subjects, or for these prisoners I capture, like Kandarius, I only seek to release my masters, the true rulers of this world. The arena, the challenges…to make sure your path came this far, and all has gone according to plan. All my subjects who would stand in my way, have been eliminated, and I have you to thank, I only had to lift one finger, and my Bride handled the rest.'

'Monstrous fiend, what plan? Is this what you spoke of Kandarius not needing me, your madness blinds your true motives!' Hernan replies.

'My motives are blind to you, but your words are true, as were mine…Kandarius was foolish, he entrusted me to keep the blade safe, and I have, until it was time for me to use it. You will forge the blade for me, and I will harness the power to conquer this realm. He no longer needs you, because I said so! If he let you go so easily, he must be weak, just as I thought he was!'

'I have told you before, Kandarius could not force me to build the blade, and I will never reforge the blade for you.'

Ja`kal laughs. 'Kandarius?! Kandarius is nothing more than a magician, head tricks and mind manipulations, that's all he is! I am the one with true power, true brute strength, only... Naumokron was too foolish to see it.'

Hernan looks at Ja`kal in confusion. 'Yes, Naumokron had three disciples, three champions; a Warrior, a Magikahn, and a boot-licker! Naumokron favored Kandarius above us, for those two were alike in their mysterious ways. When Naumokron vanished and passed into the voids for a period of time, he left us to tend Kandarius like a child, while he manipulated the Auroras. Isifier served as Kandarius's lackey and servant under Othetian, while I was sent to these deserts to deal with the barbaric Skahljah, to organize them and turn them into an army and overthrow the Baldushan, but when Shemoga intervened to protect her people, I slayed her, and drowned her in her blood, then erected the walls of Kaskopos upon her bones! Groveling to Kandarius for his help, not my proudest moment, I tricked him into crafting me a powerful tool, my beauty you see here.' He points to the Bride of Dregor, as he holds her high.

'Isifier stayed to coddle and suck up to Kandarius, and now that useless weakling is dead, and I have you to thank for that also, you make quite the servant. But you will fulfill your ultimate service once I hold the finished blade in my hands and slay Kandarius, the Dregor will be under my control, and I will lay waste to this realm of Aura and rebuild my own empire, under my reign! All will chant my name; all will sing my song with tongueless wails!' He caresses the Bride of Dregor. 'And my Bride will be at my side!'

'I will not see this happen, as I told Kandarius, I will sacrifice my life, before I see Azalir serve the Hexagus, Kandarius, or you!' Hernan cries out.

'That can be arranged, for if you will not make the blade, into the realms of Hexagus I will drag your essence and make you renew that which was broken, the Bane of Maz Dregor! For the essence of your kind has many ways to be torn apart and suffer the most severe pain, than anything alive!'

'Then face me!' Hernan draws his hammer and shield. 'By all of Aura, I'll make sure you fall, and your heart will be torn from your chest! Now unleash your weapon Skahljah Lord, or should I say, devoted disciple of Dregor!' He steps forward. 'For I stand here for revenge, to bring honor to those that you have slain, eons of tyranny and hostility, the downfall of a race of beings who have established their history and culture here since ancient times, to avenge one whom I loved, who you have tortured and beaten! For I started just as a blacksmith, a Forgemaster of Othetica, and to the Aurora Othetian, trained by Master Kerrun, and given powers by the mighty Gonun, immortalized by his hammer I hold in my hands! The blade will be reforged and used against the Hexagus and all the Dregor, to maintain the peace within Aura! My strength and determination is a testament to making that happen!'

The laugh of Ja`kal shatters the darkness, a faint bell rings in the distance, a ring of fire rises up around and about the walls of the chamber like burning ivy, and the abyss beneath reveals itself.

'Do you know what lies below your feet? This is the Pit of Razors, conceived by the ancient Dregor, a secret ritual, a celebration of battle and sacrifice to the Hexagus Lord Blodaur Ror`, and over this chasm, is where your final doom awaits, so by the will of Maz Dregor, let this be the hour were flesh is shaved and feeds the pit! That razors bathe in the blood of the fallen, your blood Forgemaster, for the hour has come, prepare, for this is the last moment you will breath, face the last enemy…for I am the last thing you will know!'

Ja`kal tosses his cape away, clutches The Bride and leaps forward onto the platform, and so the duel of fates begins, and the eye in the distance, the cool, empty reflection of the Mirror of Dregor, bears witness to the fallen and the victor. And when the hammer clashes, the Bride strikes and the thunder clasps and roars, bound higher for the skies and shatters the rims of the stars, deep into the voids of Galakaos. The spire shakes and the encircling flames rattle and wisp from the raw energy of the blow and blast of the sonic pulse that rattles the obsidian bricks and structure.

Off to the eastern sector, the narrow bridge crumbles, and the cross-shaped structure beneath their feet begins to fail.

Ja`kal leaps into the air again, and strikes forward, Hernan recoils the strike with his shield. Ja`kal lands blow after blow, and Hernan's shield begins to dissolve and shatters to pieces, devoured by The Bride of Dregor, and her insatiable appetite, for she hungers for Hernan's flesh.

Hernan is tossed aside when Ja`kal back-fists him in the jaw, throwing his helmet away. Hernan hangs from the bridge. A battered cut upon his face drips below, and for a moment in the corner of his eye, Hernan swears he can see the pit move, as though the teeth and blades react to the stimulus of the blood.

'Yes Forgemaster, the pit has awakened and hungers for blood, after eons it waits to feed!'

Hernan uses the weight of the Hammer and tries to pull himself up onto the platform. Ja`kal stands over him, and drives his horned boot into his hand, piercing through the armor and into the bone, out the palm of Hernan's hand and wedging itself into the bridge. Hernan cries out in pain, and the blood gushing from his palm, runs down the bridge and drips into the pit, the fangs and gums moan and squirm about, the ancient gaping predator is alive, and tasting its first meal in centuries. 'I believe the pit wants to meet you Forgemaster, I'll gladly oblige it!' Ja`kal pulls the boot from Hernan's hand, and attempts to kick the hammer into the pit, but the hammer will not budge. Ja`kal begins to grow angry. 'What is this, why will this hammer not move?!'

Hernan grabs the ledge with his other hand and hoists himself up. Ja`kal takes a step back, as Hernan lifts the hammer up and goes into a fighting stance. 'Only a Forgemaster can lift the Hammer of Gonun, only a Forgemaster can wield it!' He swings the hammer around, and with a solid blow, cracking Ja`kal's jaw, and shattering his face, sends him flying backwards onto the northern part of the bridge, and the structure begins to wane. He tosses away the helmet, to reveal a bruised and bloodied face, skeletal, bent, twisted, and ill proportioned, with a crack down the middle, revealing a partial inner skull ready to ooze forth from its gaping wound.

'Ah! I'll tear off your arms, I'll pluck out your eyes, devour the muscle of your heart! I will make you suffer!' He holds up his clenched fist. 'My Bride, avenge me!' The sword strikes forth, reaping puss and tearing through flame. Hernan stands aside, and the Bride screams passed. Hernan lays down the hammer, and retrieves the blade and chain upon his belt. He spins the chain about several times, cutting through wind and air, and tosses the Gleamdrill, catching the hilt of the Bride. The Bride screams and writhes, trying to break free of Gleamdrill's chain and cutting blades, as Hernan pulls her closer, but she resists the pull, trying to break away.

'Ja`kal, Ja`kal! Set...me...free!' She cries in the words of Dregor.

Hearing the cries of the Bride, Ja`kal grabs Hernan from behind, lifting him up, and crunching him like a piece of sheet metal in a grinder or vice. The pain intensifies, Hernan lunges back with a head-butt, and shoves Ja`kal's eye back further into his skull. He yells out and drops Hernan to the bridge. With a mighty tug, he pulls the chain towards him, and the Bride is forced at him, he moves away, and the Bride's hungry blade is driven deep into Ja`kal's stomach.

Ja`kal gazes down at the Bride who sticks halfway out of him, and without thought, only instinct, she feeds upon her master. Her many mouths, and salivating juices begins to absorb Ja`kal from the inside out. Hernan can see Ja`kal's life essence draining away, and his entrails emptied and fall and drip upon the bridge. 'My...Bride...don't do this...to...' Ja`kal staggers from side to side, Hernan readies himself, Ja`kal balances along the edge of the pit, his flesh is whittled down to the bone, dry and barren, sagging an lifeless, gray and cankered, as the crust of the deserts of Isa.

Ja`kal drops to his knees and grabs the Bride by the hilt. 'Do it, Forgemaster…do…it!'

Hernan needs no more motive, he does as he says he was going to do, he grabs Ja`kal with his bare hands, holds him up into the air above his head, breaks his spine asunder, and throws his body down into the razors, and watches as the teeth mangle his flesh, grind his bones, and drink what's left of his body, and his Bride, both devoured in their matrimony.

The rest of the foreign cross structure begins to crumble. Hernan takes a running leap and catches the edge of the far platform where Ja`kal's throne stands. The Hammer of Gonun already awaits him. Hernan orients his weight and heaves himself up onto the platform. He gazes up at the black stair and the mirror that waits at the top. This is the mirror that has plagued his sleep, the omen within his dreams and nightmares.

The lone glass looks down upon him, it beckons to him, and Hernan answers its call, something comes over him, the same familiar feeling when trapped within the mind of Kandarius, being tortured and mentally ripped and torn to pieces. A painful feeling, for the figure of the shadows dwells within, it whispers to him, a mental connection of sorts. He cannot disobey or ignore the call. He ascends the obsidian stairs that spiral around and around towards the top platform. The flames dance in celebration of the mirror's presence, as though it were some great deity. The language that whispers to Hernan, is the same the Bride of Dregor spoke, the ancient language, the black tongue of the Hexagus Lords that bask in the vile stomach of Wom, their Hexagus realm. He ascends higher and higher, and then stands face to face with the placid mirror. And within the center, as though coming closer from a distant realm, something approaches, at first a shadowy light, then the shapes twist, and the light bends and turns, forming into a figure the closer its comes into view. Hernan gazes into the pool of morbid lights, and is aghast at what he sees. The eyes, the armor, and the broad shape and tone, he sees his own reflection appear before him out of the swirling clouds of darkness from the realm beyond.

This shape that poses as the Forgemaster, pulls Hernan through, clutching him with an iron grip similar to a powerful vice. He blacks out for what feels like an eternity, and awakens by a clap of lightning and a roar of ominous thunder. He awakens to a barren wasteland of charred ground and ruins of ancient monolithic structures. The sky above is grey with black clouds, and the sound of the environment is harmful to the ears, and pounds the head with a loud echo as though this place were a living thing, the sounds of many creatures, their cackles and growls, snorts and slurs, and their ancient daemonic wings, and crunching of their jaws, fighting over prey and blood, blisters the soundscape of the stale, smoky air. Stone faces of epileptic eyes and cheeks and jowls infected with the touch of leprosy, stare down at him from mountain cliffs, they move and struggle about, and their mouths scream and moan at him as he walks beneath their presence, either in anger and rage, or calling out for salvation.

What this place is or has been, Hernan did not know, whether it was real or just a nightmare, he wasn't sure. The last event he remembers, was the mirror...yes, his reflection, looking at his reflection, his altered self brought him here. Off in the distance, palaces crumble and castles burn, beneath the fiery oceans and the horizons of smoke and ash. Where was his altered self hiding, watching him, he is not sure. He looks behind and around the area, there is nothing, except these ruins of a once standing, thriving civilization, and beastly shapes that skulk about in the shadows of the mountains and spires of crags and rocky hills, but there is an odd silhouette in the distance, an arc-shaped structure standing some thousands of feet, covered with jagged thorns, stabbing through the skyline, and above a void of emptiness that swirls around the top of the arc like a evil halo or worm hole, opening upwards into an infinite tunnel, a black portal. The shape of the arc, resembles that of the mirror he remembers being torn through. A bright red light spirals around within the center of the arc's massive obsidian frame.

From out of thin air, without warning, in the corner of his eye, Hernan sees the flash of cold, heated steel strike at him. A warrior with strange honed armor, and a helmet resembling a darkened sun that glows with a tempered crimson light, and pounds with the sound of a beating heart against the inside of the armor. Hernan falls to the ground, his hammer did not follow him to this realm, he has no weapons, no gear, nothing except for slacks, his bare skin, and his wits and senses. The warrior stands above him, and raises the strange blade up above his head, gripped with both hands, and a set of two more hands hang clenched and ready at his sides, the palms filled with bright lights and pulsating energy. He roars, and swings the blade to strike, then something pierces through the warriors chest, another blade.

Standing behind the warrior, is yet another, but his helmet glows with a green and yellow poison, and emits a deadly venomous gas when it breaths. He grips the dead warriors shoulder, tears him off the blade, the rib cage splinters and snaps as he is ripped away, and the poisonous warrior pushes the dark sun warrior aside. The black star sun-shape of this warriors helm glares now upon Hernan, the sick eyes glow yellow, spoiled and blind. This warrior grabs Hernan by the throat and lifts him into the air with his black, claw-like gauntlet. Hernan stares deep into the sickness of the warriors eyes, as it speaks in Dregor, then holds the blade up to his face. The blade of the weapon is twisted and curved, set in place upon a golden-jeweled hilt, and at the center of this hilt is a glowing pupil, lidless and consecrated to its evil grip with magnificent, yet terrible energy, the pummel's tip is curved outward on one side, and inward at the other, and a glowing opal is held by a golden, three-pronged claw, and set throughout the blade all the way to the point, and nearest to the edge, is a series of glowing suns, burning with an acidic green. The weapon has a ghostly visage, as does the warrior of poison, and the warrior of the dimmed sun.

The warrior speaks a final word of judgment upon Hernan's fate, and tosses him down to be slaughtered in the name of his masters. There is a thunder in the distance, and the sound of metallic hooves approaches fast in a seasoned, rushed gallop. The daemonic shape draws near, the warrior hears it coming, and turns, preparing himself for the conflict bound to ensue. The creature appears, in its full and terrifying shape, as it manifests in front of the warrior and Hernan. It is a monstrous construct of a scaled body, four legs each hoofed and standing about twenty feet in length, covered and bolted down with a metallic armor, and its long serpentine head is arched upwards and curled around two or three times, it has large Dregoric bat ears, and a short snout that heaves and spits blasts of liquid flames upon the warrior, as it dodges from side to side, avoiding the molten breath and mucus. Upon the creatures neck, are a series of several hundred rings of molten gold pierced into its scales, and a large ring riveted within its snout. A long, bloody forked tongue dripping with acrid venom, slobbers and burns layers of ground and dirt away beneath the warrior's feet.

The warrior attempts to strike, yet the monster attacks first and snatches the warrior into its jaws and tosses him about like a limp doll, snapping and breaking his bones and liquefying his guts into putrid bile that eats away the innards and fat. The sword flies out of the warriors hands and strikes into the ground. The monster tears the warrior apart, biting him in half, and the pieces scatter through the air, as the remains burn away into ghostly ash before they can land upon the surface of the dirt. The monstrosity then sizes up Hernan with jaws that drip greenish blood, that resembles masticated grass, and strikes at him.

Hernan rolls away, gets to his feet and sprints as fast as he can towards the fallen blade, with the beast in quick pursuit on his heels. Hernan lunges, and rolls forward, removing the blade from the ground with dramatic fashion of his skill. A surge of green electricity pulsates through his arm and then the rest of his body, like millions of tiny green veins spreading like a powerful nova. He holds the sword up to the darkened sky and a beam of light breaks the black clouds, and touches the voids that stretch to the outside. Then he looks upon his body, he is clad in the same armor as the other two warriors, but his armor is a magnificent ivory white, with sunlight glowing from the inside under his armor. His helmet of the sun, gauntlets, and boots are a sparkling gold, and he bears a cape which enthralls him in a warm embrace of pure sunlight, a glowing force field which surrounds his body in defense and protection.

The beast rears upon its hind legs and tries to break the shield, but the barrier only pulsates and crackles, becoming even stronger with every moment and will not give way. Hernan struggles to control the powerful beam of energy, and focuses the might of the sword upon the beast, and creature swells and incinerates in the blast of overpowering light, causing its remains to scatter about the land in falling debris of kindled flame and sloppy bits of guts that are strewn about here and there across the ground. The energy engulfs the realm in a bright cosmic explosion, and sends Hernan backwards into a warp of flickering lights and spiraling arrays of colors and voids of time and darkness, until there is no sound, he clutches tighter to the hilt of the sword, then the crying shatter of glass, as it shatters upon cold stone.

Hernan forces his soar body to move, and looks about the familiar surroundings. He is once again back inside Ja'kal's throne room, back in the dark spire, and the Pit of Razors lays dormant behind him, the flames are out, and the pit is asleep once again. The room is dark, and there is no sound, only Hernan's heavy breathing and his sweat coursing down his body, and tapping upon the floor. His own armor is once again covering his flesh, and the Hammer of Gonun at his left side, and to his other side, clutched in his right hand, is a broken blade, dull and lifeless, without power or its legacy. Hernan holds the blade up to the moonlight to examine it, to see if his eyes play tricks, but his sight does not betray him, for the broken blade, the sacred one, Azalir's remains, have been recovered.

PART XVI:

Auth's Sacred Pyre

Hernan, with hammer and mighty blade in hand rushes out from the tower, and the other worldly cloud and alternate dimension has seemed to vanish away. The spire shakes and the bricks begin to tumble and collapse with the destruction of the mirror. He rushes down the spiral stairs as they crumble piece by piece, stair by stair, and at the last ten feet he falls downwards to the sands below. He constitutes his strength and rushes down the tunnel. The darkness shakes violently beneath his feet, and he stumbles side to side against the walls. Hernan soon reaches the faint light of the end of the tunnel where the remains of the arena lay beaten, battered, charred and scorched.

The massive, wide open, fields of slaughter scatters before his eyes, over blood and bruised dirt and sand. The flames of the twenty-five headed beast still burn and have since spread throughout the area, incinerating and cremating the many bodies that remain behind, most of which are now skeletons, ash, and charred bone.

He dashes from the arena gates that have fallen from their rustic hinges and now lay in front of an empty portal frame. The Skahljah have either fled from the streets, out to some unknown desolation in the Isa desert, or lay dead, crushed and bloodied beneath tons of rubble and debris.

As the ground quakes and chasms begin to tear asunder, the sky turns bright red and the eclipse becomes a great crimson eye, and the fire begins to fall across the desert, and drops of gas and flaming rain scorch the atmosphere, and turns and twists every inhale into a poisonous fume. Hernan hears a loud creaking, crackling sound piercing the air, something moves about, something which is causing this quake. A painful, twisting shape blackens the crimson eye and holds Kaskopos in the grip of its shadow; he looks above, a large skeletal hand that drips the foul acrid liquid of the tar pits looms over his head, and burns through buildings, temples and the foul homes of the Skahljah, and erodes the filthy streets. Shemoga's remains arise, the death of Ja`kal has resurrected the dead Aurora who was brutally slain and drowned in her own blood, she has returned for her vengeance.

Her hands, those slimy fingers, some five hundred feet in length, grips down into the fortress and rakes the buildings and towers into large piles of debris, chaos, and destruction, annihilating all in her path, then the other arm rises up, and Hernan hears Shemoga's blood-curdling scream of twisted dementia and pain. Her flesh, her mind has been long torn away and dead for some eras, and the feeling comes sweeping back over her, as the thick black oil, her necrotic, spoiled blood, boils her bones and remains.

Shemoga grabs the tall, black spire where Ja`kal and his bride had fallen to the Pit of Razors, tossed away by Hernan, and she rips the opaque structure away in her powerful, titanic grip, and she tosses the structure far away, beyond the furthest horizons of Isa. Over the walls and obsidian structures, above the flames that roar and burn the destruction and crumbled piles of lost homes which dwell ominously in the wickedness of Kaskopos, the dreaded face of the Aurora appears, rears her ugly head, and reveals her true spite and pain. The sight in Hernan's eyes, makes him feel sorrow, and pity for the once beautiful Aurora, but he cannot help but feel terror for the retribution she is to bring upon Kaskopos, especially while he is trying to make his escape with the only hope that Aura has against the Grey Age.

He cannot bear to look upon her. The face of a former angelic masterpiece of creation, of a being whose powers once carried the tides and the phases of Pry, her lover, a goddess of beauty, of divine temptation towards those who were entranced by her shimmering skin as she bathed in the moonlight, within her sacred pool, until she was cut down, and fallen, scarred into the appearance she takes on to this day, the appearance she was left with when Ja`kal cut chunks away from her face, gouged out her eyes, sliced her throat, and torn her open, like a fisherman guts a fish. A curse was placed over the pool that day, and the temperature rose, and her blood turned black, she sank to the bottom of this nightmarish ravine of death, and left forgotten as the mystical flesh was burned from her bones. Brick by brick, like walls of hatred and malice, Kaskopos was built upon Shemoga, to keep her sacred memory subjugated.

But now the memories have returned, with full force of hatred which Hernan can see within the Aurora's butchered eye. Her face now filthy and charred with the tar, and disgusting as the flesh that has been melted away, the cheeks and jowls eaten by acid and acrid fumes, the lips pulled back and ripped apart. Massive worms covered with spines and many eyes and teeth writhe and crawl, chew and salivate throughout her skull and rotten, exercised stomach. Clumps and strands of thinned black hair cling upon a rotten scalp ulcerate with heavy burn patches, cling to their decayed roots. The right eye is gone, long disintegrated, but her left eye bulges and hangs by a thin cable of veins and arties, whose blood flow has long halted. Shemoga's shrieks are stark like a prehistoric beast under a silent, fiery red sky, from a time when the outer-worldly stars and planets could be seen from grounds and hills, from the mountain tops and lakesides, before the dark clouds developed, and overcast all Aura into a shadow of doom, a terror to the dwellers of the sands, and pain upon memory, to witness such grotesque horror.

Shemoga digs her claws in, drives her nails in deeper to the fortress, penetrating the crust. Hernan rushes through the final street, rounds the corner, the front gates are in sight. The roads and sidewalks are scraped away behind him, gathering under brittle nails of a titan brought back from the realms of the dead. He rushes through the portal, runs across the bridge, and leaps over the boiling pits and lands to the other side. Hernan distances himself away from the crumbling fortress by some yards away, on the far side of the shifting dunes, atop the hills of sand. There, he turns and watches as Shemoga pulls the fortress of Kaskopos down into the depths of her blood, and only a ravine of boiling black sludge remains in the shifting sands of the Isa Desert.

Roaur stands upon the watch, looking out towards the horizon and sees a distant figure approaching, the scorching sun rising at his back. Hernan approaches closer to the Baldushan tents and extinguished campfires, and the leftover smoke that rises in the morning lights, and wisps away with the breeze. There, on the outskirts of the encampment waits his armored companion with hammer rested across his arms. They say nothing to one another at first, but simply smile.

'What took you so long?' Roaur asks in a joking manner, knowing with his heart that Hernan would return.

'Ja`kal gave me some trouble, but it was nothing I couldn't handle. That bastard deserved what he had coming to him! And now he lays in pieces at the bottom of a pit, and the ancient bile of some beast melts his flesh!' Hernan replies. He looks about the camp, the Baldushan all stand in attention of his presence, glad and relieved; astonished eyes filled with tears and happiness, for Hernan, their savior, has destroyed Ja`kal, the Annihilator, the Warlord has been slain. Hernan holds up the broken blade for all to see.

'Hernan, you have it!' Roaur exclaims.

They cheer Hernan's name, and celebrate his honor. Roaur holds him upon his shoulders and carries him through the applause of the crowd that reaches out to him. But for Hernan, the victory is bitter sweet. Roaur puts him down, as the crowds circle around and congratulate the Forgemaster. Hernan looks at Roaur with the dreadful eyes of a man who has lost. 'The dead?' Hernan asks in a calm, solemn voice.

'We had pyres lit throughout the night, but…except for one…' Roaur replies. Hernan notices the row of many stacked rocks and make-shift stones where the dead were burned upon with belongings and offerings, for some of the family and friends of those who have been taken, stay at the foot of the burned bodies, morning and weeping, some have fallen into slumber, dreaming of their loved-ones faces that are still alive and interact with them once more before passing onward from this life, though they are only kept alive within that dream world very few understand.

When Roaur said that there was one they have not burned, he knew. 'Asla.' Hernan feels a tear roll from his eye and down his cheek, as her beautiful face enters his mind.

'I knew you would want to see her one last time, so I placed her body in a safe place.' He points to a large cave hidden under the cliff face. Roaur escorts him. Inside the cave, they descend a set of crude steps made of stone down into the cavern where Asla's body rests upon a large slab of stone, carved out from the floor many centuries ago, for this was once a burial mausoleum for the Baldushan. Hernan approaches her still body and feels his legs begin to buckle, for this scene seems so unreal to him. He holds her body close to him, trying to warm her, for she is trapped, frozen in a far gone and distant time, a place where her essence is still in sleep. Her beauty, her once bronze skin without flaw, those eyes, her hair…now her shell, her mortal coil lays slain and scarred. Hernan lays her back down, and stands to her side and kneels down on one knee; he runs his fingers through those once soft threads of jet black hair, now turning grey and lifeless. His attention is fixed upon her, but he speaks aloud to Roaur.

'I never did tell her Roaur…'

'Tell her what?' Roaur replies.

'That woman in the forest, tied to the tree by those vines, the life being sucked away from her through nightmares and infernal dreams…that was Asla's mother. Asla was telling me about her, how she taught her about medicines and healing. She knew that her mother was dead, but I did not tell her…I did not tell her I saw her, I spoke to her…I did not want to tell her how her mother died, I felt the pain would have been too much for her to bare.' He is deep in thought for a moment. 'I only thought it was right, that maybe I would be able to tell her someday if I could. Now she'll never know, for the whole family, the mother, the father… all of them are dead.'

Roaur had no words to say, what could he say…to comfort Hernan's pain and loss? He simply remains silent, which seems is the only true response one can give in these situations. Hernan carries her up to the edge of the cliff, accompanied by Roaur, to where a clay pyre stands, a sacred symbol of the ancient, long forgotten times of the Baldushan, where mighty emperors and kings where cremated, and their ashes would bellow out of a chimney tipped with the carved and chiseled head and figure of a stout and curious bird, with smooth black pearls for eyes, and a crest of diamonds upon its breast. The jeweled wings are outstretched to catch the sun's rays, as the sacred Auth, the carrier of the dead, flies Asla to its realm beyond the skies and past the stars. Mists of faces and ethereal shapes and forms twist around her burning corpse, lifting her upwards, and Auth's mighty talons of shimmering gold, flies her to the sun, a tangled mesh, insane, divine.

"As Auth flies his children to the sun,

Into the warm embrace of Lota,

Our sons and daughters have come."

Hernan hears a flutter at his back like great wings, and claws sink into the dirt. He turns and looks upon a familiar face. The being pulls back a red hood, and L`or reveals himself. Hernan greats the Asyndian. 'L`or you have returned! I've found Azalir, we have the blade!' Hernan holds out the blade for L`or to see. 'It is as Airical has foreseen, the blade has been recovered, and the portal destroyed. And now we come to it at last, the final stage of the journey, the reforging of the blade, and the return of the one…' L`or speaks softly to himself.

'Then we don't have much time, where will the blade be taken, and how will we begin to renew that which was broken?' Hernan asks.

'There is a place where we can go. Far across the southern seas, past the domain of the Sasparians, is an ancient land where a powerful tool, an anvil of divine power is said to be hidden away. This island very few have ever set foot upon, and few eyes have seen. Neither Civilian, nor Gormon has ever seen or been to this place, Asyndians eons ago used to take pilgrimages there, to give offerings to Sasparia, the Aurora who watches over the vast oceans and seas. Shemoga was her sister.' L`or replies.

'Sister?' Hernan says.

'Yes, and her sadness rages the calm waters, tidal waves destroy passing ships taking the southern straits, and her people would pirate and steal the fallen cargo for themselves, and take prisoners to their palaces and underwater cities, so we must be on our guard.'

‘Where can we find a ship? Are there inhabitants of these shores still, or have they all long since fled or been killed by the Skahljah?’ Hernan asks.

‘The villages have long been abandoned, except for a few more archaic groups of Skahljah still skulking and prowling about the area.’ L`or holds up his finger with caution. ‘The Skahljah that were under Ja`kal’s rule were deadly, but the feral Skahljah, the berserkers and barbarians of the desert are deadlier, for they do not rationalize, they don’t think, nor feel, they are pure instinct. The ship we are looking for is at a dock further south-east, in the village of Shugoa, the Bindock is a war galleon captured by the Skahljah, it was once used for siege by the Gormon.’ He turns to Roaur. ‘Do you know anything about sailing Master Gormon?’ L`or asks.

‘My father had books on sailing, and the ancient galleon wars. I am not one of the folk who lived north by the waters and inland seas, the fishermen Gormon who would hunt Friemisk and other sea creatures, but I could figure out how to run her, just give me a good navigator and we’ll be set to go.’

‘Then ready yourselves gentlemen, for tomorrow we make for the coast of Shugoa.’ L`or announces to them. ‘With Ja`kal slain, these people should no longer worry about the constant attacks, for under Auth’s shrine they should be well protected, and the remaining Baldushan guards should be able to keep the situation under control.’

That night, the three stay outside by the fire. ‘Even though this has been a blow upon Kandarius, I fear the news does not get any better, for just a few days ago as I flew over Othetica, armies were marching within the gates of Novilon, armies of the black armor, the Dregor were slaying and burning all those in their path, the guards could not hold them back. They formed ranks in front of Othetian’s palace, where Kandarius spoke to them, in the vile, cursed language of the

Hexagus, his cold roar echoed into their heads, a command to make ready for something big, for I could not decipher all the words to know what he was saying.' L`or says to them.

'However, I have better news. West of here, in the lands of Runegard, an army forms, an army led by a young Captain of Othetica and the five Drog Riders. Armies of Gormon and Asyndian gather to form a final defense against Kandarius's reign; they only await the final weapon, Azalir, the Sword of Ages.'

An army, led by a captain of Othetica? Hernan wonders who this captain is, could it be possible? 'L`or, who is this captain you speak of?'

'Captain Cezius Cabriel, the one who brought down the Mirym attack upon Treefort, and beheaded their chieftain Glenheim, and now the chief's nephew joins our cause, for they have seen through the black mists of Kandarius's deceit and corruption.'

And that's when Hernan finds out that Cezius is still alive, and has regained the former honor that Kandarius had taken away from him.

Part XVII:

Sasparia's Storm

Hernan, Roaur, L`or, and a battalion of Baldushan soldiers to assist with manning and operating the ship, traverse the last remnants of the desert, for the soil begins to become more fertile, and patches of grass and sewn crops begin to blend into the scenery. The closer they come to the sea, the greener the area becomes.

With that statement, the group ascends a hill covered with yellowed weeds and crab grass within long strands and blades of unkempt brush and grass. The air smells strong with salt, and the reeds rattle and rustle upon the wind. Over the far horizon, is a vast open plain of sea and ocean as far as the eye can see, a marvel to behold. The skies above are a smoky blue, and overcast with darkened clouds, the morning sun now passing into afternoon. Faint rays of light shine through, piercing onto the beach, turning dull, dry sands to speckles of golden dust and shimmering highlights. The pale tide washes upon the abandoned shores of Shugoa, the fishing village looms in the wake of tidal waves and coursing winds.

Far out upon the edge of the reeds, are the remains of a broken, ruined pier, and a dock left in shambles and disrepair, a dock made of sandstone and decayed, weathered mortar. Anchored to the dock by a hulking hide of rope, some two feet in thickness, and maybe hundreds of feet in length coiled like a mighty guardian snake, is the titan of vessels, a god amongst ships, slayer of sea serpents, a ship that has been through more sea battles and maritime warfare than any other vessel carried across the waves. The Bindock courses upon the tides and sea, its battle ground, its field of war and massacre, where the blood of its victims gushes forth and settles upon the bottom of the sea. Dried blood and encrusted bile that's picked at by the ravens and sea vultures, stains the haul, from a boarding that has been turned into a massacre. From the blood soaked masts, hangs the rotten head of a decapitated sea creature several yards in length, and many tiny shell fish and crabs have crawled their way up the planks and timbers, to reach and devour, and pick away the expired flesh piece by piece.

The Bindock's massive boards and planks are impenetrable, a Fausengard galleon from ancient days now long passed, now only an empty shell, and a barren cargo haul without crew or captain to lead her into war once again, and steer her course into victory, and annihilation of her enemies, legendary, undefeated status. The Bindock is armed with heavy cannons upon the sides, hidden under opening and closing planks in the sides of the ship which reveals them whenever an enemy is near to strike and extinguish, sending the ship down to the depths.

Mounted at the stern and at the front of the ship, are two heavy ballistae, which are loaded with heavy bolts molded from pure bronze and tipped with jagged, serrated arrow heads about five feet in length, fitted upon shafts about twenty feet long, tipped at the opposite end with silver fletching. The ship itself stands several stories tall, fifty feet wide, and about ninety feet in length, from stern to the forward. The crew would have had to climb some hundreds of stairs to reach the higher platform of the Bindock.

Hernan, Roaur, L`or, and the soldiers cross the dirt streets, and past the abandoned shacks and homes of Shugoa, the smell of the sea becomes overwhelming with the stench of rotten fish, and what smells like decayed flesh. The living conditions of these people were deplorable, Hernan and Roaur, as well as the other soldiers grasp their faces tightly, covering their mouth and nose, but the fowl air is too strong for them to stomach, a few of the soldiers rush behind the buildings and vomit their bile of sickness across the decrepit dirt. After everyone recomposes themselves, they move forward towards the pier, the mighty titan of the sea lays in sight, towering above all buildings and houses of the village.

They follow along the most direct street, following the captain of the soldiers who interprets the Baldushan language written poorly from a white chalky substance, that's been etched and scrawled across swelled boards and signs from one who was illiterate, boards that have been ruined and warped by the sea air and caked on with barnacles and fish bones. But as they go along, one of the soldier trips over something and is left behind, the others march further ahead in a quick but cautious pace. The Baldushan soldier turns to see what the object was he fell over, for it felt sort of soft and brittle, and made a snap as his leg landed upon it when his body hit the ground. The others hear a scream behind them, and realize one from their group is missing, and they go rushing back towards where the scream came from, and where the Baldushan soldier was left fallen, in front of a disturbing and grotesque sight.

Hernan and Roaur reach the soldier first and help him to his feet, the others arrive close behind. 'What happened?' Hernan asks the horrified soldier. The soldier says nothing, only simply points towards what he fell on, a corpse that looks as though it has been eaten, for pieces of flesh were gnawed away, fingers had been bitten off, the eyes slurped out of their sockets, the ears severed, and the guts torn out and scattered about. When the soldier calmed down, the others began to hear a faint noise, but was close to their position, it sounded like shuffling, tearing, and a noise that sounded like chewing and splattering.

'Wait here a moment.' Roaur walks around the back of the old shack were the body was found, and walks down a shaded alley. The sounds become louder, and sound more and more grotesque, the squishing of slimy substances and tearing of parts or pieces of something. Around the next corner, someone, a figure scarred by some form of leprosy and welts attacks Roaur, grabbing the towering Gormon around the waist, and when Roaur looks down, he hears the sound of teeth clanging upon his gauntlets, for the figure is trying to bite him and claw at him. When the teeth bite Roaur's steel gauntlet, they scatter into pieces upon the ground, broken and shattered. Roaur picks the foe up like a rag doll and throws him into the far wall. The figure hits the wall and splatters into slime and bloody, gooey chunks of flesh and rotten muscles, the skeleton explodes and bones go flying all over, the brain slides down the wall and melts to goop as it touches and lays upon the ground.

'What sort of thing is this?! What happened to that man?' Roaur asks aloud to himself. He then hears a voice from above, for L`or has been flying over head providing extra sight for him, but L`or didn't see the sudden attack upon Roaur, for these beings appear to be ordinary Baldushan people, only sick and stagger in their walk cycle, barely able to stand as if in some sort of trance or under a spell of some kind. 'Roaur, look out... ahead of you!' L`or yells back, and Roaur rushes around the corner, to witness a massacre, for several hundreds of these beings, legions of them feast upon the flesh of the fallen villagers, the Baldushan fishermen and their families, that were unfortunate enough to fall victim to such a horrible fate. These fiends were not cannibals, they were not living, they were different than those they feasted upon. Roaur could see other dead bodies rise up and join in the feast. Blood, guts, fluids, limbs, slime, and bone were being thrown and strewn across the area, and other unnamable, abominable acts of violence and maiming, torture and animalistic feasting, were taking place.

A few stopped their dinner and looked up to see the fresh living corpse of the Gormon standing before them in shock and awe. They could smell his blood boiling, and hear his heart pounding, *a fresh meal for their rotten, gutted stomachs* they thought to themselves, for these are creatures of pure instinct, they only have one need...to feed and nourish themselves, but their feasting is eternal, and their hunger never satisfied, never ending, as is the curse placed upon them, a curse not yet explained.

One by one, the creatures leave their corpses, the ones they have left slain and bloodied across the ground, and head for Roaur. 'Roaur, here they come, get out of there!' L`or yells, and soars back to warn the others. Roaur turns and hurries back, screaming for the others to move. Hernan and the others ask what happened, but he would not say, he only ran passed them in a blur, urging, pleading for them to run. Hernan looks above and sees L`or.

'Hernan, follow Roaur and run, we need to get to the ship immediately, hurry up and get yourself and those men out of there!' L`or flies off towards the ship, and Hernan and the Baldushan soldiers see the walking dead approaching, and they scramble, running through the streets towards the Bindock. The undead stumble and drag themselves along, but have an unnatural speed that keeps them moving, and swiftly, for they manage to catch up to Hernan and the soldiers, closing in on their heels. Two of the soldiers fall behind, stumbling to the ground. They try to fight off the approaching hordes, but to no avail, the creatures simply turn them into a bloody, torn apart mess, as the soldiers scream in agony as these blood thirsty beings rip into their jugular, tear off the armor, and gouge open their stomachs.

The Bindock awaits, just over the far street, on the other side of a skirmisher long-house. They reach the pier, and ascend the hundreds of steps up to the Bindock's deck. L`or is already perched on the sails above, keeping look-out, and Roaur is at the base of the steps ready to push off. When the last soldier is on board, Hernan and Roaur push the titanic vessel with their great strength, and once the ship is in motion, and a strong wind catches the sails, Hernan and Roaur grab on to a rope that the captain of the Baldushan throws to them, and they climb up, and undo the massive anchor keeping the ship at bay. They turn back towards the docks and see the dead amassing upon the edge of the pier at a standstill, their lips red with the stain of blood, while some loom too far and drop into the murky ocean depths, sinking like lead to the bottom.

At first, the seas are fair and calm, but on the horizon, there is a storm brewing, and is approaching with swift speed. The thick black clouds of the mighty typhoon are near. Faint taps and sparks of lightning strike here and there, the waves are beginning to pick up. A few of the soldiers are gripping the thick ropes latched onto the sails, trying to hold down the masts, as the wind begins to pick up. L`or sits perched upon the mast, in concentration with his eyes closed, in a meditative state, his feathers rustle in the wind. Roaur hangs onto the wheel, keeping the ship heading south along the ocean, a few miles off the coast of the western lands, but keeping their distance, avoiding the treacherous reefs and wreckage of other ships, but in honesty, and as I have mentioned before, those rocks could not harm this vessel.

Hernan walks about, observing what is going on, and planning what the next step will be once they reach the Southern Isles, how he will reforge the blade, what materials will be there to use? Gonun said he would know, for it is a natural instinct for a Forgemaster to know what to use, and where, why, and how. Hernan knew the natural metals, for example iron, steel, bronze, nickel, metal to that nature. He knows of Aeridric, for Gonun showed him its properties, by examining his hammer, and through forgotten lore found within old tomes and scripture, and through these passages, taught him how to use its alloys and work with the metal, for it is treated differently than simple steel or titanium, Aeridric is a sacred metal, very rare, and usually never seen by most beings.

Its existence has gone into myths and legends, only the Auroras, and those Forgemasters' who were trained in its craft know where to find it and how to discern its properties and what it looks like. Gonun's Hammer is made of Aeridric, and the piece remaining of Azalir is made of Aeridric, though its essence has been depleted and cooled, for Aeridric, when crafted into a weapon, burns a powerful glow, from the energy it gives off. This is the secret that allows Aeridric metal to never have to be sharpened, its glow slices through anything with its heated flame and burning strike. Even the remains of Azalir, though it no longer has its glow, is such a powerful weapon, forged for the Hero of Ages, that it still retains some of its former sharpness, and could still easily kill most foes who would be stabbed with its remains, and with Hernan's powerful strength, would make it an even deadlier weapon.

Hernan walks over towards the mast where L`or has settled himself and calls up to him. L`or awakens from his meditative state and looks down at Hernan. 'How long until we reach the Southern Isles?' He asks. L`or sits still and silent. Something unsettles him. He looks off towards the gathering dark clouds and the bolts of sparks and lighting.

'That storm...this is no ordinary storm.' L`or says. Hernan looks off to the horizon where the darkness moves across the front of hot air and heavy winds that howl through their ears like screaming banshees, driving the storm to them, and steering the ship closer and closer to the dark clouds. 'Can you smell the air, listen to the winds...' The others over hear L`or, and they all stop and gather towards the front of the ship and gaze out, they cannot hear anything. 'I hear nothing, Asyndian.' The captain says.

'There is a faint voice, for their is sorrow and mourning. The rain is tears, and the thunder is anger...the lightning, rage.'

'Is it Sasparia?' Hernan asks.

L`or nods. 'It is as I said, she has been mourning all these years over her sister's death, but there is something darker here in these realms with us. Her mind seems...twisted. There is no way to avoid this storm, our fate is bound to go through.' He turns to Roaur at the helm. 'Roaur, keep this ship as straight as you can, for a wrong turn in this storm will put us in the wrong direction, and we cannot allow for any delay, our time has run thin.'

'What of Sasparia?' Hernan asks.

'Sasparia will not welcome intruders to pass her seas. If she spots us, she will no doubt try to destroy us. But her rage and sorrow blinds her, she may not notice, but we must approach with great care.' L`or replies. They take their places and man their stations, for the storm will be upon them within the coming hour.

The waves clash and the thunderous roar of the sea rocks the Bindock back and forth, tossing the lot of them from one side of the deck to the other. The soldiers grab hold of the ropes and hang on, trying to keep them aloft, but they hear a snap, and the mast towards the rear has snapped. Roaur handles the wheel, keeping the ship steady and maintaining its course due south, but he struggles for the raging storm and wild seas clash and thrash the Bindock from side to side, for as L`or said, this was no ordinary storm. There is water, water everywhere, and all the boards did shrink, there's water everywhere but none for Hernan, nor anyone else of the crew to drink. Sasparia's curse rages on and on at sea, Hernan rushes to the side of the Bindock; a powerful wave knocks him backwards, and sends Roaur to the deck face-first, the ship begins to circle around and around, until Roaur shoves his way through the pounding waves and takes back control of the frigate.

Hernan grasps the side of the ship once more and looks out to the endless sea of waves. He hears a distant sound, a slicing and pounding upon the water, a titanic being is splashing about, and out to the distant horizon, an opaque silhouette thrashes about, it's the shape of Sasparia, her rage boils the seas and causes the waves to rise up skywards and tumble down again, filling the mouths of the crew with sea water and soaks them head to toe in a hurricane of her tears and sadness, her howls and cries scream with the winds as they pierce and shatter through the darkness. The sound is excruciating to Hernan, Roaur, L`or, and the other soldiers as they grasp their ears to muffle the noise.

Then, the dark shape of Sasparia vanishes into heavy rain, and descends beneath the waves. L`or grasps Hernan by the arm and pulls him away from side of the Bindock. 'She senses we are here,' L`or cries at the top of his lungs, for the sounds of the winds and the storm muffle his stark tone, 'Sasparia has other creatures of the deep, and they will protect their territory, and their queen.'

They look below, and heading for them is a trailing ripple of water several feet in width, it reaches the ship, and then sinks down under, before vanishing from their sight. Something begins to pound upon the ship, a forcc morc powerful, blunter than the waves, with punch after punch, the vessel shakes and rocks, and as fast as the pounding occurs; it stops, for a moment.

The stark roar of the siren cries out, and rising up from the nearby bubbles and mystical light, is the Aurora of the seas, Sasparia, ruler and seer over this dominion of Aura. Agonan once said that some Auroras do not know or remember the prophecies and the telling of the Forgemaster. Sasparia was one of those Auroras, for she cares little for stories and legends, or the affairs of Civilians, Gormons, or Asyndians, and more recently she has all but abandoned her own Sasparians, who dwell in aquatic cities far beneath the southern seas. Ignorance maybe, but could it be, this ignorance or denial is not wholly her fault, for a different cloud looms over the mind of the Aurora, not just a veil of sadness, but a mist of twisted fingers, and manipulated beings that plague the Aurora's mind.

Sasparia looks down upon them in scorn. She speaks and her voice rumbles across the waves and clouds like a gaping earthquake forming and splitting the deep sea bed.

'You dare to cross my seas! You dare to trespass in my domain, I stir my waters, I curse the tides, till all ships sink, and all beings die, and the final plague is washed away! All shall drown under my tidal waves of terror, the drowning pool is rising, and bodies will fill my seas, a debt to pay for my sister's death that you puny beings created! A debt that will never fully satisfy my blood-lust, for my storms will never cease until my waters are red, with the blood of Aura!'

Hernan, Roaur, and the others watch in awe as L`or flies into the sky and faces the Aurora.

'Are you not a protector of this realm?! Do you not hear yourself? The Dregor are poisoning your mind, and twisting your words. Your sister's death was by the hands of a Dregor warrior, not by the Baldushan, not by the Civilians, nor Gormons, or my Asyndian brethren. This is the plot of a despicable one, a monster that would see you bend to his will, and turn you into the creature he is! He uses you against us, you are under his control. If you want retribution for your sister, let us pass, for we must reach the Southern Isles! This is the Forgemaster, bound to the fate of the sacred blade, and the fate of your realm, of Aura! For he is the one who slayed your sister's murderer! Let him pass!' L`or spoke in a tone of godly proportions, matching wits with the Aurora of the sea, trying to put reason in place of sadness and rage, trying to release the poison he knows Kandarius is responsible for.

Sasparia casts down the Asyndian. Striking him with a powerful blast of energy, sending his limp body down into the sea, were his body is taken by the powerful waves. The winds howl, and the waves rise up, Sasparia ascends above the waves, her massive tail wraps around several hundred times and soars and whips in and out of the storm clouds.

'Curse the words of this vile Asyndian creature, my waves and tides will clip his wings. None control me, for I am an Aurora, a superior being over all, and none can defy me without penalty of pain and death. Your ship will be dragged down into the darkness, forgotten among the rocks and whirlpools of Plathus Czern, and the ruins of Yivv`, for I summon the deep one, the old one! My champion, my guardian, I will awaken him from his slumber, and there will be no hope left for this realm, for he and I will plunge Aura into a deep, dark watery grave! Come my chosen one...Arise Talphoon, your war is done, and your slumber is over, arise from your fallen realm, for I call you to the surface to serve me once more!'

The world shakes, and the sea bed cracks asunder. Something monstrous, colossal, something huge comes, approaching with all the fire and hate of the Aurora's rage. A large whirlpool forms and sends the Bindock around in concentric circles, faster and faster in a circular motion. Sasparia makes no motion of her goddess figure, she simply holds out her arms and hovers in concentration, muttering the words to summon Talphoon at the center of the whirlpool.

Several shadowy fins and serpentine creatures and shadows dart in and out of the whirling waves, and surround the Bindock. Hernan and the others grab hold of what they can, and hang on tight, for the motion and force of the whirlpool is wanting to knock them off balance and send them overboard. Hernan watches the shapes carefully, wondering what monstrosity they will have to face this time, what sort of slimy writhing shape will rise up from the center of that gaping maw in the ocean that spins their ship round without end.

All at once, several long tendrils reach out from the water and wrap around the Bindock. The tendrils are heads, several of them, for their razor sharp teeth and beaked faces rip into the wood and boards, the impregnable Bindock is being torn asunder, the masts torn down, and several of the soldiers are snatched up. The slimy scales and heads of the beasts twist themselves around the deck several times over and squeeze tighter and tighter, the Bindock, the ship that was supposed to be impenetrable, is beginning to crack and give way. The whites of their eyes are filled with fiery green orbs, as the slimy coating of their eye lids pulls back as the true terror of their orbs are revealed.

They rear their daemonic heads, and their poisonous fangs appear when they open their vast jaws. The thick mass writhing through the waters which resembles a tail fin whips up the waves, and beneath the murky waters, are a ring of snorting bull heads attached to where a waist should be, they moan and roar with ferocity and frustration, waiting for their serpent masters to send them the bodies of the soldiers down into the waters for them to devour, as their dull teeth crunch the bones and swallow flesh, and the rags of clothes and pieces of blood trickling armor are left to drift in a forgotten sea. But as if the situation could not become more dreaded, rising up from the depths, is a lump of scales and flesh that the serpents and a ring of the snorting bulls are attached to.

The mountainous shape takes form, and Talphoon, the guardian of Plathus Czern, King of Yivv`, and God-Monster of the oceans, arises from his domain, an ancient ruined wasteland with crumbled palaces and fallen towers beneath the waves, in the mountain ranges below in the cold depths.

The titanic merman of the ocean stands some five hundred to six hundred feet high, he wears a masked helmet made from the bones of an ancient sea monster, his eyes a piercing yellow, the armored, muscled chest built with power and defense, and his arms dominion and prowess. In his right hand, he holds a staff of sacred storms and destruction, built from the same sea monster's spinal cord, and carved with the ancient Sasparian runes.

The other hand is partially being devoured by a Tentacli` up to his wrist, a beast with eight writhing arms, with the tentacles wrapped around the wrist, all the way up to the shoulder. The bulbous head of the Tentacli` opens, splitting into four sections that peel backwards, revealing no skull, but a throat, a black hole that secretes slobber and other bile and juices. The Tentacli` is able to spray an acidic, poisonous, flesh dissolving slim. The Tentacli` is called Ioctura`, Talphoon's arch nemesis, both who are engaged in eternal combat.

Millennia's ago, Ioctura` invaded Yivv`, and waged war upon Talphoon and his ancient kingdom, for Ioctura` fought to try and supplant Talphoon and become Sasparia's champion, her new chosen one, and to make her his bride, and become the new lord of the seas. During their final showdown, Ioctura` locked onto Talphoon's arm, and the two became fused together, as Ioctura` tried to melt the arm away using the acid of his bile.

Now, Sasparia has summoned her champion, she has ordered the two to put aside this futile war of theirs, for they both serve her now, and Talphoon and Ioctura` decimate any foe, any intruder, any ship that dares to cross over the ancient kingdom were the lost war has been waging for eons, until slumber has taken hold of them, and they only arise when Sasparia summons them, and now these fiends that sail by the northern winds, in her eyes, need to be dealt with.

And now, at sea, the clash of the titans takes precedence. Hernan, the Forgemaster, and Roaur, the Gormon warrior, versus Talphoon the God-Monster, and his foe, Ioctura`.

Ioctura`'s skull opens, and sludge splatters across the ship, eating away the wood and metal rivets and plates. Hernan and Roaur dodge away but a few of the soldiers are caught in the downpour, their flesh and armor melts away in a ghastly ooze, as they scream, dying in the worst, and most excruciating way possible, as they watch their own flesh fall from their bones, and drip onto the planks and burn holes in the wood, then the waves wash them away. A large, corrosive hole is left, seeping down into the haul like a flesh eating disease, or an infected wound that spreads its sickness abound.

Hernan and Roaur jump back into the thick of the action with weapons blazing. With hammer and axe in each hand, he cleaves away at, and clobbers the serpent heads, spilling blood, ooze and water across what is left of the deck, for the battleground has almost rendered the planks to ruin, and instability. Roaur leaps into the water, and hammers and pounds away at the circle of bovine heads as they snap and bite at the Gormon. Roaur clobbers several of them into unconsciousness with the blows and thunderous slams of his hammer. Roaur grabs hold of the snout on the larger, more powerful head, the final one within the ring, and the creature bucks and whips him around like a wild bronco. Then the head bursts through the waves and sends Roaur high into the storm clouds, and he then plummets, hurdling back down from the sky, and crashes upon the deck, and through the haul, landing upon some piles of rope, and old dusty equipment used for the sea and warfare. He shakes his head, and it will take him awhile, but he tries to pull himself back up, and attempts to climb back to the deck.

Meanwhile, Hernan gets a running jump, leaps through the air, and grabs hold of the slimy, repulsive Ioctura`, catching one of the tentacles. The filthy head begins to open up once more for an acid attack, Hernan runs down Talphoon's arm, balancing himself, for the scales of his forearm, are slippery, and nearly impossible to balance one's self. Using a battleaxe, he cuts a deep chunk out of Ioctura`'s flesh, and gouges the large red opal of an eye, and the creature wails in pain from the attack, and bluish, oily blood gushes and drips into the ocean of storms and waves.

Hernan is thrown clear, towards a large formation of rocks and crags near a small isle towards the east. Sasparia looks down in rage, and can feel the pain caused to Talphoon, and she feels her powers begin to weaken, and something begins to come over her. She clasps her hands over her face, and slinks back down into the water, holding her thoughts in pain, as confusion takes hold of her. The veils begin to clear. Talphoon grabs hold of his hand in pain, and then something happens, for history changes, and the forces of the southern seas change, and takes on a new existence, an existence it once knew, but has long been forgotten. Ioctura`, the foe of Talphoon, the challenger to the thrones of the sea, dislodges himself from Talphoon's wrist, and falls, slamming with a cataclysmic splash, and sinks like lead, to the bottom of the sea, where the nomadic creatures, the scavengers of the seabed will consume the Tentacli` corpse.

It seems as though Ioctura` and Talphoon have shared a bond, for these immortal enemies were bound by a fragile lifeline, for Talphoon begins to stagger, and the titanic merman, the lord of Yivv` and guardian of Plathus Czern, the chosen of Sasparia, topples over and falls down into the whirling pool from whence he was summoned forth, causing a tidal wave that stretches for miles and miles in a seismic ripple across the top of the ocean, crashing down upon Hernan as he grabs hold of the rock face and hangs on with all his might.

The whirlpool swallows the Bindock, as it sinks down to the realm of the dead, where it has sent so many ships and the bodies of dead men in the past. In the end of it all, fate beckons her children home, and the sea has called the Bindock by name. The whirlpool subsides, and the waters turn calm. The clouds above begin to clear, and the sun shines and fractures across the water. Sasparia's rage is over, and her staggered body floats across the top of the water. Hernan watches as she begins to stir.

Hernan hears a splash from behind, and turns to find Roaur climbing up onto the rocks, soaked and worn from the battle. He stands next to Hernan, and they both look outwards and gaze up watching the dark clouds pass by, and away off towards the north.

'This is one less place that Kandarius will no longer have his grasp.' Roaur says to Hernan, who is lost in his own thoughts. 'What do you think Hernan, you look as though you have something on your mind? Is it Azalir?' Hernan doesn't say a word.

'We're almost to the island, and then the blade can be reforged, but the Bindock has sank, and we just need to find another way to get there...and L`or and the others...I fear there...' But before he can finish his sentence, a burst of energy flies forth from the water, and the Asyndian lands upon the rocks next to them, for L`or has survived the catastrophe. Unfortunately, the other soldiers have not. Roaur just looks at the Asyndian.

'I don't know why I even bothered to think you were dead.' Roaur says. L`or just chuckles at the simplex of the Gormon. He then notices the blank expression of Hernan, but can read his eyes, and can tell the Civilian has complex thoughts on his mind, complicated ideas he is trying to solve.

'Hernan?' L`or acknowledges Hernan, and slowly he turns in response.

'I don't know what it is, or why, but I feel something...I feel as though Kandarius is making our path to easy for us, he's leading us...I feel like a puppet on strings. Ever since he had control of my mind, he made some kind of connection, my nightmares, my choices, it feels as though I'm being led.'

'You call our little adventure easy? I mean, yes we've become quite proficient at monster killing and beast slaying, but I wouldn't say it was easy. This has been a long and dangerous road, and I'm exhausted.' Roaur grunts.

'I know this hasn't been easy, but it's just...he's playing some kind of sick game for his own enjoyment, his own sadism. He's having fun, before he turns all to ruin and then there will be nothing left to play with, it will be down to business for him. We have been cautious so far, and kept our feet, and paved our way, but I feel it in my bones, we've come to the point where we must be even more careful. We have almost reached the pinnacle, the point we have been questing for all this time. When we reach The Southern Isles, and the sacred anvil, once Azalir has been remade...' Hernan then silences himself.

'What is it Hernan?' L`or asks.

'There is something else...' He gathers them closer around him, and speaks in a whisper. 'There is something watching us, something following us...listening. I think you know what I'm talking about.' At first they are unsure, but then they realize that Kandarius's eyes and ears travel far, and Hernan realizes that Aumon, Kandarius's familiar, may be looming nearby. Roaur and L`or nod.

The waters open up, and Sasparia arises before them. Her demeanor is different, her eyes less dark, and the reddish glow, has now subsided and her bright pools of faint green and swirling aqua have returned. She looks down upon them and smiles, and acts as though she is seeing them for the first time.

'Wanderers...adventurers...I have not seen the likes for some time. I welcome you to my realm travelers, but where is your ship, for surely you have not swam all this distance, and with all that armor on?' She looks at them mystified, wondering how they crossed into her realm, for the seas stretch for miles and miles around.

The three of them look at each other, and realize that Kandarius's influence has left her in a state of amnesia, for she does not remember the storms, the battle, or anything else that has taken place.

'Ever since my sister died, my dreams became dark, and my sleep disturbed with omens and many faces twisting within a black mist. I feel as though I have just awaken from a long and restless sleep.' She adds.

Hernan steps forward to speak to the Aurora. 'We came this way by ship, but it has sank, we were able to reach this rock in time.' Hernan said nothing of the battle and the summoning of the God-Monster, for he felt some memories where better left suppressed and forgotten. L`or and Roaur go along with the story, and agree with what he is trying to do. She frowns, feeling sorry for the ship-wrecked company of hers.

'I am sorry for this, usually my waters are the safest, for I try to keep out all foes who would dare bring harm to my denizens and their cities. As payment for this debt, I can offer you my services, for my subjects, the Sasparians, live beneath these waves and have transports that will take you to where you need to go. Now, I will go and...Ughhh!!' A large, spiraled arrow made of coral and fossiled rock is shot into her chest.

Hernan, Roaur, and L`or turn and see a large armada of Sasparian ships that have emerged from their cities in their underwater crafts armed and prepared to kill the Aurora. Even though she does not remember, it was their cities that were decimated by the fighting between Talphoon and Ioctura`. Sasparia abandoned the Sasparians, in favor of her champion, and they have suffered for it, for now they travel in large colonies and live in their ships as they travel the seas like vagabonds. They have waited for many long years for the storms above to cease, and now they plan to exact their revenge. By spilling the Aurora's blood across her realm she was meant to protect, but because of Kandarius, she has contributed to destroying.

The Sasparians open up their hatches and climb out onto the banisters of their ships and look on as Sasparia grasps the arrow, and tries to cover her wound as she pulls the shaft away, tearing at her rib cage as it is removed. Their eyes of black pearl, filled with anger, watch as the Aurora begins to fall and keel over. She grasps for the rocks were Hernan, Roaur, and L`or stand, looking upon the entire scene in horror, as Sasparia's own people attack her. The three of them stand upon the higher rocks and yell out to the Sasparians and beg for them to stop, but the Sasparians glare back, ignoring whatever this band of misfits is saying, for they only want to see the Aurora die, for her crimes she never meant to commit, never even realized she was doing.

Another bolt strikes Sasparia, and she falls over upon the rocks. Her breathing is heavy and out of rhythm. She looks upon Hernan, Roaur, and L`or, then out to the horizon, as the armada close in around them with slow, chugging speed. The Sasparians load another bolt into the ballista, and are ready to fire. The lead vessel moves in closer to Sasparia and locks on target, the twisted head of the bolt at her face. The Sasparian leader named Fing` leaps from the vessel and walks towards Sasparia, keeping out of range to where the bolt will strike. He stands alongside the massive body of the fallen Aurora, and laughs at her pain.

‘So, my Aurora…any last words before this missile strikes the final death blow upon you…for all the pain you've caused our people?! You, the one who unleashed Talphoon upon us, and wiped out our cities, he claimed Yivv` as his own, enslaved the Sasparians, and instead of protecting us, you allowed this to happen. Many Sasparians were forced to fight his war against the Tentacli` one, Ioctura`, who brought desolation to the entire sea floor, and many fled in these vessels you see surrounding you, pinning you down, the way we were pinned down!'

'For thousands of years, my ancestors lived as vagabonds, marauders, pirates! We waited, and waited for the storms to clear, to strike you down. Like my father, and his father's before, we vowed to slay the one who brought this doom upon us, for I have laid eyes upon the ruins of Yivv`, and will one day see her halls restored, and swim across towers and lavish reefs of the days of yore.'

Fing` then turns and looks upon the odd company of the Civilian, the Gormon, and the Asyndian. 'The three of you have no business here! Leave...swim back to your lands if you must! If you don't, then we will be obliged to gut and skin you, and stick each of your carcasses upon the forward of my vessel, for I need a new figure head, and I will have three.' Fing` threatens them with the same murky laugh and deviant smile. His smile turns to confusion, for he soon notices the Asyndian has vanished. 'Where has the bird gone to!' He yells.

L`or uses his flashing speed and sores down from the sky to Fing`'s left hand side, and Hernan and Roaur look on, for they didn't notice L`or vanish either. With a clenched fist, and a roaring zoom, and rush of air that speeds by them, L`or slams the fist across Fing`'s hefty, scaly jaw, causing him to spit up a bluish, thick blood splatter. A number of the bigger Sasparians leap from their submerging vessels and charge at L`or, Hernan, and Roaur, but they flip and kick, jab and shove the Sasparians away, and toss some into the water. The leader regains his composure and sees the three figures standing over him, and the rest of the Sasparians are in worse shape than him, scattered across the rock, holding their backs, heads, arms, and jaws, soar from the beating they just endured.

But they still try to fight back, and that's when Fing` realizes he just can't win, and holds up his fist to cease the fight, and orders his fellow Sasparians to halt. Meanwhile, Sasparia's eyes fade in and out, in sorrow seeing the way her people are behaving, and why they say the things they do about her, and how they insult the company of three from the northern lands.

'Alright Asyndian, I don't know what point your trying to prove with this insult, or why you try to defend the crimes of this Aurora, and trespass upon our waters, but speak...it better be important!' Fing` snarls, but is more upset about his defeat to the three strangers.

L`or steps forward and glares upon Fing`, then looks about the other Sasparians as they stagger to their feet.

'Sasparia is not responsible for any of these atrocities to your kind, she was made to do this, possessed, and her mind corroded by Kandarius Lockmore, a Dregor worshipper, for he has already caused the destruction and downfall of Othetian, the Aurora of the Civilian people, for this man here, and this Gormon, and myself, has fought what monstrosity the Aurora became, and defeated its darkness, drove out Kandarius's power, but at the price of the Aurora's death!'

'I want all of you to listen, and listen carefully to what I say...this monster, this Dregor worshipper had control over your seas, the beasts that haunt beneath the waves, and your Aurora, your Aurora who now lays here dying in front of your eyes! And don't ask, for I know what you're thinking, how could you have known...but you couldn't , his deviance cuts deeper than you realize! If you heed what I say, and if you truly want to stop the one responsible for this treason upon your kind, then I ask the Sasparians...'

Fing` coughs up some blood, and laughs at the Asyndian. 'If you're asking us to help you, then you're wasting your time. We help no one, for we serve and assist only ourselves, we have for thousands of years, and will continue to do so!' Fing` motions to Hernan and Roaur. 'And what about this Civilian and Gormon, why does an Asyndian help them, for their kind has abandoned your own, since you wiped out half the land all those eons ago, back when having an ally meant something!'

L`or grabs the injured Fing` and lifts him off the ground by the collar of his garb, and stares directly into the Sasparians black eyes. 'Because it is this same fiend who has caused your people such nightmares to your existence, he is planning to bring about another Grey Age, to release the Hexagus Lords from the Wom, and bring about a total annihilation of us all, for only the Dregor will walk upon the dry, barren soil they will sow, and bathe in the blood and molten seas of those they burn and slaughter!' He releases Fing`, who falls to the ground.

'The Civilian is Hernan, he is the Forgemaster of Othetica. He and the Gormon, named Roaur, the greatest Gormon warrior who ever lived, seek to pass through to the Southern Isles. I am escorting them, to make sure they arrive without delay from stubborn Sasparians who seek to get in our way!'

Fing` stands to his feet, a look of anger comes over his face. 'The Civilians have long abandoned the Isles many centuries ago, and now they wish to go back...for what reason?! To claim more land for their greed, as they have taken within Aura, keeping the other denizens out of their empires!'

'Apparently Sasparians have trouble listening. Kandarius has taken over Othetica, and it's his darkness that spreads from the lands of the Civilians. The Forgemaster carries with him, the remains of Azalir, the sacred blade that was stolen from Gammafir, long thought to be lost, but was in the possession of the Dregor, and now is in our hands! That is why we travel south, to reach the Sacred Anvil, and reforge the blade.' L`or replies.

'You mean...impossible, the blade was lost! How can I believe you, for I never heard of this Forgemaster before, nor of any anvil? Then show me, Civilian. If you truly have Azalir in your possession, then you would have no problem showing me.'

Hernan undoes a golden chain that hangs over his shoulder and across his chest. He holds up the hilt, and remains of the broken blade. The Sasparians are in awe by what they are seeing, for the story was true, the blade has been found, the sacred one that was wielded by the Hero of Ages all those years ago, now hovers high above them, basking in the light, within the hand of the warrior who accomplished the impossible.

'Now will you let us pass,' asks L`or, 'will you let us stop the coming darkness? Will you help us bring down the Dregor and Kandarius's reign of terror!? Fight for us, fight for the Runegard, and all will be restored! We will stop the Dregor and bring down the Hexagus, but we need all the allies we can muster. Are you not a part of this realm, of Aura? I know cruelty has taken affect over you and your own, all of you, but if we make things better by beating down Kandarius until even his own shadow hurts...then the lives of all the Sasparians can feel better!' L`or exclaims in a dramatic speech to Fing` and the other Sasparians.

Fing` walks over to the dying Aurora, and leans his head upon her long arm, and places his hands upon her, saddened by what he has done, by the mistake he's made, for it was his command that put a bolt into Sasparia's heart and chest.

'My Aurora...what have we done...we did not know, and neither did you...can there be peace, will there be forgiveness, for if so, I will still bear this scar always upon my mind, until my body decays and my essence passes on into the halls beneath the waves and coral...' The other Sasparians huddle around her, leaving the vessels to drift upon the waves. She tries to speak to them, but her speech is weak, and she can only whisper, for her chest wheezes as she inhales and exhales. A faint trickle of blood runs down the corner of her lip, as she speaks her last words to her people.

'There are no tears, no apologies, no sadness or anger, no guilt...no grudges held...just make sure my death, and the death of our kind, our cities and realm, are avenged. Return Sasparia to its former glory, when we ruled the seven seas, and our waves were pure...and the ships' sails were carried...upon the...wind...'

Sasparia passes on, and her altar fades to grey and crumbles, for within the clouds of Athilnovia, within his ivory throne room, and perched upon his diamond throne, Airical's sadness is deepened as he watches the golden leaves fall from lithe and curved branches of the trees around his palace, and the bright skies darken. His thoughts descend further into an abyss, he feels...if this force, this power continues to gain ground over him and the other Auroras, there will be no return, and they will be locked away in that place, that nightmare, where Othetian had been kept for so long.

Fing` shuffles over to Hernan and looks upon the Civilian's chiseled face, and bruised lip. 'For the love of Sasparia to be renewed, and for this order to return to balance, we announce that we fight along your side! To avenge the wrong that has been done, and to take down this slimy, black sea snake called Kandarius, that you speak of! We sail to the Southern Isles, for we need to leave on the tide, our ships breath water like us, and use fins to power there way though any opposing waves or force. Come, for you have never truly swam or sailed like a true Sasparian, but today is your lucky day, for the chance may never come again. Now, all aboard, and we'll show you what sailing is all about!' The three of them board Fing``'s ship, Hernan turns back to the lifeless Sasparia.

'And what of her?' He asks.

Fing` bows his head in sadness.

'This…the sea was her realm in life…may it take here now…in death.'

Part XVIII:

Azalir

The waters bubble and foam, giving off a bright teal and crystal colored light, as the vessels of the Sasparians arise from the ocean, for their destination is in sight. Fing` walks over to the sealed door, where they would normally keep prisoners that cannot breathe underwater, and he opens the lock and mechanism, and tells his three passengers they have arrived where they wished to go. One after the other, Hernan, L`or, then Roaur, who had some trouble fitting through the tight, narrow passage due to his size, exit from the haul of the vessel, and out into the open air. They look out upon the water and see the islands before them and the armada of Sasparian underwater war ships from behind. The center island has mountainous peaks that reach upward some miles towards the clouds, and the lands are covered with thick forests and lush vegetation and flora, not to mention the many species of fauna which rummage and have made their habitats within this environment.

'Fing`, take Roaur and myself to the island, we we'll explore on foot to see if we can find the anvil. L`or, cover us from above.' Hernan orders and the others agree to the command. Fing` signals for the other ships to stay, while they continue on and sail towards the beach. Meanwhile L`or flies out across the waves and up to the furthest peak of the mountains, and looks about the vast scope of the island and the smaller surrounding island chains, he can see much, but cannot see through the thick trees below.

Hernan and Roaur reach the island and continue on foot. 'Wait with the ship Fing`, Roaur and I can handle things from here.' Hernan says.

'You won't have much to worry about, nothing other than the wild beasts have lived on these islands since the days you Civilians inhabited them.' Fing` reassures them, yet this made Hernan and Roaur think to themselves...*"Why did L`or say that the Civilians have never been here, if they did in fact, used to inhabit this area ages ago?"*

The two rush across the beach, and Fing` soon loses sight of them as they pass through the bramble of exotic trees and twisted vines. The Sasparian walks over to one of the nearby trees, and climbs up to the top, to pluck one of the fruits growing under the shade of the vast palm leaves. He grabs the fruit in hand and climbs back down; he sits upon the forward of his vessel, removes a sharp dagger from his scabbard, and peels away the thick, leathery hide of the native fruit, while waiting for the others to return. He looks up towards the mountains, and sees the Asyndian swoop down, for he must have either found what they were looking for, or he sees the others.

After hours and hours of searching the island, L`or meets up with Hernan and Roaur at a clearing in the center of the woods, where some old Civilian ruins still stand. They find nothing, not a trace of any anvil, or any traces that a forge once stood upon these grounds. 'Did you see anything L`or?' Hernan asks.

'Nothing, from the air I couldn't see anything, this forest is too thick. I flew down for a closer look, but…again I saw nothing, only these old ruins dotted across the landscape wrapped in these thick vines that may as well be mig webs. What about you two?' He replies, but sees the same disappointed looks upon their faces.

‘We searched every crevasse, every hill, every ruin, every cave…nothing.’ Says Hernan.

‘Even the keen sight of my eye could not find anything hidden in the darkest places of this island, where Lota’s tropical sun does not grant her light.’ Roaur replies, sitting upon a large rock and rubbing his one good eye he still has.

‘L`or, could Airical be wrong…?!’

‘It’s impossible…Airical has never been incorrect, Gonun himself said to Airical, that this is where the anvil was hidden, upon this island.’ L`or replies.

‘Gonun? Gonun told Airical, why was this never mentioned to me?! Roaur, did Gonun mention a secret anvil to you or Kerrun?’ Hernan asks Roaur, shocked by this sudden news. Roaur shakes his head no, and mentioning how Kerrun never heard or said anything to him. They each look back at L`or.

‘Airical mentioned that this anvil had been forgotten since the ancient days, even to Gonun himself, for even Auroras forget sometimes. Only within Airical's dreams did these visions of the anvil come to pass, now that our doom is nigh, and with Azalir in hand, has its knowledge become relevant. But I don’t understand why it isn’t here, where could it…’ A look comes over L`or’s face, he has found something out, and the islands where the key. ‘The Civilians left these islands because of the volcanic activity and quakes under the sea, which is what, split the island into pieces…I wonder, if the Anvil is…’

Hernan realized then at that moment what L`or was hinting at. ‘The anvil is under the ocean…! No wonder it has been forgotten, and no one has seen it.’

They return to Fing` and alert him of what they have to do, and wasting no time they prepare for the voyage to the depths of the sea, perilous to Hernan and Roaur, but an easy journey for the Sasparians. Hernan, L`or, and Roaur seat themselves back into the quarters of the vessel, and they submerge themselves, and head downwards, taken by the tides and descend lower and lower, until the gliding rays of light above them, disappear, and only the encompassing darkness of silent water surrounds them as they gaze out the small, circular window.

For hours, which seems like days, they search the murky depths, but without luck, or any sign of an anvil, or even a ruin or temple, since they have long turned to dust, and decayed away, eaten by the bacteria and slime that devours these particles away like acid, leaving barley a trace behind to be found or discovered by future civilizations and explorers. They were beginning to think the anvil had suffered the same fate, but they weren't sure what they were even trying to find, for they weren't sure if this was an ordinary anvil in size and make, or an odd and unusual contraption of the Aurora Gonun, but the only information L`or could tell them, is that it was created by the mountains and storms, thunder bolts and tidal waves, a natural formation in all sense, so they were seeking what would be a rather large object.

As the vessel descends down lower, Roaur's eagle eye spots something at the far bottom, not even the bottom but in the mists of a dark, yawning abyss, which seemed to hover in place, but the bottom could not be seen.

'Hernan, down further, and off to the left a ways…see it! That must be the anvil.' Roaur exclaims, pointing in the direction for Hernan to look out.

Hernan and L`or look out the window, Fing` and the other Sasparians see it as well, and they sail in for a closer look at the structure. Growing larger and larger as they flow near, is a colossus of the sea, a gigantic monolithic plateau some miles wide at the base, and stacked upon the base, is several layers one upon the other like a smooth, perfectly carved, perfectly symmetrical coal-gray titan of rock. At the very top, the pinnacle, seems to be charred and sparked with blows and pounds of great and mighty blasts, several thousands to be more exact, like a million suns crashed into the mountain, like flies to the flame, as though they could not avoid their fate. Crude thick pounds of iron ore, titanium, nickel, and hundreds of other alloys and minerals, were permanently welded on across the surface, from all the weapons and armor created by Gonun and his smiths all those eons ago.

'L`or, is that the Anvil?' Hernan asks.

The stern look in L`or's eyes was all he needed to see, and L`or replied. 'It is, the anvil of a forgotten period, hidden from all, where Gonun forged the sacred weapons eons ago to invade the Hexagus and drive them from soured lands!'

'We've found it…after all these days and nights of traversing land, forest, desert, mountains, and sea…after this long journey we've been through, we come to it at last, the climax, the final act…the end.' Hernan says with a sigh of relief.

'It's not quite the end, but we are nearer to our goal. What was once chance, has now become definite. The closer we get, the more the dark clouds above Aura will dissipate, and the Dregor and Hexagus threat will weaken, and become obsolete.' L`or replies.

Roaur, who still searches about the waters and scans the area for anything else, looks over to a cliff face about two hundred yards away and notices a massive winch made of Aeridric metal and still has a shine to it, but is covered with barnacles and seaweed, yet after all these eons sitting at the bottom upon these ancient rocks. The anvil is attached underneath by a mechanism that only the Aurora of metal and forge would understand, and is too difficult to explain with its vast networks of gears, wheels, leavers, and a primitive form of combustion not seen by those who dwell above and on land, and has never been discussed by ancient Aura histories or written about in ancient Asyndian or Gormon lore.

Roaur brings the winch to the attention of the others. This means the anvil did not sink to the bottom from quakes or tectonic separation of the isles, the anvil was hidden here on purpose by Gonun so no one would ever find out about its existence, but as has been already mentioned, he has not used the anvil since that time ages ago, he had forgotten, but was wise to tell one other, the Aurora Airical of the Asyndians, a being who has the power of foresight and remembers the recorded history of every event since the beginning of Aura and the Hexagus War, even when the Auroras came from the distant surrounding realms to bring about the end of the Hexagus tyranny. He knew Airical would remember, and the secret would be kept safe with him, even all others have forgotten and their memories fade with the past, and for all these ages, Airical has kept that secret, until the time was right to share.

They see the winch, and face a new dilemma…its size! For the winch is some three hundred feet in length, and the bolt at the center of the massive crank is the size of a small village in circumference. As strong and as powerful as the Forgemaster and the Gormon are, neither of them would be able to move the mechanism, even the entire force of the Sasparian armada would never budge the powerful gears and leavers.

For hours and hours, as day turned to night, and night to morning, a mist creeps across the bay and under their vessels that sit adrift upon the sea, and blanket the islands within an ethereal ghostly body, for only the high mountain peaks can be seen. With little sleep, and much on their minds, they ponder what to do. Every plan they think of, every idea, no matter how good at first they feel it is, has loophole after loophole attached to its scheme, and would never work. But unbeknownst to them, something stirs in the deep; something swims about the waters around them, hiding its bestial fins underneath the fog. A foe once thought dead is now rising, eclipsing the vessels within the towering height of his shadow. Talphoon has returned.

Everyone mans their stations and prepare for combat. Hernan, Roaur, and L`or draw weapons and ready themselves. The serpent heads, now regenerated, rise from the water and mists, and his right hand as well, has reformed itself, from where Ioctura` had dissolved its bone and flesh, and was cleaved away by Hernan, now swings down by his side fully functional and all appendages and muscles operational. He no longer wears the skeletal helmet of the sea monster he destroyed, and has lost the powerful staff he bore in his grasp. The snorting bull heads peak above the waves, no longer snapping or crunching, but simply stir in the calm. Talphoon swims over to the tiny ship were Hernan and the others stand looking up at him, he sinks down lower to their level where his yellow eyes, as large as two moons, stare face to face with him. The waves he makes, rocks the boat away, but Talphoon picks it up in his gigantic palm, and lifts the ship up, as Talphoon rises back up out of the water. The titan of the sea, speaks to them in a shaking roar, yet sophisticated in its tone, and not brutish and threatening as it once was.

'You may call off your Sasparians and put down your arms, for I am your enemy no more…I feel as though my mind has cleared, I can think clear again. But the memories are still strong, and I wish to right what I have wronged. Long was I a protector of these waters, like Sasparia and Shemoga, and I too, was brought under corruption, but the call was so powerful, I could not disobey…And now, look at what has become of all this…and now Sasparia is dead…' Talphoon speaks within his thoughts for a moment, and then continues on.

'I have been defeated by a powerful opponent, and a stout and strong warrior, the both of you,' He also refers to Roaur, 'and I surrender to you, and offer you my allegiance, if you will accept?'

'Many of our soldiers were killed by your beasts, and by all rights and justice, we should slay you! But I know these events were not your fault, or your beasts, and I think we could use the help of a God-monster with your power.' Hernan replies.

'Tell me what I can do, for I am at your call.' Talphoon replies with eagerness to help his new allies in this fight.

Hernan explains to the guardian of the seas their predicament, and he tells them not to worry, and as fast as he arrived, he was gone, disappearing in the wisp of a wave. Talphoon swims about the waters for some time, until he finds the winch and the anvil. Using his powerful hands, he clutches the mechanism with tight, white-knuckle fists, and using all his strength, the behemoth turns the leaver, with swishing pumping motions, gaining momentum with each crank and grind of the gears.

The world begins to tremble, the vessels above capsize and the Sasparians are scattered about the water. L`or takes to the sky, and Hernan and Roaur wash ashore one of the smaller reefs. All around, the seas ripple and bubble and the oceans part as the coal-gray anvil rises from the water, and ascends into the sky, and soon the far off pinnacle is lost beyond the clouds of Tundrok's realm above, and the vast base of the anvil is a solid dark slab that bridges the ocean and touches the edge of each island. After about an hour of the mountain rising, Talphoon halts turning the winch, as the last of the anvil is revealed, and the quakes and tidal waves cease. Hernan and all the others, swim over and climb upon the smooth, glassy surface of the anvil, and traverse across, sliding and falling as they proceed, soon reaching where the ascent to the pinnacle begins, for it stretches high above, beyond the thick clouds and into the realm of stars beyond the summit.

At the bottom of the anvil, where they stand, there are vast caverns and tunnels, much like a mighty fortress or keep where long lost secrets of the old world once resided and prospered, but now only thick waves of water and sand rush out and down finely carved steps and drip from empty halls and formed windows. Towards the top, they notice small working blasts and bellows where wood and coals would have been heated, for this was not just an anvil, but its own forge as well.

They look upon and gasp at its marvel, for it seems much larger out of water, than within. The colossus glistens in the morning sun. The mists begin to clear, and Talphoon arises once more, and swims over to Hernan.

'Is there anything else you require?' He asks the Forgemaster.

'No…at least nothing I can think of at the moment.' Hernan replies.

Talphoon tosses down to him a large curled up shell with a tassel of leather tied to each side for carrying. 'Use this to call for me if you need my assistance, for it will stir the waters, and I will follow the tide to where you are.' He bids them farewell and submerges himself, to wander the seas until he is called for, as he searches for whatever fate may bring.

Roaur walks up alongside Hernan. 'And now?'

'And now we get to work, Roaur.' He calls to the other Sasparians, and makes the announcement that he and Roaur are going to ascend the anvil. However, they first try to figure out how they will rekindle the long, barren and damp coals that would have heated the forge, but above the base, within the body of the mountain, just under the crown, the sound of some combustion engine roars, and a mystical flame ignites to burn the sacred coals. As Gonun said to Hernan, and Hernan already knew by the teachings of Kerrun, Forgemaster's have their own tricks and secrets, and this flame does not extinguish itself, but rather lays dormant until the air awakens it to melt and burn, roar and grumble, like an ancient beast from its slumber. All the tunnels and windows of the anvil's bowels and exterior are a complex system of exhausts and vents to keep the flame burning once ignited. The blaze is a towering inferno, as though the entire mountain were blazing in a cloud of swirling flame and smoke.

L`or flies about the anvil's perimeter, looking for a way up, and spots a set of stairs carved into the western cliff, and points out the discovery to Hernan and Roaur. They waste no time, and gather what few supplies they managed to hang onto and are about to begin their climb, when they realize they lack one vital, key ingredient…the Aeridric metal to reform the blades shape and structure. L`or then informs them, the entire mountain is made of Aeridric, for that is the reason for all the carved away chunks and layers of flats. This, in fact, is the only source of Aeridric metal in all of Aura, which is why the mineral is extremely rare, and very, very few have ever heard of or seen it first hand, or have been able to study its properties, meaning Gonun and his smiths are the only ones who have ever seen this colossal mound of sacred mineral.

But to break Aeridric is nigh impossible, for it is the hardest, most durable substance in all the realm of Aura and the Galakaos, and once the mineral is blasted in the furnace and shaped, a mythical ceremony takes precedence and makes the creation immortal and undying. There is, however, only one way to break raw Aeridric, and that's with another Aeridric weapon. Hernan raises the Hammer of Gonun, and slams the face of the blunt weapon down into the base of the anvil, causing a rift, a long and wide crack to form across the area. From this crack, a huge chunk of Aeridric breaks away and Hernan heaves it up onto the base near his iron bound, drog-scale boots.

Hernan lifts from the front, and Roaur heaves and carries from the back, and together they both lug the large piece of Aeridric up the many stairs that seem to stretch endlessly upwards towards a never ending pinnacle. The furnace swelters about them with thick, hot sweating air that blisters their rough skin, as the heat blasts upon them, feeling as though their armor is melting upon their flesh. The piece of Aeridric becomes hotter and hotter by the hour, and begins to burn their palms and fingers, making the burden of carrying this rock painful and uncomfortable to bear, but they trudge onwards and upwards still, undaunted, not fazed by the impossibilities of their task, with only one goal in sight. After days and days of marching and climbing, taking that final step, they at last reach the final frontier, the pinnacle, the peak, the crown of the Anvil King, the Forge Impirium.

Hernan and Roaur set the piece of Aeridric down near the center of the peak they stand upon, next to the anvil, and look about their surroundings, for they are well above the clouds and the entire realm of Aura that encompasses all the horizons onward in all directions. What they see below is vast plains of land and hills, desert colossi of Isa that lies of towards the north, and far beneath them, are the silent waters of the ocean that lay still, just a pale mirror of still water, reflecting light upon the most minute ripples.

Above them, looms the Galakaos, like a midnight sky that fades and blends into atmospheric space which stretches endlessly beyond the realms of Aura and across the Galakaos, where eternal limits of time are unbound and free. Though, the stars seem to shine less bright as of late, for even the potent, most sinister darkness, the one not seen by the naked eye, the sort of darkness that creeps near and behind you within the shadows but never reveals its true shape, this darkness covers all aspects of space and time.

The anvil is set like a massive, solid smooth surface, a table without legs, but is connected as one piece to the furnace maw. The blemished anvil is large in size, much larger than Hernan or Roaur, the size large enough for Aurora Gonun to use.

At the back of the anvil, set against an Aeridric wall, is the maw of the furnace, a gaping shape of wide jaws and jet black, charred teeth like those of a beast, and from the throat roars the flame breath of the forge within. Jutting outwards from each side of the metal beast's maw are rows upon rows of massive tubes and metallic pipes that smoke and bellow thick clouds of gas and sweltering blasts of heat pumping with churning, ramming force and power, releasing the exhaust of boiling Aeridric alloys and the breaking and tearing of the ancient gears from within whose friction burns with each crank and turn to pump energy into the fires that burn brighter than a thousand suns.

Within a special setting upon the sides of the anvil, are several tubes ranging in a variety of sizes from small to gigantic, which are filled with icy water gathered from the ocean's depths, each tube getting larger and wider in circumference the closer they form near the maw at the back of the anvil.

Hernan looks at Roaur, and Roaur nods back. 'Well…let's begin.' Hernan says and the two of them begin to work immediately, for until they can finish the blade, the darkness will keep getting stronger and stronger until it engulfs all.

The forge provides them with the necessary tools, such as special types of tongs, molds, several sizes of bellows and hammers, calipers, piles of rivets and bolts, thick and small gauges of nails, rope piled into tangled masses, talc, lime powder, piles of nickel, bronze, copper, and iron ore, as well as steel and titanium, as well as other anomalies of the forge that even Hernan has never seen, nor did Gonun or Kerrun ever mention, for their use and secrets were lost with the anvil, but Hernan and Roaur keep what they know and have learned at heart, and proceed with their work, for the reforging of Azalir has begun.

They put on their thick leather gloves and heave the piece of Aeridric into a large iron pail, where they melt the alloy down into a liquid that shines with a silvery, bright glow, and gives off a bluish flame, a mighty imbuement from the fires of the gaping maw, an enchantment that will follow the blade's molecules throughout the rest of the process. They boil the metal down to its liquid state, and while Roaur stands upon the anvil and uses a large pair of tongs to reach for the pail, and pull it away from the fire, Hernan places the mold for the blade upon the anvil and leaps upon the surface. He holds a second pair of tongs and places the vice around the pail, and on a count of three, they heave the mighty girth of the bucket up, and pour the volume of blazing metal into the mold. The Aeridric fills the mold quickly, rushing and weaving in and out of the smooth carving within, not leaving any air bubbles, and forming a perfect shape, symmetrical and precise.

They bind the mold, with a strand of the mystical rope, and attach the sarcophagus to a chain mechanism, and place the mold back into the fire, where it burns and absorbs the full effects of the anvil's sacred properties. After a period of time goes by, they pull the mold out by the chains, and lower the forging palate into one of the larger pools of ice water. The water sears and steam evaporates into the vast space above them, they wait, count to themselves, and then remove the mold from the water, and it is placed back upon the anvil. They cut the ropes away with a special knife, and like the exhumation of a corpse, they remove the lid of the mold, and there before them, lays a renewed, reborn blade.

They work throughout time upon their knees, kneeled before the altar of the Anvil King, and Hernan hammers away for many days and many nights with Gonun's Hammer and Roaur holds the blade turning and guiding the strikes of Hernan's blows upon the Aeridric, while also assisting with heating and binding the two pieces together, and with the final twang upon the Aeridric blade, it is done. Azalir, the Sword of the Ages, the blade lost to time, captured by the Dregor, the blade brought back from a long forgotten realm beyond the Mirror of Dregor, and now in the hands of the Forgemaster, is complete, at least the shape and form is complete, there is still the matter of renewing its power, for the jewels and the eye upon the center of the hilt, are dim and lay without power, the essence that makes this sword the mightiest weapon of them all.

Above their heads, an ethereal light begins to form, and glow and pulsate, an aurora borealis takes shape, transforming into a shimmering sheet of ever changing colored light across the Galakaos, and around them, the clouds shift colors and sparks of lightning jolt through the electrified, pulsating air. The jewels and eye upon Azalir begin to glow, for they have called forth to their masters of Aura, the many essences which travel through wind and grass, fire and water, soil and rock, seasonal harvests, living creatures of all kinds, the elements, pulsate within the hilt of the blade, absorbing the powers of Aura, drawing them within. The energy of the essence pulsates through the veins of the blade, and perfect it.

Azalir raises high into the abyss above towards the borealis, and hovers there in mid air. Hernan and Roaur behold its majesty with awe, and their eyes filled with the beauty by what they witness. Then, in a burst of light and a blinding explosion, which turns the dark sky into day, they close their eyes and raise their hands over their face to block the blurring bright light, more potent and more powerful than the brightest star. When the light dims, and the force of the explosion is now settled, and the Galakaos has returned to its balanced equilibrium of night, and the clouds reform into their menagerie of different clusters, and fluffy shapes upon the tide of the sky, reverting back to their usual patterns and movements as they glide upon the winds heading due west towards the sea in those distant lands.

Hernan and Roaur, once more, stare upwards to the vast dome above their brows, and they look, their eyes mystified, confused eyes ponder their mind and surroundings, and then within, to believe what they could not see, did not see. It was impossible, they thought to themselves, this cannot be happening, they were yelling to themselves. *"Why...what happened, what went wrong?"* They pondered and thought, and wondered aloud to the other, but neither had the answer. Azalir, had vanished, nowhere to be found, no trace, no sign, nor trail...nothing to show of its whereabouts...lost, gone!

L`or has witnessed this entire event further away from the anvil, from a distance, flying about the area, and he too was cast down by the spell of light, and the blindness of the explosion. Their hearts sank, for Azalir was gone, the most powerful weapon, and their one hope, has vanished from their grasp, and where it went, no one had any idea.

Hernan and Roaur descend the anvil's stairs, back down to where Fing` and the other Sasparians have awaited their return. There were questions from Fing' and the others, referring to the blast of light which shook the mountain,

"Where was the sword, what will happen now, what was to be done...?" But neither of them knew, nor did L`or have any idea of what was about to take precedence. Fing` could, however, see the anguish look within the Gormon's and the Civilian's eyes. The tired look of anguish and a sickened air of disgust was about them, for the two could only think about the worst ideas of what could happen now that their salvation could no longer be grasped by the hilt, and their victory, to plunge the blade deep into Kandarius's heart, was no longer an option, and then they thought of Kandarius, and what would happen if he found Azalir once more, they thought about what would happen to them and all of Aura, and the deep pit in their stomachs only became more sick, and their minds clouded over even more.

Their accomplishments, all their progress, was now lost and gone, *"all for nothing"* they were thinking to themselves. Their questions were still ten-fold and many. L`or was asking Hernan and Roaur what happened, what went wrong, while Hernan was asking L`or, drilling him for answers, why the sword would disappear, where would it go, is it still even in this realm, or a time a place like that of the Mirror of Dregor, where Hernan first found the blade, Roaur was at L`or's neck, and a fight was about to break loose, but the Sasparians calmed down the three travelers, trying to hold reason amongst the companions, but no one knew, and the Sasparians were caught in the middle of this confusion.

Once again, here they were caught in a dire situation, and for days and days, pondered furtively on what to do. But Roaur was not helping the matter, and today, he lunges out at the Asyndian, thinking his powers had something to do with Azalir's disappearance, but Hernan caught the massive, spiked-armored fist of the Gormon's wide hand, and held him back.

'Roaur...control yourself! Can't you feel it...the black mists of his presence looms all about us! This is what he wants, he's just toying with us, manipulating your thoughts and feelings...' Hernan yells, trying to get the Gormon under control.

At that moment, one of the Sasparians sees something approaching in the distance, great wings, flying fast and heading in their direction. L`or recognizes the shapes, for a small band of Asyndians approaches them. The three land upon the anvil base where the others stand. L`or recognizes them as his own brethren, not the outcasts who still dwell in the Greywaste, and he is the first to greet them. One Asyndian is a deep purple color, and his feathers tipped with a bright yellow highlight, the other further back is red, similar in color to L`or, but his feathers are much darker, and the third, a hefty, more muscular Asyndian, whose feathers are forest green, and tipped with a bright teal that reflects the sun's rays, the leader, steps forward and returns L`or's greeting. His tone is neither good, nor ill, but he speaks urgently, and at a quick pace.

'L`or, it is good that we have found you and the Forgemaster. Uthar `ra has sent us immediately, for something has happened and you have to get back to Runegard as quickly as you can!'

'What has happened?' L`or asks.

'The sword...Azalir has appeared in Runegard!' The purple Asyndian exclaims in an excited voice.

Hernan and Roaur over hear this and rush towards the Asyndian. 'What do you mean, Azalir is in Runegard!? How...when...how could this be?!' He asks.

'The blade appeared yesterday, it stands at the center of the city, but is surrounded by a strange field of light, and the blade is wedged into a mystical stone. The stone is causing the energy field around it, and no one can get near it.' The Asyndian replies.

'Why can't anyone get near it?!' Roaur asks.

'Our general says that it waits for the wielder to come, it waits for the One, the Hero of ancient times to claim and wield it once more, for he says that the Hero is near, and will soon reveal himself! You must come as fast as you can!'

'Return to Uthar `ra, and tell him we are on our way, and that we come with reinforcements, the Sasparians have agreed to help our cause. We will be there when we can.' L`or replies to the Asyndian.

The Asyndian nods, and the three take off, and fly back west, to Runegard to relay L`or's message, and to inform the King of Runegard to expect more troops. But this moment has come at last for Hernan, for this whole time, and for a while now, he has thought to himself, that once the blade has been reforged, once Azalir was whole again and in the hands of where it needed to be, he wondered...what would be his fate now, what would the future hold for the Forgemaster, now that the forging was over and done? What was his purpose now? What other quests and tales were spoken of, but lost in these prophecies of old, that the Asyndians and the ancients of the time foretold...?

Meanwhile, let's go back in time a bit, to the post-war at Treefort, and the events which took place after and surrounding the execution of Glenheim, chieftain of the Mirym tribes in the north. On the other side of Aura, General Cezius and an escort of Treefort soldiers, and the Drog Riders, are en route to Runegard, traveling along the eastern roads, going due west...

Part XIX:

Runegard

The Civilian army marches along the vast western road through the mountain pass upon their mighty hoft steeds and carry their spears and shields, swords and clad in armor, that clangs with each stomp of the hooves upon the stone roads, roads which separate each area in a triangle formation, with Greenhaven back east a ways in the distance, Runegard off in the west, ahead of their path, and Mirym further to the north, out of view over the other side of the snow-capped mountains. The blizzard-covered peaks rise upon their right side, higher and higher as the road leads them around a wide bend near the base of the mountains. A light, brisk snowfall covers upon their red faces and beards, as they ride under a cloudy sky and overcast of storm clouds, for the sky seems closed in and small, as if they were looking up from the bottom of a well.

"Stone by stone, wall and tower, we garrison our soldiers,

Brick by brick, sword, and shield, we defend divided nations,

To fend off jagged spears, and bring down shaded legions,

Of Dregor is our purpose. and surround Aura in the protective armor,

Of iron and steel, diamond, and titanium.

Tonight we die for Aura, we fight for the world!

Tonight the armies of all will band together, and Runegard will show its true might!

And maybe tomorrow we'll see the morning light..."

The snow lays upon the grass around them in a thin, inch thick layer, a light frost compared to the Glorial Tundra and the vast snowy plains which are hundreds of feet in thickness and their layers, the cold, barren plains where the Mirym dwell and migrate from area to area following their herds of Mirym Beasts, creatures that are about twenty to twenty-five feet tall, and are covered on their entire body and all fours with thick, burly layers of fur, and two long horns protruding from their head, and they move extremely slow with heavy steps, for they weigh about one thousand to two thousand pounds, and the females weigh more by about five hundred pounds, and when pregnant, their girth increases. The Mirym depend upon these creatures for their meat and fur, and for transportation across the icy realm.

Cezius and the Civilians have never had to endure the hardships of the Mirym, but in the days to come, all realms may yet feel the finger of execution by the Dregor, if they don't keep their feet, eye up the road ahead, and watch their backs.

They march over a steep hill that leads upwards a ways and at the peak, they can see a clear, vast, and distant view of the entire area for miles and miles around. Off to the southwest, the dark grey shadows loom over the Greywaste and the lifeless crust of what was once Asyndian territory, now home to nothing but land urchins, twisted creatures that feed on anything that moves, living underground, and hunting where the shadows are the darkest, for their two pale eyes are extremely sensitive to even the slightest glance of light, that is why when they hunt, they bask under their shells, and feel the vibrations of the ground, for the smaller critters to approach, and when near, the urchins open their shell, and pounce upon the unsuspecting prey with pincers and claws unleashed.

And feeding upon the urchins, are the fallen Asyndians, the ones who were left behind and never made it to Athilnovia with the more aristocratic Asyndians that follow under Airical. These are the creatures who served Naumokron, and they will sweep down upon the urchin shells, and tear the bugs from their homes, and carry their food back to their dens, holes, cliffs, or Naumokron's black fortress, and there they will tear the creature to pieces and eat it while still alive, as it squirms and twists, and cries out in pain, then silenced at the jugular by the kill strike of the Asyndians that hunt them.

Just ahead of Cezius and the other soldiers, off in the western direction, stands Runegard, beyond the plains, the cornfields, gardens, and the outlying farmlands and pastures where the cattle and livestock graze, off in the distance upon a rocky acropolis, surrounded by thick forests far below, and mighty towers that dot about the landscape, built in key strategic areas, patrolling and watching for any attack, and the two largest and tallest towers are based at the top of the acropolis, guarding the gates and walls. The wall itself stretches for miles and miles in each direction, north and south, and around in a perimeter of the stone buildings, shops, temples, and structures dedicated to the Runegard and their formation including banners of majestic blue with the symbol of their king embroidered upon the fabric and threads used to design and create them. At the front gates, and upon the forts and castle, are flags made in the same fashion as the banners, and stone idols of the king and Soldiers of Virtue who have died for a cause to form the Runegard and protect the king's lands, where erected.

Cezius rides at the lead of the marching troops, some hundreds follow behind, while the rest are still stationed back at Treefort as a precautionary measure, for the threat of the Dregor is still present, and their actions anonymous and erratic. Also with them are the hundreds of Mirym warriors, who met them at the cross-roads some miles back after days and days of travel, and marching at Cezius's side, is Glenheim's nephew, Brihem, riding upon a dark grey, and spotted white hoft, the size of a great mare in stature.

Shoranna and the other Drog Riders patrol the skies, keeping an eye on the shadows from the south and east, and from the rear, towards the direction of Othetica. From the way they witnessed how the Dregor move about and sleek past Lota's watchful eye, in the shadows of their master's dark hand, and deranged influence, they weren't taking any chances.

The sentries of Runegard see the army approaching, and that General Cezius Cabriel rides at the lead. The Asyndian alerts the Gormon's at the gates below and to the Civilians upon the north tower, and a horn is sounded, and bellows deep and through the air for miles around, catching the ear of Cezius, Brihem, and the others. The two husky Gormon gate masters, crank and turn the wheel and chain, and the thick mighty gates of bronze, hardened oak planks, and silver riveting across iron bands give way. The mechanism creaks and the metal grinds as the gates open inwards, and a long, colossal draw bridge unfurls and gaps a deep and vast ravine below, bridging the chasm between the acropolis and the steep hill upwards to the gates.

All within the city, Civilians, Gormons, Asyndians, one and all, cheer and praise the return of their own, but those who did not return will be mourned throughout the night, by those who have survived them. Some refugees and families have come to Runegard and have settled throughout the years and centuries, but the fortress within the realm is primarily a military instillation, so those whose families are still living in their own lands and homes, word will be sent to them, written and signed by King Edrin, ruler of Runegard and those within his realm.

King Edrin is not an Aurora, but a Civilian mixed with a Gormon, and he received his lessons on politics, history, speech, writing, combat, defense, and many other skills from the Asyndians who would fly down from Athilnovia and tutor him and his people. Edrin learned from an early age the importance of all races and to learn to respect all, so when Airical came bearing the idea of creating a force to unite the races of Aura if the threat of the Dregor ever returned, he agreed to make Runegard the base of operations, for all were welcome within his walls, and were free to council and discussion. Plus, Runegard was settled under the clouds and mountains upon which Athilnovia was settled, high up in the sky, out of reach of all, except for the Asyndians who could fly and reach her walls and golden towers.

Even though the greeting was warm, the air about the area is cold, and the grim gloom and tone was set under the eyes of all within. Even though the battle at Treefort was won, the war was still far from over. The situation was on the minds of everyone...what was Kandarius planning? What was he waiting for? Where would his next strike be and when? Why...would such a deadly and powerful force stay hidden in the shadows and not strike outwards at the armies building in Runegard, where all have gathered in unison? *"What was he waiting for?"* was the question every Civilian, Asyndian, Gormon, man woman and child...was repeating to themselves. Even Cezius and Brihem were curious what the sorcerer was up to.

The soldiers settled back to their rooms, warm beds and baths, rest houses, temples, to their wives and husbands, and children, for the many men and women were exhausted and ready to sleep in a comfortable bed after being stuck in the trenches and behind the barricades of Treefort for so long.

Cezius and Brihem went to the palace to speak with Edrin immediately, for the Mirym were already receiving punishment and threats, and if it wasn't for Cezius, they would have been rounded up, and Brihem would suffer the same fate as his uncle Glenheim, but Cezius would not allow one Mirym to be touched, and the Gormon, Civilians, and Asyndians scoffed at the general and kept away and went to tend to their own who have returned after so long, and the Mirym were left alone, crowded along the streets, twiddling their thumbs in an unfamiliar place, with beings who are alien to them, and their barbaric, savage ways, and they, the Mirym, being alien to the others as well. They sat and waited for what was to happen, if the king would spare them, and allow them to join the cause and fight for the Runegard, to have their lands open to them once again, and to escape the cold, harsh waste of their northern homeland.

The soldiers guarding the throne room open the doors for Cezius and Brihem, and they rush in and across the dull, gray stone of the floor. The throne stands empty, for Edrin resides over at the far window and looks out upon the vast courtyard below. Cezius and Brihem approach the king. Edrin turns and looks upon them with a smile, but is confused to see Brihem standing alongside the general.

'Cezius Cabriel…I was wondering when the magnificent general would once again grace my halls,' He gives Cezius a warm hug. 'It is good to see you again old friend!'

'And you, King Edrin…It's good to see your still in good health and standing with all that has been going on.'

'Thank you Cezius. When Airical came and told me that the Grand General of the Runegard armies was going to be you, my heart leapt, I said to myself, 'Damn it, now we have a chance at this war, these Dregor bastards won't stand a chance! Then when I saw the armies of Treefort returning, I knew our troops did it, and then I saw the Mirym as well, and I wondered what was going on, why we marched together in unison,' He looks upon Brihem, 'for I was under the impression that the Mirym wanted to rid the Civilians from Greenhaven, by destroying us all, and joining with the Dregor to rule over us all, perhaps this Mirym can explain.'

Brihem stepped forward and spoke. 'I can explain, King Edrin. My people were deceived by the lies spilling forth from the black tongue of Kandarius Lockmore! He poisoned the mind of our Chieftain, my uncle Glenheim. Cezius has showed us the error of our ways, and my uncle had to pay with his blood.' He kneels to one knee and bows his head. 'I have offered my allegiance to the Grand General Cezius Cabriel, and now I and my people offer our arms and blades to the King of Runegard, and all the Gormon, Asyndians, and those who dwell in a realm free of Hexagus and Dregor rule! If you will accept my honor, for I give my life if I must. The Mirym give their blood to the cause of Aura!' He stands and raises his spear towards the king. Edrin waves for him to lower his weapon, and nods in agreement.

'The dark one is cunning, and his influence slips through on the haunches of a silent, black cat. Welcome to Runegard, Master Brihem, Chieftain of the Mirym and warrior of the northern ice lands. Go to your people, and tell them no more harm or insult will come to them, by law; you and your people are under my protection. Go to them, and tell them they may use the north-west tower for their quarters, I will send for my subjects, to bring them food, drink, and whatever they may need, for we are an army now.'

Brihem stands at attention and bows to King Edrin, then leaves the throne room, and heads back to the Mirym, to collect his people and head for the tower, while being escorted by two Asyndian soldiers to make sure all goes well and they remain safe from any unsavory thugs or those who would want to try and harm the Mirym.

‘And now Cezius, or should I refer to you as Grand General of Runegard…I have something to show you, something that I think you’ll be quite pleased with…if you’ll just follow me.’

Edrin leads Cezius over to the window he was looking out of earlier, and they walk out onto a wide open balcony. The balcony oversees a great courtyard below, and within the vast high walls and columns holding up great temples and buildings, while around the area, stands line after line, legions and legions of Gormon and Civilian troops, and high above the white clouds break, and the golden light rushes outwards in a ethereal, mystic power, a force of good that has not been felt in a long while. The gates of Athilnovia have opened up, and flocks upon flocks of Asyndians clad in light battle armor, wielding sacred spears and scepters imbued by the magical essence of the Twelve Altars that still stand, well at least ten do now. They land upon the grating at the top of the walls, and emerging last from the golden sky of dawn and dusk, is the Aurora’s general, Uthar `ra the one who will be second in command to Cezius.

His angelic, mystical wings of gold and brown cascade across the sky, spread in all their glory. His yellow eyes of the two suns burn with a sacred glow, revealing his aged and wrinkled Asyndian years, all the eons upon his furrowed brow are exposed in contrast to the dark shadows under those two suns, the dark sides that have long since seen a golden day. His robes flutter and whip through the breeze from the east, and the bronze helmet of dazzling tassels and feather’s glistens from the light. He hovers for a moment, then touches his talons upon the cold stone of the Runegard courtyard.

The sight is an amazing one to behold, for Cezius has not seen anything like this in a long while. The soldiers face towards him, in concentration and battle-ready, prepared to fight, prepared for attack, prepared for war. Some fifty thousand strong surrounds him, all built from Gormon, Asyndian, and his own Civilians. He was speechless, and doesn't know what to say, but to only react in awe. The sight of the sparkling, dazzling array of the Asyndians guarded and surrounded by Airical's light was a beautiful sight to behold, and the pride of the other soldiers, made him feel strong inside, and Airical's general, Uthar `ra has come to Runegard. This made Cezius feel deep within that something was about to happen.

He turns and looks at Edrin. 'Your troops are at your command and ready, Grand General.' Edrin says to him.

That night, all was quiet. The Asyndians were perched upon the high towers and walls, some asleep, and some were keeping a secondary watch. The Gormon patrolled about the hills and forests beyond the walls, and within the courtyards and tunnels of Runegard, the two largest Gormon, even wider and taller than Roaur, stood watch at the gates. The Civilians kept to themselves within the palace and courtyard interior, guarding the throne room and the hallways, and on the other side of the city, the Mirym settled into their new quarters, but the transition for them was not so easy, for they were not used to these beds and brick walls, and windows, and these tables and chairs they used to hit against one another for sport, until Brihem had to get them under control and teach them to act in a civilized way.

Cezius was at rest for the first time in a long while in his room. For most of the night he rested, but his dreams were evil and haunted, demented and corrupted, as though a blood-red veil covers his sight, constricts his breathing, and slows his blood to a cold, dead flow, but something stirs him, and he awakens from his nightmares of terror. He takes this as an omen, that something doesn't feel right to him. His door is flung wide open, one of the Civilian guards calls to him, telling him to come, for something stirs in the courtyard, an odd, blinding light colors the air, and brightens the sky.

All gather to the courtyard, Cezius, Edrin, Brihem, and all the servants, subjects, and soldiers surround the area. Their distance is kept back, except for Uthar `ra, who is kneeled before the light that floats above him, surrounded by blue and green flames, and smoking fire, and shifting palettes of textures and voids that open and close above his head, above where all can see. Uthar `ra sits with his legs crossed together, as he is locked in deep concentration with the thoughts of the light, for they seem to be almost communicating telepathically.

All the others can do is watch, while the guards maintain the distance of the curious onlookers, except for Edrin and Cezius, who are allowed through. On the other end of the crowds, the Mirym show up, and the guards tell them to let Brihem through, he hurries over to Edrin and Cezius.

'What is this, what is happening?!' Brihem asks.

'We're not sure, the guards saw this light appear in the courtyard, and when we arrived, we found Airical's general sitting here. It seems like he's communicating with it. Cezius?' Edrin says in reply to what he is witnessing.

Cezius only shrugged and shook his head, for he did not know what was going on, or what this strange light was. After a while, Uthar` ra stirs, and stands up, hovering into the air. The light lowers itself to the ground, and bursts into a dazzling array of sparks, and when the lights clear, a tall stone slab remains, but the mineral of the stone is not of any Edrin, Cezius, or anyone else has ever seen. But that is not what amazed them or the crowds, for within the altar of stone, was a massive, two-handed blade, with a twisted golden hilt, encrusted with magnificent jewels as majestic as the sun's glow, and bearing a great eye at the center of the pommel. The stone covered about fifty percent of the blade, for it seems as though, it's jammed into the stone, and will not be moved.

One of the mighty Gormon tried to get near the blade to try and pull it from the stone, but Uthar` ra tried to warn him, and of course the Gormon ignores the general's warnings, and places his muscular hand upon the hilt. He laughs to himself, and for a second, nothing happens. But when he clasps his other hand around, and tries to move the blade, a jolting force of energy pulsates and tears the flesh and armor right off the Gormon's bones, and nothing more than a pile of ashes and crumpled pieces of metal remain near the sword and its stone base. Now, a green sphere of magic surrounds the blade, protecting it from anyone else who tempts the same fate as the dead Gormon.

The people are horrified and run back to their homes, but the soldiers, Cezius, Edrin, and Brihem remain, fascinated by this magical device that stands before them. Then, like a bolt of lightning, it is clear to them, they realize what stands before them.

'Great Asyndian general…is that…is that the sacred blade?! Is that Azalir?!' Cezius asks, mystified by the sword, for he is finally seeing the blade he has only heard of in legends and song, yet is now before his eyes.

'It is, Airical has sent me for the moment when the hero will come, and the time is almost nigh…he is near, I can sense his presence…he will be here soon.' He motions for a few Asyndians to stand by his side. He whispers something to the dark green Asyndian in their native tongue, and the three fly off with great speed.

'Then Hernan has succeeded, the blade has been remade! Now what do we do?' Cezius asks Uthar `ra. But the

Asyndian remains silent. 'What were you telling those Asyndians, where did they go? What is about to happen?'

Uthar` ra turns with a stern eye and looks at the General with a hard, serious stare.

'Azalir was destined for one bearer, the one warrior, the Hero of Ages. It senses that the One will appear in this spot, so this is where Azalir has chosen to be, to wait for the one to come and reclaim that which will be wielded against Kandarius and the forces of Dregor! The Hexagus shall not regain foothold in these lands, I will make sure of that, to protect our Auroras. Once the Hero reveals himself, it will be all over, for Maz Dregor will be spinning in that black realm of his, clawing to get out...but he never will! It is your duty, General Cabriel, to make sure these troops guard this sword with their lives, for if the Dregor do come, they will strike hard, and they will strike quick, and we must be ready for them...are we!?'

Cezius looks about at all the troops that reside within Runegard and he nods back. 'We are!'

Part XX:

The Greywaste

For five days, the Sasparian vessels travel the far, southern coasts of Aura, setting their course for the western coast, along the desolation of the Greywaste, and then to the Runegard docks. The armada passes over rough seas, and sharp, jagged rocks upon each side to the right, and to the left, for these seas are more rugged than the eastern seas and the Plathus Czern. The waves wash upon the planks and toss the ships asunder and about wildly. Some of the ships were wrecked, and the Sasparians swim to the other ships where they are brought aboard.

They pass the iron-handed peaks of the Azaroth Mountains upon the far banks to their northern position, were the Azimoth dwell. Far away, in the bleak distance, upon the misty crags, reside Mothral Tower and the walls of the Aziia Castle. Swarms of Azimoth could be seen in the distance, gathered around the pinnacle of the tower's spire, for something deeper, more sinister has stirred them into a fuzzy mesh which resembles a distant moving cloud of flies. After the battle upon Kaskopos, the fight for their lands, and struggle for their freedom has become more personal and involved, not just an alliance to their Baldushan hosts, but to the Dregor that have begun to march upon their territory, for the banners of the dark ones are beginning to rise in the east, for Kandarius's troops have begun their march, to achieve their Reich, and leading the armies, is Athian Dor by land, as his black drogs Abhor and Femog cast their terror across the skies.

Unknown to Hernan and the others, beyond the mountains of Azaroth, upon the dunes of Ampurzum, are the caves and fortresses of the Raumkat, a sophisticated, evolved race of prowl that think, speak, and wear thick hide armors and iron helmets riveted to the bone by blasted heat and horns coated in the blood of their prey they catch from the hills and rotten trees dotting their lands. The Raumkat guard their lands with a ferocious territorial instinct, but their ancient Warlords hold a blood-pact with Kandarius and swear allegiance to the Dregor worshipper. Now the Raumkat wage war upon the Azimoth and lay siege to Aziia Castle in a brutal struggle for survival and to conquer territory, to add another finger to the black hand which begins to clutch around Aura.

The tropical lands and seas of the Southern Isles were behind them now, the warm and humid weather was becoming hot and molten, the heat rises over the oceans and an acrid steam looms above the waters, as they become still, not calm cool waters, but a death creeps over these boiling seas that bubbles as thick as oil. Up ahead, off to the furthest part of the southern horizon, volcanic lava, and air as hazardous as poison, and black smoke spews from gushers of magma and obsidian island chains, swallowing the area in a black cloud that casts it's shadow over all the sea and Greywaste.

About two hundred kilometers due north and leading east a ways, a gigantic crust of black earth, an island of shadows and opaque desolation rises over the waters, and against red skies, molten geysers, and clouds of black skulls, where dark winged hofts with devil eyes and their dark masters sit upon their thrones of despair, stir above in dark castles with hollow halls that scream of torture and death. For these fortresses reside upon forgotten land, a land of utter black soullessness and charred decay, where death is abound and hunting his way through the flames of the fiery, nightmarish realm beyond the blue seas and green trees of Aura. This is a place that has become one with the Greywaste for all eternity, its harbor to suffering, anguish, terror, and regret for the eyes of one who gazes upon such a foul place.

For this is where the unresting, undying essence and remains of Foameater boils, Reignkiing, the summoned of Maz Dregor and the Hexagus Lords, the one who left all Asyndia barren, drowned the land in its retched destruction, and cleansed the land of all, down to nothing but lifeless soil, black sands, clouds of ash, and without life, except for the foul creatures who crawled from their holes and creep across the decayed peaks and cliffs to dwell and find solitude within such a domain of inhospitable madness.

The Sasparians keep their ships as far away from the remains as possible. The hollowed out eyes glare down upon them, and the monstrosity's titanic claws are submerged halfway into the water, but only the two largest ones can be seen, the other hundred or so lay deep down in the volcanic depths. The armada must sail under one of the claws to miss the obsidian reefs of solidified magma jutting from the coast. The revealed part of the claw stretches some miles high above them. The claw curves in over their heads, and upon their scales and crust, black vultures and other foul, unnamable creatures carry their prey to feed their grotesque young they have bred in animalistic rage, anguish, sorrow, and bitter despair. Their caw is a threat to the Sasparians far below, warning the ships and vessels to go no further, to keep away.

Fing` leads the armada forward, and they pass under the hulking arch of the claw that curves over top of them forming a deadly point that drips a molten substance from the tip. They watch the shadows move across the surface of Reignkiing, scuffling and scratching, for the creatures that lurk upon Reignkiing's bones, the many beasts and urchins that writhe and move about, are constantly surviving, feeding, existing within these plains. These slimy, many legged worms, with red eyes upon their entire body which stretch across their many-appendage figure that crawls across the walls and climbs the distorted, disfigured body and face of Reignkiing, as well as the haunches and colossal, wide dome of its shell, eating upon the dry, rotten bonemill, as well do slugs, migs, and these serpent-like insects with slivering tongues about ten feet long from tip to throat, with rows of razor sharp fangs. These beasts hunt and kill one another, but they seem to ignore the ships that pass by under Reignkiing's shadow of death, or is it, they haven't caught wind of their scent just yet?

'Row on an easy stroke, we must pass unnoticed.' Fing` orders to his crewmen.

The steam of sulfur and oxide, and the smell of suffocation hinders Hernan, Roaur, and L`or's stench of blood and sweat that attract the urchins and other abominable creatures, but the stark cries from the winged fiends above echo louder, especially from one of the larger creatures, the alpha, he puffs his chest and spreads his black wings out, and the blood-red eyes glare deep into their own eyes. Fing` raises his arm, and signals for the ballistae to be loaded. The feathers of the beast begin to transform into a figure, the arms and legs morph, and a being of black malice swoops down upon the vessel. Half way, it almost reaches the ship, the fist drops, and the bolt screams through the air, and within a moment, the brass bolt tears through the creature, splits it in two, and the remains are cast towards the boiling seas, but half of this creature lands upon the vessel.

The right part of the body crisps and fries as it sinks down into the depths, while Roaur walks over to the other half upon the deck, its entrails and guts and blood are splattered across the bronze planks and the once red eyes that glowed, are now dull and hollow, as black as the land around them. Roaur picks up the creature's remains, and with a mighty toss, throws the partial body over upon an obsidian structure protruding forth from the oil. The other beasts sense the splatter of the guts and blood, and take in the aroma of their next meal, and like a swarm, pour upon the rocks and tear and eat the pieces, fighting over arm and hands, fingers and crunching upon the wing.

'Let's hurry and get out of here…our time dwindles away!' Hernan says to Fing`.

'Row, faster…let's get through these boiling pits as soon as we can!' Fing` orders to his fellow Sasparians.

With swift speed, they pass under the claw and the nests of the vulture creatures that loom above and squawk now more wildly over the death of their pack leader. They travel onward; the seas grow more and more thick, slowing their progress. The Sasparians man the oars of their vessels, for the pumps and apparatuses that power their ships clog and coagulate, and will no longer run. Hernan and Roaur assist in the rowing, and Fing` leads them forward, stroke after stroke, the drums beat and slam on a power stroke, forcing their muscles to pump harder and harder, thickening their blood, and tightening muscles that churn with brute power, forcing their way to escape these seas, and as soon as they possibly can.

Another day goes by, and the stars are barely visible as they sense the night creeping up on their backs, for the molten skies grow dark and soon turn pitch black. Torches are placed across the helms and banisters to light their way. The seas begin to return to their normal state and consistency, as the volcanic wasteland of Foameater's remains lay behind them.

The Sasparians toil day and night to fix their pumps, while others continue the rowing, for they need to reach the ports of Runegard as soon as they can, for they are now days behind since the Asyndians gave them the message. Fing` looks out over the side and gazes upon the Greywaste off to his right, beyond the shoreline, where lighting strikes and thunder clasps, for a storm is rolling over the wastelands. Roaur and Hernan come up from below the vessel and stand near Fing`

'Now I see…this is what will become of Aura and all her realms, if the blade was never reforged…I always heard the legends about these lands from my ancestors passed down to us, about the beauty of Asyndia, to behold her crystal clear skies, wisps of thick clouds where the Asyndian would fly, air as pristine as cold water, forests that stretch ever onwards across lavish grasslands, and the towering cities of the Asyndians graced these parts, rulers of a golden land…I never thought that this is how I would see this place for the first time…how horrible, sad…? What words are there that could possible describe such devastation!'

Roaur and Hernan sympathize, for this is the first time they have also seen these badlands of ancient times. They take in the sight, only to want to look away. It is, however, L`or who has been quiet, for seeing the remains of Reignkiing and the desolation he has caused, brings back all the hurt, all the pain…for it was here, all those eons ago, this is where he, the last Sentinel, slayed the God-Monster, where the final days of Asyndia came to apocalypse and extinction, where the final battle of the Sentinels was fought, and where they fell. A place and time when the land was flooded and burned, crumbled away in the erosion and cold wind that has scalded the landscape.

Hernan and Roaur ponder at L`or's feelings and thoughts, unable to even imagine what he is going through. He stares outwards into a deep thought, a cold space of memory which he could never suppress, nor escape, for the flames of grief burn far too much and have branded his mind with the scar of that day, that moment eons ago, when he witnessed almost his entire race and the races of the other realms nearly washed away into forgotten history and obscure legend, but there would have been no one left to tell of their plight.

‘L`or?’ Hernan tries to speak to the Asyndian, but he is too far out there, yet replies without blinking, nor turning his head to look Hernan in the eye.

‘It’s like I never left this place, for I still see this graphic vision in my sleep and conquering my dreams and forcing them to die, it’s at that moment in which the nightmares are born… I see my fellow brethren dying around me, drowning in Reignkiing’s blackened gut, a pit of bile and despairing pain. The Sasparians boiled in the seas, the Gormons are washed away with the monsoons and tidal waves, mountains crumble, and our homes, our cities…crushed and crumbled down to nothing but dust and ashes, the Civilians cried for help…for salvation, a savior…but their screams were gurgled, as the massive bricks and mortar grinded their bones as they joined those they buried and cremated.'

‘It’s as though, time is frozen in this place, preserved like some demented jest, what is the purpose of a scarred land, scorned and mocked by those who look down from the Galakaos and laugh with a sinister grim beaming like the opposite rays of a cold, parched sun, with all life torn from it…like a heart from the ribs, the veins, and the arteries. This place is trapped within an eternal nightmare that it will never awaken from, a bad memory, a harsh lesson upon the backs of me and my people?'

‘What is this land here for, to show the error of our ways, for trying to know more than we can handle, and not leave well enough alone? This stands as a testament…never to be forgotten, never to go away…never to heal.’

Lor` grows angry, his eyes furrow, and his hands clench into tight fists. ‘I don’t know what fate became of that damndable warlock…that dirt of all Asyndians! I hope he has suffered, I hope he rots, being eaten and torn apart by scum like him, an insect to be smashed with a heavy iron boot, clad with spikes upon the heel! And I'll watch his body squirm and die as I squash him! I hope, with all my hatred, Naumokron suffers within his cold halls and tomb!'

Before Hernan could reply, they feel the seas ripple, and the land about them shakes, as great quakes rumble and crack Aura. Something is happening, something draws their attention towards the northwest, the clouds miles away part, and a bright bluish light rises from Runegard, warps the skies, and pierces through the Galakaos, the clouds swirl and twist round and upwards like a towering funnel cloud, a supercell. The quake pummels the rocks and mountains, decimating cliffs and land masses shift. A super-sonic blast of sound stings the air as it rings outwards through the winds that drives them back upon the waves.

'It's happening…Azalir has awakened, the one has come! The Hero has revealed himself…it is only a matter of time now…' L`or remarks.

The beam of light illuminates the land for miles around, it lasts for a time, and then subsides.

'I wonder who it could be….who this warrior is…he or she? Do you know L`or, any ideas?' Roaur asks.

'I don't know. What I do know, is that it's someone who shares the ancient blood…a descendant of the Sacred One, the Hero from the beginning…he or she carries the same blood within their veins, but who that is…I don't know, Airical would be the only one to know…but his thoughts have grown dark of late…' L`or replies.

Then in the aftermath of the blast and lights, a red glow illuminates the sky, and seems to drip, red rain falls from above. Hernan looks upon his skin, he examines his hands, for they become covered with this fluid. Roaur, Fing`, as well as the other Sasparians are in awe and confusion, wondering what was the meaning of this? Hernan and Roaur look at one another, not sure what to think, that's when Hernan gets the idea of what this could be. He tastes the fluid, and the taste is sweet, yet the feeling it gives him is bitter, something is not right…this is all wrong, something has happened, something has gone wrong.

'It…it tastes like blood!' Hernan says as the iron dampens his tongue, and tarnishes his thoughts. He feels dizzy and falls to the floor, Roaur tries to hold him up, and keep him awake. 'Hernan, what is it…what's happened?' Roaur looks at L`or.

'It's…it's the blood, the blood of Aura has been spilled….I first tasted the rain all those eons ago, the rain of war, begins the reign of darkness…the Grey Age, has begun!'

'What, this is not possible! We remade the sword, the Hero of Ages has claimed the blade, this darkness should be ending…and you tell us it's just beginning! You better explain yourself Asyndian!' Roaur drops Hernan down, and grabs L`or, holding him in the air as he screams at the Asyndian.

'My people where right, a Gormon's head is filled with rocks, for do you still need an explanation, has He not been the reason for all this world unraveling, tearing apart our cause, our goal, what you and the Forgemaster have set out to accomplish, what the Auroras have fought to protect? Has it not become clear, has it not pierced its way through the thick wall of that Gormon skull?!' L`or's words echo through the halls of Roaur's mind, and the Gormon releases him.

Hernan stirs and awakens from the darkness of his brief fall. 'What has happened, I feel horrible…' Roaur lifts Hernan to his feet. 'It's this rain; you fainted from the taste of it.'

'How long until we reach Runegard?' Hernan asks.

‘We have the docks in sight, for the flags blow wildly off in the distance, we should reach port by morning....’ Fing` replies.

‘I’m afraid, the rain will last through the night, and the morning, and ever after, ***for when the scent of war is underway…the Dregor will rise up, to rule out the last….the darkest of days, the final act of the play, for the road has been laid before us…and the climax will only lead us on the road towards chaos and dismay…’*** L`or utters in a chilling voice.

The armada pulls into the wide bay of Runegard, only to be greeted not by soldiers or crowds of Civilians, Gormons, and Asyndians, but by silence, a deathly still that haunts the desolation. No creature, nor being walks upon the stairs, bastions, towers, or palaces of the city. Hernan, Roaur, and L`or, hurry off the ship, while Fing` stays behind to commandeer the armada. They look about their immediate area, *"where is everyone?"* There should be soldiers, battalions of troops, and those who have made residence across the towns and farmlands, there was nothing, no trace could be found of anything or anyone.

The three leave the docks, along with a small band of Sasparian soldiers, and walk through the still streets. The windows are dark, for all lights have gone out, only quiet homesteads, abandoned towers and posts are left, the lights of the palace have been extinguished. They pass through the quarters and halls of King Edrin. There is no sign of the king, or his guards, on the other end of the city, they find the towers where the Mirym where staying, abandoned as well, there was no one left, none who could tell the tale of what happened that night.

L`or flew up, and around the city from above, but he could find nothing either. Hernan and Roaur look out the king’s window to the courtyard below. ‘Let’s check out here

Roaur. I thought I might have seen something move…maybe someone has remained; they could tell us what happened.'

They rush out to the balcony, and traverse down the marble stairs into the courtyard where all those soldiers had been stationed, and that's where they find the mighty stone where Azalir stood before the mighty Runegard armies.

'This must have been what happened to Azalir after our work was complete.' Roaur says. They examine the structure, someone did indeed pull the blade from its altar, and that's when Roaur told Hernan the bad news.

'L`or told me, while you were unconscious, that the blood you tasted, was the blood of Aura, for it seems when the blade was removed, something caused an immortal wound in the realm…a deep cut that has brought about the beginning of the Grey Age.'

This news horrified Hernan, he could say no words, only the sorrow of his thoughts and feelings engulfed him. All they have been through, they fought for the lives of many to stop the Grey Age, and to drive back the Dregor, but it seems the dark times foretold, would happen anyway. The Sasparians meet up with them in the courtyard, but L`or was nowhere to be found.

Hernan raises the Hammer of Gonun above his head, and shatters the stone of Azalir to pieces in a fit of rage and distress. 'Now what is to happen, what will become of everything and all?! What doom waits beyond the shadows to strike at us, and destroy us all?!' Hernan cries out. Then, a shiver crawls down his back…for a voice from the past has come back to haunt him, a voice that brings nightmares, and fills his gut with a feeling of unease, of fright…

'Hello Forgemaster…it seems we meet again!'

From out of the shadows they come, the Dregor surround them, armed with the razors and teeth of their master, and upon their shoulders, they have slung the shackles and chains of black cold steel, that brands the wrists, and tears at the tendons in the legs.

'If you wish to know where your destiny, your fate, your…future lies, then I will be happy to oblige, for my soldiers have a special welcoming gift for all of you…'

Part XXI:

Matu`, The White Asyndian

For days, everyone waited, anxious, yet nervous of what would happen, was this battle almost over? The soldiers could not wait, for those who were from the outside, only wished to see their homes and families again. Most camped in front of Azalir outside the light of the force field, waiting for the One to arrive. Then, on that faithful day, something was beginning to change, the weather, the time, everything would be different from here-on-out.

The winds begin to pick up, for a storm is approaching. Off towards the far eastern skies beyond the mountains and passed the gathering of clouds, clasps of thunder and the deadly kiss of lightning strikes. Then beams of light break through the clouds, and the mass of cumulus part ways, as something approaches from the distance. The grass bends to the will and the direction of the winds commands, and the dry, autumn leaves are torn from the branches in the gust of harsh winds that whistle and scream like the call of a cyclone. The large, bright light of the object, like a passing, blazing sun of fiery sparks, flies over cities and countryside, and the denizens of Aura look overhead, not knowing whether to flee in terror, or gaze in awe, at the curious object. Its speeds in pace, as though it has flown across time and eons away at great speeds to reach its destination in a hurry.

The object is nearing Runegard and quickly. The Drog Riders, who were absent from the greeting the others received when they arrived at Runegard, have now reappeared, for they were away for other important business, and doing what they do, which is spying out the land, and keeping an eye out for any signs of the Dregor.

'Sorry we could not be here earlier, General Cabriel,' Durg` says, he leaps from the drog, and bows in the presence of Cezius and Uthar `ra.

'Anything to report, any sign of the Dregor?' Cezius asks.

'Other than this approaching storm and mighty gusts of wind...none,' Durg` replies, 'all seems quiet…'

The other Drog Riders position themselves along the walls, but Shoranna and Fenzir stand behind Cezius. Fenzir walks up behind Cezius and nudges him, and Cezius pats Fenzir on the head. Fenzir snorts and closes his eyes, for the scratching behind his ear feels good to the drog. Then, alerted by some presence, Fenzir's head shoots up, and he and Shoranna take to the air and hover above the rest. She sees the object approaching, gliding upon fiery wings and traveling at an incredible speed towards them. She points towards the shape.

'General Cezius, over there, to the east...something's heading this way!'

The others look in that direction, and they see it as well. Uthar `ra flies off towards the eastern wall next to some of his Asyndian troops where they watch and wait. 'This is it, he is coming…' Uthar `ra says.

'Everyone, keep your distance and prepare yourselves, I don't know what's going to happen!' Cezius orders to his troops. The soldiers man their stations, while the families and subjects are escorted back to their homes and farms by a few of the guards.

As the mysterious shape gets nearer, its figure takes shape, and the mighty span of its wings glide up and down with gusting blasts can be seen. Its blur becomes clearer, and within a matter of minutes, the great being hovers above them, for he is an Asyndian, with great white feathers of bursting light, and arms so toned and muscular, that his strength seems indomitable and unchallenged in power. A gold plate of armor covers his chest, and a kilt of scale hangs from his waist by a jeweled belt, and upon the buckle is an ancient inscription, a symbol of some far away, undiscovered land, where a long forgotten culture from days of old has been subjected to. The white Asyndian, with an easy wind, lands upon the marble of the courtyard. A magnificent shimmer surrounds his being. The features of the Asyndian are slightly different than the others of Athilnovia. The beak is slightly more pointed at the tip; the eyes are larger and brighter with odd symbols not like the ones the other Asyndians bear upon them. His features are closer to Airical, for he looks like he was once a king, a leader of his time, a ruler during a golden age and rise of power to a point of utopia for him and his race of perfect, flawless Asyndians.

The Asyndian walks across the marble upon his talons, they click upon the cold stone with each step, for he approaches Cezius, Uthar` ra, and the others. All were in awe at the magical sight, for this being, the one who would pull the sword from the stone, and take his place as the Hero of Ages, this Asyndian whose very presence gives off an energy that radiates with all the soldiers in the courtyard, a positive presence that gives them hope and a feeling of joy, the same feeling they felt when they returned home to Runegard.

He stands before the two generals and bows to them. He speaks to them, greeting them in a deep and heroic voice, uplifting and non-threatening, the voice of a leader.

'I great you, people of Aura, for I am the one you have waited for! I have heard the call of my ancestors and followed the instincts within my blood! Azalir has called to me, and here I am, Matu`, the Light from beyond Aura, I have come to claim this weapon, and to lead you into battle to rid you of this darkness once and for all!' The soldiers cheer for Matu`, for his words spark something in them, every Asyndian, Gormon, and Civilian feel they can win, that they can drive back the Dregor threat, and the Hexagus have no chance of returning, to reign and cause desolation to this land where peace was established, and will return, when the darkness has been cleansed away with the tide.

'And now…I shall take the stand, and carry on in the steps of my ancestors, and ancient Hero of old, and claim that which is my destiny!' The crowds cheer and roar with applause. '*My destiny…and Aura's fate…*' He whispers to himself. Matu` makes the long walk to the stone, he passes through the force field that encompasses the energy of Azalir. And there he stands, face to face with the hilt and the pommel, Azalir gleams within Matu`'s eye. Sweat beads down the face and brow of every soldier, including Cezius, Brihem, and the others, wondering what was going to happen as they gazed on at this epitomous event.

They hold their breath; Matu` grasps the pommel with one hand…then his right. Fenzir, and the other drogs stir about, something is troubling them, they sense something the others cannot, something doesn't feel right to them, something agitates their smell, and they let out a low bellow and a growl. 'Fenzir…what is it?' Shoranna asks as she tries to calm the drog down. 'General Cezius…something isn't right, something is terrifying Fenzir, something's wrong!' She cries out, Cezius turns, and a heavy force heaves against his chest and knocks him and everyone else to the ground. They look up and see that the blade has been removed from the stone, and Matu` holds it high for all to see. A bright blue blaze surrounds the white Asyndian in a field of sparks and blasts to the sky, deep into the vast space of Galakaos, illuminating the area for miles around, for even Hernan and the Sasparian armada could see the light from the south, and feel the powerful waves of energy that ripple outwards like a seismic wave.

Strike after strike of lightning pulsates and pounds Azalir, and the energy radiates and spreads through his blood and veins. His eyes turn bright white, and spark with electrifying energy. His body shakes and convulses, but keeps his death grip upon Azalir. His muscles twitch violently and shake, the veins expand outwards, as though they're about to burst, the energy seems it cannot be contained…until, all comes to a halt, the beam of light subsides, and everyone is able to reorient themselves and stand to their feet. All eyes are upon Matu`, who is glowing, but not the yellow glow of a golden hero, no…he is surrounded by a red burning energy, and those white eyes, glare red, piercing into the soul and insides of everyone around. Their joy, turns to fear, they begin to feel sick, some even buckle to their knees and vomit, and many of them wail with powerful migraines and burning insides.

'Heh heh heh…hahahaha…!' Matu`'s laugh chills them to the bone, the sky is turning red above them, and a down pour of rain falls upon Runegard and the lands all around in a shower of gore. Crops die; live stock is wasted away, left in piles of a bloody mess, with skin and bones eaten away. Cezius wipes the rain from his face, and looks upon his hand. 'This…this is blood, blood rains from the skies! What…what sorcery is this!' Cezius approaches Matu`, but the red field surrounding him drives him back, burning through his armor and forearms with scars resembling deep ulcers. Cezius falls back, and Fenzir catches him, before he can hit the hard marble below. Airical's general, Uthar` ra now steps forward.

'What…what kind of hero are you? What hero brings harm to others, rains blood from the skies, darkens our hearts with his laugh?!' He draws his weapon. 'What are you…what kind of sick game do you play?'

And Matu` speaks again, but his voice has changed, he speaks in a voice familiar to Cezius, a tone so familiar to Cezius, he realizes what was happening, but it was the words, that truly drained the color from him.

'Game…why, I play no games…I'm here to claim what is mine, what was always mine!' Matu` cries a daemonic laugh that would haunt the ears of everyone within Runegard for the rest of their days. Almost immediately, Cezius knew that voice.

The figure of Matu`, the white Asyndian, begins to change and distort, for they've been fooled, they were all fooled! The descendant of the ancient Hero was never a being named Matu`, but to their horrific shock, the white Asyndian transforms into the tall, pale and lithe form of the Dregor worshipper, the voice of Maz Dregor…Kandarius was, all along, the descendant of the Hero from eons passed.

'This cannot be, this is impossible! There is no way you could be the one! The One was supposed to be an ancient Hero, a bringer of peace who was supposed to destroy you and wipe all your wretched kind from Aura, to that black abyss with your masters!' Uthar `ra cries out.

Kandarius chuckles, humored by the Asyndians anger and disgust. 'Why, I'm a bit disappointed. This is how you would greet your hero, the one who will bring you from your squalor and darkness, and show you what the true light really is?! Lead you to true salvation, to live and love under the rule of the true Lords of this realm…for the Hexagus can now return, for the blood already fills the oceans, and will soon grow their twisted crops and raise their beasts and creatures from the decayed stomach of Wom.

‘The Gormons will die before we are ruled by your foul idols!’ One of the Gormon yells out.

‘The Asyndians as well, we’ll never surrender to your tyranny, we will die fighting.

Kandarius laughs. ‘You lower denizens are so amusing, but in all seriousness, you will die in due time, but you must help me first, for I have work for all of you to do…’

All at once, every soldier, every able man and woman charges at him with swords and spears raised and on target for Kandarius’s heart, firing arrows and raised shields in defense. With little effort, Kandarius unleashes a force that strikes at their hearts and nerves, forcing them to fall to the ground. They hold their chests, and squeeze their bodies, for they feel a severe pain like no sword wound, mace strike, or hacking or cleaving of an axe could amount to. Their hearts gush as though they are about to burst forth, and their heads throb and sicken their kidneys and liver, and every other internal organ within the abdominal wall.

‘Now that I have your attention, and you are calm and collected…I would like to speak. Bear in mind that I have your hearts gripped within my fist, and one squeeze will bring instant death, but I will only make you suffer, for I cannot kill all my slaves, then I will have no one to work. But before we continue, let’s make some introductions. First, these are my friends I would like to introduce to you…’ He looks to the walls, and from the western wall, Othyus leaps over with several thousand Dregor at his command, and the creature Aumon sits upon his shoulder. From the east, Krel and her Dregor cross over the Runegard threshold, and burn in their wake, and tear apart houses and buildings, and collapse towers to the ground.

The Dregor surround the armies from all sides. 'Second, I believe you all know who I am, for I sense my presence has grasped the attention of all Aura, even if you couldn't see me, I was there among you, for I see all, more than your dying Auroras, and I bear more knowledge than that fool who sits above, dying upon his throne. Once I am done here, I shall pay him a little visit, for I have not seen my good friend Airical for some time.'

This causes the pain-stricken Uthar` ra to leap to his feet; he stands, face to face with Kandarius, glaring the sorcerer down. 'I will not let you go near the Aurora, I am his sworn defender, and you will not...' Kandarius strikes the Asyndian with Azalir, and his pieces explode and scatter across the entire city and the surrounding fields and woods, as the bloody chunks sprinkle down with the blood rain.

'Well, that's a relief. That Asyndian was beginning to irritate me!'

'You monster...I can't believe...you set this all up! The tomb of Vos`ul, now the sword! I wonder what pain you have brought to Hernan?! What manipulations and strings did you pull on him?!' Cezius shouts at Kandarius as he struggles to his feet.

Kandarius hears the voice, and a smile comes over his face. 'Ah, General Cezius my old friend, I'm glad to see you're still alive and well! Why, I thought you were a goner for sure, but it appears I was wrong for once, Hahaha! But in all seriousness, it is good to see you again.' He walks over and helps Cezius to his feet, and places his arm around him. They walk together for a stretch. 'Now, let's talk about current events...ah yes, you were asking about your friend the Forgemaster...I am happy to say he is just fine, and your Asyndians delivered their message as commanded, well done to them! Too bad they became a snack for my general's pet drogs, but drogs have to eat too, you know! I will say that Abhor and Femog were quite satisfied.'

Cezius shakes Kandarius away.

'Ah, and as you can see by my new weapon here, our good friend the Forgemaster has done his job as I had asked him to do, and I must say he and that Gormon really exceeded my expectations, they did a fabulous job, wouldn't you agree?' Kandarius runs his finger down the blade of Azalir. Cezius does not reply, but simply glares upon him.

'Oh, it's okay General Cezius. You once took orders from Othetian, but now you follow me, Otheian is out of the way, as is Shemoga and Sasparia, and soon the rest will fall to their demise.'

The news of Othetian's death strikes harshly across Cezius's ears.

The Dregor go from soldier to soldier and lock them up with shackles and chains upon their legs and wrists. One of the Asyndians tries to fly away, but a black arrow strikes him in the back and he falls back to the ground, and is splattered across the marble courtyard.

'Well now, this is no good, we can't have you Asyndians flying off like that. Othyus, Krel, what shall we do? We can't have them flying, but we need them to work…any ideas?' Kandarius says.

'What are you going to do Kandarius!?' Cezius clenches his fist in anger.

'Well, I don't know. Let's see what my Persivators decide to do.'

And in horror, the Persivators raised their weapons, and proceeded to cut away the wings of all the Asyndians. The order was given, and the Dregor went to each one and slashed away their wings, and stopped the bleeding with torches of blue fire, damaging and killing the nerve so they would never grow back. The Asyndians struggled, but nothing could be done, they could not be helped, they were too weak, too crippled by Kandarius's blast to resist and break away.

Cezius and the others could not believe their eyes, they could not believe the brutality, the inhumanity that was being displayed in front of them, they watched as the Asyndians were being stripped and torn of their pride and gift of flight. But while this was going on, Cezius looked back and noticed the Drog Riders where gone. Had they fled like cowards, or did they have something else in mind, a plan? Only time would tell if they would return, or have fled in shame.

'Now, for my final act before we must get to work, because time is, well…my time isn't short, for I rule this land now, and I can take all the time I want. I wouldn't bother calling for your Auroras for protection, for they are too weak to defeat me, I now possess more power than any of them could ever hope to attain. I will now show you the true form of Kandarius, behold! Feast your eyes, for this is what true power is, this is what…all encompassing greatness gains…this is what I am….!' He tears away his robe, revealing a pale naked body scarred with symbols burned and branded into his flesh, down his back, on his arms, across his chest, and along his spine. Kandarius slouches and crouches down, holding himself in a fetal position as his body is surrounded by red sparks and lightning. He claws and slices his flesh, his skin flakes away, as purplish scales begin to form around the areas of dead patches where muscle is revealed. Thick black hair forms around his wrists and ankles, and around his midsection. The muscles pulsate and extend outwards and become strong and as thick and hard as solid titanium when flexed.

From his skull grows two horns like straight razors, and

more durable than bone or any common metals. Two black wings rip out of his back and extend outwards some twenty to thirty feet in wing-span. His eyes turn completely red, without pupils, without an iris, only two pools of bright blood-red that glow. Kandarius elongates his completed body, and poses, strutting his power, for his final transformation has finished, and the evolution of the vile enemy has reached perfection. Perfectly toned, reflexes honed to any movement, any speed or reaction. His height increases by about ten feet as he towers over all around him.

Within his left hand he carries Azalir, but its appearance has changed; the jeweled suns burn a cold red, and the hilt and pommel have charred and turned black as the ashes that spread from the Greywaste with the cursed winds. The blade is engulfed with the flames of the Hexagus; the power of Kandarius has twisted and manipulated the weapon to his will, a weapon, an artifact once meant to be a weapon used against evil, is now their ultimate weapon.

'Ah, I feel incredible…better than I ever have! At long last, after ages and ages of waiting, striking from the shadows is over! Now the true Lords will return and there will once again be true order as each realm is clutched within the Destroyers grasp, as he emerges from beyond the portals of Daskar! And I...I shall ascend and be among my Hexagus Lords!'

'Order?! Your masters writhe and twist within the bowels of a fallen serpent of shadow, as they crawl from her rotten womb on crusted black nails filled with the dirt of malice, nurtured as her darkened, corrupted being! All you'll bring is tyranny and rampage!' Cezius cries out against Kandarius.

'Yes, my old friend! Only can we find true order, through tyranny and malice, only the war under the blood rain will cleanse the world of all infidels and weakness! Only death can bring about new life, a life without weakness, but filled with perfection, the perfect balance of power and domination, for the ones strong enough to wield that gift!' He back-fists Cezius across the chest, and shatters his armor to pieces, splintering, shattering those pieces across the marble, and some are thrusted into Cezius's breast and through the stomach.

Kandarius calls for the Dregor to move forward and close their prisoners in, and split them into several groups. The Dregor pass around thick black chains, corroding and dripping the vile sweat from the palms of their hands, and finish chaining the prisoners. They place the last of the locks upon the chains, and the prisoners are lead to carts pulled by mammoth-like beasts, burly and broad with short faces and concaved eyes holding ruby-like jewels within them. Two large tusks protrude from there bottom gums, and their teeth are flat and grimy. They snort and stomp the ground, for they feel the loads are getting heavier and heavier, as hundreds and hundreds of Civilians, Gormons, Asyndians, and Mirym are loaded up for transport.

During their round-up, Athian Dor arrives upon the back of Femog, while Abhor stays within the skies and circles the area. Femog lands in the courtyard near Kandarius. Athian Dor approaches his master and bows, kneeling to one knee to honor his presence. 'My Lord Kandarius!' He says. Kandarius commands for him to rise.

'My Lord, I must say…the new you, is absolutely exquisite…none will resist us, none will dare oppose us!'

'Thank you Athian…I need you to take Femog and Abhor, and find those five Drog Riders! They think they got away unnoticed, but I saw them head east, see if you can track them down…' Kandarius orders his war general.

‘It will be done! I will make sure to destroy them!’ Athian replies.

‘No…all in good time, I want you to spy on them, and see what their planning, see where their destination is…then report back to me, and we will go from there.’ Kandarius replies.

Athian nods in understanding, but then he sees Abhor heading towards them, wings curling in as he lands and runs to Athian’s side and speaks to him in the language of the drog. Athian listens as Abhor speaks. Athian looks up to Kandarius.

‘It seems…the Forgemaster has arrived, and it appears he has some company with him.’

‘Then we will prepare a welcome for them. Hide the carts, and keep the rest of the prisoners hidden. Make sure they find their way to this courtyard. I want to thank the Forgemaster personally…’

They carry out the plan. The Dregor soldiers round the several hundred prisoners left into the larger buildings and bind their mouths so they cannot call out. The rest of the full carts are sent away to specific destinations, for they will mine and build the rest of the stone and blood needed to finish Kandarius’s creation, his new palace, and the portal to summon forth his masters of Wom. The Hexagus Lords will once more desolate their terrain. It is only a matter of time before the Arc of Daskar is complete.

Part XXII:

The Arc of Daskar

And so begins, the Reign of Darkness, the Age of Depression, when the suppression of the Dregor has begun. The lands change all across Aura. The black clouds spread from the Greywaste and cover the entire realm. Cities are decimated; palaces of the emperors, kings, and warlords are destroyed and broken down into nothing more than ruins. Villages and farms burned, and Civilians, Asyndians, Baldushan, and a large handful of Gormon are taken as slaves and prisoners, while any who resisted the force of Kandarius's power, were punished by means of severe pain and torture within their black and foul dungeons of dank grim and flooded tombs were exhumed corpses float and bob up and down in thick streams of sludge.

Mighty temples and steeples were pillaged and grinded down under fire blazing tanks, machinery created within the blast furnaces of Dregor forges and factories of industrialization. Marching among the hordes of Dregor and chaos, are gigantic automatons of horrific stature, standing some one hundred to two hundred feet high, who trample and crush fleeing citizens under their tarnished bronze feet, grinding their victims under their boots, cutting their victims screams off at the climax of the most excruciating pain, and when the foot lifts up, nothing more than a pile of blood, goop, and a sloshed mesh of intestines and splintered bones remains trampled into the dirt. Every now and again, the Dregor slaves must scrape any leftover flesh and body parts off their feet and toss them to the Slaths to finish.

These towering machines were built to resemble their Dregor counterparts, not breathing, not thinking, nor feeling, but controlled like a marionette by the sinister hands of Kandarius.

Also among the ranks of Dregor soldiers, warriors, and just huge battle–brawlers wielding five-ton spiked maces, are large hulking beasts with four legs like tree trunks in thickness, long serpentine necks, their heads like a lion, with a mane of black hair, covered with riveted dark armor that shuns the light and absorbs the night. These creatures, called Stryder Walkers, spit fire and acid, and devour those who try to flee, they tear apart livestock, incinerate the birds that fly in the air overhead, and rip apart farm houses and turn green land to ashes and smoldering flames.

While the destruction and terror reigned, at the heart of Aura, a new fortress was built upon the ruins of Gammafir`, the bricks mined within the mountains were formed and shaped, and over a period of time the black fortress Daskar, the sister city of Kaskopos from Isa, was completed, and was where the throne of Kandarius would be. Its black spires and spikes wrought and twisted up to the skies and would guzzle the first drops of the blood rain, as the liquid dripped and cascaded down over the palisades and smoothed walls and rigid edges.

Novilon had been abandoned and left in ruins. The palace of Othetian crumbled, the streets were littered with the bodies of Civilians, and only bands of refugee Skahljah and some Dregor patrols in the streets and ruined towers remain within the walls of Novilon's massive boundaries.

But, the fortress of Daskar looms within the shadow of the towering jaws to oblivion, for beyond Kandarius's fortress, towering with a height some miles high, is the black archway, the Arc of Daskar, the portal to the guts of Wom and the Hexagus realm, where the Hexagus Lords will once again pass and walk into this realm. This is the same structure Hernan saw within the realm of Azalir, crowned with thorns and ridges and inscriptions of dark lettering. Only a few more steps are needed to complete the structure, and all the preparations will be in order. At the foot of the Arc, on a pinnacle of rock, is a stone where Azalir will be placed to fuel the energy needed to open the barrier and let the Hexagus through.

Around the area of Daskar, thousands and thousands of slaves mine brick and stone from the obsidian mountains and quarries. These slaves, these scrapers, numbered in the millions, they are scattered across Aura for different purposes, whether to erect the many black fortresses and bases of the Dregor and their generals, many of these fortresses hover over vast lakes, land, and oceans to the south and east. The scrapers build these fortresses upon crumbling, decayed islands which float by Kandarius's power. Their masters and overseers will whip them and beat them more, as they construct and lay foundations to the sentry towers and guard outposts, upon crumbled ancient Asyndian ruins.

Soon, across all the land, the black banners of Dregor were soaring under dark skies and blood rain, with desolation as their base, and upon the wicked embroidered material, is the crest of Hexagus, the symbol which hangs around Kandarius's neck. Upon his necklace, the symbol of the Destroyer, Maz Dregor clashes with the winds, ruffles in frenzy, the banners, flags and black still of Aura, prepare for his coming. And in the mists of it all, the Arc of Daskar stands as the symbol of doom.

The Dregor begin to push further north, along the southern tip of Fausengard. Roaur and Brihem have been placed upon a cart along with others, to the mines far in the southern desert. The Gormon and Mirym are blood enemies, for even though they have tried to make peace for Runegard, the battle of their ancestors still rages within their blood, and if the battle with the Dregor were finished, their quarrel would resume.

Cezius and King Edrin sit within a cell at the far bottom of the dungeons at the base of Daskar. They await their fate, and execution dooms their sleep, but fuels their thoughts on what is to be done, if there is any chance left that they can find.

There is, however, one last defense, one final stand which still remains, for the newly established Ruins of Otoni has been packed and stationed with fully armed, fully equipped Gormon warriors ready for combat. Along the northernmost edge of Fausengard, on the tip of the Great Divide, the Drog Riders hide out of sight upon the cliffs. By night they travel and gather all the soldiers from the Gormon cities, capitals, villages and towns that they are able to muster, so the defenses can act as a thick shield, and then a powerful ram head of battering steel and mauling force to drive the Dregor back.

At the front lines of the armies stationed behind the walls of Otoni, are the Gormon captain Hideron and his father Hindrinj, a mighty Gormon clad in gold drog scale and wears a helmet with several horns around the brim. He wields a double-bladed axe with a ten foot shaft, and a blade five feet long, and a three foot width from tip to tip, blade to blade.

Beyond the far edge of Otoni's borders, another leader of the black armies, named Bolaug, and his Dregor forces, automaton machinations, and black Stryder beasts, amass and prepare to siege and exterminate. Shoranna, Durg`, and the other Drog Riders swoop down over the heads and red eyes of the Dregor armies with lightening fast speed, raining fire and the elements upon the Dregor, but barely making a scratch in the brute forces.

Bolaug and the Dregor armies quicken their pace, and march at a swift rate over the rough tundra, and rummage and stomp through the cold creek that runs along the outer walls of the city from east to west in each direction for miles. The tundra slopes downwards and then flattens out across a plain for about a half a mile until it reaches the city of Otoni's most outer wall.

The blood rain has not yet reached the Otoni ruins, but the Gormons could see the thick black clouds of the ash storm and the red skies approaching. For Fausengard, it is a still, cold day; snow was beginning to fall over the tundra in a light coating across the ground and buildings. The winds whistle through the halls and ruins like hollow bones and skulls that speak from beyond the dead, from realms that keep secrets, where cities of death and ruins made of decay and skeletons cry out to live again, to place their ethereal hands and feet within the cool pond of life once more, and feel the shiver down their spine.

Bolaug and the thousands of Dregor line the hill, and form ranks upon ranks some miles across the tundra each way. They come to a halt, as Bolaug holds up his spiked iron knuckle in a clenched fist. 'Form ranks, stand your ground! Bring forth Gurgurldog!' Bolaug calls for the ancient horn, a black twisted cone that spirals this way and that, a black husk rigid and scratched from warfare and battle, for this horn once stood upon the head of the Dregor Ram of the same name, Gurgurldog, the guardian of the Guand Sewers were the Hexagus kept their prisoners. Gurgurldog was a black goat some two hundred feet tall, one hundred tons of sheer ramming power, and its breath was a deadly flame. Its wings were shadow like a bat, but were too small and insignificant for flight to take place.

During the imprisoning war eons ago, Agonan and a force of some thousands broke through the defenses of Maz Dregor's fortress, and broke the Hero free from his imprisonment. While the ancient Hero and the Aurora's troops escaped, Agonan and Gurgurldog fought to the death above a high cliff, a mountain of dusk and shadow where the beast rested and always kept one piercing green eye open for intruders to dare and pass his guard, and when they did, they were incinerated and flesh was torn and melted away. Gurgurldog kicked and bucked, rammed and sprayed his flames across the winds and through the air, attacking Agonan with everything he could to kill the Aurora, but Agonan raised his sword and charged.

He slammed the beast's head away with a strong punch and back fist, then drove the sword deep into the chest of Gurgurldog, shredding and tearing the heart, as the fowl, murky blood splattered across the rocks and ground all over the area, and the sword was removed with a twist and wrench, then pull, cutting across the ribs and spine. Agonan tore away the right horn, and wears it across his neck as a call for battle. He lifts the goat's dead corpse into the air, and tosses the remains to the valleys and canyons below, were urchins and voracious, carnivorous beasts ate away at the meat and innards. Later the body would be discovered by the Dregor, and the left horn was torn away, and now used upon this battlefield as weapon of war.

Bolaug walks over to Gurgurldog, shoves away the Dregor who carry it, and holds the large horn in the air upon his spiked chest-plate clasps the base of the horn, and the area around the mouth hole. The Dregor crouch down and prepare for what is about to take place.

Hideron calls for the Gormon to be steady, and to arm their spears and axes, to be ready for anything, defense, a charge, whatever may happen. That's when they see the black object being carried out from among the vast hordes. A curved writhing shape which looks like a horn, which confused the Gormon as to what they hope to accomplish with this farce, for a horn, they thought, would not get the Dregor anywhere, and would surely make the battle a little easier than the Gormon thought could be possible, but the veterans, the Gormon warriors who have been around awhile, know the Dregor, and have seen the way they fight, dirty and from the vantage point, unfair, uncaring, for they slaughter to win, no matter what method or practice is implemented to use. Even Hindrinj and Hideron know they're up to something, and they were about to find out. Even the Drog Riders hold their attack for they know what is about to happen. Some Gormon break their rank, for they think this is some sort of joke, just a mind game on their behalf, but before Hideron orders them back to their places, the deep bellow sounds out, and the ground beneath them shakes.

When Gurgurldog was slain, it is said that his dying wail was collected, and locked away within the horn, forever screaming and echoing out from whatever realm his essence is condemned to for eternity. A horrible echo of a dying, squalling beast branded with pain and misery of his bones crunching, flesh tearing, eye's plucked out, leaving hollow craters, and wind and ice that bites and claws in constant assault at the beast's back.

This very sound, this very pain that torments Gurgurldog, roars and sunders, shakes the skies and breaks Tundrok's dome above, the grounds and crust crack and split open, and the walls come crumbling down, the defenses of Otoni break, as thousands of Gormon fall through crumbling brick and mortar from the walls, and the forces beneath the walls, scatter and avoid the falling debris, as a blast of dust and choking debris and smoke fills and clouds the area. Bolaug holds his hand up once more, ready to give the charge, and as the smoke clears away, to the Dregor's shock, thousands and thousands of hulking, lumbering, armored Gormon shapes and silhouettes come barreling and pouring from the rubble and debris, over the broken, fallen wall with weapons drawn, and the sweat of war beads from their head, and the blood of war churns and stomps through their hearts and minds. Axes drawn, pikes outright and tempered, are ready to slay the black, working gears of the Dregor armor, and splatter their skulls across Aura.

Bolaug and the Dregor charge, and at the center of all the chaos, the clouds meet, and the hordes battle under the shadow of the Arc of Daskar. Blood and steel braze the banners, and the realm of Lota, her watchful eye glows red, a tear of blood shows itself this day. Hammers bash, and axes send the black armies soaring through the sky and crashing upon rocks and hard soil, as they trample over bodies, the battering plow; the shovel-headed kill machine that wedges and gouges through the enemy ranks and legions of dark armor, forces its way to the snake's head, the hulking armored tank Bolaug, who bashes and slaughters Gormon left and right, he is untouchable. Hindrinj engages the tall, mace-wielding Dregor warrior, and the two clash axe against mace, warlord versus king and emperor.

Hindrinj knocks back Bolaug to one knee, and dazes him, his shield is down, and Hindrinj raises his axe to attack, to deliver the final death blow, but out of nowhere, a stabbing pain jabs the Gormon King in the back of his leg, and he staggers a bit, but still, he keeps his axe raised high. He goes to swing once more, and then, another arrow strikes him, this time upon his right shoulder, and the axe begins to lower, but he will not give up, he will not let a few arrows take him down, Hindrinj will not fall to this Dregor scum. Fausengard will never fall to the Dregor and ignoring the pain, raises the axe for one more shot, to decapitate and cleave the warlord in two and splatter his skull across the dirt. But, this would be the final attempt, for screaming through the air, at a velocity so ferocious that none could deny its force, a large boulder slams into Hindrinj's back, sending him tumbling across the ground like a rag doll, snapping and tearing bone, muscle, and limb, paralyzing him indefinitely.

Hideron hears his father's cry, and charges through the hordes bashing and slamming those who try to stop him, out of his way. Bolaug gets to his feet, and walks over to the limp, motionless body of Hindrinj. The tear filled eyes of the Gormon king looks upon his fate, as the curdled, bloodied mace of Bolaug is raised into the air.

In an intangible gurgle and roar, Bolaug drives the mace down into the Gormon's skull, crushing his helmet like tin, and blow upon blow, after blow after strike, hit, slam, and bash, Hindrinj is slain, his beaten corpse is left mutilated, and Bolaug stomps the body down, and places his boot of teeth and gnarled spikes upon the Gormon's chest, and cries out a blood-thirsty, conquering battle cry of victory.

Then, a force of unbelievable magnitude tackles Bolaug and lifts him into the air. Hideron has him in his grasp. He forces Bolaug to drop his weapons, and he starts from the top of the hill, and takes a running start, and gaining velocity, he slams head on into the Otoni walls with full force and adrenaline hatred. Hideron slams and pounds Bolaug's skull into the brick over, and over, and over. All that's left is nothing more than a meshed, shrunken head, a greenish ooze stain across the wall, and the blood splattered over Hideron's armor and face. He slams the corpse down to the ground, and walks back over to his father. The Gormons chase off the rest of the Dregor, along with the Drog Riders scorching and blazing their bodies to ash and burning pieces.

The remaining Gormon warriors circle round, and mourn their fallen king, as he passes on in the arms of his son Hideron, who is now the new King of Fausengard, Emperor of the Gormons. They stand and salute their new king. After a time has passed, and Hideron has left his father's side to be alone, Durg` approaches Hideron and reports that they have gathered an army in secret further north, and they will march with the Gormon army when ready.

‘We must scout out all the mines and prisons, and free the Runegard army that slaves at the quarries! We have to regain our strength and our numbers quickly, for Kandarius will strike back, hard and swift, he will not wait for the siege to come to him.’ Durg` says.

‘Now that Kandarius has the Sacred Blade in his possession, it will not matter, he can bide his time and do as he pleases. Where are Captain Cezius and the King?’ Hideron asks.

‘They are kept in the lowest dungeons of Daskar. Roaur and Brihem are being taken south along with the Mirym…’ Arro` says.

‘Let the Mirym stay slaves!’ Hideron says with scorn.

‘Do you see that over there,’ Shoranna points towards the Arc of Daskar, as it can be seen for some distance off, ‘The vile scum that sits upon his black throne, Kandarius is our enemy, these Dregor fiends are our enemies! Not ancient blood wars and feuds!’ Shoranna cries.

Hideron scoffs.

‘She’s right, get your soldiers together, we will ready our troops to the south and message back and forth to plan our final assault. And Hideron, I am sorry for your loss, we will make sure he receives a proper burial. We will mourn his passing.’ Durg` says, placing his hand upon Hideron’s shoulder.

He turns and looks upon the cold, placid corpse, of his battered and bruised father. ‘Has there been any news of the Forgemaster?’

He looks upon the others; the Drog Riders shake their heads. ‘We don’t know, no one knows what happened to Hernan, or where he is?’

They turn away from the battlements, and gaze upon the brooding Arc, the gateway between annihilation, and a world which crumbles around them. The Forgemaster is nowhere to be found, but there has been a victory here today, and the black clouds of blood rain hovers above the Arc of Daskar, just on the borders of Fausengard. For they know where their next target lies, for the Arc must be brought destroyed.

Part XXIII:

The Cleansing

Far atop Athilnovia, upon his crumbled throne, once golden, but is now faded to a lifeless, colorless stone slab, a shell of its ancient glory, a mold of old legend. Airical sits slumped to one side, his feathers once a bright light, now have turned to shadows, eyes that were ablaze with the Aura fire, have been extinguished. He turns and watches as the shrines crack and drain of their mana essence, for his life fades, it's only a matter of time before his final hour, and his fall.

The Asyndian populations flee and scatter about the city, as Athilnovia's golden buildings and breath-taking architecture begins to crumble and fall from grace and hierarchy, rubble cascades through the sky and clouds send forth like heavy rain and tumbles over mountain slopes, and litter and pollute the vast plains below. Any villages and towns beneath are crushed and obliterated as the rubble falls and avalanches from the highest peaks, and are carried away with the stone and mortar in the destructive path.

Airical whispers of his fears and realities, of the fate that has befallen him, his Asyndians, and all those who live upon Aura. Kandarius, the deceiver, has fooled them all, a wolf in sheep's skin that not only bites, but swallows all in a bloody roar, wrath, to conquer, and war, for division...Aura falls and the black hand tightens its grasp. He feels the power of the Dregor growing, the Arc is almost complete, it won't be long before Aurora blood is cleansed and the Hexagus infect the life force once more.

Airical whispers of an ancient saying, not of prophecy, but of doubt and paranoia, that speaks of the Destroyer's return, Maz Dregor, whose force will blast a hole of darkness into Aura so large, that this time, it will never be fixed, never recover, never renew. The Destroyer will strip all of their history, culture, choices, and their overall being, and their very lives. Nothing will be left, nothing will carry on to new generations and future eyes can never see, they will be blind of what once was, and never will be again, *'a time when the sun actually shown upon Aura?'* A child shall say, his or her flesh cold and dry, dead and gray, and lips cracked. A time when the sun's rays warmed Fausengard, Othetica, Asyndia, Sasparia, and all other places and lands, no matter how large or how insignificant. The Destroyer shall tear everything away, rend the life from all and leave the shriveled heart to pump without blood, without feeling. All will be stripped down to none, one and all, to no one...

Athilnovia, a star in the sky, a cool breeze like water,

The purest and blue, for life in the golden city, a

gem polished and imbued, a city of immortality, a

city that will never die.

Athilnovia, where the Asyndians fly, and none shall weep,

and none shall cry.

Athilnovia, above Aura you glide, the clouds of cotton and mists

swirl and twist, a sweet kiss upon the jewel's ruby lips,

Emerald eyes, and sapphire skies, a city of serenity,

a city... that sparkles in the eye.

Athilnovia, where stood the altars of my bride,

Now all fades, and stripped of pride.

Athilnovia, shall fall from the sky, a piece of our life falls,

like fire from the domes above, a corpse who lost all but his skull,

his identity to remind us all...we hear the whispers,

we read the signs...the cleansing has come, and all shall fall...

Athilnovia, the city in the sky, Athilnovia, where the Asyndian flies,

Athilnovia, Aura's jewel, Aura's pride...

Athilnovia, here is the end,

for the Cleansing begins...

He feels the cold wind at his back, and the clouds reap and moan above like tortured faces in the sky.

'So this dark day has come at last...Reignkiing was only the beginning for much larger things...and now you've won, you will finish your master's orders, and the Hexagus will be free once again...a problem your ancestor handled all those eons ago...Who would have thought, that our savior, our final hope, would be the guiding hand...to destroy us!'

Airical turns to the shadow of Kandarius that looms above, upon the edge of the temple, looking down upon the Asyndian with the eyes of a predator.

'Your dark power has destroyed all visions and senses of mine, or I would have known, I would have seen right through you! Your power is strong indeed!' Airical says.

Kandarius swoops down in front of Airical and walks closer towards him, smiling and holding Azalir drawn in one hand. 'My power is stronger than you realize Asyndian!' He grasps the slouched Aurora by the throat and holds him in the air. 'My influence stretches far beyond clouded mists and simple doppelgangers.'

'Indeed it has.' He chokes from Kandarius's tightening grip. 'Look at your handy work, look around and about you! The Twelve Altars have all but crumbled to their ruin! But one is still whole! When Athilnovia is lost, and when we fall, the magnitude of the city will cover Aura in a desert of eternal night as ash covers the sky and poisons the air! Then what will be left of your land?!'

Kandarius laughs. 'How sentimental, Asyndian! I'll tell you a story...I was not as I am now...I was once, just a young boy who would go on adventures through the woods and traverse the unknown! I used to be afraid, but it was my determination, my power that gave me bravery, I cast aside all the weakness, and I could do so much more than I was ever capable of!'

'I would love to feel sentimental, but it is our feelings and sentimentality that makes us weak! For they are our worst enemies, and if we are to ever grow and become strong...then we must cast such feelings aside! And then true power will come!' Kandarius grins with a sadistic smile.

'Now that you have your true power, what are you going to do? Go on, do your worst, and use your power and finish me off, finish what you began! Well...what are you waiting for?!' Airical irks on the beastly figure of Kandarius.

Kandarius drops Airical to the ground and points to the altars, and tells him to watch. 'Just keep your eyes over by the altars, and watch. I want you to see for yourself, I want you to see the final moments of your world become extinct in front of your eyes...it will only be a matter of time! Athian Dor, Othyus, and Krel are on the hunt as we speak...'

'The hunt for what...?' Airical cries, but the answer then becomes all too clear to him...

Over across the mountains east of Fausengard, Othyus and his troops of doom, the forces of darkside, storm across the rugged terrain and through the valleys beneath, then across the summit burning and decimating villages in his wake. They make the march upwards, towards the peaks and the top of the mountains, where the prey resides, resting beneath the rocks and rubble in secret foreclosure.

His troops make their base of iron contraptions holding up ragged, blood-stained tents covered with black dirt and sludge, and covered with a heavy coating of blood. Othyus and several hundred Dregor make the ascent upwards at the very top, to the jagged crags and barren oasis of crust and boulders dry as a bone from the airy climate of Fausengard. The Dregor troops take and round up any live stock they can to drink of their blood, for Porphyria, a shriveling blood condition will soon set in, and only the flesh and meat of the living will quench their thirst for plasma, and their hunger for death and decay.

They take with them gigantic chains and heavy leather whips, and shackles that would bind the arms and legs of a mighty giant, and bring down a titan of epic proportions. Othyus and the Dregor leap across, climbing over the cliffs, along the edge, and over the crags of teeth. Othyus stops, for within this area along the cliff, the rock has changed, something is different about this particular patch, and there, standing in front of him, is the first tree, the first tree that had been planted all those eons ago, the tree that grows upon Niffrok's back. He orders the troops to stop, and without further delay, they carry forth jagged saws and torches, and they cut the tree from Niffrok's back, and hack it to pieces and burn the branches down to ashes, and they feel the dirt and mountainside move and tremble, for they have disturbed Niffrok's sleep.

Othyus climbs down upon the side of the mountain, and uses his mighty blade arm and drags it across the rocks, tapping and jabbing in particular places. He growls for the Dregor to ready the shackles and chains. Lower he goes still, and beneath his feet he sees an odd rock formation jutting outwards like spines upon the back bone of some beast or creature of marine origin.

Lower still, until the spiny rocks lay just beneath his massive boots, as he places himself upon a tight ledge to get his footing in place, readying himself for what will happen next. Gently, he runs the blade down the side of the rock, leaving a long scratch carved into the side of the mountain. And when he reaches the spines, he slices them away...and the mountain again stirs. Shaking and rumbling, gravel and debris roll from the top cliffs, and travel downwards in an avalanche, a downpour of dirt and dust.

A low roar echoes outwards through the sky, and within the cliff before Othyus, a huge, gaping eye opens up, a massive pupil of impressive circumference and diameter. The pupil dilates from the darkened clouds above, and the brown and grey, mystical orb turns and looks down upon Othyus, and the cliff's shift, and an angry brow is shaped in the rock, for this Dregor has awakened the Aurora from his slumber, his long forgotten sleep that has lasted through the ages, but now, Niffrok is awake and enraged.

Niffrok spoke in a long, drawn out roar. 'Who dares....what is the meaning....of this!'

Othyus raises his sword, and drives the blade straight into the pupil, and rips the iris to shreds. Niffrok cries out in pain, as the sword is removed, and the mystical blood of the Aurora is spilled to the valleys below. Othyus leaps away to the other cliff face next to him, avoiding the further rock slide and explosion as Niffrok's hand emerges from the cliff to grasp his eye. His head, arms and legs, then his entire body rises out of a sea of stone, and there the gargantuan size of the titan of Auroras is gazed upon, by awe to many who have never seen such an amazing sight, but to the Dregor, the prey has been found, but Niffrok would not go down without a fight and struggle.

The Dregor swing the chains and shackles through the air, as the gigantic rock being raises his arms to pound the scrawny little black things which dare to attack him, but the black hooks snag his wrists, and he is pulled down to his knees. The Dregor run up and bind thick iron chains around his ankles, over his fur boots, and squeeze as tight as they can. They pull him to the ground, and bind him to the rocks, for there is very little he can do. The power of Kandarius has weakened the essence of the Aurora. The Dregor use the spiked whips and lash and attack Niffrok without mercy or feeling, tearing through his fur armor and tunic with the sleeves torn away, leaving bloody gashes and burning cuts across his back.

Othyus runs upon the chest of Niffrok, his tunic is ripped open, and Othyus drives the blade into his chest, through the lower rib cage, and past the blood and spewing bile and gore, he reaches in and tears the veins and arteries away, and pulls out the Auroras heart!

Othyus heaves it up with both arms clenched tightly around it, blood spews forth from the gaping incision within Niffrok's chest, and splatters over the Dregor and Othyus's golden armor. It runs down the bronze gears and wheels of the automaton being, like a candle that's all but melted away, and only a faint glimmer is left. A glimmer in Niffrok's eye, that slowly fades, and the Aurora's life passes.

Airical looks upon the altars. He notices something is happening at the far end. Kandarius brings Airical's attention to Niffrok's altar, it begins to fade and crumble down into rubble, and the dust blows across the tainted marble floor.

'Othyus has torn the heart away from Niffrok, the forgotten one. Now the cliffs shall corrode, and become weathered with the taint of the Greywaste, the peaks shall blacken the cursed sun, and there will be no tomorrow.'

Airical feels the blow to his heart and his balance begins to stagger as he crosses the floor, his talons clicking upon the marble. A tear of blood excretes from his eye, and drips upon the floor with an echo.

Meanwhile, the stars beam across the clouds, but no light pierces the darkness that spreads and engulfs across its path. The blood rain continues its forecast over dirt and mud, coagulated and grimy. A spark clashes across the sky, and then another, for a battle rages that none but the quickest of eyes can see.

A soaring bright glow glimmers across Tundrok's dome, and behind is a red flash, then another red flash streaks by. Athian Dor has tracked down Lota and Pry, who are also of the Asyndian line, kin to Airical. Lota's palace and realm upon the sun has been destroyed and ravaged by Dregor who fly upon the backs of drog, led by Athian Dor, now the bricks of her city crumble and burn beneath the molten energy the sun sets off. Her dazzling wings and the glaring, burning eyes of revenge upon her beautiful face, burn and twist her delicacy to madness and rage, but she two has been affected by the curse of the Grey Age, the darkness that spreads from Daskar and the Greywaste, and she runs and tries to avoid the burning hostility of Femog and Abhor as they chase her down, like two wolves closing in on a lame deer with a bleeding leg.

Trailing close behind, Pry glides after them at a mach beyond comprehension, upon glimmering wings, blue as the starry sky, and wrapped around his face is a mysterious shawl and a hood. His hands and feet are bandaged, but his yellow eyes are focused upon his two targets, as he tries to save his sister's life. The two drogs close in, Pry flies alongside Athian and Abhor. Athian pulls out a large black crossbow, and fires a bolt straight through Pry's heart. He stops, his wings and body weaken, then he feels he is about to collapse, and spiral downwards, and then he is released, as Femog grabs Pry's limp body with his talons, and twists his neck with those long, jagged claws upon scaled hands, and Femog releases the Aurora, as he falls, and slams downwards through the black clouds, to the mass of land, the rotten shell of Aura below.

Lota stops, and turns, she cries out in agony, reaching for her brother's body as it falls out of sight. She pays no heed to Athian as he leaps from Abhor's back, and lands upon her chest. Athian grasps her throat tightly, Lota tries to release him, pry the death grip away, but it is no use. He removes a curved dagger of jet steel and ruby eyes upon the scabbard, and drives the blade into her throat. Her breathing gushes with blood, and radiating waves of excruciating pain. As Athian watches the blood trickle from the corner of her lips, he notices she smiles, and the blood is spat across his half-iron face. He removes the dagger from her throat, and swings it around and drives it into her heart. The smile turns to a gasp, and her breathing ceases, and her life is ended....

Airical watches the altar of Pry become decimated to ash, and then Lota's shrine expires to dust and rubble, then trickles down the steps and reaches Airical's knees as he kneels before the life's work of his beloved Y`nahlia, crumbling, destroyed before his very eyes, as his beloved Aurora's perish, and there is nothing he can do.

Towers of Athilnovia continue to crumble in the far off distance. The city now lays barren and all but wasted away. Asyndians have either fled to other distant lands, or like many, lay buried beneath the crumbled towers that have fallen to the ground far below. Lightning and storms tear away the sacred foliage and flora that has grown atop Athilnovia for eons and eons, since the city was conceived. Winds scream like wild banshees and sirens who have taken their true form, for no sweet singing will be heard, only the sounds of fallen man, slayed women, and tortured children, for none escape the Grey Age and its skeletal hand.

'Lota, the sun, will shine no more. And the moons of Pry will no longer guide the weary traveler in the night sky. Soon the stars will fade, the oceans will cleanse the east, for the Aurora's fall...is almost complete.' Kandarius laughs at the wretched, twisted shape of Airical as he crawls upon the steps, breathless and weak, for his heartbeat is failing him.

'Just kill me! I will look at this no more...I will not see this land fall, just end this now!' Airical shouts.

Kandarius walks over and places his daemonic foot upon Airical's chest. 'You will die when I say you will die! The forces of Athian have conquered the sun, the Dregor amass to bring down Ezik`al, the Tower of Pry upon the largest moon. The Galakaos is almost in order. But continue to watch, as the final few Auroras are done away with.'

Airical watches on, but he doesn't know how much longer he has, for the sands of time trickle down and down more and more, every grain a moment, and every piece of sand closer to the end of the hourglass.

At the summit of Bal Sador, within the tower, Tundrok sits upon a granite throne and ponders with a mind of darkness, and a crown that causes no more storms, no more rain, for Kandarius and his dark essence brings about a revolution in the new climate, of a red sky and shaded Aura world. The doors to his fortress begin to pound and thunder. The doors begin to split and crack, then the red lights beam through the creases, the rustic iron doors burst through, and the Dregor rush forth with pikes and axes, hammers and stakes, chains and torches. The battering heads are thrown aside, and Tundrok steps from the throne to make his stand.

He slams and stomps the Dregor with his mighty boots, and slams several through the tower walls, and sends them spiraling to the canyons below, and the corpses are washed away in the cold rivers. Several of them have climbed up the side of the tower, and burst through the spire with a massive net, and they toss the threads of impenetrable strands over Tundrok's head and the weights upon the sides, massive bones taken from God-Creatures slain in the past, bring the Aurora down to his knees, and massive sludge-covered nails are driven into the net to hold him down.

The small, unassuming figure of Krel walks into the tower, with her mace in hand, and a large rolled up parchment within her grasp. She tosses the parchment in front of Tundrok's face, and two Dregor unroll the parchment to reveal a map of Aura. She then tosses a large knife to the floor. Tundrok looks upon Krel, and wonders what she is up to.

She speaks in a raspy, rattling, throaty voice. 'You will tell me the location of the hidden forge!'

Tundrok remains silent. The Dregor take the torches to his flesh and stab and drive them deep within, beneath the skin. He still refuses, so then they take large branding pikes tipped with thorn-covered skulls and brand and singe the Aurora's right eye. He screams and lets out a great bellow and pain-induced writhing growl.

'Where is he?! Where is Gonun?! Where is the Lost Forge?' She asks again, this time with less patience emanating from her slivering tongue.

Tundrok tries to break through the net but cannot rip or tear the threads or fray them just enough for him to reach his hand through, grasp the scrawny, little Dregor witch and smash her and crush her to pieces.

He still will not speak. Half-blind, he laughs and spits at her, covering her in gross amounts of saliva and spit. She wipes away the insult from her helmet, and turns the dark, sullen eyes upon the Aurora, who has made a great mistake. She motions to the Dregor with a devilish looking weapon in his grasp, an antenna of sorts. He crawls upon Tundrok's shoulder and grasps tightly as the Aurora tries to knock him away, but the insidious automaton reaches the head, and stabs the antennae into Tundrok's skull, as he winces with pain as the blood trickles down his brow, over his nose, across his lips, and stains his grey beard red.

Krel raises her hand, and by the powers of her dark lords, and the will of Kandarius Lockmore that has been invested within her, she summons a brutal storm of lightning and a battle roar of thunder like the drums of war that thunders in the deep. A blast of lightning strikes the pole, creating a shock wave through Tundrok's body, so painful, so irritating to his flesh and muscles, bones and will, he begins to spasm and shake violently, smoke begins to fill the vast columnar space of Bal Sador, emitting upwards like an industrial chimney.

The lightning strikes again and again, he cannot take much more, but he fights, Tundrok tries to fight off the pain and burning of his flesh, as he scars and blisters, he feels his eyes begin to melt, and blindness begins to set in. He raises his hand, the jolts of electricity surges through him, and his fingers cast bolts and his hands and body are cooked, his insides destroyed. Tundrok's hand falls slowly, and the final wisp of wind exasperates from his lungs, and travels as a call upon the wind, a call for help, but the winds lead to nowhere but desolate sands and haunted deserts overseen by a messiah of black clouds, and the Arc of Daskar.

The pieces of his flesh crumble over the map, and burn it to ashes from the heat emitted by the scorching, blasted electricity.

Krel is agitated for a moment, but then gets an idea. She calls to her subjects to bring the Slaths and have them try to get a scent, for Tundrok and Gonun are brothers, and they would try to follow the Slaths, to see if they could find the Aurora scent, and this would hopefully lead them to the forgotten Forge of Gonun.

The Slaths lead them through dangerous, rugged territory, much different than the way Hernan, Roaur, and Kerrun went, but the extreme sensitivity of the Slath's sense of smell was able to catch something, and they followed and marched onward. They massacred all life in their wake, animals, Trau`ls, denizens, it did not matter, for they had to keep moving, for they were on the trail of catching the most elusive of Auroras.

Gonun was at the grind wheel, smoothing the hammer he carried in his grasp, so it would give any enemy a good smash across the head. Kerrun sat at a small table near the edge of the woods, and made sketches of the surrounding area for use in his book he was writing, mapping the area in every detail, for the study of this place has been his ultimate goal, and to record it for future references in his research of Aura.

Something strange begins to happen however, for the sun within the grotto never rises and never sets, never moves at all, but something strange caught Kerrun's eye while he was sketching with his set of pastels and instruments. The shadows began to shift, for the sun...was going down. He closed his book, and stood to look at the sun, it was indeed sinking, and the color has changed, it was no longer the mild yellowish orange ball of flame it once was, for it was fading and burning out, like a candle in the diseased wind.

Kerrun approaches Gonun, who has noticed this as well. They look at one another, and then they look at the fading ball of light, as it falls behind the mountains.

'Aurora Gonun...its happening isn't it...they are here aren't they?!' Kerrun asks.

'So, the Grey Age has begun...the Forgemaster has failed then...!' Gonun replies, the disappointment sharp in his voice.

'No this can't be, I won't believe that! I trained that boy, he would never let this happen, he has the determination of a stubborn lion! Something else must have gone wrong, I can feel it in my old bones, and my mind whispers that something else has happened!' Kerrun sharply replies, defending Hernan, his friend and student.

'The ancient barrier has been broken through, but it is not time that will ruin this sacred place, it is those in black armor, waving their black flags! The Dregor are coming!!' Gonun shouts.

And they are correct, the Slath have discovered the Aurora's scent, and were marching at a faster pace. Gonun and Kerrun watch the fires within the forest burn higher and higher, and the snow melts away, and the clouds above part to reveal a blank, starless sky, and with an exhausted moon.

'The sun has faded, Lota is no more…The moon casts no light in the dark, Pry has fallen…and…and the stars sprinkle their heavenly glow upon Aura no more…no more! Tundrok!' Gonun's heart fails him, for he knows without stars, the essence of his brother Tundrok, has been taken and wretched from his body.

'But how…how did they find the forge, there are none who know its location other than my son Roaur, Hernan, and your kin!' He starts to think about Roaur, and what could have happend to him, what was his fate in all this disaster, for he traveled closely with Hernan as his right-hand.

'If Kandarius wields the force of Azalir, than he can summon enough power to do anything he wants, and manipulate things the way he wishes, and none can disobey or refuse, for the power is a drug, and his servants and subjects are all addicted and blind. When that black influence roots the dark branches within an individual's mind, he is lost. Like what happened to Othetian, and many others before.' Gonun says.

The sketches and notes are tossed aside, and Kerrun replaces them with two hammers in each hand, and Gonun wields the hammer he was polishing. The flames rise, the tree trunks burst with explosions and splinters that scatter across the area and the Dregor march through with Krel at the head. They surround the Aurora and the wise, old Gormon and close in their ranks tightly. Gonun swings the hammer down and smashes the oncoming hordes and Kerrun tosses the hammer at Krel who catches the weapon in her hand with little effort. She looks at the hammer curiously then immediately charges at Kerrun, who is unable to defend himself fast enough, as she drives the hammer into his skull with immense blunt force. Kerrun drops to the ground upon his back, nearly dead, but his helmet over his brow protects his life by a sliver of a thread. Gonun is too busy trying to fight of the Dregor that crawl over him and try to wrestle him to the ground.

Krel stands above Kerrun, who is hemorrhaging badly, as he gurgles and coughs up blood that has filled his lungs, by the blow that severed his spine into pieces and splinters. She grasps his robes in a fistful and looks into his eyes, with her cold, lifeless stare, for Kerrun can see no eyes, only hollowed black holes within her helmet.

Kerrun spits at her and laughs. 'My son…will avenge me! I know he is still alive, for a father has these instincts…and he will kill you! You and your entire horde…he is the greatest Gormon warrior alive…remember his name, for he will bring about your demise!'

Krel gurgles in a sinister whisper. 'And what is this pathetic child's name?!'

'Roaur! My son…my pride…my…Avenger!' His eyes close permanently.

She remains silent, and tosses the lifeless body of the Gormon to the ground. 'Burn the rest of the area! And chain that Aurora down, let's make this quick!'

Gonun is held upon each side by the thick chains, and he is kneeled down in front of Krel, who stands before him. Gonun looks and glares at her, trying to get away, but suffers the same fate as the others. She places her mace upon her belt, and uses her jagged gauntlet of sharpened knives and points to tear through bone and rib and pulls the beating heart from Gonun's chest. She holds it up, the Dregor yell and chant her name, and then she tosses the heart to the ground and steps upon it.

'The heart of an Aurora is nothing more, than the dirt under my boot!' She smacks the Aurora across his face, over and over, until nothing more than a bloody pulp is slung over dead, the chains are let go, and his corpse falls upon the dirt of his grotto, where he lays in a pool of his own blood.

Airical watches the statue of Tundrok crumble, and then Gonun follows in its wake.

'No…not Gonun! Tundrok too!' Airical whispers to himself, but Kandarius can hear every word, every lip movement he makes. Airical lays upon his back clutching his heart in pain. Then, above the altars, the statues and carvings of the All Father, and the All Mother, Kathaxes and Asyndiis, begins to crumble away.

'No! Mother…Father, they cannot give up, they cannot fade, for the balance of all the cosmos rests with them! What have you done Kandarius…what have you done?'

Kandarius sits upon the step near Airical's clenched body. 'New order is not of one realm, but of all the realms and the Galakaos. Their spirits have weakened and abandoned you; they know there is nothing more that can be done!' Kandarius looks at the remaining altars. 'Well, there are only two altars left…that last Gormon sheep…and you!' He points to Airical with his sinister long finger, and the blank stare of those red eyes, and a furrowed brow. 'But, I have decided…'

Airical looks upon him with wide eyes.

'It will only be a matter of time before that last Aurora of the Gormon is captured and slain, so I have decided to end your life…here Aurora, once and for all! And when you die, the power keeping this city aloft will fade, and then it will crumble and fall! Are you ready Asyndian?'

Airical stands to his feet, and tries to lunge at Kandarius, but Azalir is driven through his chest, and Kandarius holds the struggling, writhing Aurora in the air with one hand upon the scabbard. The stark cry of Airical shatters outwards to the lands below. All workers of the mines cease, all armies halt their march, and all goes quiet except for the echo of the Aurora's death. Kandarius tosses the body away, and Airical goes soaring through the air, and smashes into his own shrine. The debris fall and crumble upon him, and his feathers and bones are crushed, leaving his lavish robe covered with fresh blood that flows out in a puddle, and cascades down the stairs like a waterfall, and gushes across the floor.

Kandarius holds out his broad arms, and begins to rise into the air, his black wings take him above, ascending higher and higher. He parts the clouds, and watches as the golden city of Athilnovia, in a soaring ball of smoke and flame, debris and scattered golden pieces, trail from the descending mass of the island in the sky.

Eyes across the world look on in horror, the Dregor legions with pride, as the city falls from the sky, for the Aurora of the Asyndians…Airical has died. The Asyndians fall to their knees in tears and terror, shock and numbness fills their bodies, the Gormon weep and lower their heads in sadness, and the Civilians cannot believe the horrors that fill their eyes, the sight they see is the worst nightmare come true.

Athilnovia burns away, as it almost reaches the grounds below, the mountains and hills, trees and plains have sealed their fate, for decimation is imminent. The Sasparians watch far away hidden within their submerged vessels, and far away, upon a high cliff within Fausengard, overlooking the ruins of Otoni as the troops of Hideron pick themselves up and clear their fields of the dead and slain, Agonan watches…as Athilnovia crashes into Aura, the impact shakes the world, and all are rattled and knocked away, the air is taken from their chests, and their legs are crippled from the earthquakes and volcanic eruptions. Agonan kneels and covers his eyes, for the collision is so powerful, the rocks and rubble soar for tens of thousands of miles away from the impact point. And after days of shaking and earthquakes, he can finally look and see, for the land has been decimated severely. There are no trees, mountains have crumbled, and rubble covers many who have been caught in the blast as the rocks rain down from the sky.

Huge geysers and craters emitting volcanic steam and activity, pour their poisonous gases into the sky and air. But off towards the center of what was once Aura, an ethereal dome of powerful magic, a force field of energy surrounds something, and as the smoke clears away, Agonan can see the erected, the completed, Arc of Daskar, and the Daskar fortress which protects the structure. The power of Kandarius has created a dome to protect the Arc from annihilation by the impact of the fallen Athilnovia.

Agonan returns to the forge to find his brother and Kerrun, to warn them of what's going on, but he has arrived far too late. He checks the body of Kerrun, there is no pulse, no response. He morns the loss of his friend, but then he turns and sees the mutilated body of his brother Gonun. He kneels by his side, and holds his brother's hand, lays his head upon Gonun's back, and weeps. But when he turns the body around, and sees the gaping hole in his chest, the anger is one million fold, the veins in his face, neck, and arms emerge like great pythons. He lays his brother down, and covers the body with the blanket from the large bed near the forge.

He picks up the body of the Gormon, and places him upon the grass under a tree that still has some green to it, for the fire the Dregor created, came and went, leaving hardly anything left of the grotto or the lost forge, what has been charred and burned, and the fires extinguished.

He does however, find the book that Kerrun was sketching in, and has luckily avoided the fate of the inferno that scorched the area. He places the book safely within a pouch upon his belt, and if Roaur is still alive, he will return it to him, for it his rightful possession now, but how he was going to explain his father's death, he was not sure.

For many days and weeks, Agonan traverses the land, keeping hidden from the Dregor, for they will no doubt be after him. He tries to find his fellow Auroras, but discovers that each one, as he comes across their domain, has been slain, even at Bal Sador… he finds his other brother.

'These bastards! They killed them all…I'm the only one left! The Grey Age has begun, but it will not be completed!' He rushes over the dusty terrain, and passes through a valley, where he sits and ponders, plans what to do next. He has to somehow help with the Gormons and The Drog Riders to form a final assault, for he is the Aurora of Warriors, of Soldiers…and if there is anyone who knows how to fight a war, it is Agonan, even if it is their last. For he is aware, this is the final stage, this will be the final war, and there is much to be done.

Part XXIV:

The Final War

Kandarius stands upon the palisades of Daskar, and looks out upon those who mine and slave at his quarries. The Gormon hammer away at brick, the wingless Asyndians grovel and cry at the loss of their entire civilization, and the Dregor troopers have to go around with whips to get them back on their feet and working. Behind Kandarius, walking up the obsidian stairs, are the chugging steps of Othyus, and his sister Krel following closely behind, they have arrived back from their hunt and cleansing of the Aurora blood. Meanwhile, from above, Athian Dor has also returned. Femog and Abhor perch themselves upon the nearby spires, and Athian Dor walks across the causeway and stands next to Kandarius, and they both look out to the grovelers and slaves below. Then Othyus and Krel approach.

Kandarius turns to look upon his general and his Persivators. " I am proud, of all of you! We have achieved a victory here today, that will be the milestone, the catalyst for our new beginning, our rebirth!'

'Thank you, Lord Kandarius.' Athian says. Krel and Othyus bow in agreement.

'What of the Warrior, what of Agonan?' Kandarius asks.

Krel kneels, and bows her head. *'We've looked everywhere for the last one, but he eludes us at every turn.'* Krel stammers.

Kandarius turns to Othyus, who just shakes his head no. Then he faces Athian Dor.

'The Aurora has even managed to avoid the eyes of Femog and Abhor, not even they could find him.' Athian replies.

Kandarius gets this look of anger and rage upon his face, and his purplish flesh seems to swell and his red eyes burn. He grips Athian and lifts him up in a fit of rage and stares him down, and Athian cringes in fear as to what will happen to him. But then, Kandarius just tosses him to the ground and laughs at him.

'You should have seen the look on all your faces! Hahaha! It does not matter, that Aurora has no more power here, he is no threat, but if you do find him, you may still oblige my wishes and kill him as you see fit!' The three then laugh with him.

'There is more to report...Bolaug failed to capture the Ruins of Otoni, his forces retreated and the Gormon still maintain the area south and further north of Fausengard.' Athian says.

'Oh who cares about those old ruins and dusty crypts! Let them have it, when my masters are released, then they will not be around any longer, they will be buried there!' Kandarius replies.

'If I may ask my Lord, what are we waiting for, we should commence the ritual as soon as we can. The Arc is complete, and you have Azalir...what else is there to do but bring our masters into this realm?' Athian says, wondering what Kandarius was up to.

Kandarius walks forward and looks upon the Arc far above their heads, and then he looks down to the altar before him, the altar where Azalir will be placed within the slab, and the power will generate the fields and connection to the stomach of Wom, and the Hexagus Realm.

'First...I have someone to thank...for if it wasn't for him, none of this would have been possible...'

He hears a voice behind him, as one of the Dregor troops marches up the stairs and calls to Kandarius. 'My Lord, we have the prisoners on the field, and are ready to proceed with the executions!'

Kandarius looks at the blood red sun. 'Is it that time of day already, I almost forgot, very well, let's have a look at them, shall we?' Kandarius walks over to the ledge and looks down, and in the middle of the quarries below, at the front gates of Daskar, stands in chains and stripped of their armor and legacy, is General Cezius and King Edrin. Cezius looks up at the daemonic shape of Kandarius and grits his teeth in rage. Kandarius turns back to the soldier.

'Go back down and place the King's head upon the slab, I really don't know him, nor do I care, so let's get rid of him first then. Ready the...oh, better yet, bind his hands, and hang the king upside down, wait for my signal and we'll put a slash across his gut and watch his guts spill, yes that sounds more interesting than just plain old, ordinary beheadings, eh?'

'Yes Master!' The Dregor soldier bows and marches back down the stairs. Kandarius, Athian Dor, and Othyus and Krel watch from above as the soldier passes on the orders, and they take the king and bind his hands immediately and string him upside down upon a rusted metal scaffold. He cries for mercy to Kandarius, then the pleading turns to curses. The miners and slaves recede back, some watch to see what is going on, the other Dregor surround the scaffold in a circle chanting for blood to be spilled. The Dregor have to tackle Cezius, for he jumps them and tries to stop this madness, and he too, shouts curses towards Kandarius.

The executioner, a massive Dregor with bulk and stature walks forward with his sickle drawn, he stands in front of Edrin and tears away the rest of his clothing, leaving a bare and naked body exposed to all. Many cover their eyes, as the sickle is raised into the air, he looks up and awaits for the signal. Kandarius holds them all in shock and terror for a moment, to make their skin crawl and blood run. He holds them in a grip of terror for a moment more.

'This will be most entertaining Lord Kandarius. I'd say give them a bath they'll never forget! Plus, the Dregor look hungry, for it takes much energy to whip those bastard men, women , and children into shape and slave till they collapse.' Athian suggests.

Kandarius nods, and the Dregor slices across the abdominal wall, then hooks up across the stomach and through the chest and ribs. Blood sprays forth covering the area in a bath of plasma, and the guts spill everywhere on the ground, the large intestine is left hanging and unfurled, but the rest splatter about, and clump upon the ground in a mess, but that mess is soon cleaned up, and sopped up with the greasy vile tongues of Dregor, for they lash out for the innards, while others tear the body from the rope and then crack the bone and split and tear and rip the corpse to pieces. The Gormons, Asyndians, Civilians, and Mirym watch in horror as the legions of Dregor consume and gobble the remains of their dead king. But soon, there is nothing left but a splatter of dry blood within the dirt.

Cezius, enraged, tries to break loose of his binds, but the Dregor hold him back, but his death stare is on Kandarius still. 'Athian...go down and invite the general up, for I wish to speak with him in private.'

'Yes my Lord.' And Athian descends the steps. Cezius readies himself as he sees the dark figure with half a face of flesh, half a face of iron, walking his way. The same man, Athian Dor, he saw speaking to the Dregor and twisting the mind of Glenheim, with strings wielded by Kandarius's will.

'My master, Lord Kandarius Lockmore, wishes to speak with you, General Cezius Cabriel. If you would follow me.'

'You tell that scum to piss off! The only thing he'll say to me, is when he begs for me to kill him, cause I'll beat his face in until he wishes he was dead!' Cezius retorts in answer to Kandarius's invitation.

Athian walks closer and backhands Cezius across the face, knocking him unconscious. The Dregor guards let him drop, but Athian catches him, and tosses the general over his shoulder and carries him up the stairs back to the top of Daskar. Athian throws him down to Kandarius's feet, as Cezius stirs from his unconsciousness. He looks up in a blurred daze, and sees the vile shape and black wings of Kandarius looking down upon him. Cezius struggles to his feet, and looks around. Standing there are Athian Dor, Othyus, and Krel all looking upon the general.

'Like I said... you weren't cut out for the role of General!' Kandarius laughs. Cezius tries to run at him, but Krel slams him down to his knees, stopping him dead in his tracks.

'What do you want scum! This freak with half a face said you wanted to talk to me, so...talk!' Cezius snorts. Athian just grins at the Civilian's weak threats.

'Well, I did want to talk, but now that I think about it, I think it better if I show you, what do you say?' Kandarius says.

'I say piss off!' Cezius spits at Kandarius's feet.

'Ah, its good after all you've been through, you never lost that sense of humor and charm.' He clutches Cezius by his shackles and hoists Cezius's arms above his head. 'I think you'll like this, so just hang on, this will only take a second...and a thought!' And within an instant, Cezius and Kandarius had disappeared.

Cezius feels as though he's been out for some time, his eyes open, and he finds himself laying upon a cold obsidian floor, a floor of polished black marble, and blank walls of the same stone stretching upwards around them, and closing into a point towards the ceiling. The room is vast in size like a royal dining hall they had back within Aurora Othetian's palace. He wipes away the dryness and tears of his eyes, and looks to the front of the room, where a contraption, a mechanism which resembles a torture rack with chains and nails, upon the sides are gears and leavers with switches and pipes that steam. Cezius walks towards it, for he has never seen anything like this before.

But when he gets closer, he notices a familiar face, is strapped to the contraption by rivets and binds, clasps across his wrists, ankles, and neck, with several needles and contraptions that are stuck within his arms and chest, and upon these needles are tubes that run into the machine, then out either side of these massive pumps, and into the walls. Cezius climbs upon a small ledge and looks at the pale shape, his body is thinned, and his eyes are closed and sunken in. Several deep gashes are across his chest from some form of horrible torture, and through the pumps and the tubing, runs his blood, as it is being sucked out of him and into the walls of this place, whatever this place is. Cezius looks at the figure and says only one word.

'Her....Hernan?'

The voice of Kandarius speaks to him from the shadows. 'Yes, that is the Forgemaster.'

'What, what is this place, what is this machine, what have you done to him?!' Cezius asks in complete shock and horror which fills his mind.

Kandarius steps forward from the corner of the room, and his feet clop across the floor. He stands to the side of this machine. 'You are at the very top of the Arc of Daskar, General Cezius. Now, as for our friend, the Forgemaster, he is giving his blood, to give life. You see, in order for the portal to open and for the Hexagus to be reborn from Wom, the Arc needs to be a living thing, in order to, 'Give Birth,' in a manner of speaking.'

'Give...Birth?! Cezius asks with a confused look.

'Yes, the Forgemasters blood is running through these tiny artificial veins that are circulating through this entire fortress from top to bottom, and when there is enough blood circulating, then Azalir will be placed within the stone altar, and these two forces will cause a connection between this world and the realm of my masters, and all this on the Forgemaster's blood!'

'You scum! This is a fate worse than any death!' Cezius cries out. 'Why him?!'

'Because he shares the connection with Azalir, he gave his sweat to forge the blade and now he must give his life, for this was the destiny of the Forgemaster, for he will achieve immortality through the blood of the Hexagus, for the greater good of order! I guess you will never understand, that I only want the best for this realm, and what this realm needs is its order back, why, look at all the incidents that have happened without the Hexagus around to keep us in line.' Kandarius says.

'What has happened? Everything that has happened is because of your malice, your darkness, the grasp you hold over all, manipulation and deceit that has destroyed all civilization and brought all to slavery!' Cezius cries back in rage.

'Now are we really going to have another one of these discussions like before when I was right and you were wrong? When will you learn, if my ancestor hadn't destroyed order and supremacy, we would still be in control, and there would be no desolation or war, for with order and tyranny, none fight back, rebellion is suppressed, and peace is kept! You made myself and my Dregor do this, led us to having to destroy everything and start over. It's a mess I know, but this was all necessary.'

'My master Naumokron was careless, and nearly destroyed everything, Naumokron was only supposed to cleanse the Auroras, not the entire land! A misunderstanding on his part, that's all it was. We will rebuild the Greywaste.' Kandarius replies.

Cezius growls. 'I don't' believe one word of it!' He lunges, but a bolt of energy knocks him back against the far wall.

Kandarius walks forward towards the mechanism and looks upon Hernan. 'The time has come, the blood circulates, and all that is left, is for the power of Azalir to be placed within the stand, and then the words of the black speech must be uttered...and then, may my masters walk this world once again...'

Far across to the east, Brihem and Roaur work day and night without rest, and very little food and water. The collapse of Athilnovia has left them with double the work, for the Asyndians of their camp have committed mass suicide by leaping into the vast ocean and drowning themselves. The other Mirym keep close to their chief upon the high ridge, while further below, Roaur works toward the mine entrance. They speak very little to the other scrapers, and simply give each other dirty looks.

Roaur is unaware of a figure approaching him. He hears a whisper from behind, and turns to find an old Gormon digging near him, but he did not notice him before. He is bent over with a large hump, a ragged one-piece cloth over top his thin body, and his great white beard is dragging along the ground covered with dirt and dust from the ground and soot from the mines, when he swings the pickaxe, sometimes the beard gets in the way.

'Hey, psst! Hey…I got news.' The old Gormon whispers.

Roaur gives him a confused look. 'What news?'

'Keep yer eye on the sky, I've seen em, big black wings, spread like a bat's but way bigger, way…way bigger! Their watching us waiting to swoop down, and carry us off to their lair…one by one!' The old man began to shake, as the tremble could be heard in his voice.

'What's watching us…what are you…' Roaur looks over to one of the spires and sees an odd silhouette jutting out from the tower. Then he turns to the cliff off to the north, and there he sees it, what the old man was afraid of, it was a drog sitting there, as if the beast were waiting for something to happen, keeping a eye on things, and then he saw the figure upon the back, and that's when he knew these weren't random drog hunts, these are the sacred Drog Riders, and it seems they're waiting for their chance to strike.

Roaur looks over to Brihem upon the far ridge of the quarry, but he isn't paying attention, only hammering and chiseling away at the stone. Night time falls over the desert, and the scrapers continue to keep digging into the night, meanwhile many of the Dregor are fast asleep in their watch towers and within dark huts. Only a small force patrols the area, keeping an eye on things. Two of the guards upon the northern watch tower vanish as a quick blur shoots by, then the guards upon the eastern spire vanish as well.

The old Gormon stays watchful, and sees what is happening. Terrified, he rushes out from the quarry and screams 'Drogs! Drogs, we're under attack!' This causes a panic to break out, and the other prisoners and diggers run in all directions and cover their heads. Roaur rushes out behind the old man shoves him down, trying to get him to shut up. Now the Dregor have awaken, and they hear the cry of the old Gormon and come running out wielding crossbows and longbows. They fire randomly into the air, but the speed of the drogs are too great, for they can't hit anything.

Durg`, Shoranna, and Arro` fly in and incinerate the Dregor and their crossbows. They take out one legion after the other; Roaur even lends a hand bashing a few with his fists. One of the Dregor whips him, causing his exposed arm to bleed from the massive blow and gash. Roaur grips hold of the leather strap that wraps around his bicep like a snake, and pulls the Dregor over his head, whips him around in a circle, and slams him into the obsidian walls.

The Dregor are scattered and they abandon the camp, leaving the prisoners free. Shoranna and the others land near Roaur, and Brihem and the Mirym remove their pick axes and machetes from Dregor skulls and join them at the bottom of the quarry.

'Greetings, master Gormon! You and these people are free. The children and their mothers will be taken back to Otoni, but those who are able to wield a blade, all the able-body men and women must come with us, for a second resistance is just about ready to march upon the black fortress of Daskar, and we could use your hammer.' Durg` says to Roaur.

'Ah ha! That's what I like to hear, action and fighting! No more of this mindless hammering and being whipped by these pathetic insects!' Roaur rushes over to the nearby guardhouse and kicks in the door, he's in there for a few moments, and then reemerges with is armor upon his skin, and his hammer within his grasp.

'We are ready to fight as well!' Brihem says to Durg`.

'It is good to see you again Brihem, we will need you and your Mirym.' He brings Brihem and Roaur closer. 'This is not a war between Mirym and Gormon, this is a fight for all of Aura, against Kandarius! Put aside your differences, and blood feuds. There will be a day when we may break all bonds and alliances, but it's not this day. What say the two of you?' Durg` asks in announcement.

Roaur and the Gormon that have rallied behind him, stammer for a minute, while Brihem and the Mirym delay and wait for the response of the Gormon. Meanwhile, the Civilians watch on, the tension becomes so thick, and so tight within the air, you can cut it with a knife.

Then, Roaur makes a move first, and puts out his hand. 'The Drog Rider is right, because I have a bone to pick with that son of a bitch, and an eye as well!'

'As do we all.' And Brihem shakes the Gormon's hand, and in this historic moment, the Gormon and Mirym mutually agree to become allies.

'Where are the other armies?' Brihem asks.

'There are two legions of Gormon, led by Hideron, which will be heading from the north, they are joined by a force of Civilians that we located at a fortress further west, and from that direction, the Treefort Civilians are marching as we speak.' Shoranna says.

'There is a force of Sasparians off the coast of Runegard. Their armada may still be there, I don't know.' Roaur says.

'Okay…Hurg`, you will go to check and see if the Sasparians are still alive, and tell them to take the inland Lith`Yl River, it heads straight for the heart of Aura, and they can encircle the fortress from the south.' Hurg` and his drog take off for the west to find Fing` and his Sasparians.

Roaur approaches Durg`. 'Master Drog Rider, have you seen Hernan, or know what has happened to him?' He asks.

'We don't know, we were hoping he would be here, but there is no trace of him, it's as though he simply vanished. But we did find this.' Durg` tosses Roaur the horn that was given to Hernan from Talphoon in case he needed help.

Roaur felt sad within his heart. 'I have not seen him since we were captured at Runegard all those months ago, and I have feared the worst. What about L`or? He was in the city with us, but then he just vanished right before the attack.'

'The Asyndian, in our scouting, Arro` saw an Asyndian fly south, almost heading back towards the Greywaste, why... I don't know, or for what purpose.' Durg` replies. 'But we have to get our ranks formed, and ready for the siege, we've managed to capture some heavy artillery and catapults, plus the Gormon will be bringing some trebuchets they're wheeling over the hills and roads. And as a secret weapon, we've spotted two Skahljah tanks over beyond the ridge, abandoned and unguarded. The beasts that pull them are still alive and moving.'

‘Those will come in handy. If one of your drog's takes me and Brihem over to their location, I know how to get them beasts under our control, and we’ll join up with you. What do you say?’ Roaur asks Durg`.

‘I think that plan may work Durg`,' Brihem intervenes, 'We’ll give it a shot, and attack from the east, while your Riders, my people, and this band of Civilians and Gormon will attack from the south. Yes, it sounds like a good plan, attacking from all sides and surrounding the Dregor in a tight grip they won’t be able to escape. I say let’s execute.’

Meanwhile, while the clouds gather, and the armies reform their ranks to prepare their final siege upon Daskar and Kandarius’s domain, upon a high mountain top, overlooking desolation and volcanic lava spewing from Aura, L`or sits upon the rock in concentration and meditation, thinking within his thoughts, communicating with his inner self.

‘This is where it all happened...all those eons ago. Reignkiing nearly drowned the world within his malice and cruelty. My brethren, and myself, the Sentinels, flew far over Aura and above all below, it was for them we fought for, they were our purpose, we were guardians of the Twelve Altars, of my Sacred Lady, the Altars were a symbol of peace, and a milestone in our civilization...but now, the Sentinels are gone, killed by Reignkiing, and Y`nahlia has been slain, the Altars gone, and Athilnovia, the last of my culture, the last remnants of a broken race, has fallen and burns within a crater of Aura. Now the other races have begun their fall, and what is my purpose now, Airical and all the Auroras have been slain...what else is there?’

His golden wide eyes open, the winds blow through his red feathers, and the hot air can be felt creeping up the mountain from the magma within the crust. *‘There is only one thing left of me, if I cannot die for my Lady, or my Aurora, then*

I will die for my people, my friends, and my land, my land of Aura!' He stands to his feet and walks out to the edge of the peak and looks out to the Arc of Daskar, and Kandarius's fortress, the blood within him pulsates, for he does not care anymore, he only wants to see the downfall of Kandarius, the downfall of the Dregor, and to prevent the return of the Hexagus Lords.

He glides into the air and hovers for a moment, and then flies towards Daskar, ready to fight to the death, even if it is his own.

The Drog Riders carry supplies back and forth between the northern and southern armies, readying and arming the men and women with weapons and armor, and Hurg` and the Sasparians sail down Lith'Yl with the tide that carries them. Hideron and the Gormon and Civilians line across the cliffs above Daskar, just above a steep hill, out of sight from the Dregor that patrol below. The titanic Automatons march back and forth across the walls, while the Stryders and their keepers patrol within the perimeter of the area.

Hideron commands for the trebuchets and catapults to be brought closer into firing distance. Off towards the west, the Runegard troops from Treefort take the western bank, and keep their eyes open, waiting for their signal to attack. The southern troops reach their destination, and meanwhile Brihem and Roaur drive the Skahljah fire tanks to where they need to be. Now the Drog Riders have to maintain communication between each group and make sure each move is set, each troop is ready, and they will give the signal. Hurg` and the Sasparians are ready, they signal south. Shoranna and the southern armies are ready, they signal east. Arro' and the Treefort soldiers are ready, they signal north, Durg` and Hideron are ready, they signal west, Augr` has made sure all catapults were loaded and ready to fire, and Roaur and Brihem were ready. All is in place, and the lines steady themselves.

Then they see something stir below, for Kandarius is walking across the top of Daskar, towards an altar of stone, an altar where Azalir will be placed to open the Arc, the Arc of Daskar that towers high above all the armies, almost as tall as Gammafir once stood.

'The shadow of the tower makes the men and women nervous, for it gives off a life of its own. See the light that pulsates around it, it's not natural, something powers its essence.' Durg` says to Hideron.

'How will we bring down such a structure?' Brihem says to Roaur.

Roaur laughs and smiles to himself. 'You know how you want to bring down a structure like that? Brick by Brick!' Roaur replies with the smile becoming broader. Brihem just looks at him.

'That's how me and Hernan would do it!' He replies to the confused look upon Brihem's face.

'We can't wait much longer, what is your leader waiting for? Soon Kandarius will have opened the portal.' Fing` says to Hurg`.

He doesn't respond, but is none the less thinking the same thing.

The Dregor stand in lines and ranks, facing Daskar and the mighty Arc towering before them. Kandarius approaches the altar and draws Azalir from its sheath. Upon one side of the altar stands Athian Dor and his drogs, while on the other, are Krel and Othyus. They stand at attention, in a ceremonial fashion. Kandarius lifts the blade into the air, and prepares to drive the sword into the obsidian stone.

Durg` raises his arm to ready them for attack, they wait, he's about to lower his hand with a sharp cut, but he notices something. Hideron sees it as well.

'Durg`, what is that light heading this way?' Hideron asks.

'I don't know, but it's coming fast.'

Kandarius and the others sense it as well, for the energy radiating from its powerful shell can be felt across the land. The blast lands upon the top of Daskar and faces Kandarius, whose eyes are wide with shock and confusion.

'What is the meaning of this…who dares?!' Kandarius shouts.

The golden orb around the being clears, and it is revealed to be L`or, who has traveled from the Greywaste.

'I stood face to face with the annihilation and chaos of ancient times, and I will do so again, for I am a Sentinel, the last Sentinel! And I will make my last stand here, against you Kandarius!' L`or removes a set of double daggers from his sash and twirls and swings them, ready to face Kandarius.

'Very well…if it is death you wish Asyndian, then let it be so!' Kandarius replies back.

Far upon the cliffs and hills, Durg` gives the order, 'Charge!' is cried out, and from all directions, Gormons, Civilians, Sasparians, and the Drog Riders, all armies rush forth from their trenches and charge down the hills and across rivers to engage the Dregor in the final war.

'What is this? Ha, attack if you dare, this futility will cost you all your lives!' Kandarius cries out to them all, and he and L`or engage in combat as L`or dashes at Kandarius and strikes again and again, then blocking Kandarius's strikes back at him.

'Leave this Asyndian to me, kill all the others! Leave none alive!'

Krel and Othyus leap into battle and charge at the incoming soldiers from the south, while Athian leaps upon Abhor and Femog and flies up into the air.

'Catapults…fire!' Augr` cries out, and the ballistics and boulders fly through the air and smash and crash through the walls of Daskar and legions of Dregor, crushing them to bits.

The catapults and trebuchets barrage from the west and to the east the Runegard plow through the hordes of the black flags, the Sasparians fire bolts and cannon fire from their ships that decimate and blow the Dregor legions to pieces. The southern armies march forward and engage a thick wall of Dregor, and to the left flank is Othyus smashing skulls and slaughtering Civilians and Gormons, and to the right, Krel destroys the Mirym.

Up over the ridge, Brihem and Roaur blow through the hordes and alight and burn the black flags, running over all Dregor in their path. They blast through the enemy lines to try and save the others from being slaughtered by the two Persivators.

Hideron and the Gormon from Otoni burst through and gouge and smash all in their path like the same battering ram pattern they formed to clear through Bolaug's army, but then a force of Dregor comes from behind their ranks, and they are surrounded, they fight for their lives and defend themselves trying to drive back the offenders.

Meanwhile Kandarius and L`or continue their duel that leads them up to a higher tower complex, and far beneath them, the armies continue their war and battle for the future of the entire Galakaos. Kandarius strikes at L`or, and he dashes away, flying into the air, and the blow crumbles the tower down to the ground, crushing those under a pile of rubble who were unlucky enough to be caught in the ruin. While in mid-air, they lock weapons and lock eyes, their teeth grit, but then Kandarius smiles at the Asyndian with his wicked sharp teeth. L`or can see his reflection within those bloody eyes.

'Do you think you can beat me…if only you realized, I haven't even been trying!'

The familiar of Kandarius, Aumon, appears upon his shoulder and leaps upon L`or's face, scratching and clawing at the Asyndian. Aumon jumps away, then L`or's eyes widen, as Kandarius strikes the daggers away, and L`or's arms flail away, and Azalir is driven through his chest, and out through his back, the tip covered and dripping with his blood!

He cries out to the skies above, as Roaur and the others watch from below, they scream out to him, calling his name, but Kandarius pushes the body away and L`or falls to pinnacle of Daskar, and lands upon the obsidian, twisted, broken, and dead.

The tides begin to turn, and the Dregor now have the upper hand. The Dregor strike back hard and the numbers of the soldiers start to dwindle. Then, upon the western spire, Abhor and Athian Dor look down upon all as the war rages on. Femog circles above taunting them on. Then, from the ground below, Durg` and the Drog Riders ascend into the air and circle around the foes before them. Femog then holds his ground, and Athian and Abhor take off into the air.

Femog and Abhor glide idly next to one another, and then the two seem to morph together, fusing their bodies and their left and right wing is absorbed, leaving them with a pair of talons, two long arms and claws, a single tail and rows of jagged spines across the creatures back, but there are two heads, two elongated slimy necks. This new creature is faster, stronger, and more powerful than before, for Femhor is born, the mutation of Abhor and Femog.

Athian rides upon Femhor's back, his armor now covered in long spines, and a bulky helmet ridged with razors and two large pincers covering his broken face. He wields a scepter, a long black pike with a burning red eye at the end which emits red lightning and balls of energy which emit rays of blood-thirsty light.

Femhor vanishes, and the Drog Riders scatter. They dash from area to area; their velocity stirs winds as powerful as cyclones and hurricanes, blasting sands into the air and causing sand devils to swirl and spin.

'Augr`, do you see him anywhere?!' Durg` cries out.

'No, nothing.....!' Augr`'s response is silenced, they turn to his direction to see him and his drog fall to the ground. Shoranna rushes to where he was flying, she turns to the corner of her eye, and sees Athian for a brief moment, and then he disappears. She hears a scream cry out, it sounds like Hurg`. Another of her companions has been slain by this mad being. She can hear his laugh as she weaves in and out of the clouds looking for him. She runs into Arro`.

'He's playing with us...! He's too fast, I can't...AHHH!' A bolt of red sparks strikes Arro` and his drog, and they to, fall from the clouds. Now only her and Durg` remain. She frantically searches the area for Durg`, and she finds him, he's crouched down below upon the side of a mountain. She hovers above him.

'Durg`, the others are dead...'

'Shoranna, get away, you have to hide or he'll see us...' From behind, Durg` can see the shape of Femhor and Athian behind her. He points the scepter straight at her.

'Shoranna...behind you!' Durg` cries out. She turns and sees the bright light coming for her. Durg` and his drog fly into the air, and shove Shoranna and Fenzir away, and Durg` takes the full blast. He is decimated into ash and his pieces fall. Now all eyes are on her. She orients herself, and the two circle around in the sky.

'Well, four down and that only leaves you my darling!' Athian laughs, a shadow and gurgle echoes through the massive helm.

They charge at one another and sparks crackle and clash throughout the sky like fireworks, smoking and creating a dazzling array of lights as they strike at one another and the two drogs slash and bite each other. Femhor latches onto Fenzir's shoulder and tears at the muscle. Shoranna jumps from Fenzir's back and onto Femhor to attack Athian. The two clash blades and slash back and forth. Then, Athian blocks her attack, and grabs her by the neck.

Athian descends into a free fall, and when he nears the bottom, he tosses Shoranna into a massive pile of dirt, and Fenzir is slung down next to her. They both lay unconscious and defeated. Athian Dor washes his hands clean of them, and returns to Kandarius's side, but, he does not realize, there may still be some life still breathing within Shoranna and Fenzir.

The battle grows weary, and the Dregor round up the troops and separate them into groups. The fire tanks have been destroyed by Daskar cannon fire and the beasts slain; Femhor swoops down and wipes out the catapults and trebuchets with one fell swoop of his claws and wings. The vessels are boarded and the Sasparians are chained and brought upon land where they're placed with the others. Roaur and Brihem as well, they are shoved to their knees, and standing before Roaur, is Krel.

'You...Gormon! What is your name?!' She growls at the battle weary Roaur.

He looks at her. 'My name…is Roaur, the greatest warrior in all of Fausengard! We've already faced once before, gave me a nasty welt on my head you scrawny little bug! I am the greatest Gormon warrior who ever lived!' He boasted. 'And I know who you are, I never forget an ugly mug when I see it, and that's just your helmet, I'd hate to see what lies beneath.'

Calling his bluff, she throws down her mace, and lifts the helmet from her head, and beneath is a face so beautiful that even Roaur is awe struck. She was a blonde with short spiked hair, and a tattoo across the side of her face and head; her eyes were very pale and seemed to glow with a faint blue light. But her face was perfect, no crease or wrinkle, neither age, nor blemish affected or altered her appearance.

She is silent for a moment. *'I have a message for you, from your father!'*

'My…my father?' The look upon his face was grim, but then he realized, if they hunted down the Auroras, then that would mean? 'What happened to him, what did you do?!'

'Before he died, before I slayed him! He told me you would be his avenger, ha!' She slaps him across the face. *'Even if you could break those chains, you wouldn't have a chance!'* She turns and walks away.

'You slimy bitch! I'll kill you; I'll rip your head from your shoulders!' Using all his might, Roaur heaves and pulls as hard as he can, and with a mighty tug, he pulls the bands apart, throws them down. He charges at Krel and grabs her from behind by the neck.

'I'll tear off that pretty head of yours!' He cracks her spine, and she becomes paralyzed and falls to her knees. He twists and snaps and with a quick tug, he rips the head from her shoulders, and drags the spine along with it. He looks at the horrified eyes on her face, and then gives her a big kiss right on her lips and tosses the head away. The Dregor try to charge at him, but Othyus raises his hand for them to halt.

'Ah, we have a new challenge, eh?! Let's go then, I'll take you down like your sister, but just remember, the larger they are, the harder they fall! You're my size, and we fall pretty hard!' Roaur threatens Othyus.

Othyus raises his sword in the air, and twists the blade off. Five Dregor carry to him a large hammer head. They lift it onto the arm and Othyus twists it on. Upon closer look the hammer is carved into a mammoth bronze fist.

They waste no time, they charge at one another and grapple each other in a bout to the death. Roaur punches and jabs Othyus across the bronze helmet and puts quite a few dents into the metal. Othyus staggers back, then retaliates and tackles Roaur to the ground. He mounts on top of him, and Othyus begins to pound the heavy bronze fist down into the face of the Gormon who killed his sister, but the sister who killed Kerrun, and whose hands are stained with the blood of Auroras.

Othyus continues to pound away upon the Gormon, cracking ribs, and splitting bone, but Roaur will not give up without a fight, he grabs the fist and shoves it away, then with a hard right hook, he knocks Othyus back, he lays upon the ground dazed. Roaur walks over towards Othyus and stands above him. Roaur recovers his hammer that was sitting on the ground near some terrified Dregor.

‘Now, here’s a taste of my hammer!’ And Roaur just wails down upon Othyus, breaking and cracking his armor away, and soon tubes begin to leak fluid, gears break through and crack away, springs and leavers soar abound, and the twitching of Othyus’s arms cease and his life force is kaput.

‘Your Persivators are dead, now what dark master!’

Kandarius walks to the altar and raises the blade; he slams the sword down into the stone, and an eruption of earthquakes and volcanoes takes precedence. Kandarius turns to Roaur and the others of Runegard, Gormon, and Civilian and speaks to them all. ‘This is what I’ll do!’ Kandarius raises his arms, and the winds fall silent, for only his voice is heard as it radiates outwards. All are brought down to their knees, and they grasp their ears for the sounds emanating in the air and within their minds pierces their very spine and soul. It is too unbearable for them to listen.

The necklace around his neck begins to glow, and the red eyes roll over light blue, and the energy flows into the air, for the Hexagus are ready, they amass upon the edge of infinity and time, waiting to be reborn into a world that was once theirs, their law and their rule.

“I raise my hands; I speak these words of praise!

For now is the time, for the womb shall be opened,

And to this desolation you will be reborn, to this desolation you will build a new,

A kingdom, an empire, a reign that twists and subdues.

For none will resist, a rule under clenched fist,

Shadows and the fogs will clear, from a land that once resided beyond the mists,

From the gaping womb of Wom, into this world returned to you,

For I am your servant, oh Lord Maz Dregor,

And I call upon the power of Azalir, to allow these most powerful of beings,

That have been banished by my ancestor,

To return this world to tyranny,

Where order will again rule….."

The gaping maw, the Arc of Daskar begins glow, and the red elixir of the Forgemaster is sucked away from his veins. He awakens in a mad scream and cries from the pain and the burn as the blood is pulled from him, through the tubes of the machinery. The pain is so severe, so intense, his head whips back, he screams to the black ceiling above, imagining the sky beyond, and pleading for help, his head whips forward breaking the strap around his neck, he slumps over and his pulse beats with a weak and slow rhythm. He slips into a coma, and slips into a vision.

Cracks and channels within the arching structure emit a faint orangish fire that pulsates between the waves of blood, and the blistering inferno. The stench of flesh and iron is strong in the air. The Dregor forces and the Gormon and Civilian armies gaze high above. Super seismic waves and clasps of lighting and thunder roar throughout the skies and yawning roars bellow forth from the abyss that opens up, for they are almost here, the Lords of Hexagus are so close to revitalization.

A green ethereal glow, a sheet of mystical energy forms within the arch, and a swirling bright light opens up, and before them, they can see deep into the other side, the outer realm, the black, soggy pit of Wom, the realm of Hexagus where the

Dregor and their masters have existed, waiting for this moment, waiting for this very day, and now it has finally come.

The red carpet is laid out, a stream of blood gushes forth from the Wom, the waters have broken, and the placenta is unleashed. A long, writhing hand reaches outwards, a hand upon an arm some three to four hundred feet in length. Then another one emerges, and then another, and three more emerge from the dark realm. A bursting heat and soggy, disgusting smell emits with steam. Then a long, titanic head that rises upwards, lunges out, and then the full figure of the first Hexagus Lord appears in full. It is Ter` Urkar, he has four heads, and each faces in the four cardinal directions, his armor is of a material not of this realm, and his feet have two clawed toes, and each hand is covered with fur, as well as his heads, also covered with hair and fur. They bear a Dregor diadem upon each one. The monstrosity looks down upon all the creatures he towers above. He looks at a large group in front of him made up of Civilians and Gormons, chained and guarded by the Dregor, Ter` Urkar raises his monstrous foot, and crushes them in a single stomp that shakes the realm.

The other Hexagus Lords follow, one after the other in a march of the titans, for these beings are enormous. Their height reaches the limits of the sky, their weapons genocide, their will destruction. Ter` Urkar stands to the far eastern side of Daskar, then the Hexagus come through one after the other. Taigus Sor` spreads his massive wings and soars into the air. Blodaur Ror` stomps through wielding a gargantuan, titanium axe and his hoofed feet stomp and clomp massive craters into the dirt.

The rest of them emerge from their long dark decay within the stomach of darkness, Garogmog, the serpent of Terror and Dread, a curse to all eyes who gazes upon him, Ilskull, a plague of death and desolation, a creature of many eyes and arms that ensnare and burn the flesh away, Malgo

Dul, who carries a battering mace in each arm and a tail that stings and infects the veins of Aura with every strike, Torkon Duk, with footsteps that char the world and bears a hammer that can erect chaos and destroy hope as well as bone and flesh, Adomon, a creature that engulfs all life and laps the blood from his foul and crusty lips, Skaraloun, a feisty creature born of fiery rage and temper, but freezes all the living and all the land in glaciers and icy destitution with her winds of frost and blizzard, Droth, a blade wielder and dark-plated warrior of the vile putrid and disgusting puss under Wom's flesh, Cycolog a beast with a single eye, and his Siamese twin Opolok, who are bound at the face by a twisted mass of flesh, but they have a barrier protecting them that rips the flesh from the bone of any who get to close.

They encircle the vast open area, towering over all. They await their master, the one who will revert the land of Aura back to its archaic beginnings all those eons ago. The ground shakes, and the blood begins to harden and crack with the fissures that open up. The hordes of Dregor and Aura soldiers run for their lives, avoiding the fallen stones and erupting lava from beneath their feet.

And through the portal, he comes…the Destroyer, the harbinger of death; the tyrant of all life…Maz Dregor has come. His three heads and serpent necks emerge, and his long claws grasp at the gateway and he pulls himself out. He sprays a deadly blast of fire, incinerating all in his path. Brihem and Roaur take cover behind a large mound of rocks. Shoranna and Fenzir stir from their unconsciousness, and climb over to the edge of the rocks to see the horror that lays before them.

None of the Dregor stop to bow to their masters, for they are terrified of the monstrous beings. The Hexagus have no allegiance, no sympathy, no mercy or pity. Kandarius walks forward and calls to the Destroyer.

'My…my master! Is it really you! At last, you have returned, you and the Hexagus are free once more!' He cries.

Maz Dregor snorts and turns to the insignificant shape of Kandarius, and pierces him with his massive yellow eyes. The roar and speech of Maz Dregor is so black it would swallow an abyss of nothingness. He speaks only of the black tongue, the language of the Dregor, but this is how it translates into Civilian words.

'Ah.....Kandarius....my long....time....friend!' He furrows his brow. *'You...and....Naumokron....have done.....well!'* The last word causes mountains to shake and fall to pieces, crumble into valleys and black rivers.

'Ha, Naumokron had nothing to do with this! The Asyndian was weak, I was the one who released you, me!'

Maz Dregor chuckles, as though he were pleased. *'Ho...Ho....Ho, indeed you did....you orchestrated quite the elaborate scheme.....didn't you?'* His tone then changes drastically. *'Now... I can exact my... revenge!'*

Kandarius looks upon Maz Dregor confused. 'Revenge...What revenge do you mean?'

Maz Dregor laughs again, this time in a more sinister fashion. *'Do you know...why I chose you...Kandarius...?My plan was, when I returned to Aura, I would enact my vengeance upon the bloodline of the One who cast me out of my world, the one who bears that sword in your hand!'*

Kandarius walks closer. 'What are you saying…I was the one who brought you here, released you from that vile womb you have been rotting in for nigh a thousand eons!'

'Yes, and I thank you Kandarius, but that sword is who you are, your blood, you wield Dregorbane, Azalir, the sword

which banished us. You have served your purpose, Kandarius; the rest is for us to sort out! For I knew if I corrupted the One, the ancestor of my enemy, You! Then the blade, Azalir, would be corrupted, and I would have no...more...weakness!' Maz Dregor grasps Kandarius in one hand, and then he takes a huge chunk from Daskar, and within the rubble inside his palm, is Azalir.

Athian Dor flies into the air upon Femhor and they try to attack Maz Dregor, but he catches Femhor in between the thumb and index finger, and squeezes, turning Athian and Femhor into crushed bone and iron, with a dripping blood stain leaking to the ground.

'Pesky little thing! Are these the company you keep Kandarius? They are weak and insignificant!' He wipes his finger upon a mountain top, and focuses his attention back to Kandarius.

'Now, to do away with this, for you see...your black power, or should I say...my black power, has desecrated the full power of this sword, it no longer has any affect upon me...it...is worthless! And after our summoning....its power has faded.' He takes the sword, and tosses it into the mouth of his middle head and swallows. *'There will be no more trouble out of this blade.'*

Kandarius forces his way out of Maz Dregor's gasp and flies through the air, and into the mouth of the middle head where the sword went to, and he forces his way down the throat, in search of Azalir. Maz can feel the movement cease, as though he has drowned in stomach acid and bile, and the blade corroded with him.

Part XXV:

The Hero of Ages

Hernan lies in twilight, for he's not sure if he's alive or dead. He opens his eyes, and the light is bright, too bright for him to see. He holds his hand in front of his eyes to block the source of light which seems to be all around him, cascading away all shadows and all darkness from his surroundings. He doesn't seem to be walking, but floating, weightless and free. He sees a figure approaching him in the distance. As the figure gets closer, she becomes clearer to him. It is a woman, but he does not recognize her. Her hair is dusty brown and her eyes dark pools of oak, she wears a suit of fur and light armor with a head band. Upon her belt, he sees something; his old hammer, Niron, is upon her belt.

She stands near him, face to face, and places her hands upon his face. Her hands are soft and feel soothing to him and her warm smile comforts him. He looks deep into her eyes, and he sees himself, his soul within hers.

'M…mom?!' He whispers to her and she smiles.

She shakes her head yes. Hernan begins to cry, for he has not seen his mother in years, for she died when he was very young, and now here she stands before him.

'Hi son…I just want to say that I'm proud of you, and that you can win this battle, this victory will be yours. I have this to give to you.' She hands to him Niron.

'This hammer was once mine; I used it to help Gonun forge weapons, for he taught me, as he taught you. I was his apprentice, and he gave to me this hammer. I knew that you would not be ready for your destiny at such a young age, so Kerrun took you in, and I told him to give you this hammer when you were ready to use it.'

'The Hammer of Gonun was the tool to forge Azalir, but this hammer will be used to forge the greatest weapon of all, the weapon that will vanquish this evil once and for all! For the sacred power within, is more powerful than any metal or vice.'

'What power is that?' Hernan asks.

'Craft and skill, hard work and dedication, for it is your skills and your true potential that Niron will bring out, and it is your hard work and dedication that will craft a weapon to cut through the darkness of this tyranny. Hernan…it is the love for what we do, this power, it is the love and the goodness, the truth of the heart that suppresses tyranny and power. Now, let us work together, the team of Smith-Mother and Forgemaster, to create the true Weapon of the Ages.'

Hernan takes his mother's hand, and they pass into another void of this sacred, unknown realm. The Forgemaster and the Smith-Mother pass through the white streets and ivory towers of Arla, the City of Light, for in the skies, he could see the soaring Asyndians and the magnificent beings of elder times and legends that have long passed from the realm of Aura. The mighty castles and towers rise high above at dizzying heights, but give a breathtaking view of the entire realm about them, from gazing out of one of the highest towers.

She leads him to a mighty citadel carved into the side of a vast white mountain, and from the massive chimney breaths forth not smoke, but a majestic light and a mist of pure air. 'What is this place mother?' Hernan asks.

'Why, this is the Forge of Arla.' She replies.

'The Forge of Arla? I've never heard of this place.' Hernan replies, curious to hear more.

'None have, only until they see it for themselves, for this city is sacred, and only those who have passed, gaze upon its beauty.'

The pure marble doors open before them, and a blinding light emits upon them from within, blinding Hernan's wondrous eyes shut.

'With fires of Mystic Flame, Anvils of Gold, and the mighty bellows of the Arla Furnace, the Forge awaits the sacred Forgemaster, and I am proud to say, that he...is my own son. Come, and we will do this together...' The two enter the forge, and the doors close.

Cezius awakens and stands to his feet. The destruction and shaking outside has disrupted his balance, and he presses himself against the wall to keep himself standing. The blow Kandarius landed upon him was severe, but he remembers where he is and the situation at hand.

He looks to the machine, and sees the limp body of Hernan. The pulse reader signals, that his breathing has ceased, and the blood has been completely wiped from his veins. Cezius frantically pulls at the gears and levers and pries the cords from Hernan's veins. There is not one drop to be spilled; the Arc has taken his life.

Cezius lowers him down upon his broad shoulder and holds Hernan's lifeless body within his arms and weeps for the passing of his friend and comrade.

'No Hernan, no! So many have died, so many have…' Then something begins to happen, for Hernan's body begins to disappear from Cezius's arms and fades away, into the realm where he walks with his mother, the Smith-Mother.

‘Where…what happened to him?’ Cezius asks himself as he clutches to nothing. He wipes the tears away from his face. Another pound against the Arc starts to crumble the structure, as tiny fragments start to fall from the ceiling. Cezius realizes he must find a way out of this place as soon as he can. He notices a small crawl space off to the right hand side of the room and leaves through that space. He squirms his way through a long and narrow tunnel until he feels a cool breeze upon his face, then a bright white light up ahead blinds his eyes.

Once outside, he could see far below all that has happened in his absence. Bodies were scattered and bloodied, for he could see that a final march was ordered, a final battle, a final offensive. But the most horrifying sight of all, was that of the titanic beings, the three headed devil Maz Dregor, and the twelve Lords of the Hexagus realm. Kandarius succeeded, he has released his masters upon Aura, but he does not see that wicked beast anywhere.

‘Cezius, jump on!’ He looks just below him, and there is Fenzir and Shoranna. He leaps upon Fenzir’s back, and they soar down to the far ridge where the others have run to escape the monstrous Hexagus. Cezius looks up and sees the clouds are starting to part, and light is rushing through, not the light of the sun, but a light of some other source.

‘Shoranna, what happened to Kandarius, where has that scum slunk to?!’

‘Maz Dregor betrayed him, and devoured Azalir, and then in a mad panic, Kandarius leapt into his throat after the sword. He’s probably burning away in the most painful way.’

A satisfied look comes over his face and fills his eyes.

‘And…the Forgemaster?’ Shoranna asks. Cezius shakes his head no.

‘I could not save him. He vanished, he passed on…’ His look of pleasure turned once more, into tears.

‘I’m sorry Cezius…’ She replies.

Then a blast shakes the sky and breaks the dome of dark clouds. The mystical light breaks through, and all sound ceases in a bursting blaze of what sounds like torches incinerating. The light blinds all around, the Hexagus cower under the blazing sun that gets nearer and nearer to them.

‘What is this…..!’ Maz Dregor roars, his serpent tail curls around the Arc, as he climbs up to get a closer look. Of all three heads, none could see, neither could Taigus or Ter` Urkar. They were at the mercy of the graceful light.

Then, the falling sun hits the ground miles away beyond the mountains far off to the north. The light subsides, but a glowing orb echoes light that floods over the landscape. Then, the heavenly being leaps into the air, and descends downwards in an aurora of majesty, as the figure spreads his wings and puffs his chest of solid ivory armor of the mightiest kind, he holds out his arms and within his right hand, is a weapon forged of a substance that has never existed upon Aura, only within the Realms of Light, the place where the Auroras dwell, may this precious alloy be found and crafted. The weapon, a double-bladed sword of crystal blades and a pommel of glistening ivory swelling with ancient craft and style, that shone brighter than a thousand suns and pierced the black hearts of every Hexagus. The mask upon the beings face was of the majestic alloy, but encompassed with twelve tails of the sun’s rays that glimmered and danced about.

The eyes of the figure shone pure and true, focused and ready. He landed upon the blood soaked ground and looked about him. He said no words; he did not speak, for there was only one thought upon everyone’s mind, the True Hero of Ages has come, and now the darkness will be expelled, and there will be a cleansing of all things black, and the purity and peace that the Auroras once held true, will become an ideology once more. Many did however wonder who this being was, but then Roaur rushed upon the rocks and cheered his name high and loud for all to hear, for he knew his friend better than anyone else.

'Hernan! Hernan! Hernan…!' Roaur cried over and over, and the others cheered and yelled and praised as well. Then another blast hit the crust of Aura, and standing next to Hernan, the Hero of Ages, was the last of the Auroras, Agonan, with blade drawn and armor ready and branded for war. He now stands the same height of Hernan and the Hexagus Lords, some several thousand feet in height.

'I knew the time would come, when the true force of Aura would reveal himself, and that is when I would make my final stand, alongside the Hero as I did all those eons ago! You hear me Maz Dregor, this time you won't be banished…you'll be destroyed permanently! That black womb of Wom, the darkness can no longer shield you!'

Agonan shifts and turns, and with a mighty attack, shatters the Arc with a swift cleave of his blade, scattering the pieces all over the land. Obsidian and blood falls from the skies.

Roaur, in all his excitement, blows the horn of Talphoon, and the call has been made, the beasts have heard. From all corners of Aura, the call is answered, and the God-Monsters arrive with as quick speed as they can. Talphoon arrives by the massive river and the inland sea, Bapheme erupts from the tunnels in the ground, as well as Kraunmig, and Thogmig crawls over the horizon, Aburdom the flying God-Turtle by air, as well as many others, sacred beasts that have long protected the natural order of this realm, for they come to help the Hero and make their final stand against Maz Dregor.

'Everyone…run, move, move, move!' Hideron cries out, and the armies get away from the area, for a battle of epic proportions is about to take place.

'Attack!!!!!' Agonan cries and the God-Monsters leap upon and tear at the Hexagus. The battle stretches across the entire world of Aura and lasts for many days and weeks, across the black deserts, into the charred and decayed woods, and through the skies, as Aburdom and the other flying beasts attack and bring down Taigus Sor. Agonan slices and cuts apart several of the Hexagus in a bloody rage, and takes down Blodaur Ror in a bloody duel, for he cleaves the head of the burly warrior titan clean away from his shoulders. Talphoon drowns the Hexagus in waves and powerful blasts of energy and radiating pummels of his scaled fists and atomic breath from his lungs, and his serpents ensnare and squeeze Hexagus bones to dust, and Thogmig ensnares them within her web, while Kraunmig stings and injects his venom into their curdled veins.

Ter` Urkar is beheaded three times by Agonan and the final head is cracked, and the spine twisted, along with his many broken arms. Taigus Sor falls from the skies, from a shattering blast by Aburdom, Garogmog has been cleaved in two by Kraunmig's mighty pincer. Droth is dragged down into the depths of Aura by Bapheme, Thogmig has Adomon, Torkon Duk, and Malgo Dul wrapped in titanic cocoons that hang across the sky and she feasts upon their vile black blood, and drains them of all their bile and insides. Ilskull is sliced in half by Agonan, and Skaraloun is chewed upon by the ring of snorting bulls that eat at her scaly flesh beneath the waves and devour her limb by limb. Many of the other God-Monsters have either been killed or mortally wounded. And Cycolog and Opolok have split themselves in two by fleeing from Agonan's blade, who shattered their protective field, and in the end, they did themselves in.

Meanwhile, Hernan and Maz Dregor stare each other down. Hernan and Maz Dregor clash against one another, striking back and forth, but the dark powers of the Destroyer have lost their effect, for the light has burned and desecrated his lands where his powers ruled from the curse of the Grey Age, and the black lands of the Greywaste. Hernan slashes the right head away as it explodes into a pile of ash, then the left head, and poof…gone. And he grips the final head with his golden gauntlets, and slices the head away!

With a final furious scream, a scream that weakens the last fiber of Maz Dregor's sinister heart, the head flies high into the sky, and the skull and flesh melt away by the Hero’s light.

One after the other, the rest of the Hexagus remains, the flesh and bones, freeze and turn to stone, and they crumble down into gray dust and chalky powder, that is taken with the first winds that have returned to Aura, not the winds of the evil that have darkened the sun and the skies, but the natural winds that have once caressed this green land.

Many of the God-Monsters have been slain, and the others return to their darkness and lairs, to keep secret, for their time is over. The last Aurora stands before Hernan, and shakes the hand of the mystical warrior.

‘Let the Civilians and the Gormons, and all beings and races of this realm rule with peace and happiness, for my time is done, and I will move on, maybe head north across the Great Divide...You are now the savior of this world and its protector, so with that…I will leave you…’ But before he leaves, he takes out the tiny book, and holds it within the massive grasp of thumb and index finger, the notes of Kerrun that he kept within the pouch upon his side, and tosses it down to Roaur.

‘Here is your father’s book…I think you should have it now.’

Roaur walks over and attempts to pick up the book which contains all of Kerrun’s notes and sketches of Gonun’s lost grotto, but before he can, the little beast Aumon rushes out and grabs the book. Roaur rushes upon him, grabs the little monster with his massive hand, and throws Aumon so far that he flies off over a cliff, and vanishes beyond the darkness below. Agonan laughs, and with that, the last Aurora leaves them, he bids his friends farewell. And so, he travels north to cross the Great Divide, to reside in the lands with the Rauks in Raukmar.

There is only one thing left to do. The majestic, glowing figure of Hernan walks over to what remains of the body of Maz Dregor and jabs his fist right into the stomach, feels around, and pulls out the body of Kandarius, as he squirms and tries to break free from Hernan’s grasp. Kandarius is immediately blinded by the light emitting from the Hero.

Hernan spreads his mighty wings, and takes Kandarius high into the sky, and they pass beyond the eternal realms of the Galakaos, and into a world of light. Hernan holds Kandarius in the palm of his hand, and the Dregor Worshipper bends to his knees, and he pleads to the Hero, but the pleads are soon followed by curses. But Kandarius's fate is sealed, and his death is long overdue.

Kandarius’s flesh begins to burn and sizzle away, the smoke begins to rise from his body as he is burning alive by the powerful light. The flames spark, and spread across his corpse, his wings burn and shrivel away, the black skull beneath his flesh shows through, and the skin and scales incinerate.

‘No….No…AHHHHHHHHHHHHHHHHHHHHH!!!!!! !!!!!!!!!!!!!!!!!!!!!!!’ These are the final words Kandarius will ever speak, as his ashes and remains pile in front of Hernan upon the palm of his hand.

The people below, Gormons, Civilians, Sasparians, the remaining Asyndians, and all others look to the new light above, the new guiding light that will lead them into the next age, for a new eon has begun here today. The Gormon return to Fausengard, Hideron is officially crowned the High King in place of his father, who will rule the Gormon into a new period of wealth and prosperity for all of Fausengard, the likes of which they have not seen since the ancient times. Roaur is asked to be the General of his armies, but declines and retires to live out his days in Stonehaven, giving up battle and continuing his father's studies, delving deeper into the mysteries surrounding Aura's legends that his father had only just barely scraped the surface of, for he soon becomes Roaur, the most knowledgeable scholar of the Gormons within the realm of Fausengard, for many will travel from far and wide to seek his council.

Cezius reestablishes Othetica and the cities of Novilon and Cysiiros, creating a new kingdom for the Civilians, and Shoranna is named his right hand. They rebuild the palace of Othetian, and propose a new Construction and Reformation Act to rebuild and reestablish the Runegard. Many Gormon and the remaining Asyndians populate Othetica, creating a vast and expansive empire beyond the borders of the original land that was ruled over by Aurora Othetian. Shoranna will fly into the skies and continue to return to the meeting place upon the cliffs of Greenhaven to remember her fallen comrades, but Cezius does not realize yet, that a new Drog Rider has been conceived, for Shoranna has yet to tell him. For this child, has been chosen by the grace of Y`nahlia's essence, and deep within this sacred grove of Greenhaven, a drog has been born.

Brihem and the Mirym finish their migration from their icy barren lands and slowly populate and establish Greenhaven, where their culture begins to evolve and change into a new race of Mirym, and the realm has been named The Greenrym, were they live off the green grass, the shade of the forest, and the waters of the unfrozen, fresh lakes and rivers.

The Sasparians never returned to the ruins of Yivv` as Sasparia would have wanted, and so they continue to traverse across the many seas as wanderers and leave the realm or Aura and her people behind, in search of a new beginning for themselves. The Azimoth have driven back the Raumkat to their hills of Ampurzum, where they whine to their prowl deities and lick their paws and wounds in defeat. Without the guiding black hand of Kandarius and the Dregor, they are helpless little kittens.

The land slowly over time heals and cleanses itself and forests and trees regrow, and lakes, rivers and oceans purify, and the population of fauna and other species of animals and insects return to their habitats. The Greywaste however, has been scared for all eternity, a scar upon Aura that can never be healed.

Sadly though, for many Asyndians, they have reached their end, they feel their life and presence has expired, and sadly in masses and groups, they give their bodies to the Great Divide, so that they can spread new wings, and fly again, to be with their fellow Asyndians and feel the warmth of their Mystic Lady and see their Aurora once more and fly within the crystal skies above Arla, the City of Light.

As for Hernan, he now stands as a beacon, a light to all of Aura, a symbol upon every weapon, every sword, and every shield, within every story and poem, that he never gave up, he never gave into the black will of those that would try and stop him, and harm those he cared about. He has felt loss, he has felt pain, in his eyes there is sorrow, but there is also pride and accomplishments to be proud of. He has come a long way from his humble beginnings and has emerged from the caterpillar's cocoon as a being, a deity, an example to follow.

This is the story of the Forgemaster, and how he became that which his heart has always shone… a hero.

Epilogue:

Song of the Forgemaster

'I'm neither fiend nor foe, but just a simple traveler of these parts, one who wanders the realms under the sun and sky, and under the pale face of the moon. Guided by the watchful eyes of the stars, and the rain held at bay by the mighty hands of the trees, whose ancient roots drink of the cloud's majestic tears.'

'All I seek, is to tell this tale and search the realm for song and lyric, rhyme and synonyms, story's that shift and sway, for this land has changed greatly since I have last been this way.'

The old man of the hut looks upon the stranger, his robes are foreign and odd, the markings upon his arms, and the symbols tattooed upon his face seems out of the ordinary, different from the usual passerby.

This old man of the hut sits quietly, staring upon the stranger. He looks at the staff laid upon the ground in front of where he sits. Upon the tip is a strange orb-like sphere with a dim glow, casting a strong reflection of the fire upon it. He did not know how to read the curious man, nor could he remember the stranger's name, or what he calls himself. After a moment, the old man speaks.

'What did you say your name was again?'

The stranger laughs. 'Which one, the first, the second, maybe the fifth or sixth if you wish, for names are many, and I have many names!' The stranger replies.

The old man shakes his head. 'Never mind, it's not important.'

He shrugs to the stranger of many names. 'I really don't know what to tell you, for I have only resided in these parts for…going on now ten years. I understand your eagerness for tales and songs, stranger; but I am unsure of the doings in these lands, plus I'm not good at telling stories. My wife and I came long after the war, after the darkness lifted. All that happened some two to three hundred years ago.'

The eyes of the stranger lifted and widened.

'That is what I what I want to know! About, the war, the final battle between the ancient warriors of Aura and the Dregor, the second coming of the Hexagus Lords, the histories of the ancient Civilians, Gormons, and Asyndians, for these are events truly worthy of song and poem!' The stranger exclaimed.

A voice came from outside the hut; it was the old man's wife.

'The soups almost ready!' Her voice crackles at a high pitch.

'I'm going to eat with my wife now, stranger. If you wish, I invite you to join us, at least I can send you off with one of my wife's fine, cooked over the fire, meals.' The old man offers the stranger from foreign parts.

'Thank you, but I will take my leave, I thank you for your time, and this most excellent, warm ginger mead. I will go now, and leave you to your business.'

The stranger and the old man leave the hut. The stars of the vast, open Fausengard sky shimmer across the rocky tundra, and the fire the old woman had prepared sparks and crackles in the cool night. The old man grabs for one of the wooden bowls laid aside and dips the ladle into the hot pot of soup she prepared and he pours some into the bowl, blows on it, and sips at the broth.

‘Is our visitor here going to stay and entertain us by the fire? There’s some good soup I just made,' She motions to her husband, 'He’s already guzzling it down, ah if you want some, you'd better get it now or he'll guzzle it down by the bowl!’ The old man’s wife says.

‘No thank you, I am off now, heading away to the west, that’s my best guess. Then maybe south to the libraries of Novilon, the ancient Othetica city, for maybe I can search there the many shelves and sanctums, but my luck in finding stories, has turned quite sour. It seems that my search continues with no luck after each and every hour.’ He replies to her.

The woman chuckles at the stranger, at his funny robes and tattoos, and the amusing way his words rhyme.

‘Do you know the way upon the southern road? The trail from here on out can be confusing to pass at night as when it does in the morning.’ She turns to her husband, who is wiping away his beard and setting the bowl aside.

‘Maybe you ought to show him the way?’ She says.

He falls silent, and looks up at his wife’s stern eyes looking down upon him. He hesitates for a moment.

‘I what?’ He stammers.

‘The night air is bitter and cold as ice, and I would not deny, I lose my way easy, and a guide would be nice, for I have not seen Novilon in many years, and I’m excited for the news there, that may greet my ears!’

‘But…I’m not sure of the way!’ The old man says.

‘Not sure! You’ve been traveling these parts to and from the empire, and far between for fifty odd years now! You know the way like the back of that wrinkled hand of yours!’ She says.

The stranger looks wide-eyed. ‘Fifty? He told me ten! I thought his answer sounded rather shifty.’

‘Ten, eh? He must have been feeling generous, usually it’s five, and sometimes he’ll give you, “Oh, only just arrived!’ His wife cackles at him, and then gives her husband that glare of hers.

‘Oh, very well. I’m sorry for the deception stranger; I’m just tired in my old age and traveling becomes increasingly difficult, but I’ll admit you charmed me and my wife, and I’ll get the hofts ready, and we’ll start as soon as I finished my meal, first I have to get another bowl.’

‘Thank you and I do appreciate this! Yours and your wife's kindness I will surely miss.’ The stranger replies.

The old man places the reigns upon the two hofts, the one the old man rides is white, and the hoft for the stranger is a brown steed. He turns and wave’s goodbye to his wife and he and the stranger ride off towards the horizon, on the long road, for the journey to Othetica is quite a ways from where they are.

As the sun begins to shine up over the far hill, it's marvelous shimmer glistens upon their faces, for their first night of travel is just about ahead of them.

‘Do you remember the Forgemaster? Who became the hero of all, and had returned guided by the light in Aura's most desperate hour! When the deceiver, Kandarius used his deception, to fool all and reign with his dark power?!’

The old man shakes his head and smiles. 'Why, the Forgemaster was the greatest of all Civilians, if it weren't for him, the Gormon Roaur, the Civilian Cezius Cabriel, the Drog Riders, and the many who gave their lives to save Aura, we wouldn't be speaking right now. If there is anything I can give to you stranger, storyteller, whatever you want to be called, I can give you this. This is a song passed down by my Gormon and Civilian ancestors, it's about the Forgemaster and his deeds:

"Sit quietly my child and listen,

For the tale I tell, is a story for the ages,

For behind these words,

The legend of the Forgemaster turns these pages.

Each story a marvel, a tale told in stages,

From the time he faced the Drog,

To when he reforged Azalir, and the New Weapon of Ages.

A master of the flame,

Metal and steel at his command.

The Forgemaster wields, the Forgemaster bends,

His armor and weapons are legendary throughout the land.

Now listen carefully my child,

To these words that I say, for these words are the tales,

The legend of the Forgemaster is underway...."

The old man has finished his song, and the stranger looks at him wide eyed and says. 'Do you have a quill and some ink, and a parchment that I may right that one down?! I mean, to hear these words aloud... for I don't want to forget the magnificent words of the Hero of Ages, for his story will be the main subject, to grace my book's pages! For this will truly be, a story for the ages...'

The End

www.ingramcontent.com/pod-product-compliance
Lightning Source LLC
LaVergne TN
LVHW012338100826
845148LV00018B/2726

9780615821436